The path, which was narrow and tilted downward steeply through high brush, soon came out on a rocky beach where the river was both wide and fast-flowing and looked deep and rather ominous.

I walked slowly in the fading light, eyes on the ground looking for stones that might be granite, then saw something that wasn't rocks. It took my brain a few seconds to compute the unexpected sight into a moccasin-clad foot and, beside it, another.

I screamed before I could stop myself, jerking back and looking up at a tall Indian who was utterly motionless, as still as the stones or the sand, and as silent, standing on the edge of the bushes.

He looked at me sourly and then said slowly, enunciating each work separately, "How, white squaw."

"Well, at least you have a sense of humor," I muttered.

Also by Elizabeth Atwood Taylor
Published by Ivy Books:

THE CABLE CAR MURDER
MURDER AT VASSAR

THE
NORTHWEST
MURDERS

Elizabeth Atwood Taylor

IVY BOOKS • NEW YORK

Ivy Books
Published by Ballantine Books
Copyright © 1992 by Elizabeth Atwood Taylor

This is a work of fiction, and all characters and events are either imaginary or used fictionally.

Library of Congress Catalog Card Number: 92-4225

ISBN 0-8041-1138-3

This edition published by arrangement with St. Martin's Press Inc.

Manufactured in the United States of America

First Ballantine Books Edition: June 1994

10 9 8 7 6 5 4 3 2 1

The only difficulty is that the more I tell of the history and traditions of the whites, the more I question whether they are fit subjects on which to instruct the Indians. The Kot-e-meen class was so shocked by what I told them of ancient Rome that I was very much discomfitted. Lewis Hilding, aged twelve, wept over the story of Little Red Riding Hood and kept saying in a trembling voice, "But the old woman. The wolf got the old woman."

—Mary Ellicott Arnold and Mabel Reed,
In the Land of the Grasshopper Song

It seemed so very easy in this country
for someone to get killed....
—MARY ELLICOTT ARNOLD AND MABEL REED,
IN THE LAND OF THE GRASSHOPPER SONG

ONE

THIS PART OF THE TRAIL RAN ALONG A LOWER SPINE OF THE
continent, only three thousand feet high and very hot, in August; hot even in the shady stretches created by large pine
and fir and madrone trees. The trees are old and tall, part of
the Pacific Crest Hiking Trail that runs two and a half thousand miles from the bottom of California up to Canada.
They're protected, because of the trail, from the bulldozers
and chain saws elsewhere set to work by Congress and the
Forest Service in their endless desire for more-more-more
board feet of timber from the National Forests.

The hikers, a girl seventeen and a boy eighteen, were
practiced backpackers but they were tired. The trip that had
started two weeks before in southern Oregon was the longest they'd ever attempted, and they made it even longer by
leaving the trail to find more private places to camp and
look around. A big short-haired brown dog ran ahead, tire-
less and apparently indifferent to the intense heat. A smaller
dog like a black mop came along behind, panting.

It was so hot, the girl thought unhappily, and the river
still so far below, just when a swim would make all the difference. But the map showed they should come to a creek
soon, Tomkins Creek; they could jump in and get cool
there, rest a while.

She was a plump, soft, brown-skinned girl with bright
electric blue eyes, and the boy loved her. He'd loved her

1

for almost two years now, he thought as he watched her struggle up the narrow trail ahead of him: long, silky light brown hair falling down around the sides of her backpack to her waist and then the lovely curve of her hips . . .

The trail tilted up again, suddenly and steeply. Breathing heavily, they climbed almost a thousand feet—sometimes the trail seemed almost vertical. Their faces grew red with the effort, with heat and thirst, with a growing hatred of climbing. When the path finally leveled, the girl stopped and drank greedily from a canteen. Then she adjusted the heavy pack and turned to complain in a tired singsong,

"How much *farther* is this damn *creek*, Bobby? You *said* we were almost there *hours* ago you sure it even *exists*? Won't be all dried *up*? I bet it is and we'll just keep walking and walking and *walking*, walking to San Fran*cis*co, walking to Argen*tina*, walking to the Ant*arctic*—"

"Hey—we *are* almost there," the boy panted, realizing with an oddly satisfied feeling, as he went past and took the lead, that he loved her even when she was cross and whiny. She always got that way when she was tired, but otherwise she was the most good-natured girl. "I just checked the map again," he added soothingly, "we'll be there any minute—oh wow, *look*!"

Beyond a last fringe of trees was a meadow where two large-eyed spotted deer stood with heads erect, listening— then bolted white-tailed into dark woods at the far side. It was an enchanted place of softly waving grasses, of sweet-smelling blue and yellow and white flowers, of bird song— and the sound beyond of water racing over rocks.

The girl, shorter than the boy, had to catch up and go in front again to see, missing the deer but hearing the water. "Thank God," she sighed, undoing her pack, "let's leave our stuff and go *swim*!"

"Don't leave it here, though—we'll just have to come back. Let's put them over there under those trees."

"Yeah, okay." She quickly crossed the meadow, hardly seeing its loveliness for the sound of the creek beyond.

"We must be pretty high again," the boy said as they

leaned the packs into the shade of a thick clump of bushes, "around four thousand feet. You can tell by the vegetation—it all changes about four thousand feet—"

Coming in over his words was a funny soft, plopping noise, or maybe the sound of a hundred thousand butterflies flying by fast and close together. The girl saw Bobby's sweating, serious face crumple in total blank surprise as he fell back and red liquid spurted out of the center of his chest. There was a loud *boom* and then another sound of the thousand butterflies and another *boom*. The girl stood frozen; what she was seeing had no reality, no meaning, was not possible, but finally the warnings from her brain reached her muscles and she turned and dived for cover. It was too late. The first bullet spun her around and the second knocked her backward into stiff bushes that caught and held her three feet off the ground. Bright blood began to drip onto the dry summer dirt of the Pacific Crest Trail.

The blue eyes, dull now, watched the man walk up a few minutes later, watched as he leaned his rifle against a tree, and watched as he took a large gleaming knife from his belt. He looked at her a long moment, then squatted down and took hold of Bobby's sun-streaked blond hair, held the head up with it and began to cut. It took some time, but finally he was finished. He held up the trophy for the girl to see, with a smile that invited her to be interested, or impressed. Then he put the thing in a plastic bag that he shoved down deep into a brown canvas pack. He stood and started toward her.

She shrank back in terror. He was all blurred and he seemed huge, his eyes were huge, his mouth huge smiling down at her while her life bled away, smiling as he took the knife and slowly cut her blue cotton shorts open and then her pink nylon pants beneath, smiling and looking into her eyes as he carefully pulled apart the cut flaps of cloth and unfastened his belt. With shaking hands he undid the buttons on her white shirt, opened it, placed his hands on the full young breasts and moaned softly. Then he pulled his hands away, lifted her off the bushes and lay her carefully on the ground.

The girl had never felt so bad before; she wanted her

mother to come and make her stop hurting stop the terrible pain in her head make this horrible man stop touching her. Then she didn't see the man but only a blur of tall pine tree directly above bending in the breeze, bending toward her, and she began to confuse it with her mother, her mother bending over, the cool hand on her forehead and the comfort. But it was not her mother; it was the man who was murmuring, "That's right, honey, that's it, baby" as he rammed himself inside her. A small whimpering cry and another small gurgling sound, the blue eyes flashed that brilliant blue again, then clouded as the man gave one loud cry.

Soon he pushed himself up, zipped his pants as he looked around, listening. Nothing: no birds, nothing. Then he remembered the dogs. Where were those damned dogs? How could he have forgotten them? "Here, boy," he called softly and sweetly, then more urgently, "Here boy, atta boy, come on. . . ." He listened again but still nothing. Well shit. But they'd starve to death out here, anyway. And the noisemaker he'd stretched across the north end of the trail, it would've warned him if anyone was coming. That was the only likely direction anybody would come from and even that was a chance in a thousand—no need to worry, no need at all. Though constant alertness was always part of the drill, he'd lost it for a few minutes there but no real harm done. . . .

He went to the boy's body and nudged it over with his foot, leaned down and pulled a slim wallet from a back pocket. He flipped through and saw it had both their driver's licenses, $283, and a list of post offices near the trail where supplies could be mailed ahead. He added the wallet to his pack and then walked around the area slowly, looking at the ground and kicking loose dusty dirt over the debris, but he wasn't very concerned about it. Animals would most likely come before more humans passed this way, and if anyone saw him in the area later, farther down the trail, there'd be no reason to connect him with two half-devoured corpses found days or even weeks later.

He searched quickly through the packs and found what he was looking for, the things he'd seen them pick up back at the mine. The lid of a small round container—tin, surprisingly shiny—that had held opium a century or more before. And a large piece of old blue glass with raised lettering that had once been part of a French champagne bottle. He added them to his pack, then went back to the girl and knelt down. Was she dead yet? He took her chin in his hand and moved the wobbly head back and forth. With a vague, unfocused look to his eyes now, slack-jawed and nodding contemplatively, he took the long, silky light brown hair in one hand and held her head up as he had the boy's. He leaned over and picked up the knife.

He had just begin to cut when the silence was interrupted by a faint *chop chop chop chop chop* coming closer fast, getting louder. He stopped cutting and looked up as he wiped the blade across the girl's tattered shorts *chopchopchop chopchopchopchop* much louder as he pushed the knife into the holder on his belt and stood. He was sure he could take 'em easy enough if they landed but ... maybe better not. Something glittered. He stooped and picked up a gold chain, grabbed his pack and the gun and disappeared into the woods, running toward the creek.

Why the fuck *didn't I drag 'em off into the bushes first?* he raged, partly at himself but mostly at the helicopter. Had the chopper seen anything, seen him, seen the bodies? *Was that girl dead—Christ I should've made sure!*

The chopper was almost deafening now and it was landing, must be setting down in that meadow! He skipped over the creek on a series of conveniently placed stones and raced down the trail. He'd got clean away; he was smart; he was fast; he was still better than anybody! Ambush!

He was flying high, almost too high for his own peace of mind. He felt so good it was hard to remember to be careful. He stopped, made himself stand still and listen. The chopper was a good distance behind now, putting out just a small sound from its idling engine. Smiling, he remembered how easy they'd been to track. He'd followed them a lot longer than necessary but it had been fun and anyway, the farther away, the better. How easily and quickly he'd gotten away when things went wrong, how much smarter he was than just about anybody else, always had been! He continued quickly down the steep path hoping he might come across the dogs, but there was no sign of them. As he came around a sharp curve he stopped abruptly, turned momentarily to stone by the sight of a little girl walking toward him.

She was tired that afternoon, but not as tired as the hikers had been; she'd been running around these woods all her life. She was hot though, and discouraged at not finding any of the gold pieces left on the trail by the Indian children of long ago. She'd have to find the nuggets—and the way to buy her grandmother another house—some other day. She was thinking about how it would be when she got to the creek and could jump in when she looked up and saw the man standing by the big rock where the path curved, just standing there and staring at her in a real funny way. The sun was behind him and she couldn't really see his face, but as he smoothly lowered the rifle something had already warned her and she was gone as suddenly as she'd come, slipping into the bushes and disappearing as easily, and as absolutely, as if she'd been a rabbit, or a squirrel.

The prints left by her small bare feet were clear on the loose dirt of the trail, though. She wasn't a rabbit and he hadn't imagined her. He panicked, started to run, but then got hold of himself and stopped, told himself to think, not fly off the deep end. Had she heard the shots? The chopper? Anyway maybe she'd never connect him with the dead kids back there. If she didn't find them herself and if the goddamned snoops in that helicopter didn't find them they wouldn't be discovered for days, maybe weeks.

But what if she *had* heard the shots, seen his face? What if whoever was in the chopper *had* seen the bodies, was back there now loading 'em up and calling for help? Anyway he couldn't take chances; that's why he'd survived this long—because he never took chances. It was why he was alive and all those others, those others the last place and the place before that, were dead and he wasn't.

He ran down the trail and pushed his way into the brush

where she'd vanished. But he was much bigger than she was, and he made so much noise breaking through the close-packed branches that he soon realized he was wasting his time. He hurried back to the trail, stopped a moment, listening, sensing, then ran downhill again, at last squeezing himself very quietly behind a big clump of bushes. He waited for a few minutes but decided he couldn't afford to stick around—that chopper could conceivably have half an army headed this way by now.

He came out and turned off on a faint downhill trail. Okay. That little girl. What did he know about her? From around here somewhere the way she handled herself, looked part-blood. Faded pink and green check dress too small for her—poor family. That would make it easier. They might not bother much if she disappeared, probably had plenty more where she came from. . . . No. Better make it look like some kind of accident. That way if she did say anything before he got to her, it wouldn't seem connected, wouldn't draw attention to whatever she said, emphasize it. Kid that age, be a piece of cake. About seven or eight probably. Find out where she lived, take care of it today or latest, tomorrow. Now, what *kind* of accident?

This made him think of Larry, and for a moment he saw Alma, quite clearly, standing on the porch there in Spokane calling Larry, always calling that little runt Larry. He smiled, thinking about what had happened to Larry. And nobody ever had the least little suspicion—except maybe Alma. But she never *knew*, never said anything. . . . He could rig up something like that, when he found out where the kid lived.

It was time now to think about the next five minutes, the next hour. He firmly squashed out the picture of Alma on the porch; he couldn't afford to think about Alma very often, or for very long, ever. He made an effort and replaced her image in Spokane with the scene around him: tall trees swaying in a light breeze, sugar pine cones lying big on the ground, a flash of blue ahead and a loud racket as a blue jay squawked his outrage at the approaching intruder. He took the gun from his shoulder and sighted on that small electric blue brightness—funny thing, same color as that girl's eyes.

> ... *they came before national forests,*
> *before the* word *forest—black, shaggy*
> *beings emergent from millions of*
> *forested years without benefit of*
> *manufacture or legislation. ...*
>
> —DAVID RAINS WALLACE,
> *THE KLAMATH KNOT*

TWO

THERE ARE STILL BEARS IN CALIFORNIA, AND ONE OF THEM was looking directly at me. He was about twenty feet away and I thought I could read the thoughts moving briskly behind the small bright eyes, in the massive dark furry head:

"How hungry am I, mhmmm? Long time since breakfast ..."

He started toward me, one step, then another.

"Go away, *go away!*" I waved my arms and yelled, trying to remember if that's what you're supposed to do with bears—or was it you're supposed to stand perfectly still and be quiet? The bear was only fifteen feet away now, moving slowly, but bears can move fast if they want to. He was between me and the house and as he came nearer I screeched out a terrified *"Help! O'Reagan! Com'ere!"*

The bear paused and I looked desperately around for something to rattle at him, make a loud noise with, but there wasn't anything in reach. As he moved closer all the colors around me became intensely bright and yet out of focus except for the bear. Another few steps and I'd be able to reach out and touch him—worse, he'd be able to reach out and touch *me*. With long, curving claws that looked *very* sharp. I wanted to run but wasn't that another rule, not to run? Because a bear can easily outrun a person?

O'Reagan stuck his head out the door and then quickly

disappeared back inside. As the bear started toward me again, O'Reagan came out on the porch with a shotgun.

"Very *slowly* start moving sideways to your right, Maggie—very, very slowly, that's it. You want to end up at that catalpa tree over there. That's it, just a little farther."

About six feet away now, the bear looked around at the sound of the new voice, looked back, seemed undecided. One of his ears was torn half off, I noticed as I sidled sideways. It was healed but dangling. . . .

"Okay, stop," O'Reagan continued softly. "Stay right there and *don't move* unless he comes after you; if he does climb up that tree as fast as you can and if I have to, I'll shoot him."

The bear looked around again at O'Reagan standing on the porch pointing the gun at him. Perhaps he understood, for he turned and shambled quickly off, and soon had disappeared into the woods behind the house.

My knees felt watery and tired of holding me up. I sank down to the ground and leaned back against the tree. My heart was beating wildly and I tried taking slow, deep breaths to calm it down. This made me start coughing, small, mild coughs that hurt like hell. O'Reagan hurried over, still carrying the gun, and said reassuringly, "They're not really likely to attack, these bears they have around here—but you should maybe keep some old pots and pans by the woodshed in case he comes again and you're outside. Always try that first, anyway. If you shoot and don't kill him . . . well, then he really would go after you. You okay?"

"I'm . . . fine. You think he'll come back? I wouldn't want to shoot him, he's been living around here since long before I came. How old do bears get?"

"Pretty old I think." He nodded at a tree behind the house, heavy with ripe apples. "He may come back, probably after the Granny Smiths. Be real careful with your garbage—don't collect it outside and don't dump it around here. There's what they call, in their wisdom, a 'refuse disposal site' about halfway to Scott Bar. If he keeps bothering you, call Fish and Game. They'll come trap him, take him farther away. But once he sees you're here to stay, he'll keep away, I think. Probably been making free of the place because it was empty. Want a hand up?"

"I think I'll just sit here a minute. Thanks."

He opened his mouth to say something else, changed his mind. Looking down at me with a worried frown, he said only, "I'll finish packing up, then."

I watched him walk to the house, then looked around me. One old cabin in a clearing in California mountains so far north they are almost Oregon. The place had belonged to O'Reagan's Aunt Bessie who'd died here in April. She'd died as she had lived, quietly and with no fuss.

It was now the end of August. One morning about a year earlier, I'd woken up in my San Francisco apartment so weak I couldn't get out of bed. Later when I staggered to the bathroom, that twenty feet I'd never given the slightest thought to before was like the last bit climbing Everest. Getting back to bed was just as bad. I hurt horribly all over. My heart was pounding away in an odd dysrhythm. Was I having a heart attack? Making it to the phone in the front room of that long, thin apartment was out of the question. Finally the next morning my partner, Pat O'Reagan, showed up to see why I hadn't come to work or called, why I didn't answer the phone. We had a big job going at the time, and our work sometimes creates enemies.

Five weeks later, there was still no diagnosis.

"You're just depressed. You have to *push* yourself, young lady, get up and *about*. You'll never get any better on your *back*."

Several thousand dollars later, another doctor ran some new tests and said I had a "new" disease variously called Epstein-Barr virus, Chronic Fatigue Syndrome, or Yuppie flu, the names adding insult to injury. The disease itself wasn't actually new. The sister of Henry and William James is thought to have languished most of her life away with it during the last century, but the doctors had only recently discovered it. At first I was terribly relieved to have a name to put to what was wrong, until I realized the doctor was also saying there was no cure or even any treatment except bed rest. A cluster of viruses that wears down the immune system, of unknown origin. I was told that the illness would probably come and go for the rest of my life. The doctor also said I'd probably have times of feeling near normal. He said people didn't usually die of it unless they committed suicide. Oh, great.

"When you're tired, rest. Avoid stress. Don't push yourself; that's the worst thing you can do."

Every time I'd felt better and determinedly gone back to work, the illness had slammed down on me again like a stack of bricks and I'd failed to do what I'd set out to do— every time. I lost the sense that I could count on myself, the sense of myself as a competent person.

After eight more months and fifteen thousand more dollars spent trying everything rumored to help, I'd heard of a doctor in Arizona who'd developed a treatment that actually seemed to get people well. I'd gone to see him and now was getting medicine by mail, had periodic consultations by phone. He'd said it might be a year before I could work again, maybe more. So I'd decided to try living in the old cabin left to O'Reagan by Aunt Bessie. It would be a lot cheaper than San Francisco, and the doctor thought the clean mountain air, combined with a healthy diet, would speed up the process, help the immune system rest and begin to heal itself. No chocolate, plenty of squash and brown rice—life was looking bleak.

The cabin is at a place called China Bar on the Scott River, six miles before the Scott empties into the much larger Klamath. It's a clean, fast-running river that stays icy cold most of the year because of melting snows from the high Marble Mountains to the south. These few miles of narrow river canyon, edged with steep tree-covered mountains, are barely populated now, but they once contained "three thousand voters"—which in those days meant men, and men with white skins. The considerable number of Indians, Chinese, women, and children went uncounted because they didn't really count. They couldn't vote or even testify in court.

I'd learned something about the area from Aunt Bessie when O'Reagan and I visited her several times after we began our partnership—a small but increasingly successful private investigation agency. The white men and the men from China had come for gold, taking out $20 million worth between 1850 and the end of the century—$20 million at the value of the dollar at that time. The Indians were here because that's where they'd been living when the whites came. A good many were killed directly by the whites, shot just for fun sometimes. But the majority died off from white man's diseases they had no immunity to: malaria first, from *Anopheles* mosquitoes infected by the white trappers who came for beaver furs in the 1820s, 30s, and 40s. After the trappers came the miners, bringing measles that killed one out of every two Indians in the Klamath country in 1852, and tuberculosis and alcoholism followed. I could readily identify with those poor Indians, given the fix I was in myself.

By 1852 Scott Bar, three miles downriver from me, was already a thriving boomtown. But soon the easy gold was gone, and travelers described the place a mere twelve years later as dilapidated and half-deserted. Today that "pioneer" main street with its big hotel and its bars, the butcher shop and the laundry, the general stores and the Chinese joss house at the end of town can be seen only in the black and white photographs at the Historical Society. The area is home to about fifteen families, and from an original Indian population of around fifty thousand, there isn't one pureblood Indian left in the Klamath country now. Nor one Chinese person.

I'd liked Aunt Bessie, liked her deep caring about plants and trees, her enthusiastic knowledge about the history of the area. I'd also liked her spunkiness. The first time we visited, she suggested we take the bicycles out of the shed and go for a ride. I'd not ridden since college, and heaven knows how long it had been for O'Reagan, but we both managed to get on and wobble off: Aunt Bessie, at eighty, couldn't manage it.

"Oh, I'm just too old," she'd said disgustedly. "I've left it go too long, I'm just too *old*. You two go on down the road; don't let me stop you. Please!"

So we'd ridden off a short distance to satisfy her, then come back to find her up on the bike and bumping down the rocky driveway after all, pleased as punch. Aunt Bessie had worked as a schoolteacher most of her life, had never married or had children, and O'Reagan said he wasn't surprised when she left him the property though she'd never mentioned it.

That day, sitting out front on the grass, resting and thinking about bears and Indians and gold miners, the place was, as always in summer, very beautiful. Roses so old they are no longer in the catalogs bloomed pink and red and white and cream along an old-fashioned bent-wire fence, mixed with sweetly smelling yellow honeysuckle. High mountains to the north changed from green to dark blue as they receded into the distance in ranks ordered as pyramids, some of them white-topped with snow even in August. The air was the clearest and cleanest I'd ever known, and I felt for a moment that living here maybe wasn't going to be so bad, after all.

Diana, my part-coyote German shepherd who's pretty old now, pushed open the screen door and walked over, stiff-legged, sticking her cold black nose in my face. I rubbed her head behind her big coyote ears and told her all about the bear and that she was to stay away from him—or maybe it was a her—if it came again. Even though Diana doesn't hear so well anymore, I believe she gets the meaning somehow. A faint drone overhead turned quickly into a loud, disturbing noise and I looked up and saw a helicopter circling slowly over the woods behind the house.

O'Reagan came out with his suitcase and put it in his battered BMW—bought long ago, before they became de rigueur in California. He glanced up at the helicopter, stood watching as it flew off. "Forest Service," he commented, "hunting marijuana. Though a lot of 'em grow it themselves." The sound droned away and soon the silence was as deep as if the noisy intruder had never been there.

I got up and went over to the car. "That it?"

"Yeah. All set. Remember, anything you need, call Nancy Odum—the middle-aged cousin? You won't be kindred souls but she's a decent sort and wants to help, means well. Also remember the sheriff in Happy Camp worked in San Jose with me. We weren't exactly drinking buddies, but he'll remember me. Call him if you should need that kind of help. And call the other cousin, Jim Pepper; you'll like Jim. He's just your type. Pity he's married, and to such a bitch. Maybe you can liberate him."

"*Sure.*" Nobody, I was convinced, was ever going to be my type again, not unless I could get well. And married men were not my idea of fun anyway.

"Activist, not into Central America like you but he fights for what he believes in. An environmentalist."

I noticed a tiny trickle of interest raising its irrepressible head in spite of myself.

He continued. "Don't just stay here all alone; it's too isolated. Call them. Nancy and Jim. They're expecting to hear from you, both of them."

I glanced around at the cabin and its outbuildings, the grassy yard and fruit trees and flowering fences, the dark woods. There was a deep and peaceful silence; even the birds and insects were quiet and for the moment we could have been the only two creatures alive in the world. Three with Diana, sitting now by the car and giving us anxious looks. She hates suitcases, and people leaving. I looked back into O'Reagan's worried gray eyes, this good friend and business partner of mine, and smiled. "I'll be fine. Okay, I'll call them. Don't worry. And thanks—for everything."

He nodded and put his long, strong arms around me in a tight hug, looked down and almost said something but didn't, let go. "I left the gun loaded. Keep it somewhere safe but handy because if you do need it, you might not have time to load it. And watch out for rattlesnakes."

"All right."

"Talk to you soon then."

He got into the car, shifted into first and headed slowly down the narrow, rocky drive, not looking back.

Walking was tiring, and slow. My lungs hurt; my heart was pounding. I went inside the house, into the small room with the faded wallpaper of roses and blueberries, and lay down. I fell asleep almost immediately and dreamed of a large yellow fish moving slowly, very deep down on the bottom of the sea. But it was strangely hot down there, and I kept thinking it shouldn't be, it was all wrong, it should be cool down there on the bottom of the ocean, it was all wrong and with the feeling of wrongness came a deep sense of indefinable anxiety.

THREE

WHEN I WOKE UP, IT WAS COOLER. THROUGH THE WINDOW
I could see that the sun had dropped behind some big pine
trees and wasn't hitting the cabin any longer. I felt drugged
from the long afternoon sleep, and reflected that I had no
reason to get up if I didn't want to. What was that dream?

The harder I tried to remember the faster it slipped away,
and I found myself thinking instead about the unpacking I
still needed to do, the books so I'd have something to read
tonight. But the clothes could wait until tomorrow . . . or
the next day, or the next. Was I going to be able to get well
here?

The phone rang and I got up, glad of the distraction. It
was Nancy Odum, O'Reagan's relative who lived thirty
miles farther down the Klamath River in a town called
Happy Camp.

"I got to thinking—did you know about the murder out
back of your place there?"

"Murder? Out back of here?"

"Yep. Right on that trail up behind the cabin. I didn't
know about it yet when I talked to Pat—usually I hear early
anything happens, I got a cousin works dispatch at the sheriff's, but she's on vacation. Anyway I got to thinking
maybe you wouldn't have heard—unless you brought up a
TV? I know Bessie didn't have one, didn't like 'em."

"No, I don't have a TV. What happened?"

16

"Well, the thing is, see, living alone there the way you are, you need to be on the lookout for any weirdos—particularly any *Indian* weirdos."

I wished she'd just answer my question but she seemed to be enjoying drawing her story out, almost a kind of teasing. "What happened?" I asked again. "Why particularly Indian weirdos?"

"The victims was *scalped*, that's why—one of 'em, anyway, and the news said the murderer started on the girl too but then he ran off when the helicopter came."

"Scalped?" I tried to drum up some patience, but I've never had much in the best of times. Maybe she wasn't very smart, I told myself, didn't have a brain that could tell a coherent story. "What helicopter? *Who* was scalped? What happened?"

"Two young hikers, real pitiful—day before yesterday, it was. Nobody knows who they are yet, but the sheriff says they was hikers. They had backpacks and like that but no ID. And the girl was *raped*. Up behind your cabin. There was a Forest Service helicopter flying around out there, saw something looked suspicious, so he landed and found 'em. Girl wasn't dead. He got her to the hospital real fast and they said on the news she may live but she's still unconscious, so she can't tell 'em anything. Boy blown to pieces and scalped, girl shot and raped and he'd started on her, to scalp her, too, but the helicopter must've scared 'im off."

"Oh my God." What she was saying suddenly took on a reality; the images danced in my head, repulsive. I wished I hadn't answered the phone. I could still be lying quite comfortably in bed. I tried to push the ugly scene away, make it all matter-of-fact, factual. "Right behind my cabin?"

"On that trail up there behind your cabin," she repeated with obscure satisfaction. "There's a sign for it on the highway a little farther down from your place—what's it called?"

"The Pacific Crest Hiking Trail, you mean?"

"That's the one. Hikers, and scalped—you better be extra careful. You got Bessie's gun, don't you? You see any Indians around, you tell 'em to git. Show 'em that gun, and keep it loaded."

"O'Reagan left it loaded," I said slowly. First a bear, now Indians that scalped hikers. A nice peaceful quiet place to rest and work on healing. "Where is the girl? In Yreka?" That was the nearest town of any size, the county seat.

"Now that they're not saying. Thinking the murderer might try to finish the job before she can describe 'im, they said on the news—if he knew where she was. She's in a coma, but if she should come out of it."

"That makes sense."

"Well, I'll be over to see you by and by. Not tomorra, tomorra I got to can all day if I don't want the plums to rot. And then I got to go to my sister's down to Orleans; her husband's sick. But later this week—you let me know if I can bring you anything. Pat said you been real sick. There's a freezer out back, in that little shed with the pointy roof next to the woodshed. Fill that freezer up and you won't have to get stuff brought from town so much. Happy Camp's closer for you, but Yreka'll be cheaper. You got my number?"

"I do, yes, Nancy. I'll look forward to seeing you later this week then."

This was far from true—all I really wanted was to lie down for maybe the rest of my life and not have to talk to anyone at all, particularly someone I didn't know.

After we hung up I went back to bed but was too restless to stay there, and got up. I started to unpack the box of books, just to put my mind on something, but I couldn't think about the books, where to put them. I paced the room, Diana looking at me from her bed in the corner. Had it been a big mistake to come up here?

I went out to the porch, sat down in one of the old rockers O'Reagan had brought out from a spare bedroom. I didn't want to think about Nancy Odum's call. I had enough problems of my own and I decided to think about those instead. Right this minute, for instance, instead of rocking my life away I should have been in Nicaragua like last summer. I'd liked Nicaragua, maybe loved it ... the early morning streets full of chattering children in their clean raggedy clothes, going to school in an area where, before the Triumph (as they all called it), there'd been only one school and that private. Then after the Sandinistas slowly and painstakingly got ten built in the area, enough for everyone, two of the new schools were blown up along with their teachers and children by the Contras. . . . I could still feel the rasp of that hot southern sun on my arms, working under dear ancient Santiago's direction. How to lay bricks, so much easier than the awful *bloques*. Sifting dirt through a screen for the *mixcla*. . . . Silvia's great cooking in spite of the impoverished ingredients, at the end of the day. Sitting in frail chairs on that dirt-floor porch, talking to the kids, Carmenza, Yalili. They'd all been working for something they wanted very much, valued. What would happen to those high hopes, now they'd finally been beat down to their knees, made to cry Uncle?

But as I sat there slowly tilting forward, tilting back, the feelings of anger and frustration passed into a more immediate sense of anxiety, almost fear. I began thinking about the hikers again, the weirdo who had done it. About the girl in a coma. Would they be able to keep where she was a secret from the killer she could presumably identify? That would depend a lot on who he was.

I *really* don't want to think about that right now, I told myself firmly. O'Reagan had found some old diaries, I remembered, when he was going through Bessie's things. I'd look at those. I went inside and brought them out to the porch. They were like school composition books, mottled blue and white covers and each neatly dated on the front with a spiky backhand script in black. I checked the end of the first entry but it wasn't signed Bessie, it was signed Jane. A wind came up and blew in the trees, rattling a loose

corner of the tin roof, but I soon ceased to hear as I entered
the world of June 15, 1938.

> Today is my seventeenth birthday. If only I could be-
> gin this book with the announcement of my engage-
> ment to Jed. He did ask me to dance Saturday, but like
> a grown-up playing with a child. He danced a lot with
> Alma Spencer again. He doesn't treat her like a child
> and she isn't one single day older than me, in fact
> she's 27 days *younger*. These horrid little-girl dresses
> Mama makes me wear don't help. Alma had on this
> pale beige clingy thing that just about showed every-
> thing she had, and with spangles—where she gets the
> money, I can't imagine. I know they don't have any
> more money than we do. Is it just jealousy that makes
> me think her an inferior person and not worthy of dar-
> ling, wonderful Jed? No, because I have always
> thought her mean, and sly, too, ever since we were in
> first grade and she stole the colored pencils. But
> Mama's calling, dearest diary . . . Love, Jane

Who was she? A younger sister of Bessie's? Seventeen. I'd
been seventeen once. The world had looked scary but wide
open, too, waiting to be conquered. The conquest all tied up
with finding the right man, his loving me forever. The man
had seemed to be Charlie Westerly when I was seventeen.
He was from Long Island, a junior at Yale, but he visited
a grandmother for Texas summers. Yale! He was cynical
and sophisticated, completely alluring, different from the
boys I knew. He'd even taken me out, once. We'd all been
down at Port Aransas, the unfortunate mother looking after
us girls had broken her big toe, was in pain, wasn't keeping
such good track. Some grappling in a car at the beach to
the sound of the crashing waves, which I thought was like
being in heaven. A night swim in the dark mysterious
ocean, the phosphorus flying high and bright almost as my
heart. Had I ever loved anyone so again? A hundred and

ten percent? Like the girl in the diary and—what was his name?—Jed. The next entry was July 1:

Jed is to go to work on his uncle's ranch way up in Washington after the Fourth. If only he would ask me to go with him! But even if he did, how could I leave Mama? Still, if he could once really *see* me, things would work out somehow—I know they would. I have Great Hopes for the picnic—Susanna is going to lend me a party dress, it's pale blue organdy with a low scoopy neck. I'll leave the house in my usual stupid gingham and change at her house. Cross your fingers, dear diary—Jane

I tried to remember what I had worn that night all those years ago. But the dress, surely my favorite at the time, was as long gone as Charlie Westerly. How had Jane's borrowed dress worked out? The next entry was July 5:

I am the happiest of mortals!!!!! He stayed with me the *whole time* when we all went to look for the Indian celery. The thing about the dress worked, I know it did—I think he hadn't really noticed until then that I'd changed one whit since I was twelve years old. But here is what happened. Susanna and Billy and Marvin went on ahead and I suggested we take a side path where I knew there was sure to be some Indian celery and there was, a large patch growing under a big oak tree. We were digging some up and then Jed put his hand over mine. I was scared to look at him! Then he put his other hand under my chin and pulled my head up so I *had* to look at him but pretty soon I couldn't look anymore so I closed my eyes—then he kissed me!!!!! He has the bluest eyes, just the color the ocean was, with the sun shining on it, that time we went over to the coast above Eureka when Daddy was alive. Anyway, after he kissed me, he looked kind of surprised and he just looked at me and then he said,

"Guess we better be getting back, Janey." He held my hand until we caught up with the others and afterwards he stayed with me and went and got my plate of fried chicken and later the watermelon. And at the dance, he asked me to dance *six* times. He danced some with Alma, too, but I could see she was put out. And he danced the last dance with me, not her. Oh I am so, so, so happy, dearest diary. . . .

If Jane was still alive, she'd be over seventy. That could be Bessie's younger sister, but I'd never heard Bessie mention her, or O'Reagan, either.

I went inside and got the Historical Society book, took it back to the porch and flipped through the pages, looking for a Spencer family or a Jane Thornton. Some Spencers living up Mill Creek in the 1920s were mentioned, and there was a family of Thorntons photographed on the porch of a Victorian house that no longer existed, but no children's names were given. There were three girls, though, about the right ages to have been Bessie, a younger sister Jane, and the one who'd been O'Reagan's mother. I'd met her before she died but couldn't remember her name. I couldn't find a Jed or any specific mention of either girl. A reminiscence about the Chinese in Scott Bar caught my eye.

A peculiar thing about the Chinese when they were going to and from work, was that they never walked side by side. They always followed one another in a sort of trot. A large company would be strung out for several hundred yards. They always carried a long pole on their shoulders. If I remember right there was a lunch pail on one end and a pot of tea on the other. I have heard there were several thousand at one time between Scott Bar and the mouth of the river.

Did their ghosts walk sometimes along the road now, single file and trotting, with long poles carrying ghosts' lunches and celestial tea?

It was getting too dark to read. The sun was long gone behind the mountain and the world had drifted into that magical soft twilight time that I almost never even noticed, in the city. The shadows in the yard were long and dark now; the happy summer feeling of the afternoon was gone, my sanctuary turned somber, even threatening. I closed my eyes, seeing the ghostly Chinese miners trotting along, seeing Jane and Jed holding hands, seeing Alma in her spangly dress . . . but images of those hikers intruded. An ugly puzzle that once would have been right up my alley but now I had no energy for anything like that. Still, why shoot a couple of hiking kids? Why scalp them?

I didn't like Nancy Odum's ready explanation that it was some Indian. Why not? Because I identified with them, my fellow lousy immune systems? Didn't like the way they'd been pushed around and robbed and murdered by my own ancestors? All I really knew about the local Indians were their names: Shasta and Karuk. O'Reagan himself is part Karuk, courtesy of a great-grandmother. He'd said to call his cousin on the Indian side of the family, Jim Pepper. I knew from O'Reagan that this cousin was a couple of years younger than me, thirty-six or -seven. That he lived far up a mountain road above Happy Camp, was married to a woman O'Reagan had instantly taken a strong dislike to. He'd been the first to study the Karuk language systematically and get it written down; now he taught it to others. He also worked with the tribe and other local groups in environmental-protection matters, and sometimes worked construction for additional money. Should I call him? And say what? I couldn't decide, found myself drifting off into a state of semiconsciousness as gray and indistinct as the twilight around me.

I was startled awake by Diana's loud barking. Something moved down by the gate. Even as my body prepared for flight, I saw the shadowy figures were a small girl and a couple of dogs. She seemed to be trying to drag them away and they were resisting.

"Hi," I called out. "Don't be afraid; I'll put my dog inside."

After I pushed Diana into the house, I went to the gate and saw the little girl was indeed trying to convince two rather nervous dogs to go with her.

"What's the problem? Can I help?" I asked her.

Big-eyed, thin-legged, and dressed in a skimpy, not very clean dress of pink and green checks, she stopped pulling at the dogs and looked up at me with open curiosity. "They was on the trail up there. You livin' here now at Miss Bessie's?"

I hesitated. Living here? Might as well admit it—to myself. "Yes. I live here now. My name's Maggie. What's your name?"

She mumbled something I couldn't quite catch. "Did you say Mimi?" It seemed an unlikely name somehow for this particular child with her round black eyes and high cheekbones, but she nodded.

"I'm tryin' to get them home, but they won't come. They's too tired, I guess."

"You want me to help you get them up to the porch? They're probably hungry. I'll get some food. After they eat, they might be more ready to travel."

A relieved smile swept across the thin little face and she began pushing the dogs through the open gate. "That's it, doggies, that's good," she murmured encouragingly. I helped, and they did come along as far as the steps.

"You stay with them," I said. "I'll get the food."

In the kitchen, Diana pacing excitedly beside me, I looked hurriedly around. Something they could digest easily would be best—the soup. There was a big pot on the stove, chicken and vegetables that O'Reagan had put together for lunch. I grabbed a couple of tin bowls and half-filled them, then closed the screen door on Diana's intensely curious face and hurried outside.

Mimi took a bowl and we put them down before the dogs: a big one with short crinkly-brown hair who seemed to be all ears and staring, panicky eyes; the other a little black mop, tangled and burr-filled. The big dog started lapping noisily and ravenously. The small one, after looking up as if for permission, took a tentative lick, then another, and soon was eating as greedily as her companion.

Mimi watched with great concentration. How Indian she looked. Was she Shasta, or Karuk? She seemed a very serious child, but then a smile lit her face like a floodlight as she nodded approvingly and said, "Boy, they sure do like that soup!" She gave a small contented sigh, looked up at me, looked away.

"You live around here?" I asked.

"Up the mountain. I been livin' with my granny 'cause my mom . . ." Her voice trailed off. After a few seconds, she continued briskly. "Yesterday we went down to Redding to see how can we keep our cabin from the piss-firs. We just got back this afternoon." She pressed her lips together and, for so small a creature, looked suddenly quite ferocious.

"The piss-firs? What's that, some kind of tree?"

"Oh, don't you know? They not trees, they those men at the guard station, wear clothes all the same, tell everybody how they have to do with the trees and all like that."

"You mean the Forest Service? They have a headquarters or something in Scott Bar?"

"That's them. They tryin' to tear down our cabin, and Granny, she go down to Redding to talk to the big boss there. She say it don't do no good, though. She say they probably tear it down and nothing we can do. Maybe not till next summer, though. But if I can find some gold, I'll buy us a new house where the piss-firs can't come tear us down."

I felt awkward, stilted, a false cheer creeping into my voice. "I sure do hope you find some," I said helplessly. "Is it just you and your grandmother who live up there, or are there other people?"

"Well, sometimes my mom and Hank lives there. He's her boyfriend. They like to travel around or sometimes they stay at Hank's place in Redding—my mom don't like to keep in one place. Sometimes I go with 'em."

"What do you do about going to school when you're with your mother, if she moves around so much?"

Mimi looked down at her feet, which were bare and brown and dirty, and clearly didn't care to talk about school; or maybe it was her mother that was the sensitive subject. "Where do you think these dogs came from?" I asked to spare her further embarrassment. "They must belong to somebody, don't you think?"

"I dunno. I ain't seen 'em around here before. But there was some people got killed on the trail up there. . . ." Her voice trailed off as she considered this bizarre and interesting fact.

"You think the dogs belonged to them?" The grisly images took over my mind again for a moment, and I shivered, saw the poor dogs running terrified into the woods, coming back after the helicopter had lifted their owners away, abandoned far from home, not knowing where to go. I pulled my thoughts back to the little girl, the dogs here and now. "I heard nobody knows who those people were or where they came from."

"Nobody does, I guess. My las' dog, he got killed. Granny says a good dog keeps bad peoples away. But Prince," she added thoughtfully, "he couldn't keep the piss-firs away."

"Do you want to name them?" I asked. "It'd be easier if we had something to call them."

Mimi sat back on her heels and considered. "Prince. Prince for the brown one. He's a boy. And—and—Little Dog for the black one. She's a girl."

"Okay. Those are good names." The dogs were curled back-to-back now, asleep. And no matter what we did, we couldn't get them to stand up.

"They just won't come," Mimi said. "They just *won't come*."

"Why don't you leave them here, get them tomorrow."

"Okay," she agreed slowly, "okay, I guess so. Only . . ."

"Uh-huh? Only what?"

"Well, I is the one found them, so they, so they . . ."

"So they're really your dogs?"

She nodded, looking relieved to have gotten this delicate point across.

"Right," I said. "They're yours unless someone turns up who, umm, who they belonged to before they belonged to you, right?"

Of course, the hikers were never going to turn up to claim them. But maybe their parents would want the dogs back. Their poor parents.

"Okay," the little girl agreed. Then she walked off into the moonlight, a small but competent person who seemed quite unafraid of the dark woods and whatever they might contain between here and her grandmother's house.

> ... the new thing presented by fate
> seldom or never corresponds to
> conscious expectation.
> —CARL JUNG,
> THE ARCHETYPES AND THE COLLECTIVE
> UNCONSCIOUS

FOUR

THE NEXT MORNING THE VISITING DOGS WERE STILL ON THE porch and looked hungry, so I gave them more soup mixed with some dry dog food. They gulped it down while I told them what fine creatures they were and that everything was going to be all right. Then I let Diana out and they all sniffed and wagged tails and seemed to get along fine.

I settled myself in the rocker and wrote down the previous night's fragmented, troubled dreams. Running down a strange, unknown street in diagonals and bumping into someone, apologizing but they stayed angry: "Can't you *watch* where you're *going*?" The sound of the bike in the distance and David, my husband dead these five years, arriving earlier than expected at the cabin we used to have in the Trinity Mountains, my happiness turning to dismay as I saw he'd brought along another woman he seemed to be interested in—or wasn't it David, after all?

Diana raised her head, then all three dogs raced barking to the gate. Mimi opened it and came through, the dogs greeting her like their all-time favorite human they'd given up on ever seeing again. After she got them calmed down, she ran up to the porch and said excitedly, "Guess what happen? We had a big splosion las' night and Granny say I like to got killed, only I didn't 'cause I put the switch on with my magic stick!" She grinned and did a little excited dance step.

28

"A splo—explosion? What switch?"

"When I put on my robot doll, *blam!* All the lights went out—still out. We usin' candles. All burnt black around my robot, too. She's ruint, completely ruint." She added with relish, "Granny say I be burnt black too, 'cept for my magic stick."

"Oh, *Mimi!* What—how did it happen?"

"Don' know, we never had nothin' like that before. Granny say she just can't figure it out. But it was lucky I pushed that switch with my stick."

"It sure was. Is that it?" I pointed to a long, polished piece of some dark, hard wood lying on the ground. She'd been dragging it behind her.

"Uh-huh, my mom give it to me las' year for my birthday." She picked it up and stroked the smooth wood. "Guess it protected me all right—my mom say it's a special medicine stick."

"Is your grandmother getting someone to fix the wiring so it's safe?" I was worried, uneasy. Also irritated. I didn't want to worry, be responsible. I just wanted to rest, be at peace, get better. At the same time, I liked this little girl, wanted to have her in my life up here, make a real connection—if I could summon up the energy.

"Granny say we just use candles for now. She pull down the handle on that gray box outside on the wall. She say that way we be sure we don't have no more problems till Hank gets up here. Hank can fix just about anythin'."

"That's lucky. Well . . . want to bring the dogs and walk down to the river with me?"

"Sure!" she said happily, and we headed across the road and down a stony, tree-lined trail to the river.

There was a small sandy beach at the end of the path, the water in front wide and deep and very green. A high rock wall rose almost straight up on the other side. I sat down and leaned against a log, looking upstream. Huge gray birds, ospreys, circled between high white canyon walls where a few trees clung precariously along tiny ledges. I watched the high, drifting birds, breathed the clean, pure mountain air, and listened to the silence. But for the rushing water and the occasional cry of a bird, or the dogs, or Mimi, it was absolute. But worry crept into the silence. I didn't like the idea of Mimi living in a cabin with wiring so decrepit that a toy could explode and nearly kill her. She'd left the water now and was walking back upstream along the edge of the river, peering down intently at the ground. I was bored with sitting and got up to help her look for whatever it was.

"Did you lose something?"

"I'm just lookin' for some gold."

"You think there might be some here?"

"I don't know—but I'm lookin' just in case. Usually, I'm lookin' back up in the mountains—you know that trail goes over to Tomkins Creek? I been lookin' there."

"Why there?"

"Well, Granny told me the Indian children round here, long, long time ago it was when they families went over to fish at the creek, the kids took along these big pieces a gold they found lyin' down here by the river. They used to be a lotta gold just lyin' aroun', before the miners came. Granny told me the kids thought it was pretty. They used to beat it out flat in big plates, like. Anyway sometimes they got tired a carryin' it, it was heavy, so they hid it on the trail. If I can find some, I can buy us a house where the piss-firs can't tear us down or make us move, see."

"Uh-huh. You find anything yet?"

She reached into her pocket and proudly showed me a small glittery white rock that did indeed have a gold spot about the size of half a dime embedded on one side.

"That's terrific, Mimi. I sure do hope you find some more. But you know what?"

"What?"

"I don't think you ought to be walking around on that trail to the creek right now—that's where those people were shot." I touched her arm, tried to make my voice urgent, to communicate the danger to her. "It isn't safe. Do me a favor, don't go up there until they catch the person who did it and put him in jail. Just stick to the trail up to your place, okay? And if you see anybody coming, maybe it would be a good idea to hide until they've gone past."

She ducked her head, looked away. "I'm not goin' roun' there right now, anyway," she mumbled.

Suddenly a helicopter was overhead shrieking its war games, breaking the spell. I hated helicopters. They still made me think of Vietnam, old people and thin, small women carrying dead babies, running with their children from their burned villages, trying to escape, gunned down. More recently it was the Middle East, 35,000 they said at first, then the word crept out it was maybe a hundred thousand and most of them civilians. Women and children and old ones running, screaming, this time it was the desert not the jungle. Soon they stopped screaming, stopped running. Uncle Sam up there in the sky, our boys obeyed what almost everyone agreed were brilliant orders, computer-directed, invincible, untouchable. But it had been a helicopter that saved the life of that girl camper. Nothing was as totally simple as I wanted it to be, to cut down on the chaos I saw wherever I looked.

I gave Mimi her stone and we headed back to the cabin. When we got up there, she looked down at her feet and murmured, so softly I could hardly hear, the disappointing news that Granny said the dogs better stay at Miz Bessie's for now—her Granny wasn't feeling good. Her heart was "actin' up" and they had to go back to town for some tests.

I didn't need two more dogs, but I didn't like the idea of sending them to the pound, either. Or of breaking Mimi's heart.

That evening, a report on the radio said that the "partially scalped and nearly murdered young girl hiker" was still unconscious and that the police were working on several leads.

Angry, vicious barking woke me the next morning. I leapt out of bed, thinking the dogs had gotten in a fight and I had to break it up before they hurt each other. But they were protecting the property against a heavyset woman standing by the gate, afraid to come in.

I grabbed a robe and went out to calm the dogs, then led her past: It was O'Reagan's relative Nancy Odum, bringing three large boxes of saltine crackers and four jars of home-made gooseberry jam. She was a large, pale woman with bulging blue eyes and a distinct mustache above full, pro-truding lips. She wore heavy dark polyester slacks though it was already a hot day, and an unfashionable short-sleeved green shirt that made her skin look yellow. But she was smiling and friendly. She told me she'd decided to come before she went to her sister's, after all. She said no thanks to my offer of tea, and as I put away her gifts she asked, "Did you hear they found out who those poor things are as got scalped and murdered and raped on that trail up there?"

"Did the girl die, then?"

"Well, not *yet*. But I don't think they expect her to pull through. They was from up in Oregon, anyway, having their vacation before school started up again. They was headed for Hayfork—the boy's father lives there. Both the parents're divorced, the father was gonna drive 'em back home. After he got to thinking about the TV story, he called the sheriff, and that's how they found out who they were." She paused to catch her breath.

"Do they have any idea *why* they were attacked? Or who might have done it?"

"Must be some crazy Indian—they was scalped, like I told you, and nobody never heard a no white man scalping nobody. A lotta these Indians around here ain't much good, if the truth be told—between drinking and drugs, and fight-ing and stealing—though a course they don't know if it's some Indian from right around *here* or else from farther downriver. There's a reservation down there in Hoopa."

I remembered she was related to O'Reagan by marriage on the non-Indian side of the family. I was curious what she counted as Indian, since she was apparently very fond of O'Reagan, but couldn't think of any tactful way to ask. In-

stead, I told her about the dogs, that they might have belonged to the hikers.

"Oh my goodness! Isn't that something! You better get
their parents' addresses from the sheriff then. You don't
need two more dogs to take care of, health problems
you've got."

"Do you know their names, the parents?"

She shook her head. "Seems like they did say on the
news—I saw a interview with the girl's mother. But I
don't ... Stephens. Her name was Stephens. You call the
sheriff in Happy Camp; they'll have the address. Now have
you seen any rattlesnakes?" I shook my head. "This is rattlesnake country, you know. You keep an eye peeled for
'em."

She repeated her assurances of help and then disappeared
back downriver to the oddly named town of Happy Camp.
Was it a particularly joyous place, its people smiling and
laughing all day long? Or maybe a lot of gold had been discovered there once and that was what the happiness re-
ferred to. About the only thing I knew about it was that a
lot of Indians, or anyway part-Indians, lived there: Karuks.

I called the sheriff's office and told the deputy who I was
and why I wanted the addresses.

"Boy's parents are gone back east someplace, I mean
they live out here but they left. You could write the girl's
mother, I guess."

"Fine. If you'd give me her name and address."

"Mrs. Hallie Stephens—"

I'd only ever known or even heard of one other person
named Hallie. And she had a daughter who would be about
seventeen now. "Did you say *Hallie?*" But that was ridiculous; of course it wouldn't be her.

"That's right, H-a-l-l-i-e Stephens, S-t-e-p-h-e-n-s."

"What's the daughter's name?" I asked out of curiosity.
"The girl in the coma?"

"Girl's name? Girl's name is Sally."

Oh God. Sally ... I sat down abruptly, my knees turned
to mush, my heart racing.

"Is she—have you heard anything recently on her condition?"

"No, ma'am, far's I know, she's still in the coma."

"I think I might know the girl's mother; we were pretty good friends. Could you give me the phone number?"

"I'm sorry but I can't do that, ma'am, just the address. It's uh . . . three seventeen Rockland Way, Gold Beach, Oregon. I don't have the zip."

I tried again to talk him into a phone number but got nowhere. After we hung up I just sat there for a few minutes, thinking about the Hallie and Sally I'd known when I worked in film in San Francisco. How long had it been? Six years, seven? A little more. Hallie's name had been Morgan then, a single mother who also worked in film. Sometimes I'd kept Sally for her, taken her to the beach, the zoo—she had loved the gorillas best. She'd been five, then six, time had gone fast, soon she was nine, ten. I'd loved Sally. Always a bit on the pudgy side, she'd not lost her baby fat, not when I'd known her. Those bright electric blue eyes of hers; she'd had beautiful long, thick hair. They'd moved away.

They'd moved to Oregon, not Gold Beach . . . Grants Pass. Maybe they weren't the same people, but with Hallie's habit of heading at a dead run from one disastrous relationship to another, her last name could be anything by now. I remembered the perfect oval of her face, the beautiful bones. That sunny back room with all the windows at her place on Haight, corner of Ashbury. A little oasis of the sixties still, finally disappearing even in San Francisco, which had held on longest. Hundreds of plants, light filtering through green like in a jungle. Sharing a joint one afternoon, Hallie laughing. But serious underneath. "Shit. The terrible things that keep happening to me, I think I must have been *Hitler* in my last life." The move away from the city had been intended as a new start, to change the karma, to make the bad things stop. Then David had been killed and I'd started drinking heavily, soon was doing little else. We lost touch.

I called my office—or was it ex-office?—and gave Harold, the secretary, the Gold Beach address. He looked it up in a Criss Cross directory—worth its weight in gold to a detective—and found the phone number. I dialed but got no answer. I tried again, in case I'd done it wrong, but there was still no answer. Maybe when I reached this woman I'd find out she was another Hallie, her daughter another Sally—people I'd never known and didn't have to worry about, care about. But I had a heavy feeling in my solar plexus and my hand was shaking as I put the receiver down.

> We are affected when a dog travels
> hundreds of miles to go home; salmon
> have traveled millions of years. That
> they die after spawning makes the
> quest seem all the more heroic, and all
> the more tragic the possibility that
> the quest will be thwarted by dams which
> will silt up and become useless in a
> century or two.
>
> —DAVID RAINS WALLACE,
> *THE KLAMATH KNOT*

FIVE

AFTER LUNCH I TRIED THE NUMBER AGAIN, BUT THERE WAS
still no answer. I was feeling restless so I shut the dogs in
the yard and got into my elderly Karmann Ghia. It didn't
want to start but finally caught, and I headed it for the post
office.

The river canyon widened out at Scott Bar, creating a
peaceful, old-fashioned-looking place that reminded me of
an illustration in an old children's book. Grassy yards with
flowers and big leafy trees surrounded four or five old
frame houses, a couple of them beautiful, shabby Victorians. Then there was the post office, the old iron bridge, the
bell-towered white schoolhouse, and that was it except for
the new Forest Service guard station.

The old houses sat quietly as they'd done for so many
years, but the two-way radio at the guard station was
hooked up to an enormous speaker and suddenly blared
loudly, as it had every time I'd passed that way, smashing
the peace and serenity like an angry fist shattering a mirror:
ten-four, ten-four, ten-four, more war games. The guard station reminded me I wanted to call Jim Pepper. See what I
could find out, if anything could be done about Mimi's

cabin. It was nice to feel a little spare energy for a change. To be able to think about something more than just basic survival. I definitely seemed to be doing better up here. Or maybe it was those homeopathic drops. . . .

It was a hot day. One green-uniformed young man was slowly mowing the guard station's lawn. Another was desultorily doing something to the wood-plank fence. Neither was paying any attention to the radio.

The post office was a small, brown-painted wood building with boxes that opened outside onto a narrow covered porch. There was a small bulletin board by the door, empty. I tacked up a note about the dogs, with my phone number. Mimi might consider this the act of a traitor, but if the dogs belonged to someone who loved them, they'd be frantic with worry.

I went inside and introduced myself to the postmaster, who said he was Bill Dawson and very happy to make my acquaintance. He was somewhere the other side of fifty, short and balding and round-faced with glasses thick as Coke bottles. But he was also barrel-chested, with big muscular arms. He looked strong and in good condition. He reached immediately into a box on the top row, not having to stop to think which one was mine even though I was such a newcomer.

"One for you today, young lady," he said cheerfully, handing over a thin letter that I saw was from O'Reagan. "How're you liking it up at Bessie's? You got enough firewood? It doesn't look that way today, but winter's coming before too long. There've been blizzards here, times nobody could get in, nobody could get out. Did you know that? Blizzard of 'fifty-two, for instance—1852! Pack trains couldn't get through and those miners nearly starved, ate the leather tops right off their boots, boiled 'em. Bet you've never been that hungry, am I right?"

Weird guy, something kind of endearing about him, though. "You're right." I smiled. "Never so far have I been that hungry. But I have plenty of firewood. The shed's full, already split down for the stove."

"You'll be all right then, that's a nice big shed. Bessie Thornton always was a real hard-working woman. Missed around here. I'm feeling her loss this time of the year particular—many's the time we used to go for steelhead, her and me. I always made sure to be here when they run, even when I was living elsewhere."

"You were a friend of hers, then?"

"That's right—she was my high school hist'ry teacher, and I did yard work for her. That's when we started going fishing. Her and me, we always got a real good catch—she knew all the best spots."

I'd gone fishing with David once, in that clear rocky stream way down below our cabin—the first time since childhood summers spent along Texas rivers. As an adult, I found I hated having to kill them. Bash them with a rock on their helpless, terrified heads, gasping for water in the foreign air. After that David went by himself. I just ate them.

"Steelhead are some kind of fish, right?" I asked. "What's so special about them?"

"Some kind of fish! Steelhead are *trout*—but they're a lot bigger than stream trout. They live in the ocean. Furthermore, they're the most delicious, best-tasting thing God ever put in a frying pan. They come up here all the way from the ocean to lay their eggs, did you know that? They have to come back to the creek where they were born, to the *exact spot* they were born at, way up in the mountains. Those fish have been coming up here from the ocean like that for millions of years, scientists say—but nobody knows *how they know where to go.* How in the world do you suppose they ever got started living that way? Those fish are really something, the way they travel, am I right or am I wrong?"

He was a terrible talker, but I loved odd bits of information like that. I shook my head and smiled. "Oh, you're right. You're absolutely right, Mr. Dawson."

"Call me Bill; everyone around here calls me Bill. We don't use last names much on the rivers."

"All right, sure. So, Bill, you must know a lot about what goes on around here. What do you think about the attack on those hikers?"

His wide, cheerful face became suddenly serious. He shook his head slowly. "Now ain't that something? We never had anything like that happen around here. Even back in the old days, it was plenty wild—you might want to have a look in Bessie's Historical Society book, that'll give you some idea—but we never had anything . . ." He hesitated, looking for the right word. "Anything *nasty* like this. Filth! Got to be some outsider, that's what I say."

"Some Indian outsider?"

He straightened a pile of junk mail on his counter. "Looks like it, doesn't it?" He shrugged. "Anyway, I don't recommend you to go walking around back up there, Maggie, not till they catch the son of a bitch."

A man had come in so quietly that I hadn't heard him, though the room in front of the postmaster's window was very small, until Bill looked past me and said, "Afternoon there, Sam, how's the world treating you today?"

"Can't complain, can't complain, Bill. Got a box full of government checks for me today or what?"

Bill turned to reach into the appropriate mailbox and I murmured, "It was nice talking to you," and went outside. On the porch a thin, elderly man with spiky gray hair was looking through a pair of binoculars into a late-model white car parked in front of the post office. He had on muddy leather work boots and needed a shave. As I came out he lowered the glasses.

I quickly read O'Reagan's letter, a typical factual account of what was going on at work, his hopes I was feeling better and settling in. Had I called Jim Pepper yet, Nancy Odum? O'Reagan never talked about his personal life, though he had one of sorts—a son who lived with the mother. He saw him sometimes. And he was attractive to women. There were always women scattered about in his life, trying to dig themselves out a permanent niche. But no one had succeeded since his ex-wife. O'Reagan and I were pretty close, but even I didn't really know whether his detachment was because she'd been a horror or because he still loved her. Perhaps both.

I looked to see where my box was and noticed the numbers only went to fifty. The man who'd been inside came out, fat and red-faced, about forty, and paused to read through some mail. The old guy with the binoculars unobtrusively sidled close enough to look down sideways and read right along, too. The fat man gave a sudden start, looked up and glared, said, "Pardon *me*," and stomped off to his car. The curious man was unperturbed. He looked at me with interest.

"You're the one living in Bessie Thornton's place now, ain't you?"

I said I was.

"I hear as how you're a friend of Pat O'Reagan who inherited the place, is that right?"

I said as how I was.

"What did you do before you came up here—I heard as how you was a PI. Is that a fact?"

I admitted that it was and retaliated by asking, "What's *your* name?"

"Joey Brown, pleased to meet you. Your name's Elliott, isn't it? Maggie Elliott? I knew old Miss Bessie many and many a year. How long you plannin' on stayin'?"

I said I didn't know but had no plans to leave. He was sort of sweet, with his insatiable, completely out-front curiosity.

"Well, what about these murders—you hear about those hikers gettin' attacked, one of 'em killed, the other one still in a coma?"

I nodded.

"Well then, seein' as how you're a trained professional PI, maybe you'll be the one to find the killer."

"More likely the sheriff. Anyway, I'm up here to rest, not work."

"Sheriff's people are all right for some things"—he shook his head—"but I wouldn't bet money on 'em, this

kind of real hard-core *crime*. You know? Think about it.
They never come up against anythin' like this. That's why
I thought, person like you, person experienced in this sort
of thing, probably stand a better chance of figgerin' it out."

"What do you think it's all about, Joey?"

"Well, I don't deny I've given it considerable thought.
What I figger is, it's either some crazy lunatic *or* somebody
not so crazy. Somebody with a reason. If we just knew
what it was, it'd all make sense, you know?"

"Like what, for instance?"

He shrugged. "There's rumors old gold's buried up there.
Ever hear of Indian Mary?"

I shook my head.

"She used to disappear back up in those mountains,
come back with U.S. government gold pieces. Way
back, some Indians attacked a pack train carryin' sol-
diers' pay, killed 'em, buried the gold somewhere up
there. It never was found but then old Mary maybe knew
where it was. She must've, way she always came back
with those gold pieces."

That's a story for Mimi, I thought. "When was this?"

"Well, that I'm not sure, I'd say maybe a hundred
twenty–thirty years ago. People tried to follow her but she
always ditched 'em. She's long dead now, of course. But if
the killer could be found—why maybe it'd lead right to that
old gold! You know? Give it some thought, why don't you?
See what you come up with."

I kept trying the number I had for Hallie and not getting
an answer. I became a regular listener to the radio
newscasts—usually I avoid the news like I'd avoid a con-
tagious disease—but the girl in the coma was no longer
mentioned. Surely that meant she hadn't died. Wouldn't
they have said so? I tried to picture Sally, a larger,
seventeen-year-old Sally, lying in a hospital bed breathing
steadily. Opening her eyes, smiling . . . but images of the
horrible attack kept intruding.

I got out Aunt Bessie's Historical Society volume on

Scott Bar again, wanting to fill my mind with something else. To replace images of Sally hurt, Sally dying, Sally a vegetable with pictures of that old Scott Bar. There were some funny letters home by a man named Lucius Fairchild, who later became governor of Wisconsin:

> This Scott's Bar is decidedly the Roughest place and the miners the most Rowdy drunken set I have ever seen in my life. Every night some party is on a spree whooping and yelling around town, fighting, swearing, breaking the Rum holes up, etc. . . . There are 4 stores, 3 Pie shops, one Bowling Alley, one Hotell (a one-horse one) and my market, all of which except myself, keep licquor for sale, in fact, it is the staple article here, the very staff of life. . . . Now that I have seen the true nature of women when freed from all restraints of a polite society, seen their licentious behavior without curb or decency coming from any vestige of character, I will never marry.

Had he stuck to his plan? A bachelor governor keeping the girls' hopes up, and their mamas'. Probably they'd just mildly flirted, those licentious women.

You make up your own song, your own special song—you get your power from that.

—LEAF HILLMAN,
KARUK TRIBAL COUNCIL

SIX

LICENTIOUS WOMEN, I WAS THINKING AS I WASHED DISHES the next morning and heard the sound of tires crunching up the drive, the dogs barking. I went to the door and saw a sky blue Chevy pickup and an Indian getting out of it. He opened the gate and leaned down to pat the growling dogs, talking to them calmly, then continued on unconcernedly toward the porch. He was a big man, two or three inches over six feet, with wide shoulders and a rather stocky body, but he moved with the ease and grace of an athlete. He was wearing clean, faded jeans and a blue work shirt and I suddenly felt a little licentious myself. I pushed open the screen door and he stopped just below the porch.

"I'm looking for uh, Pat O'Reagan's partner, is he home? I'm Jim Pepper, Pat's cousin."

He was very good-looking. And the inner man just my type, according to O'Reagan. My heart beat a little faster; I couldn't help that. But how in the world had O'Reagan managed to tell him about me and not mention I was a woman? And why? "I'm his partner—I guess he must not have told you to expect a woman. I was meaning to call you, in fact. You want some coffee?"

"Sure. O'Reagan didn't say, I guess I just assumed . . ."

"Come on up, I'll get the coffee."

When I brought it out, with microwaved cinnamon rolls from the freezer plus linden-flower tea for myself, Jim Pep-

43

per was sitting in one of the rocking chairs and rubbing Prince behind the ears, talking softly. Prince looked like he'd died and gone to heaven; Little Dog and Diana were looking needy and pitiful, so I gave them a few pats and soothing words to even things out.

"Nice dog. What kind is he?" Jim asked.

"I'm not sure. He's a stray, maybe belonged to those hikers who were shot. But I think he's a Chesapeake."

He looked up, interested. "The hikers who were killed? Why do you think so?"

"A little girl found the dogs wandering on the trail a couple of days after it happened. She told me she'd never seen them around before. I put a note up at the post office, but nobody's claimed them so far."

He nodded and said nothing more but just sat and rocked, sipping coffee and eating a cinnamon roll, looking off at the mountains which I did, too. I didn't like to stare, but this was the closest I'd ever been to an Indian, not counting Mimi, which was somehow quite different. He looked very Indian anyway, though I knew there were no full-bloods left in the Klamath country. He had the very thick, very straight pitch-black hair, dark eyes, hooked nose, and high, wide cheekbones seen in indigenous peoples from the top of Alaska down to Tierra del Fuego. Did he have a ruined immune system, too, like the Indians of old? We could live happily ever after except for taking turns being sick, perhaps. But O'Reagan had said he was married, a big obstacle to the plan even if our immune systems were perfect twins. Also he looked quite healthy.

He sat silently sipping his coffee, seeming very relaxed. His dark good looks appeared to include absolutely no sense of vanity or self-consciousness.

"O'Reagan's my second or third cousin 'removed,' " he said finally. "Whatever that means." His voice was slightly husky and with some other quality I couldn't pin down that made it appealing, sexy. "I never met him till last year when he worked for the tribe on that Nevada land deal."

O'Reagan had been hired, I remembered, because of his

own Karuk connection. And they'd been pleased, he'd gotten what they wanted. After another silence, I asked Jim what he thought about the murder. "People, or anyway some people, seem to be blaming the Indians," I commented.

"I wonder if even a dumb Indian would point a finger at himself like that."

"The scalping, you mean?"

"Yeah. Happened somewhere near here, didn't it?"

I nodded. "Up behind the cabin and I guess it would be . . . south."

He waited, then prodded gently, "And? You look upset or . . . what is it?"

"I didn't know it showed. . . . I think I know the girl. I think her mother is a friend of mine; we'd lost touch," I blurted out. "I've been calling but don't get an answer. And maybe it's not the same people."

"Girl's still in a coma, how long's it been now? Almost a week?"

"About that. They don't seem to have any idea who did it."

"Except that it was 'some Indian.' I'm sorry, if it's the people you know. The mother's probably at the hospital. Wherever they have the poor kid now." He took a sip of coffee, put the cup down.

"O'Reagan gave me your number," I said. "The little girl I told you found the dogs? She lives with her grandmother farther up the mountain. She says the Forest Service is planning to tear down their cabin. The grandmother talked to some Forest Service honcho in Redding but apparently it didn't do any good. Do you know anything about that? The little girl's name is Mimi, that's all I know."

"I don't know who you mean, no. Or the particular cabin. By law, the Forest Service isn't allowed to tear down anything over fifty years old until a complicated review is made, to determine historical value. Lotta times, if a place is getting along toward fifty, they tear it down quick before it gets to *be* fifty years old and they have to submit to some accountability. That might be the case here. If you can find out the grandmother's name, I'll check it out for you."

"Thanks. I think they've been there a long time."

"Maybe something can be done, then. Usually it can't. But what I came about, I wanted to let you know we're having the Deerskin Dance tonight. O'Reagan said you're interested in things like that."

"Oh, I am."

"It's our New Year's—what we call the world renewal."

"Ah. What is that?"

He leaned forward and suddenly became quite talkative. This was a subject he apparently liked expanding on: "Well, see, during the year the world gets tipped off axis, and therefore bad things happen. Sickness, natural disasters, people hurt—murdered, maybe—all caused by the imbalance in the world. So we put the world back right side up because if we didn't, it would get to the point where things would get so bad nothing could survive. That's the old belief of the Karuk people."

"And the dance puts the world straight again?"

"Not exactly. First, the world's put right by the prayers of the medicine man. He has to fast, stay in the sweat house. Then he goes up on the mountain to different sacred places, makes special fires with wood he gathered by hand, because it has to be wood no ax has touched. He prays for there to be a lot of acorn, a lot of salmon, deer, plant food for the next year, and not much sickness. He walks up the mountain every day to a different place—it's bad luck if you see him, *dibee chrahcup*. Anyone who sees him isn't supposed to survive the year. Bit by a rattler, maybe, or the person will crash his car on the cliff and drown in the river, something like that." He paused, finished his coffee. "It started night before last. Anyway the main event's tonight, if you'd like to come."

"I'd like to very much. Where is it?"

"Down by Clear Creek, what we call Inan, that's a few miles the other side of Happy Camp. What I thought was, I could get old Steve Henry to pick you up—he lives a few miles up the river, up your river here, the Scott. I have to go by there anyway, so if you'd like I can arrange it. O'Reagan said you've been real sick; I didn't know if you'd be driving."

After Jim left, bidding me *jimmie co yap*, I had lunch and tried Hallie again. I realized when I thought about her, I thought Hallie, not Hallie Stephens. Because I was already sure it was the same Hallie. This time I got a machine that told me I'd reached the number I had called and instructed me about the beeps. I left a message and then took a long nap to rest up for the evening of Deerskin Dance, which Jim said might go on all night.

Steve Henry arrived a few minutes after 6:30. He was a little elderly man with wrinkled pale skin and small blue eyes who wasn't Indian-looking at all. He was so shy I could barely hear his mumbled "How d'ye do" and he merely nodded his head to indicate that I was to get into his new green pickup. After a couple of comments to which he responded with only a nod, I leaned back and enjoyed the changing scene in silence.

We passed through Seiad Valley, a tiny place surrounded by fields of yellow mustard flowers beneath blue-green mountains, then Happy Camp, which was larger and not so pretty. After that, empty wild mountain country. Finally Steve turned left on a nondescript dirt road and parked by several other cars, most of them old and beat-up. We walked past a group of Indian men standing beside an old Dodge van, and I followed Steve through the fringe of brush to a grassy bluff that looked out over the wide brown river. A lot of people were milling about and others were seated or standing around small fires. I followed Steve to the far edge, where two young women were stirring something in a huge cast-iron pot. He mumbled something and left, clearly intending me to stay. I felt awkward, out of place. Almost everyone else I saw looked Indian. I didn't know anyone and I didn't belong there.

"Jim Pepper invited me to come," I offered tentatively, "and Steve was kind enough to give me a ride down."

"You're the detective?" the shorter of the girls asked. "Work with Jim's cousin—what's his name?"

"O'Reagan."

"Yeah, Jim said you might come," she said noncommittally. "We're making acorn soup. You want to help?"

"Sure—what can I do?"

"Follow that path there down to the river, you'll see a place with a lot of rocks. Gather up some big ones— softball size, more or less. Try and get the granite ones. They're to put in the soup to heat it up; the other ones break sometimes when they get hot."

"Okay. How many?"

"Many's you can carry—we got a big crowd tonight."

"I feel awfully pleased to be able to be here," I said shyly, and the girl, who was somewhat overweight and had broad, plain features, stopped looking serious and rather disapproving and smiled.

"We are glad to have you here," she said courteously.

I headed down the path, which was narrow and tilted downward steeply through high brush, and soon came out on a rocky beach where the river was both wide and fast-flowing and looked deep and rather ominous.

I walked along slowly in the fading light, eyes on the ground looking for stones that might be granite, then saw something that wasn't rocks. It took my brain a few seconds to compute the unexpected sight into a moccasin-clad foot and, beside it, another.

"Eeech!" I screamed before I could stop myself, jerking back and looking up at a tall Indian who was utterly motionless, as still as the stones or the sand, and as silent, standing at the edge of the bushes. He had a hard, mean look.

"Oh!" I said, catching my breath and feeling foolish but also still unaccountably scared.

He looked at me sourly and then said slowly, enunciating each word separately, "How, white squaw."

"Well at least you have a sense of humor," I muttered, "after scaring the life out of me."

The barest glimmer of a smile appeared around his mouth and his flat black eyes, and I saw that he was younger than I'd thought, probably not much over twenty.

"Would you mind telling me which of these rocks are granite?"

But he turned without another word and disappeared into the brush and the twilight.

I chose some baseball-sized gray rocks I hoped might be right and took them back to the girl at the fire. She looked at my offering and picked out two from the others. "These're good. Go see can you find some more like these."

By the time I'd made several more trips, the soup was boiling and I helped ladle it out—not into the Karuk baskets that I'd read about, so tightly woven that liquids were cooked and served in them in the old days, but into white polystyrene cups. People then went on to another table where grilled salmon, various casseroles, and pies and cakes were laid out in great abundance.

As I helped myself to the food I spotted Jim Pepper across the field, listening to the dour Indian who'd surprised me down by the river. Then the guy who'd snubbed me walked off and Jim sat down with a small group. I went over, feeling shy of intruding but less so than with any of the other groups sitting around eating and talking quietly.

Jim looked up, smiled, patted the blanket beside him. "You made it. Sit down. How do you like the acorn soup?"

"Don't know yet." I took a small sip and said noncommittally, "ummm." Rather like thin oatmeal, it was basically kind of tasteless considering all the trouble it is to make. I sat beside him and asked, "Who was that tall, sort of mean-looking man you were talking to just before I came over?"

"Tall and mean-looking?" He thought a moment, smiled. "Ruther Bradshaw, you must mean. You know him?"

"No. I saw him down by the river, is all. I just wondered."

Jim hesitated, then said soberly, "Ruther was telling me he happened to see the *fut-a-way-non*—the medicine man—going up the mountain the last day."

"He's not supposed to survive the year, you mean, because he saw the medicine man?"

"That's the old belief. Ruther says he doesn't believe in all that old stuff, but he seemed a little nervous about it."

"I don't blame him." I followed Jim's gaze to a high bluff across the river that caught the sun's last rays. A group of boys with bows and arrows were throwing things into the river, and on the dark bank below, in the light of flaring torches, I could see other Indians, all men.

"What are those kids throwing?"

"It's—they're throwing stones into eternity. They follow the medicine man around and shoot arrows at certain targets, then on the last day they throw those stones into eternity."

I felt no wiser, but let it go. I was feeling relaxed now, comfortable, at home here. It was almost dark where we sat, and fully dark but for the flaring fires on the beach below the bluff where the boys were throwing the stones into eternity. The men down there were naked to the waist, wearing what looked like boxer shorts or bathing suits, with beaded belts and long necklaces of what Jim said was Indian money—elk teeth and snail shells. They were putting on elaborate feather headdresses that moved and swayed mysteriously in the light of the burning torches.

"Look!" Jim commanded, and I saw flashes of white in the torchlight. "There're the white deerskins! *Poofitch dahko*—they're very old, handed down in certain families—those tongues, they're beadwork."

The white deerskin heads were carried on poles, the beadwork tongues flapping as the men climbed into a long dugout canoe. They remained standing as it was pushed off, while at each end seated rowers sent the boat slowly against the current, upriver. A sound began, a deep, guttural chant:

ai ai, ai ai,
ai ai, ai ai ...
ah yeh, yeh yah
ai ai, ai ai

The rowers stilled their paddles while a costumed medicine man, bare to the waist like the others, came to the far bank, stood tall and still for a moment, then dived into the water in front of the swaying, singing men in the boat. After a long time, his dark head popped up and he swam over and climbed back up out of the river on our side and was lost in the watching crowd.

The standing men in the boat began chanting louder and the swaying, dancing bright-to-darkness movements began again as the end men dipped their oars and headed the boat slowly upriver. People got up and moved to the edge of the bank and Jim and I followed, running, trying to keep up with the canoe.

Suddenly, I slipped and fell. Jim caught me, then steadied and held me against him a moment. We stood still as the crowd surged around us, looking at each other for what seemed a long time, and then he let me go but kept an arm around my shoulders as the people from behind pushed us forward.

I was thinking it had been a long time since anyone had looked at me like that when he abruptly took his arm away, but we continued rushing ahead very close together in the pressure of the crowd. The canoe turned around and drifted downstream past us, then pulled in on our side of the river and came to rest.

The men with the white deerskins got out and went over to the far end of the flat. Jim bent his head toward me and said softly, "In a little while, they'll dance over there. Let's get the blanket and find a good place for you to watch."

There were small fires at random intervals all over the field. Huge moving shadows would appear, temporarily become an ordinary man or woman, then turn into monsters again before fading out in the flickering light-darkness of the fires and the torches. The air smelled of the fires, the fresh, sharp scent of pine trees, and the full, ripe smell of the river. Jim laid out the blanket on the ground in front of the gathering dancers, murmured, "I'm in this," and went off.

The men were sorting themselves into two long rows that faced each other, each one holding a fairly large branch. A man crouched at each end with a large jagged stone in an outstretched hand. The white deerskin heads swayed on their poles as the men began a low chanting:

ai ai, ai ai, ai ai
ai ai, ai ai, ai ai

The two men at the end leapt out and began to cross back and forth around each other, crouching and turning between the rows of chanting white deerskins, circling and passing in perfect rhythm. Then I realized that the taller dancer was Jim. As they passed each other they held the flints up high and the white deerskins behind them swayed higher still as the low guttural chanting grew more intense. The slender younger dancer was graceful but Jim's dance had an added power and authority that was compelling and very dramatic.

hi ya hi ya
hi ya hi ya
hi ya hi ya

The little beaded tongues glittered and the naked torsos glistened, the waving headdresses and the white deerskins swayed; it all mixed and blurred together in moving pieces of light and dark and color and sound that were yet all of a piece, a unity. In the red light of the torches the ancient chanting grew louder, the lines of men lifted and stamped one foot, then the other, while one or another stepped forward and sang special but to me incomprehensible words or sometimes let go with a bloodcurdling scream. This went on for a long time. Then, abruptly, it was over.

"Pretty good dance," someone next to me said, and I looked around in the softly growing light, blinking, trying to reenter the twentieth century and realizing with surprise that I wasn't tired at all. Some small boys were fooling around, mock dancing where the real dance had been, while the dancers took the white deerskins off the poles, rolled them up very carefully and packed them away, but I didn't see Jim among them. Steve Henry came up behind me, however, touched my arm shyly and then turned toward the parking lot.

I followed, thinking about those moments in the running crowd, the sudden unexpected intimacy. I wondered about the new year ahead, what it held up its sleeve. Would I get well? Would Sally regain consciousness, not be too damaged, be given back the rest of her life to live? But whatever was on its way, the Deerskin Dance was done, so at least the world was right side up again.

"*Ai ai, hay yah,*" I hummed; how had it gone? "*Ai ai, ah yay yah.*"

It is true we have killed many white men.
The Modoc heart is strong. The Modoc guns
are sure. But hear me, oh muck-a-lux!
The whites are many. They will come again.
No matter how many the Modocs kill,
   more will come.
We will all be killed in the end.

—KIENTPOOS, 1873

SEVEN

I SLEPT UNTIL MIDAFTERNOON WHEN THE PHONE WOKE ME; IT was Jim Pepper.

"You be home for a while? I'd like to come by."

"Sure, great."

"I'll be there in about forty-five minutes."

When he arrived the dogs leapt and clamored, but he patted them rather absently and greeted me with a blank, all-business sort of face. There was no trace of those moments when we'd run with the crowd along the river. Just as well—I reminded myself briskly that I was sick and he was married.

"You remember the guy you were asking about last night, Ruther Bradshaw? You said you saw him down by the river."

"I remember."

"They've picked him up. They're charging him on what everybody's calling," he added quietly, "the *Indian* murder. I think he's being railroaded because he's got himself the reputation of the town bad guy. And he's Indian. And they needed to arrest someone."

"Do you know if they have evidence of any kind?"

"Nothing real far's I know. They got a warrant and went through his place, found some fancy camping equipment. He claims he bought it at an army navy place down in Redding. Of course the store doesn't remember, and Ruther doesn't have any receipt. They ran it by the girl's mother, who apparently couldn't identify the stuff one way or the other."

The girl's mother: Hallie. But she hadn't called back; there was still a chance it wasn't her. I'd left a couple more messages. "Where was he when it happened?"

"I talked to him this afternoon. He may have an alibi— that's why I'm here. He didn't tell the police but he did tell me: He was with a woman all that day, over in Tulelake. Together the whole time, most of it in bed. Uh . . . her husband was away. They made sure nobody saw him."

"Difficult . . ."

"Ruther doesn't want to get her in trouble with her husband. Says the husband could get violent—with her. The poor guy's in love, wants her to get a divorce and marry him but she's undecided, has a couple young kids."

"Does he think she'd admit to being with him?"

"He doesn't know, said she's pretty scared of her husband. We had an emergency meeting of the tribal council—a thing like this is bad for all of us, undoes months, maybe years, of work, efforts at expanding the communication between the Indian community and the whites. Not to mention we don't want to see any Indian get railroaded, and Ruther's not such a bad guy, really. The tribe would like to hire you to talk to this woman. Find out if they were together that day, and *if* they were—if you could get her to swear to it."

"O'Reagan told you I've been sick—but I should be able to do that much. Why me, though? Why don't you do it yourselves?"

"Well, the woman's white, for one thing. We thought it'd probably be better if someone like you approached her. Also another woman might have a better chance. Then you being a detective, and we think so highly of O'Reagan from the work he did for us last spring. You're his partner, and you're here."

"All right. Sure. I'd be glad to." We settled on a fee,

lower than my usual since I didn't have an office to support, and then I asked, "Does Ruther have a lawyer?"

"Just the public defender at this point, and I don't think he's much good, or very interested."

"Well . . . listen—get the lawyer to subpoena the sheriff for everything they've got on the case. Tell him *everything* they've got . . . okay? Tell the lawyer you've hired me. I'll go through it."

"Okay, but you won't need to do that if we find the woman and she'll swear to the alibi."

"But if we don't or she won't, the subpoena will take a little time."

"Okay. All right. I didn't know it was possible to do that. And if you don't get what we want in Tulelake—maybe you'd see Ruther? There might be some other leads that I missed."

"Sure. Where is Tulelake? That's a town?"

"Yeah, over by the Lava Beds, the old Modoc country. You know that area at all?"

"It's been a while, but I went camping there once."

I'd gone with David, after we'd been rained out camping on Mt. Shasta one July, Panther Meadow. A freezing river of rain pouring into that green tent we had, about three o'clock in the morning. It got us up fast, packed in record time. David thought it probably wouldn't be raining over at the Lava Beds; they're on the dry eastern side of California. We could hike one of the volcanoes or, if it was raining, go look at the caves. I was wet and cold and wanted to go home; we ended up quarreling. But we'd gone, stayed a couple of days and I'd liked it there. Jim's voice brought me back.

". . . place, isn't it? Anyway, this woman's husband works for the Park Service. It's maybe a three-hour drive from here, maybe a little more."

"I suppose—the sooner the better?"

He nodded. "Funny thing, remember I told you Ruther saw the medicine man go up the mountain the last day?"

"And so Ruther isn't supposed to last the year?"

"Not only that—he saw him slip and *fall down* going up the mountain; he's an old man. According to the old beliefs, that's bad not just for Ruther; it means the world gets made wrong when something like that happens, and then everybody has trouble the whole year, Indians and everybody." He shrugged. "Well—when could you go?"

"Tomorrow, I guess." Oh shit. How was I going to get well in a year like that? A world gone wrong for Indians and everybody. But it was the only year I had. "Tomorrow," I repeated, "if my car will start. I haven't been using it much and the battery is a little wimpy."

"Let's have a look at it. I'm pretty good with cars."

After three hot hours, I turned on a narrow road that went along the Oregon border through marshy country with huge numbers of ducks and a sign that said I was passing through the Lower Klamath Wildlife Refuge. This dead-ended into a wider highway that took me into Tulelake. It wasn't much, just a string of tired-looking necessities along the highway: gas stations, hamburger joint, motel called Modoc Inn, but only a very desperate Modoc would have looked twice at the place.

A fat, cheerful, middle-aged woman checked me in, and wanted to know had I come to see the Lava Beds and Captain Jack's stronghold. I gathered nobody much came to Tulelake for any other reason, and I said I had. She took me to Room 15, chatting away a mile a minute about the Modoc War and telling me to be sure not to miss the caves—some had old pictures in them. She didn't seem to mind that I'd brought Diana, and patted the dog's head very nicely before she left.

The room was about what you'd expect from the outside of the motel: two swaybacked single beds and a battered night table that had never been lovely, a dreary bathroom with a tattered shower curtain—all for twenty-one dollars. I put down a plastic dish with water for Diana, then flicked on the air conditioner, which sent out musty air only a degree or two cooler than what was in the room already. I washed my face and hands and dropped the seven drops under my tongue from each bottle, looking at the mysterious labels, aurum D 30, hypericum D 4, viscum mali . . . could these weird things really get me well? But I'd been better since I started taking them, much better. I plugged in my cassette recorder, lay down on the soft, uncomfortable bed, pushed PLAY, and relaxed with a Feldenkrais tape for half an hour. I'd been pushing myself pretty hard; I needed to be careful or I'd get sick.

But after I'd finished the simple breathing exercises I felt quite restored in spite of the long drive. I was feeling pretty good in fact, though all in all, my experience the past year suggested I shouldn't trust that. I ate the chicken sandwich I'd brought from home and drank hyssop tea from a thermos. Diana got that look: I've been in a concentration camp for several years with nothing to eat, won't you give me some of your food? I handed over the extra chicken I'd brought for her.

Then I looked at the directions Jim had gotten from Ruther, which seemed simple enough: small white house needs paint, on the highway third down from the Texaco station same side, far back from the road and a big shade tree in front. Lucy Farrell's husband should be at work, but if he wasn't, I'd simply say I was selling Avon products. Unfortunately I didn't have any Avon products, so I hoped he'd be away.

When I drove up to the house I saw I needn't have worried about the husband. The curtainless windows and the bright red and white plastic FOR RENT sign showed clearly that he wouldn't be coming back today, and neither would his wife. The padlocked front door hung loose on its hinges. A two-wheeled orange plastic tricycle was lying on its side in the dusty yard, the dry weeds around it swaying in a brisk wind that said the warm weather wasn't going to last forever. There was an unpleasant, creepy feeling to the place that seemed to have to do with more than abandonment.

I wrote down the phone number on the FOR RENT sign

and checked the padlock on the sagging door. There was a big gap where the door didn't meet the frame but the hasp and lock were strong and new, so I walked around to the back. Old plastic bags and orange peels lay scattered around the steps of a sagging porch. The skins were hard and faded and had been there a while, weeks maybe.

The back door was locked, but a credit card easily pushed the tongue back. I found myself in a small kitchen with a gaping, empty refrigerator, a lidless metal garbage can full of broken dishes. Ceiling-high shelves, not very clean, had only a container of Ajax cleanser lying on its side. A large bag of popcorn spilled its contents on the counter by a sink that was old and stained. A straight-back plastic chair was turned over on the floor. I began to half-expect to stumble over a body or perhaps the whole family, mass-murdered by the outraged husband, smelling of decaying flesh. As I moved deeper into the house, though, the only smells were of mildew and age.

Beyond the kitchen a narrow hall opened onto a bedroom on each side, both of them empty and dusty and small. From the end of the hall I stepped into a fairly large living room, suddenly bright from windows that stretched across the whole front of the house. This room, too, was completely empty—no left-behind furniture, no broken knick-knacks, no clues.

I went to the smaller bedroom and peered into the narrow closet. Groping for a darker shape in the back got me a tattered yellow lion with the stuffing coming out, missing an eye. I felt around cautiously, thinking about the brown recluse spider, but there was nothing more except dust balls. The closet in the larger bedroom had a built-in chest of drawers but all the drawers were empty and there was nothing on the floor except a couple of coat hangers.

The bathroom cabinet held nothing except smears from spilled medicines or cosmetics, but on the floor of the small linen closet, under a grease-stained pink towel, I found a clear plastic bottle, empty, with a prescription label. Two hundred Prozac capsules for Jonathan Farrell, authorized by a Dr. Byron Browning and filled by a Thrifty Drugs in Sacramento. Good, good, good! Just how out of control was this guy, this husband Lucy Farrell was afraid of? Who might be traced through the drug that was supposed to be holding his pieces together? Hadn't I read something about several people on Prozac using the drug as a defense in their murder trials? It made them do it, they claimed.

Back in the kitchen, I went through the small garbage can. It was full to the brim with what looked like a whole set of cheap dishes, cream with a blue stripe, promised on the back to be ovenproof, and all broken into small pieces. I set the pieces carefully around me on the floor, imagining various scenarios in which they'd been broken. There was nothing beneath them except the scummy plastic bottom of the container.

I pulled the door to, hearing the lock click, and returned to my motel room. When I called the desk to get the number on the FOR RENT sign, the cheerful woman said that was the number of the motel. What did I want to know?

"Oh. Well, I was looking for Lucy Farrell, but the address I had is empty and for rent. Are you handling that house, is it yours?"

"Yep—they left a couple days ago, lock, stock, 'n barrel, and didn't give me no notice, neither. Course I had a last-month deposit, so I'm covered long as I rent it by the end of this month. Where'd you say you know Lucy from?"

"A friend asked me to look her up. What's their new address?"

"Now that I don't know and that's a fact. They left with just a note for me when I wasn't on shift, which I figure is what they intended. Like I said, they had the last-month deposit down so I'm okay long's I find a renter pretty soon. Not too easy round these parts, though."

"Do you have any idea where they might have gone? Or where they were from?"

"No, I don't. Musta been a important message?"

"Well, it was. I'd certainly like to mail it on if I could."

"Don't guess you can, since you don't have any address."

"There must be something—didn't she have some special friend, someone around here who might know where they went?"

"Nope, she did not—kept to herself, that girl, never did really blend in here. A course, them Park people never stay too long, don't mix much with the locals, generally speakin'. Maybe you could find out somethin' over at the office where her husband worked. Over at the Lava Beds."

"That's a good idea. Who left the note?"

"It was him as left it. He always took care a the business side."

"Well, thanks very much for your help. How late is the office open, do you know?"

"They close five sharp, so you have plenty of time to make it over there and see Captain Jack's stronghold and maybe some of the caves, too. You know how to get out there?"

I took Diana with me. It didn't take long to cover the three gas stations, the hamburger joint, the laundromat, the neighbors on either side and across the road. Nobody had known the couple well. Everybody agreed they'd kept to themselves and nobody knew where they'd gone. A mechanic at the Texaco station said the Farrells had a new Chevy ranch wagon, pale green. He'd worked on it but didn't have any record of the license number.

I drove south over the thirty miles of narrow paved road through the Lava Beds National Monument to the Park Service office. It's the strangest landscape I've ever seen: rough black rock that looks flat as far as the eye can see, except for perfect cone-shaped black hills several hundred feet high that appear periodically, or occasionally an odd chimney-shaped thing sticking up five or ten feet out of the ground.

Even though it was now September, there were flowers lingering from the summer along the road. Indian paintbrush, intensely scarlet against the black-rock background, mixed with the purple of sage, the pale blue of wild flax, the occasional yellow of a late evening primrose. In the far distance were the two volcanoes with the sawed-off tops; the one on the left I'd climbed with David. A hot climb in mid-summer but fantastic when we reached the top. A big hole up there, grotesque heat-twisted giant rocks—or was it lava? A view of the whole world.

Where do such days disappear to when they're gone? If we could find them stacked up someplace in a dusty corner. Riffle through them like a pack of cards, choosing what we want to keep.

The Park office and visitors' center was a small white building nestled among a stand of dusty juniper trees, waist-high gray sagebrush, and giant cream-colored boulders in an otherwise barren landscape. I told the short-haired, uniformed young man at the desk I'd come to Tulelake to visit the wife of their employee Jonathan Farrell but found they'd moved away—did he by any chance have a forwarding address?

A funny expression crossed his face. "Sorry, I can't help you."

"Do you mean you can't give out the new address, or do you mean that you don't have one?"

"Well, we can't give something like that out; that's private information. Though in this case," he added, unbending a little, "I'm afraid there isn't one—they left all of a sudden. He just quit."

Their house hadn't looked exactly prosperous. "Wouldn't he have some pay coming if he left so suddenly? Wouldn't he have left a forwarding address so his pay could be sent on?"

"Well . . . he did leave just before a pay period. I guess he would be owed something near a couple weeks' salary—but as I say, he didn't leave any address. I'd tell you if he had."

"If you do hear from him, would you let me know? I'm a lawyer. His wife is in line for a small legacy. It would be very much in their interest for me to find them." Pitiful, but it was the best I could do on the spur of the moment.

"We-ell . . ." He considered, apparently believing the tired tale. "I guess I could do that—if he sends any address, which I don't think he will. But in a case like this, your best bet would be to contact the state office where the paychecks come from. If anybody knows, it would be them."

I took down that address and phone number and left him mine. "Call me collect if you should happen to get the address. And thanks."

I drove over to the parking lot next to Captain Jack's stronghold, thinking I'd call Jim when I got home, see if he could have someone get an address from the Park Service, also contact that doctor on the prescription bottle. No, maybe I'd better do that myself. But soon I found myself thinking about the Modoc War, and poor Captain Jack.

The jagged outcrop of lava rock in front of me, complete with huge caves and narrow, twisting passageways, was where a ragged band of fifty starving Modoc warriors held off the U.S. Army for six months. They'd come back from the reservation in Oregon where they'd idiotically been sent to live with their traditional enemies, the Klamath Indians (". . . but they should have got along fine," a Park Service brochure asserted, "because they had similar lifestyles and were in a real sense related"). They'd asked permission to live on their ancestral land at Lost River. Refused, they'd asked if they could at least live in the Lava Beds, so barren even the endlessly greedy whites had no use for them. Refused, they stayed and fought.

I got out of the car, let Diana out. We walked up into the stronghold, where the leader, named Kientpoos but called Captain Jack, finally had given up after he'd been separated from his water supply and an army scouting party was led to his hiding place by some of his own warriors who'd surrendered. Tired of the misery of a six-month fight that had left them no better off. "Jack's legs gave out" was all their leader said.

"Tried" at Fort Klamath and asked if he had a last request, Kientpoos had said he'd like to be allowed to live until he died a natural death, but the request wasn't granted. Before they hanged him they took his photograph, standing next to a fellow Modoc named Schonchin John. So you can see him any day at the Park office, looking out at you from the sepia-tinted postcard. Both men in worn-out white man's clothes, a cap, a hat. Schonchin John looks directly at the camera, a big older man, angry and defiant. Kientpoos, a young man with a lithe, graceful body, looks to one side, lost in depression.

The night after he was hanged his body was dug up and sent to Washington, D.C., where it was exhibited for ten cents a look. It had been the most costly Indian war in U.S. history per man killed, with 160 U.S. casualties to only six Indians. It cost the United States $1 million. The surviving Modocs were sent off to the Oklahoma territory and lost their identity as a people.

Tulelake is also the place where sixteen thousand Americans of Japanese ancestry were resettled in army barracks behind barbed wire during World War II.

Now white hikers were murdered and scalped, an Indian lined up to take the drop. Chosen, as far as I could tell, for no real reason but race. Had anything really changed?

As he talked, we saw that his face was
not hard at all. It was young and
open. There is nothing to do on the
Rivers. . . . Nothing to do but be a
badman and scare everybody.
—MARY ELLICOTT ARNOLD AND MABEL REED,
IN THE LAND OF THE GRASSHOPPER SONG

EIGHT

IT HAD RAINED DURING THE NIGHT BUT WHEN I WOKE THE NEXT
day, late, the world outside my window was so clear it
sparkled. After breakfast I called Jim but he wasn't at his
office. I left a machine message about Tulelake and went
outside. It was the kind of shimmering gold and blue and
green day that made me want to walk around in it. I took
my drops and then called the dogs and set off on the trail
behind the cabin. Perhaps I'd come across Mimi's place,
pay her a visit.

The path was wet and muddy but I had on good boots,
rubber-bottomed Canadian Sorel boots, and I didn't
mind. The smells were strong and fresh and varied, of
pine and wet earth, of sunshine on bark and leaf, and
it felt good on me, too. The dogs ran ahead as a jay
squawked loudly and was answered by another.

After winding upward for ten minutes on an incline that
soon had me huffing and puffing like a very old woman
and left me feeling not quite so euphoric, the trail leveled
off and joined up with the wider Pacific Crest Hiking Trail.
The changing leaves were brighter here at higher altitude:
gold-leaved aspens and brilliant red mountain ash mixed
with the intense oranges and scarlets of plum and choke-
berry and cherry. But soon the trees crowded so thickly together on either side that the sun didn't reach through

anymore, and in spite of the gaudy leaves the feeling grew somber. I thought of the hikers, and went faster.

Soon I came to a steep downward switchback—first trail to the left—that I thought might be the one Mimi had described. I called the dogs to follow and in a few minutes saw a cabin sitting squarely in the center of a large sunny clearing. An ancient rusty red pickup was parked just beyond the house. It was higher elevation here, and cooler. The leaves of the maples and oaks were starting to turn to yellow and rust. A thin column of smoke rose slowly from a chimney at one end of the sharply pitched tin roof; a few scrawny chickens pecked hungrily at the bare dirt around the steps. Diana is trustworthy about chickens but Prince and Little Dog were looking much too interested, so I put on their leashes and hooked them to a falling-down fence.

As I walked toward the cabin, a tattered screen door swung open with a screech and a rifle poked out, a shadowy figure behind. I stopped dead, then spoke in as friendly and innocent a voice as I could manage—a Pollyanna voice, I hoped, enunciating very clearly.

"Excuse me—I'm a friend of Mimi's. My name is Maggie Elliott. I live in old Bessie Thornton's cabin and I'm hoping to visit Mimi if she's home."

Nothing happened. The silence, the rifle pointed at me by someone I couldn't see in the dark doorway, the autumn landscape—all combined to make me feel very creepy indeed. But finally the rifle lowered, backed away, and an old woman who was stooped, gray-haired, and very wrinkled but carrying no gun, stepped out and looked at me inquiringly. She was wearing a loose green wraparound dress that was much too big, as if she'd lost a lot of weight since she'd bought the dress.

"What's that you said? You live at Bessie's?"

"Yes. Like I said, I'm looking for Mimi. I'm Maggie Elliott. Mimi's been helping me with these dogs. Are you her grandmother?"

"That's right, great-grandmother, I'm Lillian Goss.

Hermina told me about you right enough. Come on in. Hermina's been real sick. She sleepin' now."

Hermina? I followed her inside, past a bearded man standing inside the door. He held the rifle, resting its tip on the floor. The room was big, with a large cast-iron stove at one end. Heavy flowered drapes, faded and none too clean, were closed and helped keep the place very warm and rather dim. A beautiful dark-haired woman sat, very still, in a chair by the stove. In a small room beyond the stove I could see a bed with a small mound that I assumed was Mimi.

"Please excuse this mess." Mrs. Goss picked up a pile of old newspapers from an overstuffed chair and put them on the floor. "I have the arthur-itis so bad I can't do much around the house no more." She held bent and twisted fingers toward me. "And Hermina, she been sick," she continued. "That child ate something or other. She been so sick I thought she goin' to die but she lots better now." She made no mention of the man or the woman, no introduction, as if they weren't there.

The man, maybe thirty, had longish dark blond hair with shaggy ends and wore some sort of aged military shirt with dirty jeans and heavy boots. Very thin, with jutting cheekbones and bloodshot blue eyes, he looked tired, or ill. Expecting attack apparently. Why? Maybe a little crazy but all to the good, I thought, for keeping Mimi safe with a killer around. The woman, younger, must be Mimi's mother. She looked Indian, with classic regular features and a strange serenity—not quite in the room with the rest of us. I pulled my eyes away from the strange couple and turned back to Mrs. Goss, who was talking again.

". . . just eat what she always eat, her pancakes and syrup in the mornin' and a little coffee, and right after that she got real sick. So I doctor her Indian way best I can and she seem to be makin' it."

"Indian way?" I asked, interested.

"Well, we has special plants we use, you know," she said vaguely, but didn't seem to want to talk about them further.

"You think something poisoned her? Was what she ate different from what the rest of you ate?"

"That's what I told you." The man spoke suddenly in a low voice, talking fast, so the words ran together. "That's what I told you didn't I Lillian? Didn't I? I *knew* it. I *knew* those wires were tampered with I told you at the time Lillian, didn't I? Didn't I know they've poisoned her?" He gave a disgusted snort and a half sneeze, then added, "Thank you, miss, for seeing it—they just think I'm crazy!" He gave a rather crazy soft laugh and, still carrying the gun, walked over to a straight-back wood chair by a round table that held the remains of some meal, and sat down. He put the rifle across his knees.

Mimi's great-grandmother looked at him crossly and said to me, picking up the thread, "I don't generally have the syrup myself. You think maybe the syrup went bad? I never knew it to do that."

"No," I said, "I never did, either."

The man sat shaking his head no no no, as if to say syrup can go bad, anything can go bad. The young woman sat still and silent, expressionless, looking off into space.

"We both had the pancakes and the coffee. Though she take sugar in her coffee and I don't—but I know sugar don't go bad." The old woman shook her head. "That was the last of the syrup, anyway, so if that was it, it can't cause no more trouble now."

"Anything can cause trouble," the man muttered.

There was an awkward silence and then I said, "I always call your granddaughter Mimi. Did you say Hermina?"

"Hermina, yes. Great-granddaughter, she is. This here's Hermina's mother—my granddaughter Clara. And that's Hank. What you say your name is? Hermina did tell me and you, too, but I forgot."

"Maggie. Maggie Elliott." I added cautiously, "I'm glad to meet you, Clara and Hank."

The woman still sat unmoving, but the man nodded and even moved his lips in a slight smile that didn't reach his eyes. Then the little bundle of covers on the bed in the other room suddenly moved and Mimi poked her head out. She looked pale and washed-out but not, I noted with relief, like someone dying of poisoning.

"Maggie," she said in a groggy voice, rubbing her eyes, "what're you doin' here? Did Prince come too? And Little Dog? And Diana?"

"They're tied up outside; they seemed a little too interested in your chickens. If you look out that window, you can probably see them."

She pulled back the curtain over the bed and gave one of her big transcendent smiles. "Oh boy! There they are! Oh great!"

"Close the curtain, honey, you catch cold."

"No I won't, Granny. It's warm outside!" She threw off the rest of the covers and skipped over to a large wooden box at the far end of the living room, where she pulled out jeans, shirt, and a sweater and began putting them on.

"You sure you feel like gettin' up, honey? How you feelin'?"

"I feel okay. I'm tired of stayin' in bed." She pulled on unmatching socks, a blue and a red, shoved her feet into some ratty-looking sneakers, and ran out the door calling, "Prince! Prince! Hello honey, hello Little Dog, I missed you. Hello, Diana!" The door banged shut.

I turned back to Mimi's great-grandmother. "This is a very nice place you have here. Have you lived here a long time?"

"Lord, yes. My folks had the rancheria up behind here and their folks before that. Back in the Indian times. Later my dad built this cabin and I come down here to live when I married."

It was hard to imagine her as a young bride, she was now so old and withered, a stick for clothes to hang on. Except for her eyes—they were black and bright like Mimi's, intensely interested in life. You could have exchanged those eyes, between the old face and the young one, and not have noticed the difference. I looked cautiously at Mimi's mother, but her eyes were lowered now, studying her hands or some internal landscape.

"My husband was a gold miner," Mrs. Goss reminisced.
"He wasn't doin' too bad, neither, but then he took sick.
Seemed like nothin' we did could help him. He was a strong
man till just those few weeks' sickness, somethin' went
wrong with his lungs. And Hermina's daddy, he got run over
by one of them big loggin' trucks, crushed his skull right in.
Seems like the men, they don't last too good in this family."

"I'm sorry," I said. "That must have made things very
hard. And Mi—Hermina said you're having some problem
with the Forest Service."

The man scowled fiercely as Mrs. Goss said softly,
"They say they plannin' on tearin' our cabin down, but we
got nowhere to go so I think we *won't* go nowhere. How
they gonna tear it down if we still be here?"

I didn't know a lot about the Forest Service, but from
what I'd seen so far, I had a feeling that was not likely to
stop them.

She continued. "We stay at Hank's sometimes. But Clara
not so well, she do better up here. Maybe someday she be
well again but I don't count on it."

"Why are the Forest Service people called piss-firs?" I
asked.

Hank grinned happily. "Story I heard, there's a kind of
fir tree they have around here. It smells like piss when it's
cut and also it's not good for anything, too wet. No good
for building or even for firewood—good for nothing. So the
Indians started calling the Forest Service people piss-firs."

He waited expectantly and I smiled appreciatively, then
he laughed. I looked over at Clara, but either she hadn't
heard or didn't care. There was no change at all. She wore
soft old jeans, faded, tight, and a dark blue sweatshirt with
sequins forming what seemed to be a Christmas tree with
presents beneath. Some of the sequins were hanging by thin
threads; others were missing altogether. There were no
lights on in the cabin.

"Mi—Hermina told me about the accident with the electricity. Must have been pretty frightening."

"Lord, that was terrible! That child come this close to

bein' burnt just black! I don't know how such a thing coulda happened, she was always playin' with that doll and nothin' never happened before. . . . But Hermina be all right, and it's all fixed now. Hank fixed it."

He said roughly, "I don't know why you don't know, Lillian. Haven't I told you often enough somebody *wanted* to electrocute Hermina. It was her toy, after all. Nobody else here plays with robot dolls, do they? I have to look after you all and I'm so tired . . . never sleep. . . ." He sighed deeply and got up.

"Why do you say that?" I asked sharply. "Was something wrong with the wiring—you think it had been tampered with?"

But he said only, "They think I'm imagining things; they think I'm crazy. But I'll take care of Hermina, don't worry about that." He walked over to the door and went out, closing it carefully behind him.

How crazy was he? *Had* the wires been tampered with? And if so, why? I could probably do better talking to him alone, maybe when I left.

Mrs. Goss and Clara and I sat silently for a few minutes, listening to the rooster crow occasionally, to Mimi conversing softly with the dogs or with Hank. It was so hot in the cabin, I was sweating.

Soon I said, "I should be getting home. I was just out for a walk when I saw your cabin. I was a little worried about Mimi—walking the trail after those hikers were attacked."

"Wasn't that some terrible thing? But you don't need to worry—Hank's been walkin' her down to the school bus and meets it ev'ry afternoon, too. Hank don't let her go nowhere by herself if he can help it. And that reminds me—we decided we can go ahead and take those two dogs Hermina wants so bad. Hank says they'll be good watchdogs; he wants her to have 'em. He already went and got some food for 'em." She shifted painfully in her chair, then got up, and I followed her to the door.

"That's great," I said, "I'll leave them here today, then." A sound behind made me look back. Clara was sprawled face down on the floor in front of her chair. Frightened, I rushed over. There was a strong smell of alcohol and I realized she was dead drunk.

When I went outside, there was no chance to talk to Hank. He went inside to see about Clara. But Mimi was ecstatic, and I left with only Diana. On the way home, I wondered about Clara, about Hank, then started thinking about what I could do next to find Ruther's alibi.

The jail was a couple of blocks off the main street, a square gray concrete mass that looked appropriately grim. I gave my name and was ushered into a small, drab room with two doors and no windows. After a few minutes, the tall young man I'd first seen feet first came through the other door in handcuffs. The policeman told him to sit in the empty chair, then locked the cuffs to a chain dangling from a metal bar on the edge of the table. He said we could have half an hour, then left the room.

"We meet again," Ruther said, trying for ease but looking surly.

"We meet again," I agreed. "Jim told you the council hired me to look for your alibi, and that she'd left Tulelake with no forwarding address?"

"Yeah. He told me."

"If I can find her, do you think she'll be willing to swear you were with her?"

He raised the cuffed hands to his face, rubbed his chin, looked past me. "Dunno."

"How did you leave things between you, when you parted?"

"Why do you want to know that?" His tone was sullen.

"Why do you think I want to know that?"

He gave a deep sigh, then his shoulders dropped as if he'd given up or at least relaxed. What had seemed a permanent scowl, as much a part of his face as his eyes or his nose, lifted, and he looked suddenly young and vulnerable.

"Jim said you're all right ... and since you're looking for her to save *my* ass, I guess I better try to answer you."

"It would help."

"But listen, I don't want anyone else to know about this, especially not the cops. If I tell you anything it has to be on that condition—is that a deal?"

"That's a deal."

"Okay . . . Lucy . . . we were in eleventh grade together. In Happy Camp. We went together that year, but her folks didn't like me—what they saw was 'half-breed.'" The stony, bitter look came back. After a minute, he went on. "They didn't forbid her to see me. I think they were afraid we might run off together if they did. But they made it real clear they hated my guts. Lucy's their only child. And real pretty—you could say beautiful. They had the idea she could do better. Which, she did, as it turned out. As far as money goes, anyway. At least, the guy's family has a lot of money. I don't think they saw much of it, from what she said."

He looked down at his handcuffed hands. "Lucy's family was real poor. Her dad managed a new hardware store that opened up but it folded; after that he didn't have a job." He moved his shoulders around as if they were too tight, or they hurt. "Lucy was only there the one year. After that, they moved away, down by L.A. Then her dad died, had a heart attack."

"What was her father's name, and her mother's?"

"Uh . . . people called him Jimmy . . . James, I guess it would be. Bertha was her mother's name."

He stared past me, at the dingy blank wall. "We wrote for a while. After she went to L.A. But I guess we just kinda drifted apart. I lived in Happy Camp and she lived down south. She went on to some college down there, got a scholarship. I went in the army a couple years. We still wrote some, at first."

He looked so sad now. I wanted to help him. But I had to ask any questions that came up—questions whose answers might make him more likely to be the killer, not less.

"What did you do in the army?" I hoped he wasn't going to say Special Forces, Green Beret, something like that. Something trained in ambush.

"MP. It was okay. I was stationed in South Carolina. Anyway when I got back, she'd married this Farrell—there was a letter waiting, telling me."

He slumped farther down in the chair. Riffling through that deck of times past, some of the cards are so painful. He looked at me, shook his head. "I don't remember where she said she met him. It wasn't the college, I do remember that. I'd saved some money in the army and was thinking we could get together again, get married. After I got the news, well, she was already married. There wasn't one fucking thing I could do to stop it; it already happened."

I let the silence ride for a bit, then asked, "Where'd you hear his family has a lot of money? Who from?"

He thought about it, shook his head. "I don't remember. She was gone . . . I didn't pay a whole lot of attention to the details."

"When did you see her again? How did you happen to spend the day with her in August?"

"Okay. Actually it was two days—the day the hikers were shot and the day before. See, I ran into her about four months ago, in May. At a bar in Yreka that has dancing, the Stop Light. Her husband was away doing some job for the Park Service. They lived in Tulelake but she was stir-crazy—there's nothing there but a couple of gas stations. Her kids were visiting his parents, so she came to town and into the Stop Light to dance. She's a really good dancer; she always loved to dance." He sighed heavily. "And I'm also . . . I like to dance." A memory of happier times passed across his face.

"She was staying at a motel—said she didn't know anyone in town anymore. She made me come after dark and we had to be real careful nobody saw us. Then, well, we started seeing each other again. Not often. I wanted her to leave Farrell but she wasn't sure, didn't want him to know. I was hoping to change her mind."

He looked down, remembering. "Another time, her husband was off at some conference or something and we spent a couple days together in Redding, that was when I bought that camping equipment the sheriff took. We thought maybe we could go camping sometime. Anyway, the end of August Farrell was away again, some Park business. She called me and I went over to her place in Tulelake. But we made sure nobody saw me there."

"Not even her children?"

"They were at her in-laws' again."

"Where do they live, the in-laws?"

"She never said. We didn't like to talk about *him* much. I went to her place because we were both broke—I had some money but I couldn't get at it just then, and she didn't have any except a little her husband left her for groceries. So we spent the two days at her place."

"And nobody at all saw you there?"

"Nobody far's I know. I arrived at night, left at night."

We sat there for a moment, temporarily out of words. I felt sorry for him. I wanted to find his girl and have it all turn out all right. "And how did you leave things between you?" I asked gently.

"She said she'd think about leaving Farrell, that she'd be in touch. But she never was. A few days later when I tried to call, the phone was disconnected. Then the police started questioning me; I could see they had me in mind for the big drop. . . . I tried to call again, called information but there wasn't any new listing."

"You didn't think of going over to Tulelake? Trying to see her?"

"Well, see, I was hoping the cops would somehow come across the shithead who really did shoot those kids, then they'd get off my back. And I'd promised Lucy I wouldn't blow it for her with her husband. She said if she did get a divorce it would be important for him not to know anything about us because that would help him get custody. She said he's got violent with her in the past—jealous rage and knocked her around. For no reason, she said, no reason. She was real scared what he might do to her if he *had* a reason. She was afraid he might even get carried away and hurt the kids. Seems Farrell can't control his temper at all, at least where she's concerned. I think she's had a pretty hard time with this guy. I didn't want to make things any rougher for her. I still don't. I've tried and tried to think who might know where she is, where she's gone. Where Farrell's family lives. They're rich; he might've gone to them. But I can't think of anyone."

"You still want her to leave him and be with you?"

"Yeah. I do. But then, there's the kids. One's three, the other one's four, I think. It's only the past six months or so, Lucy said, they started visiting the grandparents on their own. They're crazy about her kids, come pick them up, bring them back. So maybe they don't live so far away from Tulelake. But I don't know. And the bottom line is, she's afraid Farrell will get her kids if she leaves him."

"But Ruther," I said, "you seem to care about each other. Do you think she'd let you be tried, maybe convicted of murder, rather than have him know about the time you spent together?"

"I don't think she would. Wherever they've gone, I don't think—she probably wouldn't know about me being arrested. She never reads the papers or watches the news or anything like that."

"Ruther, keep thinking. You might remember something that would help. Especially try to remember where you heard about Farrell's family having money. That person might know where they live."

"I will." His face was open, the sullen look completely gone. He swallowed and then said with difficulty, "Thank you for trying to help. And listen . . ." he hesitated.

"Yes?"

"If you find her, talk to her. Tell her for me—tell her I've got some money stashed away, enough for her to get a good lawyer if she wants to leave Farrell. A good lawyer to make sure he won't get the kids. Tell her . . . tell her I'm waiting for her to come to me, her and the kids. Or . . . I have an aunt she could stay with if it would look better for her not to be with me while she's getting the divorce."

"I'll tell her," I said.

*If life has taken such different shapes in the
past, who can feel any assurance about the
future. . . .*

—DAVID RAINS WALLACE,
THE KLAMATH KNOT

NINE

As I GOT OUT OF THE CAR, I COULD HEAR THE FAINT RING
of the telephone. I ran to the house to answer and everything changed, got put on hold.

"Maggie?"

"Hallie." I knew who it was instantly. "I've been trying
to reach you—it seems like forever. How are you?" Stupid
question.

"I've been better."

"Yes. What about Sally?"

"Then you know."

"Yes, it's terrible. Oh Hallie . . ."

"She just . . . stays the same." Hallie sounded bad.
Worn-out, lifeless. In my memories she'd been vibrant,
shimmering.

I asked, "Can I come up—down, wherever you are? Or
do you want to get away for a little while, come here?
What can I do?"

"I don't—where are you, anyway?"

"Very near where Sally was attacked, oddly enough." I
explained briefly where I was and why. "What can I do?"

"Maggie, could you really? Come up here? I'm here all
by myself—" Her voice broke for a moment, then recovered. "I'm in Ashland. Sally's in the hospital in Ashland.
But don't tell anybody—not *anybody*—where we are."

"Of course not. I'll come. Tomorrow?"

77

I drove down to the post office, where Bill Dawson said he'd be glad to be a dog feeder and exerciser for a few days, and I gave him the spare key.

The last bit of that road is very steep. David and I had come up from the cabin a couple of times on the bikes. BMWs, the old R-60s. His had been destroyed with him. I'd sold mine, having no desire to ever see another. But I'd loved the bike, leaning way over into the mountain curves, the wind streaming past, the freedom. Enough time had passed now to remember that feeling. How good it was. Maybe I'd get another bike someday. An R-75, or even a 90 if I was ever rich enough.

The Karmann Ghia chugged with difficulty, slowly, to Siskiyou Summit, slipped over the top. ELEV. 4,310, the green sign said. I stayed in second, going down. Ashland has a famous company of Shakespearean actors, very good ones. David and I had seen *Richard II*. It was marvelous. They didn't just do Shakespeare. We went to *Hedda Gabler* another time. That had been in the fall—like now, a dark cloudy day. We'd stayed in a bed and breakfast that had a fireplace, made love for hours.

Today, Ashland glowed eerily in the odd stormy light, little houses sprinkled over a cluster of hilltops in the high Siskiyou Mountains of southern Oregon.

I easily found the house where Hallie was renting a room. One-story, yellow, faded, not very big, on a street of similar houses not far from the freeway. I parked, picked up my bag, went to the door. Rang the bell.

I almost didn't recognize her, she was so thin. All the bloom gone, still the marvelous bones beneath, but she'd aged. Sad eyes, a droopy stance. We hugged and she led me to a big room at the side. Cheerful, lots of windows and even some plants.

"It reminds me of that wonderful room you had on Haight Street."

"That's why I took it, I think. But sit down, or maybe we should go out. Are you hungry?"

I wasn't, but she was so thin. "Yes," I said. "I'm starving."

We went to a pizza place on an artsy street. Small round wood tables, not much light. Anchovies, peppers, and onions, and when it came it was gigantic. Hallie ordered coffee, I asked for peppermint tea. Hallie just picked at her food; I didn't do much better. I wanted to know everything about Sally's condition, but there wasn't much to know. It was all up in the air. Specialists had come, all that. But the concensus was that there wasn't one. Maybe she'd regain consciousness and be fine, or else be a vegetable, or else live on and on in the coma, or else die.

"They refuse to even guess any percentages, what's most likely to happen. But I'm holding on tight to the belief she can come out of this and be fine. What else can I do?"

We took halfhearted bites of the red, yellow, and green pie-shaped slices. The anchovy was too much, after all; the crust wasn't very good. "What about you?" Hallie asked. "Tell me about this strange illness again? I'm afraid I wasn't really listening. . . ."

We did what catching up we could in the next hour. Of course the subject of relationships came up, our present mutual lack of any. We talked about David, about a more recent relationship of mine that had faded out, about old boyfriends of Hallie's.

"Remember Phillip?"

Did I remember him? Yes. Hallie'd had a little child support back then, plus whatever she could earn at occasional jobs as an assistant film editor. She didn't make enough money to pay for much more than their rent. Those jobs were scarce and she wasn't that experienced. Phillip owned his house, a car, a truck. He had a good bit of money from some inheritance. But he wouldn't pay for Hallie to have an abortion when she got pregnant, wouldn't even contribute to one. Though he wanted nothing to do with a child, either. It was her responsibility, her fault, her problem. And he'd seemed like such a sweet guy until then.

He'd tried hitting on me next, Hallie's friend. When that

didn't work, not a week had gone by before he had another girlfriend. He was attractive, he'd made his own feature film, and girlfriends were easy to find. I'd kept Sally for a few days. . . .

"And there's no one in sight for you right now, Maggie? Some nice redneck he-man down the road a piece?"

I sighed. "The only guy in sight is not a redneck. He's an Indian, but he's married."

"How married?"

"I don't know, but in general that's not a smart path to follow, right? My partner met his wife and thought she was a bitch. I've no idea what Jim thinks of her."

We went to the hospital. It was big, connected with the university. Supposed to be good, Hallie said, sounding not so sure. She was torn between hope and an abyss.

She introduced me to the man sitting in the hall, a guard. Big guy, not much hair. Wary-looking, alert. We went in.

Sally's face was much thinner, her eyes closed. But I easily recognized her, even though her face had been seven years younger when I'd known it. Her head stuck out from the white covers along with her arms. Tubes hung from metal racks on both sides of the bed putting things in, taking things out. She'd had hair almost to her waist when I'd known her but what I could see sticking out from the bandage was cut short now, rather clumsily. Probably they'd done it here. A jagged scar, red and angry, rode the hairline across her left temple. Partially scalped, the news had said. Her lungs breathed so shallowly, pushing her chest up, collapsing, up again, they hardly made a difference in the surface of the white-sheeted bed.

Hallie pulled up a chair to one side, sat down, took Sally's hand. I pulled another chair opposite, took the other hand.

"Maggie's here, darling, remember Maggie? In San Francisco. You used to go to the beach together, to the zoo."

I joined in. "You always liked the gorillas best, do you remember? I liked them too, but I maybe liked the monkeys more."

"You're going to come out of this soon, darling. I know you are. And when you do, I'm here. Whatever the problems, getting well, we'll work them out. Don't worry. Just come back, honey. As soon as you possibly can, okay?"

I stayed for four days, all pretty much alike: eat out, go to the hospital, eat dinner out, back to the hospital. One of the nights, I talked Hallie into going to a Woody Allen movie while I stayed with Sally. But she showed up at the hospital an hour later. "I couldn't stay," she said, "I'm sorry."

When we weren't with Sally she talked about how terrible it had been, how terrible it was. About the theories some medical people have. Carl Jung had provided some early evidence that unconscious people actually are aware of what's going on. So they should be talked to; maybe you can influence them, help them come back. We'd both dropped whatever religion our parents had provided and when something like this happened, what did we have? The new gods we'd adopted, Jung and the others, weren't really much help at a time like this. I'd come to believe that there's something out there, in there. When I'd finally pulled away from the full-time drinking, gone to AA. But what that something might be, I hadn't a clue, no concept at all. Someone newly sober said at a meeting once that his Higher Power was his radiator, going on and off at its own whim no matter how desperately he turned the knob. In a little fleabag room down on the Embarcadero, I remembered. "It was definitely a power greater than myself," he'd said. Funny, what you remember. What you forget.

Hallie said the truth was, some of the time she believed Sally would recover and some of the time she didn't. Like me she prayed to unknown, faceless gods and goddesses. But she always presented the hopeful side when she was with Sally.

She showed me some photocopied pages from a book by a Dr. Andrew Weil. He was in Tucson, where there are a lot of Latino people. Hispanic, they call it down there. He said he'd seen many Hispanic children in comas, not supposed to recover. But their hospital rooms were full of life, all the relatives there, radios blaring, people talking, laughing, yelling, even arguing. And many of those children came out of their comas and were fine. He'd seen a lot of Anglo children in comas, too. Their hospital rooms were silent, only a mother visiting, a father, people speaking carefully in whispers. Those children didn't seem to recover so often, died without regaining consciousness.

Hallie couldn't have a room full of people there because of the security. But she'd seen to it that a radio was always on. She had a cassette player in the room and played Sally's favorite music over and over.

At the hospital when Hallie talked to me, she always included Sally in the conversation, as I did, too.

"How did you decide to become a detective?" Hallie wanted to know. "Does that surprise you, Sally, that Maggie became a detective? Remember how crazy she always was to make films?"

I didn't want to talk in front of Sally about people who'd been murdered. Maybe she *could* hear everything, like that patient of Jung's who was carried into the hospital unconscious, eyes closed, but later she told them the time it had been on the clock on the wall—a clock that had been three hours off at the time and fixed since. If Sally could hear, hearing about violence would be terrible. So I didn't go into the story of my half sister, and my niece. I just said I'd met O'Reagan, an ex-cop, and we'd decided to give it a try, established an agency. It had gone well, I'd worked under his license until I had enough experience to get my own. Everything was going just fine until I got sick and had to abandon my career along with my city, my friends.

One evening, I remembered to ask Hallie about the dogs.

"You *have* them? They were Bobby's—I'll let his mother know; she'll be relieved. I thought it was crazy, taking dogs along on a trip like that. But they're animal people, his whole family. His mother was away and he wouldn't even consider putting them at a vet's, not taking them."

"What was he like? Were they—he was Sally's boyfriend?"

"More on his side, I think: he'd been crazy about her ever since they met. Oh, she liked him too, liked him a lot. They were good friends and I'm sure they slept together, but I don't think she was in love with him, not really in love. She may have thought she was, for a while."

Like her mother, so many times. Like me quite a few times, too. At least if Sally came back she wouldn't have to face the loss of half of herself, murdered while she'd survived.

I told Hallie about Mimi. "Do you think they'll want the dogs back?"

"I'll find out. But I don't think so, as long as they have a good home. His mother went to her family back east after it happened. But she and Bobby's father seem to be getting together again. Bobby's murder has brought them together."

Hallie was terrified the murderer would find out where Sally was, would come back and kill her. One guard at the door was nothing, she pointed out, for a man like that.

It was my last evening. I'd taken Hallie to dinner at a pretty good French restaurant on that same artsy street, a block from the pizza place. We'd both ordered crepes. I was hungry and wished they'd bring the food. I started filling up on French bread, buttered. Finally, the soup came. And after the waiter put it down and went away, Hallie asked me what I should have offered. Except I was so afraid of taking it on, then getting sick.

Since I was a detective now, she asked, would I try to find the killer?

I sat there looking at the onion soup, wondering about my strength, how far I could trust it.

"I can't pay you anything, not right now," she said hurriedly. "The hospital ... I'll probably be in debt the rest of my life. There's a point beyond which insurance doesn't go. But I'll make it up to you."

"Don't be ridiculous. If I could find the person who did this to Sally, don't you think that would be the best pay in the world? Find them and get them put away somewhere so there'd be no question they'd ever show up here? But I have this horrible illness. I'm okay for a while and then I get sick, can't do anything. I mean *anything*. But since you don't have money to hire anyone else, anyone better—and I don't, either—of course I'll do what I can. Of course I will. But you should know I've done some work on the case already. This guy they've arrested has an alibi for the time it happened, but the alibi has disappeared and the Karuk tribe hired me to find her. But I don't see any conflict of interest. Of course, if one should develop, I'll work for you, not him."

"Oh, Maggie." Big tears gathered in her eyes, then began rolling down her face. "I'm going to miss you."

"I'm going to miss you, too. And Sally. I'll be back. But listen, you should know not only am I likely to get sick, I've never worked on anything like this. I mean, the cases I had before, there was always an obvious group of people to suspect. A fairly simple question of who benefits, going over it and over it. I don't even know where to begin on something like this."

"I'm sure you can do it. Is there any way I can help?"

"Well . . . what about . . . I don't know," I said helplessly, my mind a blank. We were silent, thinking.

"Maybe—you might keep your eye out for a small gold locket," Hallie said finally. "Sally's locket. She didn't have it on when she was brought to the hospital. It was my mother's. She was crazy about my mother. Mama gave it to Sally when she was little, then after Mama died Sally wore it all the time. She was wearing it when she left for the camping trip, but she doesn't have it now. I don't know when she lost it, of course. . . . It was only gold plate, some of it worn away, and it said 'Elizabeth' across the front."

"How big?"

"Small." She looked down at her hands. "About the size of the nail on your middle finger, more or less. You think that might help?"

It didn't seem too likely, but I smiled and said, "Maybe it will."

It frightened me, the blind faith I saw in her eyes.

*Humans have not evolved from animals; we
ARE animals, no less dependent on plant
photosynthesis and bacterial decomposition
for our survival than the lowliest flatworm.*
—DAVID RAINS WALLACE,
THE KLAMATH KNOT

TEN

ON THE WAY HOME, I THOUGHT AND THOUGHT. HOW TO find this killer. How, how? Where to start? Maybe as Joey had suggested with his tale of Indian Mary, the important point was the *place*. Someone who was protecting it, killing people who came too near? But if so, where exactly? How to find out who he was? Work on the why. Go exploring myself up there. And end up scalped, as well. Then I'd know who the killer was. How to go about this? How? I'd call O'Reagan—he was so much more experienced. Maybe he'd have some brilliant idea. I certainly didn't. The killer could be any one of the whole male population of Siskiyou County, maybe nearby counties, too. Or he might be a drifter, long gone. It seemed impossible.

A song from Sally's Tracy Chapman tape kept running through my mind, interfering with my thinking.

> *She's got her ticket*
> *I think she gonna use it*
> *I think she going to fly away*
> *No one should try and stop her*
> *Persuade her with their power*
> *Why not leave why not*
> *Go away*
> *Too much hatred*

Corruption and greed

And she'll fly fly fly . . .

I couldn't get the words out of my head, not for very long. They were driving me crazy. I told myself, it's just a song.

In Scott Bar I stopped at the post office. A middle-aged blue Cadillac was parked in front, a beautiful blonde in the passenger seat, her door open and her long, shapely legs sticking out. I tried to look as if I wasn't looking at her, while I was. She had shining blond hair that sprang out in soft curls around a glowing, suntanned face. With wide-set eyes of a clear aquamarine blue, soft beautiful skin, breasts of movie-star proportions—she was a startling sight for tiny, backwoods Scott Bar. She belonged in Rome or Paris or Hollywood. Who was she?

A man was on the porch getting out his mail, and as I came up, he turned. Did he belong with the blonde? A sugar daddy? Tall, a little stooped, he had a wide, beak-nosed, tired-looking face, lightly freckled. His light brown hair was thinning; he looked like a worn-out forty-year-old who life has asked too much of. Perhaps the blonde had done it.

But he smiled in a friendly way and said, "I'm Frank Ullrich. You're the one living at Miss Thornton's place, aren't you?"

He stuck out his hand and we shook. He was stronger than he looked.

"Maggie Elliott," I said.

"Just call me Frank. I'm happy to make your acquaintance. How do you like living in our little town here?"

"It's very beautiful. The murder has me worried, though."

He shook his head. "Know just what you mean. Never had anything like that here before. Must be some crazy person."

"Is there anyone around here you think might be that crazy?"

A look of cunning or maybe it was just amusement crossed his face. "Plenty of people around here crazy enough, I'd say."

"Like who would be crazy enough?"

"Well, not to go pointing fingers at anybody but, well, take Bill Dawson in the post office here. He's out in those mountains a lot, and you know what he's doing there? Looking for Bigfoot. Now I ask you! *Bigfoot.*"

I tried to remember what I knew of Bigfoot. Bigfeet, bigfoots? They're supposed to be eight feet tall, covered with hair, have faces like an ape or maybe a cat. They smell of sulfur. Some people claim to have seen their footprints in the high, isolated mountain forests between Scott Bar and Happy Camp. Some people claim to have seen *them.*

"And Joey Brown," Frank went on, "you know him? Walks around in the mountains all weather, God knows what for. He's a real inquisitive fellow, though; that might explain it. But they got to be crazy, don't they, what with those people murdered up there? Unless one of them is the killer himself—*he* wouldn't need to be afraid, would he?"

But I liked Bill and Joey, while something about this man made me feel creepy. I said in my best saccharine voice, "It's logical. Your thinking is very interesting on this, Frank. You have any other ideas, what it's all about?"

He looked gratified, then grinned. "Aw—I really think it's that Indian. Look at the way they were both scalped. White man wouldn't even know how to go about it, something like that. But I should be going. It was real nice to meet you; maybe I'll stop by to see you sometime."

Actually he had a kind of saccharine quality himself; something about him wasn't for real. What I wanted to say was, No, no, please don't, but I didn't want to be rude. And maybe he'd be worth talking to some more, anyway. Maybe he was the killer himself. "Sure," I said.

Bill Dawson had his nose in a book but seemed happy to be interrupted and wanted to tell me about what he was reading.

"You ever give any thought to *worms*, Maggie? Did you

know we're all *descended* from worms? Ha ha!—and not just us humans either. Why this book says all the big animal groups in the world—that's mollusks, chordates, and arthropods—show signs of being descended from worms! We've all got blood, muscles, nerves, sense organs—and fetuses that look like worms!"

Any other time, I'd have enjoyed this, but I was too preoccupied, my mind hobbling around in circles. How was I going to find the killer before he found Sally? I felt disoriented, displaced. Bill rattled on.

"But they wasn't really land animals, worms wasn't. They still got a little film of moisture all over, like they was still in the water. They can't breathe unless they have it. Millipedes and centipedes now, they was the first real land animals, come along about three hundred fifty million years ago. Isn't that something? If some of these religious groups don't like to think we're descended from apes, how do you suppose they'd feel if they knew we're all descended from *worms*? *Millipedes! Centipedes!*" He laughed delightedly. "But you got some mail." He reached up to the back of the box and handed across a thick letter, which I saw was from Jim. My heart gave a little leap, then I realized it was surely only business. The material subpoenaed from the sheriff.

"Who's the blonde with Frank Ullrich?" I asked. "I saw them outside."

"Blonde? Oh shoot, that's just his daughter. You thought he was really up to something, huh? She's a real bombshell, that girl!" He laughed happily, then grew serious. "What I hear, she's out of control, just out of control. Course with a father like that—what I hear about him, I won't even *tell* you! But I'll tell you this. Folks say the way he's treated that girl, well, it's not right, it just isn't right."

All the natives busy tattling on each other, why not. I heard the door open and I turned, to see a Chinese man just coming in. He had on new jeans, a new-looking navy blue sweater. Short, thick black hair, a broad, expressionless face. Of the thousands of Chinese who'd been here in gold rush days, I knew that not one remained. The Chinese had been a pet subject of Aunt Bessie's; she had done a lot of research on them, even published some of it. I'd always meant to read her articles, maybe now I finally would. What I'd read in the Historical Society book had piqued my interest, too. I wanted to know more. What was this guy doing here, like a ghost from the past? A modern-day miner? Looking for some of his roots? I went out as he asked Bill about his mail.

The blue Cadillac, Frank, and the out-of-control daughter were gone. Joey Brown, Mr. Curiosity, was on the porch getting mail out of his box. It was like Grand Central Station here today, Jones Beach, India at bathing time along the Ganges. "Who's that Chinese man?" I asked in a low voice. "I thought there weren't any more Chinese around here."

"Fella stayin' over at the Rainbow cabins. You know the ones I mean, over there next to the Rainbow Grocery? Arnie said he showed up end a last summer. Closemouthed fella, doesn't say what he's doin'. He ain't fishin' or huntin', but I've seen him wanderin' around in the mountains up above here. Lookin' for somethin', looks like. But what? That, I *don't* know."

The man came out, walking rather stiffly, with a slight limp to the right leg. He went past without looking at either of us. In his car he opened his mail, which consisted of a single letter, a one-page one. Joey lifted his binoculars and looked through them into the car, trying to read the letter, too.

Who was he? After a minute, he drove off and Joey lowered the glasses. "I had the idea maybe he was our killer. So I went over to the Rainbow, talked to Arnie about 'im. Though he don't look to fit with the scalpin', does he? But then, he might a done that to shift the blame elsewhere. What do you think? Course they arrested that guy from Happy Camp. He hasn't confessed, though. But you know, I've been thinkin' a lot about the killin', Miss PI. Let me try this on you. Maybe it's a *group* of killers, not just one man, I mean. This Chinese now, he might be part of some gang, a tong. What do you think? What's your professional opinion?"

"I don't know . . . more than one killer could make sense, I guess. Or one guy who's been highly trained in that kind of ambush, had a lot of experience—maybe Vietnam, or some mercenary up from Central America now they don't have Nicaragua to kick around anymore. . . ." I liked that, being able to use my favorite line from Dick Nixon. Of course, they still had El Salvador. "Or—I don't know. The thing is, *why* attack them?"

"Yep, that's it. *Why?* Think what I'll do, I'll try to keep track of this Chinese fella, help you out that way. Let you know what I find out, right? I could be your partner in this investigation, or anyway help out; I'm really good at findin' things out. Always did think the detection business would be pretty interestin', you know?"

"I'd love to have your help, Joey. You take the Chinese man, I'll work on some of the other aspects, then we'll confer and compare notes."

"Sure, great. I never had time to do anythin' like this back when I was younger, workin' too hard. Maybe I'll have somethin' for you soon."

Before I drove off, I stuck the letter from Jim in my purse. I didn't want Joey reading that one over my shoulder—which was unkind, he would have loved it so.

Back at home, I unpacked, made some lunch, then called O'Reagan. He was out, so I left a message. I opened the fat letter from Jim. It contained copies of everything the sheriff had against Ruther on the hikers. A short note said Jim hoped the trip to Ashland had been good and that he'd be in touch.

I removed the clip and looked at what they had. The initials *V, S, W,* and *P* were scattered through the report— victim, suspect, witness, perpetrator. The statement of the helicopter pilot *W,* the results from the scene of crime, lab reports, autopsy, medical report on Sally.

The warrant to search had a list of what they'd taken from Ruther's house, which included a .30-.30 and a pair of boots, along with the camping equipment.

The hospital report noted that no wallets, ID, or money were found on either V. Sally's wounds were described in detail and it was noted that she had been raped. The young caucasian male V, between seventeen and twenty, had a one-inch fragment of heavy blue glass in one pocket, old glass with a raised F at one edge.

The autopsy described the boy's gunshot wound and the scalping in grisly detail, which I skipped over fast. It was Sally's boyfriend they were talking about.

The lab reported nothing at all from the scene to indicate the identity of P. No wisps of cloth or hair that didn't belong to the Vs. The report on Ruther's boots indicated they could have been in the area where the hikers were killed. But unless there was something very special about the dirt or vegetation up there—I'd have to check—the dirt could also have come from most anywhere in the area. The gun was also negative, didn't match bullets.

The helicopter pilot's description of the scene brought it all before me even more hideously than my imagination had. I tried to put my feelings aside, concentrate on the details. There were two backpacks, which the deputy describing the scene said had obviously been searched. For what, for what? They contained nothing you wouldn't expect for a long hiking trip, about four weeks if I remembered right. The deputy noted the presence of a small amount of dog kibble with the food and several tubes of an extremely rich nutrient paste, a veterinary product that he speculated had enabled the hikers to pack less dog food.

The damaging part came at the end. A male W out getting firewood reported seeing a man about a mile down the trail from the area the afternoon of the crime. Later picked S (Ruther) out of the lineup. So that was it, why they'd gone ahead and arrested him, charged him. Ruther denied he'd been anywhere near there. I'd have to find out about that lineup. Who else was in it, whether the man had been shown pictures beforehand that included Ruther, so by the time W came to the lineup, Ruther was, unconsciously, familiar. It might also be that he'd seen an Indian-looking man, and if Ruther was the only Indian they showed him . . . I'd have to talk to this W. His name was Harry Lipscomb and he lived at 30580 Scott River Road. I was 28050, so that wasn't far. I read through the transcripts of the interrogations of Ruther, before and after arrest—nothing new.

As far as I could see, what they really had, aside from that witness who could easily be mistaken, was mostly a very strong desire for the killer to be Ruther. That witness who *was* mistaken if Ruther's alibi panned out, and I believed it would. If I could only locate Lucy Farrell.

I got in the car and drove to 30580 Scott River Road. A metal mailbox had the number, on the river side of the road. A short driveway led through a weedy yard to a small cabin with few windows. A couple of cords of firewood were on the porch. I rang the bell. I waited, rang again. But no one came. I didn't want to leave a note to call me. I needed to see this man and I didn't want to alert him.

I went home and called Sacramento information, but they had no listing on any of the names I tried for Lucy's mother or Jonathan Farrell's father. They had the doctor from Jonathan's prescription bottle, though, Byron Browning. I called his office and at first the woman who answered said I couldn't have an appointment for two weeks. When I said it was urgent and that I'd been recommended by the Farrells, she said to wait a minute and I heard muffled talking. Then she came back. "There is a cancellation," she said, "day after tomorrow. You could come at two o'clock." I said that would be fine, wondering what kind of doctor Byron Browning was. Perhaps a shrink.

I went back to 30580 Scott River Road. It was a hot, dark day, threatening to storm. A light was shining in the front room of the house this time, behind a heavy shade. He must have heard my car, for he opened the door as I came up the steps to the porch. A short man in a plaid wool shirt, he had a big head, out of proportion to the rest of his body, narrow glasses, arms too long for his torso. Sixty or so. He almost looked like a dwarf but wasn't quite that short. He seemed friendly enough, accepting my vague statement about working on the murders without asking why, who with, who for. He invited me in.

The front room was small and dark. As the door closed with a loud *snap*, it occurred to me I'd better hope *he* wasn't the killer. A sheet-metal wood stove with firewood stacked on both sides took up one side of the room, probably kept the whole house warm in winter. The lamp standing next to the window had only a fifty-watt bulb or maybe not even that, further dimmed by a white cloth shade with bobbles. The couch looked like a Hide-A-Bed, covered in something rough and gray, stiffly all of a piece and uncomfortable. I sat at one end and he lowered himself down gingerly at the other, as if he hurt. There was also a brown La-Z-Boy recliner in imitation leather, but the seat sank way down at an odd angle, as if the underpinning had collapsed. I asked him about the day the hikers were attacked, the man he'd seen. Behind the narrow glasses his gray eyes were bright and interested.

"Like I told the sheriff, fella looked Indian, big guy, dark hair and eyes, big nose—you know, how the Indians mostly look."

"Dark skin?"

He nodded. "That, too. Yeah. They showed me a bunch of pictures, photographs in those books they have. Known criminals, I guess they are. I couldn't say I recognized any, but one or two of 'em looked like it might be. One guy in particular looked familiar after a while."

I smiled. "After a while? There was more than one picture of this guy?"

"That's right—he kept turning up. Then, well, he was in the lineup, too. By then, I was pretty sure he was the one. So, that's what I told 'em. Not a hundred percent, you understand, but pretty sure."

I felt pleased that my suspicions of the sheriff's methods

had panned out. A lawyer could do a lot with this witness, if it came to that. "I can see you were very conscientious about it. Who else was in the lineup? I mean, were any of the other guys Indian-looking?"

"Why no, that was the thing, see—they were all just regular people, just this one fella was Indian. Like I say he seemed real familiar. I felt pretty sure he was the one I'd seen. They said where I saw him, it was real close to where the murder was."

"Uh-huh. Okay. Now, Mr. Lipscomb, think back to that day you were up there and saw this man—before you were at the sheriff's, before they showed you the pictures, before you saw the men in the lineup."

"Aw, call me Harry. Everybody calls me Harry." He grinned, apparently enjoying this. An old man who lived alone.

"Sure." I smiled back. "So, Harry, the day you were up there and saw this man, did you speak, or did he say anything?"

"No, he just kinda nodded at me and went on past. I didn't think nothing about it till I saw on the news about the murder. They asked anyone who'd seen anyone in the area to come in. So I did."

"Could you tell me a little more what he looked like?" I shouldn't let reverse prejudice cloud my judgment entirely, fellow immune systems or not. Maybe the killer was Indian, just wasn't Ruther. "I mean, you know, anything special about the way he looked? His ears stuck out, or they were real small? Were his eyes especially small or especially big? Set close together? Did his eyebrows grow together over his eyes—"

"Now wait! That's something I'd forgotten—fella's eyebrows *were* real bushy-like. Don't see too many Indians like that, but, of course no reason they can't be. That's right—fellow's eyebrows were real thick. I wouldn't say all the way across, though. So maybe . . . that Indian—why, I don't think he *had* eyebrows like that! How could I have forgotten a thing like that? I just completely forgot it." He shook his head. "Oh my God. I think maybe I made a mistake. I feel terrible."

He looked like he really did, too. His eyes were large and staring; his hands shook. I revised his age upward, more like eighty.

"That's all right—I can see you were trying hard to do your best. It's difficult to remember everything, especially with someone throwing a lot of questions at you. Now you can tell them about the eyebrows, and that'll help them find the right man."

He looked a little relieved by the reassurance. I smiled encouragingly.

"I feel like some kind of a fool, though."

"No, no, Harry, you're doing great. You have any idea how many people there are would never admit it if they knew they'd made a mistake? Now try to recall if there might have been something else—his ears big or little, any moles on his face, any scars?"

He shook his head.

"What about . . . was his neck long, or real short, or just medium? Same thing for his arms and legs."

"Well now." He looked past me, out over the tops of the glasses. "He was a real big fella, like I said. Over six feet, I'd say, and heavyset."

"How old about?"

"Sometimes these Indians, it's hard to tell their age. But I'd say maybe twenty-five or thirty. Fella was carrying a rifle—I didn't notice what kind."

I'm not too bad at drawing. I took out the sketchbook and pencil I'd brought, drew a face as much like Harry's description as I could.

"Wider," Harry said. "Much wider in the face, but the eyebrows, I'd say you got them about right. Something wrong with the eyes, though."

I did several more drawings and finally came up with a face he thought was a pretty good likeness. It was no one I'd ever seen. But if the guy was Indian and I showed it to Jim, maybe he'd know him or could find someone who did.

ELEVEN

WHEN I'D LAST SEEN IT, DOWNTOWN SACRAMENTO HAD
looked like the abandoned parts of Oakland—boarded-up
windows and OUT OF BUSINESS signs. But they'd had a boom
here the past few years and it showed in flashy but uninteresting new buildings, busy shops that were all *in* business
now. The address I wanted, a tall monolith of glass and
concrete near the state capitol building, provided its own
parking for seven dollars. I handed over the money and
went into the Browning building. Same Browning as the
doctor?

A very quiet elevator whisked me to the nineteenth floor.
In the corridor, wall-to-ceiling glass at each end let you
pick which view you wanted of the smoggy city spread out
widely beneath you. I checked the number directions opposite the elevator and went left to a polished wood door with
the doctor's name in brass letters. INTERNAL MEDICINE.

A comfortably quiet and subdued large room in mauves
and grays, good fabrics, restful pictures on the wall. A

white-uniformed receptionist took my name and said the doctor was running a little late today, to have a seat. I thought of my doctor's clinic in Arizona. A small waiting area with polished, bare wood floors, pleasant but no frills. And his office, small, too, an old oak rolltop desk, some books and a lot of plants. Much more *simpático* ... and they really tried there to keep the fees down. They didn't have big cumbersome egos—or many clients who had them, either. We were all too beaten down by the viruses by the time we got there.

About one hour and four *Time* magazines later, the receptionist called my name and a nurse came out and led me to a large office gotten up in the same muted colors as the waiting room, the carpet even thicker. A tall, spare man, silver-haired, stood up behind a large highly polished wood desk, cherry maybe, smiling, his hand outstretched.

"Miss Elliott. I understand Bert and Beth Farrell sent you." His smile looked genuinely warm, his cornflower blue eyes crinkled attractively in a suntanned face. I guessed he was in his late fifties. We shook hands and he said, "Have a seat, make yourself comfortable." He sat down, too, and looked across at me expectantly. "What seems to be the trouble?"

Bert and Beth. Albert? That might help, if he wouldn't tell me anything. "Well ... it's a little complicated," I began.

He nodded solemnly, sympathetically.

"Actually, I'm trying to find Lucy Farrell, Jonathan's wife." The listening face stiffened, was no longer so sympathetic. "It's important for their marriage that I talk to her without Jonathan knowing. I bring them no harm, but it's extremely urgent that I see her, and I'm hoping you will help."

He nodded noncommittally but said nothing, waiting. I took out my private detective license and pushed it across the desk.

He looked it over carefully and handed it back. "You realize I couldn't—and wouldn't if I could—tell a private detective anything at all about my patients, don't you? Do

you even know the Farrells, or how did you . . ." His voice
petered out; he waited again.

"I think it will be simpler," I said quietly, "if I start at the
beginning."

"All right." He steepled his fingers and rested his chin on
top. "You have five minutes. I'm a very busy man."

I told him quickly about the attack on the hikers,
Ruther's arrest, Ruther's claim to have been with Lucy.
"Jonathan needn't know," I said. "I can get a deposition
from her and that will be the end of it."

"And you think this fellow, what's his name, Ruther?
Odd name. You think he's telling the truth?"

"Yes. I do." I held my breath, held his eyes with mine.
He sat very still, looking back at me, looking rather stub-
born, I thought. Not a good sign.

"So what do you imagine you want from me?" he asked.

"Just a very simple thing. Jonathan's address now, if you
know it. Or his parents' address. I'll take it from there and
I'll be very careful, very discreet, believe me."

He frowned. "Careful? You'd better be, if you find them.
Jonathan has a history of violence, you know." He held a
hand up, palm toward me, as if pushing something away.
"I'm not saying there's anything really wrong with him, but
he has always been overly . . . emotional. If you do see
Lucy, you should tell her to be extremely careful he doesn't
find out about this. Only fair to warn you. But I'm afraid
that's all I can do. I can't give out any patient's address. It's
out of the question."

A flush of disappointment swept through me, and irrita-
tion. He continued. "However, if you should find yourself
in Walnut Grove, well, it's an interesting town, up on the
delta. I was born there myself." He smiled encouragingly.

Walnut Grove? I knew the place because it was next
door to Locke, only about a mile away as I remembered. I
was surprised to think how long it was since I'd been there.
To the little half house Jennifer rented as a getaway place
and let her friends use, too. David and I had gone there
sometimes. It was close enough to the city for a quick ref-

uge from hectic film editing or whatever, when there wasn't
time enough to go up to our cabin.

The doctor was smiling, waiting. I smiled back. "Thank
you very much, Dr. Browning."

From a pay phone I called information, got a G. A.
Farrell in Walnut Grove, but it was unlisted. Nothing for a
Jonathan. I called Jim Pepper to give him the good news
about what I believed to be the town where I could find at
least Jonathan Farrell's parents, but he wasn't home so I left
a message.

I called my friend Charlie, who lived in Locke. He said
he didn't know the family but could probably dig up someone who did. He said by all means stay with him, the couch
was pretty comfortable.

"Wonderful. Will you try to find out if the son and his
wife are anywhere around? And if they are, is there anyplace she'd be going the next day or so, by herself, where
we could talk without any of the family knowing? Prefera-
bly tomorrow? I'll come down now, I'm in Sacramento."

All this made me feel better, useful at last.

Sacramento had felt plastic, garish, and polluted. It was
a relief to get out on the badly paved narrow road running
along the top of the levee that edges the enormous Sacramento River. It was hot down here at nearly sea level,
about half a season behind Scott Bar. On the right was the
river, slow and gray and huge. Below on the left, dark
ploughed fields stretched as far as the eye could see. All
their contents harvested, put away by now in cans, or frozen: asparagus, spinach, tomatoes. After twenty minutes or
so, the fields gave way to neatly planted lines of big old
trees. Leafy and green still, with yellow mustard flowers
covering the ground around the twisted black trunks—the
pear orchards that surround Locke.

I turned off the levee road past Main Street to the only
other street in town, where a hand-painted sign read RESI-
DENTS ONLY BEYOND THIS POINT. I drove slowly past small
white frame houses with small green lawns and rosebushes.

I'd loved Locke, so had David. How could I have let so much time pass and not gone back?

An old, old Chinese man, wrinkled and thin, sat nodding on the front porch of the house across the street from Charlie's. I remembered him from the days I'd come here often. As I got out I smiled, and he nodded and said something unintelligible in Chinese. Locke is restful that way: Almost no one speaks English. Also restful is the town's time-machine aspect: built all of a piece in 1915 after the old Chinatown in Walnut Grove burned down and virtually unchanged since. To turn off the levee road into Locke is to travel back almost a century in time.

The early town was all things to the thousands of Chinese who'd come to build the levees and work the rich black delta land: recreation in the form of Chinese gambling houses and opium dens and Anglo-Saxon whores; home and rest in the small cheap rooms on the second floors of the Main Street buildings where the men lived the occasional moments they weren't working. Some of the workers saved up enough money to go back to China and marry; sometimes the husbands made enough additional money, after another quarter century or so of low-paid toil, to send for their wives to live with them in the Gold Mountain—which is what the Chinese of China called the United States—at Locke. The town is almost all old people now, a handful of elderly Chinese still working their plots in the big vegetable garden out back of the houses. Lush and thriving and growing the kind of inscrutable Oriental things I'd seen for sale only in Chinatown in San Francisco.

I remembered trudging up the trail through high weeds at the back of the gardens with David, up to the levee, through the strong smell of licorice from head-high lacy green plants baking in the sun. Then you come to the unused railroad tracks along the top, Snodgrass Slough on the other side, and the swimming hole with a rope from a tree we'd swing way out on, drop into the water with an enormous satisfying splash . . . the whole area back there a magical place of thick marshes, small woods, lots of wild-life. Also aged Chinese fishermen, and women, engaged in the old-fashioned kind of fishing that's done with a long pole, a worm, and long hours of patient sitting under a big straw hat.

Several cats slept deeply in the autumn sun and hens pecked desultorily in the weedy dirt around Charlie's house—a two-story dark wood structure that one of the old Chinese sold him for a hundred dollars because it was fall-ing down. He'd transformed his great bargain into a really beautiful place to live, plain dark wood walls, a lot of win-dows flooding a big space two stories high with soft yellow light, a loft at one end. Not gentrified, but simplified.

I found Charlie in the workshop behind the house, pushing a long piece of wood through a table saw. I had to walk around to the other side because of the noise, and when he saw me, a gratifying look of pleasure swept across his wide, appealing face, then a big grin as he turned off the saw.

"Hey, Maggie!" He gave me a big hug followed by a rather nice kiss. "Let me just finish this, we'll go inside." He flicked the switch and sent the long piece of redwood smoothly into the blade until it was halved lengthwise. Then he leaned the two pieces against a wall, and I fol-lowed him through a connecting door into the large main room of his house. He filled a cast-iron kettle with water and put it on the big wood cook stove.

"I've found out quite a bit about this Farrell guy. He comes from one of those really rich families that live on River Road south of town in Walnut Grove. Family owns about four thousand acres of best delta farmland—pears, to-matoes, beets, asparagus. Been here forever, by California standards. The one you're looking for, Jonathan, he's the only child. Ran with a heavy-drinking crowd. He and his pals used to ride around at night throwing rocks in win-dows and then peel off, lotsa wild laughter. Because of his family, he never got called on it—also because the smashed windows were always Chinese or Mexican migrant. Any-way, he went in the army—"

"What'd he do in the army?"

"Uh, some sort of commando stuff, not Green Berets; I think it was something else. But same idea. Anyway, after he got out he came back and went to the community college. My friend said the family heaved a big sigh of relief when he went to work for the Park Service. Where he's done okay, it's thought, through strings the father can pull with the district congressman and Senator Hedgpole, who spend a lot of their time in his family's pocket when they're not hanging out in the pockets of similar delta families. Speaking of pockets they—the family—is reputed to be very tight with their money, some would say stingy. This Jonathan has a couple cousins they're training to manage the agricultural empire. Apparently, he's not considered management material. This the kind of stuff you wanted to know?"

"It's perfect, Charlie, thanks. You interested in a job at the agency?"

"Even better"—he grinned—"he's here. With a little wifey and kids. Staying at the family manse."

"Ah . . . I *hoped* they would be. Now how am I going to get to see the wifey without the husband knowing?"

"My friend Sherry said she'd pick you up here a little before nine tomorrow. She takes their kid to a story hour at the library and the Farrell woman always goes with her kids."

"Magnificent. How about I take you to dinner at Al's?"

After Charlie went to bed I kept the light on, looking through a book about Locke, *Bitter Melon*. It had very good photographs and interviews with the old Chinese residents. Their round, foreign faces made me think of the Chinese man up north. What was he looking for? In the book, they talked about the past:

> . . . the whites would attack you with stones when you walked through some of these towns. We never dared to walk on the streets alone then. Except in Locke. Locke was our place.

But I was tired, and worrying about what I would say to Lucy Farrell. I put the book down, turned off the light, closed my eyes and listened to the sound of a branch tapping on the windowpane. Lucy . . . Lucy . . . Lucy . . . Lucy do you love me, Lucy will you save me Lucy . . . Lucy . . . Lucy . . .

Sherry and a small redheaded child pulled up in an old pickup the next morning just before nine. She had sparse blond hair cut short, wispy, and big pale blue eyes behind large glasses. I followed in my car, covering the mile to Walnut Grove in about a minute. She slowed at the beginning of town, turned left, and pulled up at a long, low building of pale beige brick on a back street. We went into the main room and Sherry nodded toward a thin, beautiful girl sitting at a big round table at the far end. She was dressed rather smartly in a skirt and blouse of the rich young matron type, but she looked exhausted, with dark smudges beneath her eyes and a sad slump to her shoulders.

"That's Lucy," she whispered. "You should have a few minutes with her, the others usually straggle in late."

My heartbeat sped up. Lucy at last. She looked unhappy, somehow bereft, not nearly old enough to be the mother of the two children at the table with her. She had high, wide cheekbones, a Scandinavian look. Shining shoulder-length yellow hair—what was that Yeats poem . . . "only God, my dear, / Could love you for yourself alone / And not your yellow hair." She was staring off into space and actually jumped when the older child pulled at her sleeve, asked her something about the book.

We went over to the table and I sat down next to her. Sherry began talking in a loud chattery voice to the only other mother who was there, and I said quietly, "Lucy, my name is Maggie Elliott, and I've come here from the Klamath River to talk to you about Ruther Bradshaw."

Her lovely face paled, then turned red, and she looked at me, then quickly turned away. I went on, trying to sound simple and clear and unthreatening. "I came here to talk to you because Ruther said it's important to you that your husband not know anything about him—but he's in trouble and needs your help."

She didn't say a word, just sat there, still not looking at me, looking down at her lap, numbly listening. "Ruther says he was with you at your house in Tulelake for two days in August. On one of those days, some people up in the mountains near Scott Bar, hikers, just kids—one was murdered and the other one's in a coma, not expected to live. The police chose Ruther as their suspect. They've arrested him and charged him with the murder."

She was listening hard, straining, and I saw tears in her dark eyes as she finally looked at me. "I didn't know," she said. "I'm sorry, I didn't know."

A stocky young woman came up to the table at that point, said, "Hi everybody. Let's get started. Betty Jo, stop writing on the table; put that pencil down." Several more mothers and quite a few children had arrived, and I said hurriedly, "Where can we talk, later?"

"I don't . . . let me—here would probably be best. After this is over."

"Once upon a time," the storyteller began, "there was a poor young fisherman who was very handsome even in his ragged clothes. One day when he was out fishing, the king's boat came across the lake and the boy saw the king's daughter in the boat, a beautiful princess with yellow hair that shone in the sun like gold. But the princess was sad . . ." Just like Lucy, I thought. There was something about the storyteller's voice—she had the children's attention totally. The adults, too. Finally she brought the story to its predictable conclusion, happier than what I feared for Lucy and Ruther.

There was a bit of talk and then the mothers gathered together children and coats and security blankets and tiny trucks. Soon Lucy and I were left alone at the table with her children. The younger child, a fat-faced yet adorable creature, was asleep in her lap. The older girl, with the beautiful blond-haired, dark-eyed coloring of her mother, seemed content turning the pages of an upside-down picture book.

"Tell me," she said anxiously, reaching out, touching my arm. "How is he? You said he's in jail? He was with me those two days, it's true; we were together the whole time. He couldn't have murdered those people. Why did they arrest him?"

"Do you remember the dates? The exact dates he was with you?"

"Of course. August twenty-first and twenty-second. How could I forget?"

They were the right dates and I let go of my last lingering, unwanted doubts.

"How is he? Did he send any . . . any message?" Lucy asked.

"He asked me to tell you he still wants you to come to him, to get a divorce and marry him."

"I wish I could," she said. She looked at the wall of books across the room and absently rubbed her shoulder. She had on a pale yellow silk blouse, very becoming. "I'm so afraid of losing the kids. Jonathan found out about Ruther. Quentin—a man my husband worked with, Quentin Adams, he was always trying to hit on me, hanging around. He saw Ruther and told Jonathan. That's why we left. Jonathan said if I ever saw Ruther again he'd take the kids and I'd never see them again. . . ." Her voice had been gradually rising in pitch, and though she spoke in a whisper her real terror came through.

"So he knows it was Ruther?"

"He—" She looked away, ashamed. "Jonathan beats me up when he's angry," she said finally. "It started right after we married. Then he's always so sorry after, says he can't live without me. . . . He gets in fights, too. . . . He's real big, strong. . . ." She took a long, shuddering breath. "And I don't have any money . . . oh *God.* I *want* to go to him but—what do you think I should do?"

I shook my head. "I can't tell you what to do. Except I'm hoping and expecting that you'll go with me to a lawyer to make a deposition that Ruther was with you those two days. Unless you decide to come back with me and tell the sheriff yourself."

"Jonathan's gone fishing with his dad over on the San Joaquin." She stared across at the books, immobile. Then she said, all in a rush, "I'll do it. If I—could you take me back with you today? Right away?" She got up and started to gather the children's things.

"What about your car?" I asked. "Shouldn't we drop it off at your house?"

"No, let's just go," she said nervously. "It'll be okay here for a while and by the time it's noticed, Jonathan will have got home and"—she shrugged—"it won't matter about the car. I'll write him. Let's just go—he'll kill me, if he can find me."

We reached the jail around four o'clock. I'd called ahead and Jim's truck was waiting in front. He jumped out as soon as we pulled up.

I introduced him to Lucy and said I'd join them inside after I'd taken Diana for a walk. She was enchanted with the suburban abundance of other-dog smells after being so long in the car, and we were gone some time.

When we returned, I put her back in the car and an officer showed me to a small room at the back, not the same one where I'd seen Ruther. Lucy's two kids were sitting quietly in a chair next to Jim and she was just handing her statement to a grim-faced cop who looked none too pleased to take it. Why? Because they'd have to start all over now? But he did take it, and then she was granted some time in the visiting room with Ruther.

Jim and I went outside and stood on the steps. It was nearly dark. The streetlights came on suddenly but the scene was still dreary and gloomy. My mind had been full of fairy tales about beautiful princesses and poor boys who lived happily ever after. The jail had squashed them, and I felt sad. Jim put an arm across my shoulder as if he sensed my thoughts, gave me a hug.

"Thanks for finding her—probably nobody else could've done it, got her up here like you've done."

"Oh . . . I don't think she ever really hesitated about making the statement, once she knew what the situation was." I looked at him anxiously. "Where will they go now?"

"She'll stay with my mom for a while, in case Farrell comes looking for them. There's a good lawyer here in town. He's a friend of mine and he'll take her case."

"What about Ruther? It won't have done him much good to get out of jail, if he's shot dead by Jonathan Farrell—who knows his name and where he's from. From what Lucy told me about him—"

"Ruther won't get out till tomorrow, then he's going to stay with me for a while. I'm living now in a small cabin out back of my mom's place."

I took a minute to compute that one, then asked, "You're living there by yourself, you mean?"

"Yeah. My wife and I split up."

There was some strong expression on his face but I couldn't read it. Sorrow, rage, what? After what seemed a long time, he continued. "I left a couple weeks ago. She's gone down to L.A., may be staying there. She once wanted to be an actress, now she just might go for it."

"Oh." My heart leapt to my throat; the information traveled in a dizzying swirl through my head. Jim—but I didn't want to think about it now. I'd think about it later, like Scarlett O'Hara. What had he said? Actress. "Does she have the talent? To make it as an actress?"

"I think I'm not the best person to judge. She has the looks, I do know that." He gazed down the street, as if his wife were standing there in front of the two-story Victorian where the street dead-ended. Playing who? Not Pocahontas. "She's pretty angry with me for leaving, even though she's the one who started it." He shook his head and looked back at me. "I don't know why I'm telling you all this."

"I did ask," I said quietly.

He nodded. "Yeah, I guess I wanted you to know. We've been married thirteen years, but it's been headed this way a long time, six years anyway. So the break seems recent, but it isn't really."

We stood for a while with no more words, with something between us that made me want to take his hand or hold him. Finally he broke the silence.

"I forgot to tell you. I'm afraid nothing can be done about your friend's cabin. It's forty-nine years old, which is why they're going after it now. I'll do some more checking, though. Maybe there's something I don't know about."

"Thanks. I hate to see them lose their home."

We stood there next to each other, each thinking our own thoughts. It was dark out now, a full moon rising over the town. Which made me think, Lunatics. "You're putting you and your mother in a possibly dangerous position, aren't you? Maybe they should come to my house. At least it isn't in Happy Camp. Farrell will be looking in Happy Camp. And the police don't have my name."

"You said he won't be back for several days—we'll think about it, whether someplace else would be better. Not your place, though. And don't worry. We'll all be very careful and no one will know they're there. It'll be hard for her, though. She likes you. Would you come down to visit her in a day or two?"

We settled on Sunday, two days away. As Jim was drawing me a map to his mother's, Lucy came out, carrying one child and leading the other. The tired, defeated look was gone. She was radiant. It made me feel all the danger was worth it.

"Before we go to Happy Camp," she said to me, "I'm going to see a doctor here to look at the . . . the bruises. I feel like a traitor, but Jim says that'll help get the restraining order and I'm scared not to get it. Also it'll help for a divorce. And I guess"—she smiled sadly, the happiness clouding over—"I already am a traitor, aren't I? The sheriff said they want confirmation from Quentin—the guy I told you saw Ruther in Tulelake? Who told my husband? They have to talk to him before they release Ruther."

"Will he give it, do you think?"

"Oh, I think so. He's kind of a nasty person, but he's a stickler for rules. I don't think he'd want to lie to the police. As soon as they've contacted him, they'll do the legal things necessary to release Ruther and drop the charges, probably tomorrow, they said. Thank God there's a little time. Thank God for that fishing trip."

> *"But why did they jump through the window?"* we asked, *"Were they drunk?"*
> *"No,"* said Essie, *"they wasn't drunk. At least not much. . . ."*
> —MARY ELLICOTT ARNOLD AND MABEL REED,
> *IN THE LAND OF THE GRASSHOPPER SONG*

TWELVE

SUNDAY FINALLY CAME. I WOKE UP LATE, WROTE DOWN A dream about being chased by something unknown and terrible, my legs like lead, my feet dragged down as if in quicksand. But aside from the creepy residue left by the dream I didn't feel bad at all, just a little tired. Maybe I'd get away with it this time, doing a little work.

I took my drops, then found Aunt Bessie's pamphlet on the Chinese and took it to the porch to read with breakfast. It began with a quote from *The Shasta Courier* of April 2, 1853:

> How these little weakly looking hombres manage to carry such loads over such mountains as we have in this region, is what we cannot precisely comprehend. However, we suppose it is done by some sort of legerdemain, as it is well known that the Chinese can do almost anything through the instrumentality of certain mystic sciences.

But soon the tone became hostile and shrill. Agitation grew to rid the country of the "moon-eyed pests." Violence and murder all through the last half of the century plus special mining taxes not applied to whites, exclusion from white schools, from employment with the state, and prohibitions against owning land—declared unconstitutional only in

1952—all combined to force the Chinese back to China. Sometimes at a dead run, for their lives.

After breakfast I dressed carefully in soft old jeans and a thin Indian cotton blouse the same pale blue, my favorite. Hoping that, as with Janey and Jed in the old diary, the right outfit would catch Jim's eye, enhance something I hoped was there at least a little . . . poor guy. Just rid of the wife and here I was right away with brand-new plans for him. If he wanted . . . Sometimes he'd seemed interested in me but maybe I'd just imagined it. I felt uncertain, nervous about seeing him again. But full of a happy feeling, anticipation, too. I gave my hair another couple of swacks with the brush and set off. It was a warm, dark day again, threatening rain.

Happy Camp has the feel of a frontier logging town still, a rough-and-ready town, a saloon town. I'm not sure why. There was a huge sawmill on the outskirts, but after that it was the usual big supermarket, drugstore, and quick-stop places selling plastic food. Behind the highway, it was all small, elderly frame houses—so why that rough, tough feeling?

I turned right on Indian Creek Road and wound uphill along the creek, which was swollen and turbulent. After the indicated eight miles, which I spent thinking of Jim and hardly saw, I turned left on a dirt road generously dotted with potholes and climbed higher up the mountain. There were no more houses. I began to wonder how I'd find Lucy and Ruther. Happy, nervous, scared of pursuit, what?

After another couple of miles, the road went through a thick stand of pine trees and then dead-ended on a lawn with a small Victorian house and a barn nestled in a tiny valley. Mist and fog clung to the mountain just behind the house and gathered in ravines below it. It was very beautiful and also very isolated. I pulled up beside a newish white pickup, noticing Jim's truck wasn't there.

I'd brought Diana, and as there didn't seem to be any other dogs around, I let her out to wander. As I walked toward the house, the door opened and Lucy came out on the porch, hugging her arms to her chest. She looked pale and nervous.

"Hi. Jim and his mother took a sheep to the vet, but Ruther should be arriving any minute. They didn't let him out till this morning, cause they couldn't get hold of Quentin—that's the guy who saw him—till yesterday."

The living room was the long section of an L shape, comfortably but simply furnished in cheerful colors, with the kitchen making the smaller leg. We were just sitting down when we heard a car approaching. We went back out to the porch and soon an elderly Chevrolet drove up. Ruther got out.

I think he didn't even see me standing there, his eyes all for Lucy as he ran quickly up the steps. They stood looking at each other but not touching and then his arms came around her and her head buried itself in one of his wide shoulders. He was talking in a low voice and she was murmuring back.

"Maggie! Come on up here. Hey, I'm in your debt. For finding her for me. And bringing her up here."

"I'm glad it worked out," I said, hoping that it had, and we all went back inside. I asked Lucy, "How're your kids doing?"

"Well—they seem nervous. I thought they'd settle down by now but they're jumpy as—as cats. All this moving around and being in a strange place, I guess."

There was a loud scratching at the door: Diana. I let her in and she lay down right by my feet, practically on them, when I sat down again. She seemed nervous, too. So did Ruther; so did Lucy now their reunion had worn off a little. I felt it myself.

Lucy's face was tired and strained. She said softly, "I wrote Jonathan a letter. Jim got someone to mail it from Yreka. He may be back by now, be looking for us." Ruther smiled at her reassuringly, was holding her hand. "I sure hope the lawyer can get the restraining order *soon*. But I ought to go check on the kids. Excuse me."

I hoped she'd get the restraining order, too. But what

good would it do, really, if Jonathan was mad as a hornet with his nest disturbed and found them? He would hardly care that it was illegal for him to be here.

Ruther went out to the car to get his things. I was thirsty and walked around the corner of the living room to the kitchen. I heard Ruther come back inside, then heard another car drive up. Jim. My heart skipped a beat or two and I told myself not to be silly. How many husbands and wives split up, only to go right back together again? I couldn't find any glasses but then discovered them in an unlikely lower cabinet. Why keep them there? What did that say about Jim's mother? Peculiar, original, anti-drinking, what? I filled the glass with water, and as I turned off the tap, I heard the front door open and slam shut again.

Ruther said in a strange voice, "What the—"

"I want to talk to her. Where is she?" said a second man's voice and it wasn't Jim's. I felt a sudden chill . . . but no. It couldn't be. Then Lucy must've come downstairs, because I heard her cry out, *"Jonathan!"*

Oh my God. I peered cautiously around the corner of the refrigerator. A big man with a pleasant smile on his face was standing just inside the door, facing Ruther, who looked stiff and tense, ready to fight. Jonathan? He was blond, blue-eyed, good-looking with a kind of little-boy charm, a crooked smile. How could this man be Jonathan? I had been expecting a monster.

Lucy was at the bottom of the stairs, standing as if paralyzed in mid-step. They were both looking at her, a scene in freeze-frame. Then she moved, walked up beside Ruther, slightly behind. She'd said he would kill her, but his voice had sounded calm enough and he was still smiling pleasantly. His right hand was in his jacket pocket, which also held something else, something heavy. None of them saw me, and I pulled back, out of sight. If he was angry as well as strong and maybe armed, and I had to rush him, I'd need the surprise. I leaned against the refrigerator door, listened.

"Well, you see, I got back from the fishing trip, dear. We came back early, in fact," Jonathan said. Was he being sarcastic? His voice sounded quite friendly, almost jovial. Jovial? Not so appropriate . . .

"The fishing was real good too, honey, since you didn't ask. Wow! There was this one big fish, musta been fifty pounds! I almost got 'im; he got off the hook at the last minute, though."

Did river fish *ever* weigh fifty pounds? Why was this guy talking about fish, anyway? I peered around the refrigerator again. No one had moved. The smile on Jonathan's face was fixed, rigid, a little garish now.

"But I got an even bigger one after that! Boy was that a fight!"

And then, still with the same fixed smile, pleasant voices, no change, he said, "Get packed, get the kids. We're leaving."

"She's not going anywhere," said Ruther, stepping toward him. "She's left you. You'll hear from her lawyer."

"Fuck the lawyer." Jonathan was still smiling. "Lucy, get the kids and let's go before somebody gets hurt." His voice was not so pleasant, more a snarl.

"Jonathan, I—"

"Do what I tell you. You're my wife—you have to!" he screamed. He pulled a revolver from his pocket and pointed it at Ruther, then grabbed Lucy by her long blond hair and pulled her to him and pointed the gun at her head. I didn't dare move or he'd shoot her. He screamed at Ruther, *"Don't move motherfucker!"* and turned the gun back to Ruther. It went off—*Blam! Blam*—but Ruther had dived behind the couch.

Another earsplitting *blam!* as Lucy screamed, "No Jonathan! Oh God don't kill him—"

He slapped her hard across one cheek, then the other, and she began sobbing uncontrollably. He held her pinned against him with one huge arm while the other waved the gun back and forth between her and the couch. Lucy was sobbing and pleading with him.

"Shut up, you whore!" Jonathan snarled at Lucy, his voice lower but somehow scarier than before. "I'm going to kill that nigger. You let him stick it in you, didn't you? And now you're down here so he can stick it in you again, but he's not gonna stick it in you anymore. He's not gonna stick it in *anybody* anymore. Come out of there you fuckin' nigger coward. I'm gonna blow you away!"

Ruther, wisely, did not come out. It was a large heavy sofa—but was it thick enough to stop the big bullets that Jonathan Farrell began to shoot into it again? *Blam! Blam!* My eyes scurried wildly around the kitchen for something I could bash his head with. It would have to be something I was really sure of because if it didn't knock him out that would be the end of us all. All the damn pans were aluminum. Why couldn't there be a big cast-iron frying pan?

He'd stopped shooting. Why? He was repeating in a low, crazy monotone that he was going to blow them away, that Ruther was a motherfucker nigger and Lucy was a whore. As Lucy tried to placate him, I pulled out the bottom kitchen drawer as quietly as I could. It screeched. But he was talking. "Where are the children? Upstairs?" Then ominously, "And *whose* children are they, you little *whore*?"

Paper napkins, cups, plastic forks, flashlight batteries, oh *God*—

Lucy was sobbing, assuring him they were his children, no one else's. I pulled out the next drawer—dish towels, then the next—a heavy iron meat grinder.

I grabbed it, wanting to just crawl under the table, but instead I lifted it high and tiptoed up behind the giant, who turned just as I came within reach. His frenzied face glared furiously and I yelled for Ruther as Jonathan brought the gun around, but by then I was too close. I dropped the meat grinder and tried to get hold of the short barrel as he swung it toward my head.

Then Ruther grabbed him from behind and they crashed around the room, rolling over furniture and the floor and changing positions so quickly that, following them as I did with the meat grinder poised, I couldn't get a clear aim at Jonathan's head before it would twist away again and Ruther's would come between us instead. Lucy was circling on the other side, a lamp held high, but she couldn't get in a blow, either. Then I thought of the gun and as I turned away to look for it, the two of them went crashing through the front window, rolled across the porch and went over the side.

It was the luck of the draw, or maybe Jonathan's greater rage, but the huge man landed on the rocks five feet below, on top of Ruther. As he raised his arm to smash his fist down on Ruther's face, I pointed the gun at him and said in a hard, mean voice, "Stop it, Jonathan, or I'll shoot you."

He looked up, eyes wild and unfocused, then seemed to take in what I was saying, saw the gun. With a grunt he pulled himself up, twisted around and raced for the trees. I couldn't shoot him. Soon he was out of sight. Ruther slowly raised himself up, looking groggy, shaking his head. He stood up unsteadily, then wearily climbed the steps to the porch, shaking his head as if loose pieces inside it were moving about.

"Ruther, Ruther, oh, you're alive, you're *alive!*" Lucy flung her arms around him and they stood holding each other for a moment, then Ruther loosened her arms and came over to where I was standing. We heard the sound of a motor, tires eating gravel, a whine as a big car took off.

"I better go after him," Ruther said, starting for the steps.

"No," I protested, grabbing his arm, "that's a job for the sheriff. And Lucy needs you here. I'll go phone."

Ruther stood shaking his head, trying to clear it. "What a mess," he said.

Through the shattered window I saw Jim's truck come through the trees and pull up behind Ruther's Chevrolet. We walked out to the porch as Jim and a tall, big-boned woman with gray hair in a ponytail got out and came toward us. She had a plain face, rather dark, but then she smiled and the smile transformed her face to something very special. Dark eyes, like Jim's but much warmer. Jim grinned and then they noticed the broken window and hurried to the porch, no longer smiling. I explained briefly what had happened.

Jim's face didn't show much. "Must've been his black Trans Am we saw back on the road," he said. "Thank God you weren't hurt." He put an arm around my shoulder, pulling me close.

"Are the kids all right?" the woman asked Ruther, then turned to me, concerned. "Are Lucy's kids all right?"

"They stayed upstairs through the whole thing. So it could have been worse. Lots worse," I added.

"Oh thank God. But what a time you've had here. I'm Jim's mother. You must be Maggie. I'm Helen."

"Oh, sorry," Jim said.

"I'm glad to meet you but sorry about the circumstances. I'm afraid your house . . ."

"I'm just glad no one got hurt. The house don't matter."

She went upstairs to see Lucy and the kids. She was about sixty, but walked like a much younger woman. She had a lot of vitality, along with a warmth and gentleness I somehow hadn't expected.

Jim was looking around the room at the damage, dazed. I picked up a chair that had been knocked over, a couple of cushions. Jim went to the phone, dialed the sheriff and told him about the black Trans Am. Helen came back downstairs and started fixing the dinner that was to have been a festive celebration of Ruther's release from jail. She said there was nothing I could do to help, so I took the broom and dustpan I'd noticed next to the refrigerator while cowering there earlier and swept up the broken glass. Jim went out, came back with a piece of plywood and started boarding up the broken window. When he'd finished, he went upstairs and brought down a blue chenille bedspread, which he draped over the dreadful-looking couch.

I went with Jim around the house to the back, then beyond the barn and along a path through thick woods to a small cabin clinging to the side of the steep hill as if it belonged in San Francisco or perhaps Greece. There was a deck with a rocking chair and then a small room that was mostly kitchen. A round table by a window looked down a wooded hillside and across a ravine to high mountains beyond, where mist and clouds in constant movement kept changing their shapes. I could easily imagine having breakfast there of a morning, Jim at the stove still cooking his own pancakes after he'd given me mine. Maple syrup, and we'd be pretty silent. I don't like to have to talk first thing, so maybe we'd be reading. He'd look up and smile, want to tell me something from whatever it was he was reading. I'd be healthy and he'd be divorced. . . .

The door closing behind us brought me back. The round table was covered with stacks of books. An open notebook had writing that ended in mid-sentence. There was a large book behind the papers with a lot of paper place markers, *Costa Rican Natural History*. What was *that* doing here? Something to do with his work or could he have a special interest in Central America, like me? O'Reagan had said he didn't, though. . . .

There were two doors, each going to a tiny room. One had only a single bed and the other, somewhat larger, a double mattress on a two-by-four homemade frame, a small chest of drawers and a freestanding closet. The far wall had shelves filled with books from floor to ceiling, while windows of all different sizes made up the outside wall.

Jim pulled a chair out from the small table and gestured for me to sit. I did, and he lowered himself to the other.

"Cozy," I said. "Peaceful, after six years of a going-bad marriage?" I added, throwing caution to the wind. "Or lonely?"

"Little of both, I guess. I built this place and lived here before I got married. Now I'm back." He shrugged. "You said Farrell drove up right after Ruther? Followed him from Yreka? Or how the hell else would he've found the place?"

He still looked upset, frustrated, angry. I wanted to reach out, take his hand, offer comfort.

"Couple of those deputies're from here," he continued. "Probably everybody in town knew when Ruther was getting out. I never thought of that."

"No one can think of everything." Maybe a change of subject would help. "What're you doing with all these books? I mean, *Costa Rican Natural History*?"

"Oh ... I'm working on a master's, over at Arcata. It's taken a long time, but I'm almost finished, a course here, another there.... Trouble is, I've got involved in too many other things. Working with the tribe, with the Shasta, with the Audubon people ... making a living." He yawned. He looked tired. "I get credit toward the degree for a lot of it, actually, I shouldn't complain."

"And here I thought you were just another pretty face."

Jim grinned, started to say something, and then changed his mind. He stopped grinning, just looked at me. There was an awkward silence and I tried to think of something to say, change the subject from his pretty face. The sheriff's witness, I hadn't told him about that. I got out my drawing and told him what Harry Lipscomb had said.

He looked at the picture, frowning. "Don't know the guy. Okay if I keep this? I'll ask around. With those eyebrows ..." His voice trailed off.

Outside, the light had grown soft; the afternoon was ending. Jim looked at the scene out the window, I looked at Jim. Well, he really *did* have a pretty face—in that moment, beautiful. Finally, I asked, "Where will Lucy and Ruther go now? And you and your mother—you'll have to move too, won't you? If they don't pick Jonathan Farrell up right away?"

"I don't know," he said slowly, coming back from some far place. "I'll have to think about it. God, I'm glad no one was hurt." He reached over and took my hand. "You could have been killed so easily—"

"Ji-im! Din-ner!"

The voice was rather far away but loud and clear. What had he been going to say? As we walked back he held my arm, letting go when we got to the back door, his mother's kitchen.

The dinner, though it was broiled salmon and delicious, was gloomy, everyone on edge. A deputy had come and after he'd taken our statements had said they'd post some-body on the road to the house, in case Farrell came back. But nobody felt safe and no one said much of anything. Helen tried gallantly and I did my best, too, but the dark mood wouldn't lift. Dessert was a rich-looking chocolate cake, which I declined with difficulty.

"We'll have to think," I suggested, "of somewhere else for Ruther and Lucy and the kids. Probably for you and Helen too, Jim."

He nodded. "Yeah. I've been thinking about that. Ruther and I can stay in the cabin. If Farrell comes back, he won't know it's there. And we can keep an eye peeled. Mom, could you and Lucy go to Patsy's?"

Helen stood, began gathering dishes. I got up to help. "I don't see why not," she said. "We'd better go tonight."

"Who's Patsy?" Ruther asked.

"My aunt," Jim said, "Mom's sister, down in Orleans. Get them all right out of Happy Camp, that'll be best."

Ruther nodded, looking satisfied with the plan. Lucy still looked scared.

As I helped Helen with the dishes, I noticed that my throat was a little sore.

When we'd finished, Jim walked me out to my car. I opened the door for Diana and then got in. "So long," I said.

He leaned in for a second, said in his husky voice, "If you don't hear from me before, I'll be over your way this week sometime. I'll stop by." He brushed my cheek with his knuckle.

"Please be careful. I wish you weren't staying here," I said. Then all the way home, where he'd touched me the skin burned.

. . . drawn out of the stream of life into
stagnant backwater.
　　　　—CARL JUNG,
　　　　　THE ARCHETYPES AND THE COLLECTIVE
　　　　　UNCONSCIOUS

THIRTEEN

THE NEXT MORNING I WOKE FEELING LIKE A DOLL WITH ALL the stuffing out—with a pneumonialike flu, a throat that felt like the victim of a neck-ax murder, and an accompanying depression that this had happened to me. Again, again.

I slept and woke and drank water from the glass by my bed, slept and woke again through a couple of days and nights, the hours and days all blurring together. Three times a day, I took the drops. I'd been getting better, I told myself. They'd help me get over this fast. Occasionally I staggered to the bathroom, and one of those times I tumbled some dry food into Diana's dish and let her out, laying my head on the kitchen table while I waited for her to finish. There was a murderer out there somewhere. I should at least keep the doors locked. I made some toast and took it back to the bedroom, but then lost interest and didn't eat any of it. Outside, leaves of maple, hawthorn, and oak were beginning to change from the deep, shady green of summer to yellow, cream, and palest orange. Yet it was still warm, like summer.

I was hiding in a garden with some friends, camouflaged as mushrooms so the bad people chasing us couldn't find us. I was part of a revolution down in Argentina and we were running down wide, empty gray streets from the military bosses who were chasing us in big, fast black cars, shooting out the windows with black plastic machine guns, the bullets spraying and ricocheting all around, some of us falling. I was running, endlessly, from the Nazis.

Loud knocking woke me. I got up and wobbled dizzily to the door. Through the glass, I could see Jim standing on the other side.

"I have to go pee," I said hoarsely as I let him in. "Excuse me. . . ."

When I got back he was making a fire, though the house wasn't cold. He put a match to the paper and stood as I came in.

"You look terrible. How long've you been like this? Here, let's get you back to bed."

Everything was going spotted and black. I swayed and he picked me up as easily as a bag of groceries and carried me to the bedroom. He looked at the messy bed and put me down carefully on the chair. "Where do you keep the sheets?"

"Bathroom closet," I mumbled.

He came back in a minute or two, stripped the bed, and started putting on clean sheets. "I called you. I got worried something had happened. . . . There." He scooped me up and put me gently on the turned-down bed, then pulled the covers over me. The sheets felt clean and smooth, wonderful.

"Thank you," I croaked.

"No problem." He sat on the edge of the bed and held the back of his hand to my forehead, eyeing the tray on the floor. "When did you eat last?"

"Not hungry."

"Yeah, well, it couldn't hurt to eat something. I'll be back."

He went out and I heard kitchen noises: cabinet doors, refrigerator door, drawers open and close. I felt the blessed relief of someone there to do the thinking, make a meal even if I didn't want it, care about what happened to me. I drifted back to sleep.

He woke me with a touch on the cheek, propped up the pillows, set a tray on my lap: buttered toast, soft-boiled eggs, a pot of jam, tea. I forced down a few bites of toast and sipped at the tea. He talked easily as I tried to eat.

"I'm doing some consulting over in Scott Valley right now," he said. "Helping the Shastas complete the paperwork to get federal recognition. I know a little more about how to put something like that together than most of them do, from working on the Karuk application."

I tried to show some interest. The room was shifting around, wouldn't stay still. "What does . . . federal recognition do?"

"Gets eligibility for certain government-aid programs, mostly health. It's urgent now; all of a sudden the Bureau of Indian Affairs is saying it'll work only with federally recognized tribes. It's really difficult to get the proof together at this late date." A bitter look crossed his face. "It's just an incredible hassle, dealing with the BIA."

I forced a few more pieces of what tasted like dry cardboard down my throat.

"All the old treaties the whites signed with them, the California congressmen in those days saw to it they were never ratified. They did the same to us. But they're turning up now, in the archives, which should help to prove they did and do exist, at least."

I put down the cup before it dropped out of my hand, leaned back, closed my eyes.

"But I shouldn't be bothering you with all this," he said. "Is it that sickness you get? Maybe you should be in the hospital."

"No. No no. I have to wait . . . it out."

"Shouldn't I at least call a doctor?"

"Maybe—if you'd call my doctor in Tucson. Set up a time for him to call me. . . . Jesse Stoff, number's on the . . . phone book."

"Sure. Look. I have to go over to Scott Valley, but I'll leave a fire going. You have a thermos? I'll put some more tea in it. Then I'll come back after I'm through over there, fix you some dinner."

"You don't need to do that . . . but if you would call . . .

Hallie, too. Number's right by the doctor's. . . . I've been out of touch for days. Be sure Sally's all right. Not worse or . . . Tell her I'm sick but I'll call . . . tomorrow."

"Sure."

"Thanks." I yawned again and my eyes closed themselves against my will as Jim took the trays and left the room.

When I woke up, I could hear kitchen sounds. Soon Jim appeared, smiling down at me but looking worried. He looked so competent standing there, so strong. I'd tossed off all the covers. The room was very warm.

"Soup soon." He went away, came back with a tray. We were quiet for a while, sipping chicken soup.

I asked finally, "What's happened with . . . Lucy and Ruther?"

"Well, Lucy and the kids and my mom are down in Orleans. Ruther and I decided not to stay in my cabin, after all. We've moved to my uncle's place and he knows not to tell anyone we're there. He's reliable. They put out an all-points on Farrell, but so far there's no sign of him. Anyway, we're all safe for now. Eat a little more of that soup."

I took a couple of sips, suddenly very sleepy again. Swallowing felt like I was breaking my throat. "It's awfully good. . . ." I yawned. "Must be late . . . want to stay here?"

"If that would be all right. I can go over to Scott Valley in the daytime, look after you at night till you're on your feet again. Hey, no argument—it's what I want to do."

I was in some kind of underground tunnel, dark and dank, and I met death: He looked like a skeleton but there was more to him than dry bones—I couldn't say what. There was a very strange feeling of shaking hands with that person, shaking hands on a deal, but what was the deal? I woke up terrified, my head pounding, feeling the dream was something that had actually happened. Jim was holding me and saying everything was all right, it was just a bad dream, everything was all right. We lay there for some time and then he started to get up. I thought of the horrible skeleton and held on to him. "No," I said, "no."

"Well move over then; I'm almost on the floor."

"You sound awful," Hallie said. "Listen. Don't worry about us, just rest and get well. Oh, I wish you could be up here in Sally's room where I could look after both of you!"

"I feel so miserable. Not to be able to work . . ." I could hardly keep from crying, wailing.

"Hey, lighten up. We both knew this might happen," Hallie said briskly, "so, it has, that's all. It won't last forever. It's all *right*. We're doing fine right now. The vital signs are holding steady—just rest, don't worry."

A couple of weeks went by, agonizingly slowly. My doctor called and sent some more drops. He said I'd get well much faster this time. But I was totally without energy and at the same time, wild with frustration that I couldn't get up and be well, work on finding the killer. I had a doomsday feeling that the more time passed, the closer he came to Sally. Circling in somehow—I was sure he was circling in on her. Finally the drops seemed to kick in after a few days and I began to feel a little better.

I called O'Reagan, hoping maybe he could come up and continue the work but he couldn't, at least not right away. He was swamped. He said he'd do his best, try to find a little time later. Meanwhile, Jonathan Farrell had never been found.

At night Jim would take Diana for a walk, then sit beside me on the bed reading through papers he'd brought, making an occasional note or sometimes writing quite a bit. But he was always gone again in the morning when I woke up.

"I talked to that deputy," he said one evening. "Remember I asked him to check where Farrell was, when the hikers were attacked?"

"Where was he?"

"In the Bear Creek area, alone at least part of the time."

"Is that near where it happened?"

He nodded. "Near enough. It could have been him. But why?"

"Did they search through his things? At his parents'?"

"Had the local people do it. Didn't find anything, though. And I passed your drawing around. Nobody knows the guy. Strange."

The trees out the window turned gold, turned crimson, turned burnt-orange and darkest red, began to fall and make large bright patches of color on the ground beneath. The air became thinner, the sky a paler blue. Yet it was still quite warm out. Jim finished his work with the Shastas. I was able to take care of myself again and he came only on weekends.

Finally one evening toward the end of October, sitting on the couch reading and sipping echinacea tea, I felt my energy come back in a kind of rush. I breathed deeply, cautiously, and realized that my lungs were pretty clear and the sore throat was *gone*.

I went over to the door, let Diana out. It was just after dark. Looking up at the sky I saw a new moon, a nail-paring moon, a thin, delicate white sail riding serenely across the dark immensity of the night, and then there was the *hoo, hoo, hoo* of an owl, sounding like it came from some much older world. Owls are messengers of the Great Spirit of the Night—but what exactly was the message?

A small shape hurried past. "Mimi!" I called. "Mimi, wait!" I went down to the gate and she came over, came inside the yard. She squatted down and hugged Diana. She had a satchelful of books, with a carton of milk and a loaf of bread sticking out of the top.

"I've been wondering when I'd ever see you again."

She looked up and smiled shyly. "I got to go—Hank's gonna kill me for bein' so late. He don't like me out by myself. He's gonna be real mad!"

"Come back soon, then," I called as she ran off, "and be careful. Hide if you see anybody!"

But she was gone, into the dark woods. And I realized I

felt fine now. I felt interested in life again. I could start handling things again. It was almost as if Mimi's sudden appearance was a sign, a signal, the decoded message of that owl.

Life rushed in, almost at once.

"I wanted to know had you heard yet about the murders?" said Nancy Odum's voice on the phone the next day.

A feeling of deja vu came over me, but Nancy couldn't be talking about the hikers. She'd already told me about them.

"Near that trail again, that Pacific Crest Trail," she continued. "Men fishin' up at Lake Crick—always been a good fishin' spot back up in there."

I didn't want to hear this but couldn't find words fast enough to head her off.

"A whole group slaughtered this time—four *men*."

I finally found my tongue. "Were they—were they scalped?"

"Yes they was, ev'ry single last one of 'em. Scalped just like those hikers. A terrible thing, terrible."

"Yes . . . horrible." I might be well again but I didn't feel ready for this.

"They can't say for sure when it happened, they all being dead quite a while by the time the bodies was found. My cousin works at the sheriff's said they think it was probably a couple weeks ago—around the middle of October. Arnie at the Rainbow Grocery knew one of 'em, said he come up every year for the steelhead. But couldn't get up here in time this year, came late."

"Four men, murdered . . ."

"*All* scalped. Now it's plain as can be the killer's from this area, all right. Some Indian. The sheriff arrested one of 'em, name of Bradshaw. But then the fools let 'im out! He's from here in Happy Camp, a bad apple if ever there was. It's a plain crime, leavin' 'im loose like that to murder those poor men."

Ruther. "Have they arrested him again? Do they have some new evidence?"

"My cousin says he had some kind of alibi what he was doing when the hikers was murdered. I guess they figure the same maniac did that who did this—they haven't arrested him anyway. I just don't know." I could almost hear her through the telephone wires, shaking her large head.

"Where did you say they found the bodies? At a lake?"

"Not a lake, it's a mountain called Lake Mountain, and a crick back up in there, further away from you than where those hikers was killed—higher up, more toward Seiad. But close enough. You're awful isolated there where you live. Maybe you oughta move down here to Happy Camp. There's a nice little house near me for rent. You be interested?"

"I don't think so, Nancy. But thanks."

Maybe the killer had made some mistake this time; maybe the sheriff would catch him. I needed to get hold of the scene-of-crime reports somehow but there was nothing I could do about it tonight. I felt restless. I was wide awake and I'd read all the books. I made a cup of tea, called Hallie but got no answer, remembered the diaries. So much had been happening, I'd forgotten all about them.

The next entry wasn't until almost two months after the happy July Fourth:

August 30. My heart is broken forever. Susanna says time always helps in the end—but I don't see how I will get *through* the time, all the long years of the rest of my life. He left for his uncle's yesterday—and Alma went with him. Miss Louise said Alma's sister said Alma is going to have a baby. At least they'll be in Washington and I won't have to see them or that baby. I know he cared for me too, he was so different after the picnic and then I felt was holding back. Now I know why. What a cheap trick. I *hate* Alma Spencer, I will always hate her.

September 20: Susanna says it's all because the world was made wrong this year. She's part Karuk Indian. She says there was some fuss at their New Year's feast—it's in August or September—and some of the ceremony didn't get done. They were all arguing. So now Susanna says the whole year will probably be just one bad thing after another. Mama says those Indian stories are just superstition and the Indian people don't know anything, that they are ignorant and backward because of not having the background and the experience of the white races. And she's still always saying, even after all these years, "I don't see why you have to have that little Indian girl for a friend, Jane Ellen, when there are perfectly good white children to play with right here in Scott Bar. Louisa Bradley is just your age and so is Alma Spencer." But Louisa is so boring and I hate Alma. Maybe she'll die having the baby.

Too bad. But maybe Jed, in spite of his beautiful blue eyes, was really not much good and Jane was better off without him? Not that that would be any consolation, of course. I got up and fixed some squash with a little olive oil and some pumpkin seeds, and continued reading as I ate.

October 17. Busy with Mama, as usual, also pretty depressed. It's been raining for two weeks straight, but now the sun's out again today, the leaves are all gold and beautiful, there's a slight feeling of hope, from somewhere. No one has heard anything from Jed and Alma.

Old Chicken Hans died last week. Mr. Morris found him dead in bed in the middle of the day when he went over to inquire about some firewood. The funeral was in the old Chinese graveyard next to the cemetery—it's so strange there, all those big empty holes where the other Chinese used to be before they were taken back to China. Chinese people must be very peculiar but I liked old Chicken Hans. He always gave us those good rice cookies when we were little. Mama said there used to be lots of Chinese here when she was a girl, but later they all left, for some reason, all but old Chicken Hans. The end of an era, Mama said. Just about everybody in town went to the funeral, even though he was just an old Chinese man who got people firewood. I think I'll walk over later and put some of these beautiful autumn leaves on the grave.

Wilmer asked me to marry him again after the dance Saturday. I told him no again. He said he'll keep asking until I say yes.

I turned several empty pages but there were no more entries for 1938.

The diary stayed in my mind, and when I went to the post office the next day I asked Bill, "Did you ever hear of anyone around here named Jane Thornton—a younger sister of Bessie's? Or a man named Jed, but I don't know his last name?"

He put a marker in his book and closed it, wrinkling his brow. Slowly, he shook his head. "Nope. Not that I remember, what do you want to know for?"

"Curiosity, mainly. How about a woman named Alma? Her family lived up on Mill Creek. She was Alma Spencer before she married but she may have married the Jed guy."

He looked down at some junk mail on the counter, idly flipped through it. Finally, he shook his head. "How long ago were these people here?"

"Well, about fifty years ago."

"No wonder I don't remember. I'm not *that* old." He grinned. "Where'd you hear about these people? What got you going on it?"

"There're some old diaries at the house. They're mentioned in those."

"Really? Say, that sounds interesting. I'd enjoy having a

look at 'em sometime, if it wouldn't be, well, invading any privacy."

"I don't know . . . let me think about it. Do you know anyone around here who might remember them, some old-timer?"

"Can't think of anybody but I'll put my brain cells to work on it. I'll sure let you know if I do."

"Thanks. Did you hear about the murders?"

He nodded. "I just don't know what this place is coming to. Four grown *men* now, all scalped. That fellow who killed 'em must be a real slick article, you know?"

"You don't have any theories on *why* it's all happening?"

He shook his head. "Just makes no sense. No sense at all."

When I went out, Joey Brown was getting mail out of his box. It felt good to see these people again after the weeks I'd been stuck at home. Joey heard me and turned, his face brightening.

"Well, Maggie—just the person I wanted to see. I've been thinkin' a lot about these latest murders—looks like I might have somethin', doesn't it? With my theory it's a group of killers, not just one? After all—four men like that. One was a cop from Oakland what I heard and a couple of 'em worked construction—they were no softies. What do you think? What's your professional opinion?"

"It could be. Do you have any connections at the sheriff's office by any chance?"

"Could be I do. I know one of the deputies there real well. He owes me a favor, in fact. You need somethin'?"

"I want a copy of the reports on these murders—scene-of-crime reports, lab reports, everything they have. Think you might be able to get them?"

"I can sure try. Maybe I'll have somethin' for you by the Halloween party. You goin'?"

"What Halloween party?"

He pointed to a handmade poster on the wall that I hadn't noticed. "Costume party at the old school Saturday night. Has prizes for the costumes and there's always lots of real good food. You ought to come. And say, I tried to track that Chinaman a couple times but lost him. Maybe you could go interview him, see can you get any information out of him. But I'll try again to follow him, see where he goes."

I decided to see if Mimi wanted to go to the party, so I went on past my drive and after a few minutes turned up a rutted dirt road that took me bumpily to her cabin. It looked peaceful and safe drowsing in the morning sun, all the edges softened by forty-nine years of time. There was no sign of the dogs and no barking. The truck wasn't there, either.

The front door was open and I knocked on the screen. Hank appeared immediately with the gun but lowered it when he saw me, then motioned me inside. Lillian was sitting in the easy chair. There was no sign of Clara or Mimi. Lillian looked pale, unwell.

"No, don't get up," I said. "I just stopped by for a minute. I heard there's a Halloween costume party at the old school tomorrow night. I was wondering if Hermina might like to go to the party with me. I'm sure between us we could rig up some kind of costume, and I think she'd enjoy it."

"Well, that be all right I guess, if she want to go. She's gone with Clara to the store now. But Hank don't let her go out walkin' these trails by herself since all these people killed—*apruan* about in these parts now."

"*Apruan?* What is that?"

"That be devil, or maybe devils, more than one for all I know. *Apruan.* Course I give the child some icknish root, you put that in your path and if they be after you, they can't cross and follow."

"I was thinking I could pick her up in my car—and maybe she could spend the night at my house after the party and come home Sunday morning."

"No need to pick her up—Hank can walk her down, and come get her, too."

"Are you all right, Lillian?"

"Oh . . . my heart's actin' up a little. But I'll be around a while yet." She turned to Hank. "Now don't you forget what I said. When my time does come, you be sure I get buried Indian way, you hear me?"

I got out the child's skeleton costume I'd seen in an old chest in the shed. I hadn't been planning to wear a costume myself but began to want one while I was ironing the skeleton. I remembered some old dresses in the back of Bessie's closet—the delicate ruffled white cotton kind from early in the century. Maybe I could be an elegant old-fashioned kind of ghost, if I could squeeze my late-twentieth-century body into one of them—which might just be possible, because I'd lost weight during the bout with the viruses.

I took the dresses out—there were four—and chose the largest, which I did just manage to get buttoned. Ironing it was a pain and I felt sorry for the women who'd had to wear clothes like that every day. As I tried to get the ruffles right, I thought about Mimi and her great-grandmother. How bad was her heart? Mimi's mother so drunk that time. Thank goodness for Hank. Were his ideas about Mimi purely crazy or might he be right about some of the things he said? Mimi really had been sick. And the electrical explosion that nearly killed her really had happened, too. Maybe I'd get a chance to talk to him when he brought her down.

> ... it all comes out as if there were
> some sequence, some logic, instead of
> moods, contractions, alternatives. The
> design imposes itself afterwards.
>
> SHIRLEY HAZZARD,
> THE BAY OF NOON

FOURTEEN

I TOOK A BATH AND THEN EVENTUALLY GOT MYSELF RATHER snugly buttoned—with seventy-four tiny batiste buttons—into the old-fashioned white dress, which luckily fastened up the front. My face was a nice ghostly hue from talcum powder, I had pale white lips, startling black-marked brows, and green and purple on my eyelids and under my eyes like bruises. Finally, I pulled on my high leather boots, modern but probably similar to what any female would have worn in that muddy mining town a hundred years ago. For finishing touches I had yellowed long kid gloves and a ruffled parasol I'd found in the same closet as the dresses.

I was just taking my drops when there was a faint knock at the door, and Diana rushed over as Mimi came shyly inside, followed by Prince and Little Dog. She was dressed in a real buckskin beaded skirt, much too large for her, gathered at the waist with a long yellow sash. She had a brown beaded band around her forehead with a large white feather sticking up. It looked like one worn by the rooster at her cabin the day before. Around her neck was some wonderful old jewelry of yellow porcupine quills, and her black eyes were dancing with excitement.

"Get *down* Diana, get *down*! Oh Mimi you look *wonderful*. Where'd you get that beautiful jewelry and that skirt?"

"Granny let me use it. She say family things 'sposed to be for grown-up people, but just this once she let me wear it—I got to be *very* careful though, and not tear it or spill nothin' on it."

"Where's Hank? Didn't he bring you down?"

She nodded. "He left already."

It was almost dark outside. Mimi followed me to the car and as we drove down the drive, I said, "Mimi. I was thinking . . . remember when that hiker was killed last summer? Right before I first met you, and you'd just found the dogs?"

She nodded.

"Where'd you find them?"

"Up on the trail—just near our house."

"Did you see anybody around? When you were looking for the gold, say maybe a couple of days before you found the dogs—did you ever see anybody up there on the trail?"

She looked at me a moment, surprised, then slowly nodded a yes.

"Tell me about it," I said quietly. "Who did you see? Was it a man, one man?"

She nodded. "He had a big gun. He was on the trail comin' aroun' where the big rock is. Then he was takin' his gun down, but I run and hid in the bushes. He come along lookin' for me, but he couldn't find me and then he left."

Oh God. "He was chasing you, looking for you? Are you sure?"

She nodded. "Well, I'm pretty sure."

"What did he look like?"

"I don't know. He had on one of them baseball hats, and his face was—the sun was behind. I couldn't see his face good."

I felt excited. "What color was the baseball hat?"

"Green."

"Did it have some letters on the front, some writing?"

"Well—" She frowned, trying to remember. "Well—it wasn't no words. Maybe some letters."

"Could you draw them?"

She shook her head. "I don't remember what they looked like."

"Do you think you might know the man again if you saw him?"

"I couldn't see him good enough."

"Was he tall or short?"

"I think maybe he was kinda big."

"Fat or thin?" I went on relentlessly, the closest I'd come so far to the killer.

"Well, he was kinda big."

"But not fat especially?"

"I don't know."

"Anything else you can think of, about him?"

"No."

If I'd been worried about her before, it was deep relaxation to what I felt now. I could so easily see the dark figure, creeping into the empty cabin while they were in Redding, setting up the robot-doll trap. A large man in a green baseball cap—but I couldn't see his face.

Suddenly bright lights were shining out into the night. We were there, a lot of cars already parked outside the old schoolhouse. A sweet white frame building with a bell tower, it was built in 1875 with one thousand dollars subscribed by the residents. Now the young children, who are few, are bussed seven miles up the highway to Horse Creek, while the high school kids travel the forty miles to Yreka.

The big main room was warm and bright and well filled with people, all the children and about half the adults in costume. I saw Joey Brown at the far end of the room, wearing his everyday clothes including the binoculars. He was eating something and listening to Bill Dawson, whose mouth was going nonstop. As Joey nodded and turned away, Bill lifted a gold bandit mask hanging from his neck and put it on over his glasses.

A small green frog with a long, thin, red flannel tongue sprinted by crying, "Ribbit, ribbit, I'm a frog, ribbit, ribbit!" and almost bumped into the gorgeous young blonde I'd seen at the post office, waiting in the Cadillac for her father. She and another girl standing beside her were dressed up as sluts in several inches of makeup, tight satin skirts with very long slits, clingy low-necked blouses, lots of costume jewelry, and high-heeled platform "come fuck me" shoes complete with ankle straps.

Mimi and I walked over to a long table that divided the main room from a small kitchen and looked over the goods: a dozen or so cakes, several pies, many plates of cookies, little bowls of candy. I helped myself to a very small piece of chocolate cake, wanting the whole thing. Mimi took a cookie iced in orange, with raisin eyes and mouth. A sheet figure with a long-fanged rubber vampire mask came up, took a cookie and ate it through the mask.

"Hello there," it said. "Remember me? Frank Ullrich. We met at the post office. Glad to see you again."

The effect was bizarre, the commonplace words in a weird high-pitched voice coming from the frightful mask. "I'm glad to see you too Mr.—Frank," I said, wishing he'd take the mask off.

The gorgeous young blonde came up and said to the vampire, "Daddy, could I stay over at Coochie's afterward? It's okay with her parents."

"Just because I made a special exception and let you come tonight, you forgot you've been grounded?" the vampire asked gruffly. He turned back to me. "Like you to meet my daughter Darlene. This is Maggie, honey. She's just moved here. And who's this little Indian girl?"

"Mimi," I said, "this is Mr. Ullrich, and Darlene." Mimi looked down at her feet.

"Say, do you have the time?" Ullrich asked. "I'm supposed to start up the musical chairs at eight-fifteen sharp."

I looked at my watch, an old one with a dark blue enamel face that had been my grandmother's. "It's just eight-fifteen now."

"Oh, that's a pretty watch," Darlene said longingly, examining it. "I've never seen one like that." A small towheaded pirate pushed forward to look, too. "Don't push, Betsy. This is my little sister."

She was round-faced, with metal-rimmed granny glasses,

a tiny freckled snub nose. Nothing at all like Darlene. She and Mimi eyed each other cautiously. "Can we go over to the tub an' try to git a apple now?" Betsy asked Darlene.

"Sure, honey. You come too, little Indian girl." Darlene took her with one hand and Betsy with the other. Mimi looked back—but surely she was safe in this brightly lighted room full of people. I smiled and nodded, and she turned and went with them willingly enough.

"I better get going. I got to organize that musical chairs. It was real nice to see you again."

Frank went off to the other side of the room and started talking to a fat witch. Mimi was still standing by the tin tub and seemed to be enjoying herself. I poured out a paper cup of acid green punch. As I took a sip and almost gagged, it was so sweet, a tall man around forty—but a glowing, solid, healthy forty in contrast to Frank Ullrich, as if they were from different species—came up and poured himself some of the green liquid. He took a swallow and hurriedly put the cup back on the table. "Jesus! Wish they had some beer."

"It is pretty horrible," I agreed.

He wasn't in costume but wore a plaid wool shirt and well-shined leather boots with the toes pointed in cowboy style. He had dark blue eyes, short, curly blond hair, and was good-looking in a freshly scrubbed, outdoorsy sort of way.

"They can't have alcohol, something to do with the insurance. I should've known better than to try drinking anything that color. I hear you're living in the Thornton cabin. My name's Robby, Robby Rowe."

"I'm Maggie Elliott. You live in Scott Bar?"

"Close enough, down in Seiad."

He had wide shoulders, slim hips, probably an excellent immune system. A cowboy type. Maybe he had a horse outside. He could pull me up behind and take me off into the moonlit night, to unknown wide-open spaces and a whole new life where I'd always be healthy, like him. Maybe he had a ranch of yellow mustard flowers in the green-blue hills. A clean, wholesome life, singing old songs around the camp fire. Something about him said single, said available. But my heart wasn't lifting to him, wasn't interested. Because I'd already given it to someone else recently?

"Seiad's a pretty place," I said. "Have you lived there long?"

"I'm more or less a native—my mother's people come from Scott Bar, go back to the gold-mining days. My brother and I still have their original claim. Not worth anything, but it's a good place to fish when the steelhead're running."

"He lives here too, your brother?"

"No, just comes up for the fishing when he can. He's here now, but he'll be leaving soon. Works down in Central America."

"Really," I said, interested. "I've spent some time down there. Where in Central America?"

"Guatemala mostly, I think. Costa Rica maybe—I get those countries all mixed up."

"What does he do down there?"

"Sells pharmaceuticals. Seems to like it. But me, suits me fine around here."

"Are you a miner?"

"No, there's still a little mining but nobody's making much. Or so they say—miners are closemouthed, ornery fellows. Crazy, every damn one of 'em. Got to be, kind of life they live. Groveling underground where a whole mountain might fall in and crush 'em. Spending all the time they do underwater, cold water too, with some half-broken-down dredging machine, losing fingers, legs, any damn thing for a chance to get rich quick and never work again—doing it quiet and secret so they don't have to give any to the government, take any responsibility."

"Musical chairs!" a man's voice called out and other voices joined in: "Musical chairs! Musical chairs!"

Loud, cheerful music blared and people circled around a row of chairs in the center of the room until a whistle blew and they all sat down—all but the small, confused ballerina in pink net who didn't get a chair in time and so was out.

What had he been saying? Secrets, finding gold and

keeping it secret. It was hard to concentrate, with everything else going on. "Any miners come to mind you think are especially crazy, more than the others?"

"Well." He looked down, scanned the cookies, took an orange one. "All about equal, my opinion."

"Are there any miners here tonight? I'd like to meet one."

He looked around, eyes narrowed. "Old Joey Brown over there, he used to do a good bit. Don't think he does much anymore, though." Joey was standing by the wood stove, talking earnestly to Frank Ullrich. Mimi was still with Darlene and Betsy, in the far corner now where a mother was stringing up a piñata.

Robby continued. "And Frank Ullrich, the one talking to Joey, there's a man desperate for money, what I hear. You know they closed the mills over in Eureka. Even management types like him got the ax. Now he's here, no visible means of support—has a couple claims he fools around with. But I don't think he's making anything on 'em. So where does he get his money, drugs?" He smiled, added, "He doesn't seem the type, does he?"

"I'm not sure I know what the type is, up here. What do you do?"

He put back his head and laughed heartily. "Not drugs! I work for the Forest Service."

"Oh," I said flatly. Was he one of the ones planning to tear down Mimi's cabin? "Some friends of mine who live farther up the mountain from me, they said their cabin's going to be torn down by the Forest Service next summer. They've lived there a long time; they don't have anyplace to go." My voice was accusing.

He shifted his weight, cocked his hip. "I don't know anything about that."

"Well, why does the Forest Service do something like that? Aren't there enough homeless without going out of their way to create more? An old woman and a little girl?"

He looked down at the table. "Can't have people freeloading on the National Forest. What if everybody wanted to live there?"

"From what I understand they were there before there *was* a National Forest. So what's it all about? It seems to me like a really rotten thing to do." I knew I was going overboard, attacking this man at a social event, but I couldn't help myself.

"Like I said, I don't really know the case," he repeated defensively.

There was a strained silence. Finally I asked, trying to be polite, "What do you do, then, for the Forest Service?"

He studied the plate of cookies again and finally chose a pumpkin shape iced in yellow. He looked at me appraisingly, took a bite. "I look for marijuana, people growing it. You hear a helicopter sometimes? That's me, usually."

"Oh! Were you the one who found—the girl hiker?"

"No, that was my partner. He talks to the mother sometimes. I guess they still don't know if she'll ever regain consciousness. May be brain-dead. What a terrible thing. How is it living out there in that cabin all by yourself? Don't you feel nervous? Those killings were pretty close to your place."

His blue eyes were warm now, concerned, as if he'd forgiven my outburst. He seemed to want to offer the protection of those wide shoulders, his strong right arm. Possibly with a silver six-shooter attached, to keep all the bad away.

"I do feel nervous sometimes in the woods," I admitted, "but I don't go out much. Especially since those four men were killed. When you're looking for marijuana—you ever see anyone else?"

"Who might be the killer, you mean? Is it true you worked as a private eye in San Francisco?"

"Just on routine things," I said, wanting to downplay my detective side, "nothing like this. But do you go near where the murders were? Who have you seen up there?" I was persistent, the life of the party.

"Let me think—in the last few months, you mean?"

I nodded. His eyes were shining. I knew that look. I get it myself—the thrill of detection, figuring things out for their own sake, so you forget even why you're doing it.

"Frank Ullrich has a spring back up there he checks on,

also a couple of gold-mine claims—I'm not sure just where. Then um, another Forest Service guy, Bob Gerald— he's chief ranger, but he likes to get out sometimes. I've seen him. Bill Dawson prowls around back in there, look- ing for signs of Bigfoot, believe it or not. Um . . ." He took a deep breath, let it out, his fingers spread out, counting. "Arnie from the Rainbow Grocery goes fishing up there sometimes. And I've seen a Chinaman—don't know who he is, though."

I needed to go over to the Rainbow, see what I could find out about that Chinese man. I should talk to this Arnie, too. Also Frank Ullrich, and the other Forest Service guy. What had Robby said? Gerald. Bob Gerald.

The music switched off, switched on again loudly. Only two elderly witches and a teenage boy were left. Mimi was still at the piñata, where a lot more children had gathered.

Robby said "You know the difference between a Indian and a Chinaman?"

I shook my head.

"When you throw 'em in the river, the Indian can swim!"

He grinned, waiting for me to share the joke.

As always happens when someone tells me a "joke" like that, my head swirled with anger and resentment and I couldn't immediately figure out just what to do. Finally I said, "I hate racist jokes. I *hate* them. Why do you do that anyway?"

The smile left his face and he looked resentful in turn. "Aw, where's your sense of humor, can't you take a joke? I didn't mean anything. Just seemed like between this Chi- naman and that Indian from Happy Camp they arrested, made me think of the joke. They released him, though. Lot of violence down there in Happy Camp. Lot of drugs. The hard stuff, coming in from outside. Man I know in Happy Camp told me the other day: 'How come everybody in the county says we're so violent down here? We only kill each *other*; we never kill *outsiders*!'"

He grinned, waiting expectantly, hoping this joke would be acceptable. I smiled back. The music stopped again. One

THE NORTHWEST MURDERS   143

witch and the boy had been squeezed out, leaving the fatter
witch laughing triumphantly.

"You mean they think the murders are drug-connected
and that's what it's all about?"

"No. No, they don't think that. What I hear is, they don't
have a clue what it's all about."

"I'd like to talk to your partner. What's his name?"

"Harvey Grove. He's almost never in the office and he
doesn't have a phone, but give me your number and I'll get
him to call you. Why do you want to talk to him?"

"Thanks." I ignored his question, scribbling my number
on a napkin. I handed it to him as the blond bombshell
sauntered up, batting heavily mascaraed eyelashes at
Robby. I looked across the room, saw Mimi and the little
sister still over by the piñata.

"Hi, Robby," she drawled, and put her finger on his
chest, ran it lightly down to his belt. "Why didn't you wear
a *costume*?"

"Yours is enough for both of us, Darlene." He looked at
what filled it, appreciatively. "Want some punch?"

I felt a hand on my arm and turned to see Joey Brown,
who was smiling, looking pleased.

"You made it, I see." He helped himself to a large piece
of lemon meringue pie and began eating it quickly. "You
finding plenty to eat?"

"Yes, unfortunately."

Joey looked around, then moved so he was between me
and the others, his back to Robby. He lowered his voice to
a conspiratorial level proper for communicating info to a
private eye. "I told you I'd see what I could find out about
that Chinaman? What he's up to? Well, listen to this! I went
over to the Rainbow cabins today, real early. When he
came out, I followed 'im. He didn't see me—I was real
careful this time. He parked up by the cemetery, took this
trail that goes way back in the mountains from there. . . ."

Joey hesitated, as if remembering the place, the trail, his
cautious following of the Chinese man. Now he went on,
still whispering, his eyes fixed on mine excitedly. "I fol-

lowed him a long way, to the same area as those murders; then I lost him—had to get back then, anyway. But I got the area pinned down now where he's lookin'. Next time, I won't lose 'im. I'll maybe find out what he's lookin' for, if he finds it himself. And another thing, someone else I decided is pretty suspicious, 'cause I saw 'im—"

Someone jostled Joey. It was Frank Ullrich, making a beeline for Darlene.

"You have to go home now. *You have to go home now!*" He was shouting, pulling at her arm, pulling her away from Robby Rowe, who looked embarrassed. Out of control, someone had said. Out of control, but with a father like that . . . I tried to think what I could I do to de-escalate the situation. The poor girl. But she didn't need me; she stood her ground, yanked her arm away.

"I will *not* go home now." She said it quietly, but something about her voice was chilling. "Stop it. Everybody's looking at you. If they knew what I know, they'd *really* look, wouldn't they, Daddy?"

Frank stood looking at her helplessly for a moment, then turned and walked off, shoulders bowed in defeat. Now I felt sorry for *him*. Darlene started talking to Robby again, as if they hadn't been interrupted. He still looked embarrassed.

I turned back to Joey, lowering my voice. "What were you saying, Joey? About someone else you saw?"

But he was looking off across the room, moving away. "Talk to you later—there's a fella over there I been trying to get hold of, need to talk to. I'll tell you about it later. Glad you made it."

He'd followed the Chinese man to the area of *which* murder scene—Lake Creek or Tomkins? But he was already halfway across the room; I'd have to wait to find out. I hate waiting. He was talking to someone now, a tall blond man in a brown sweater.

I looked around. Parents more fond or conventional than Frank were wandering around with cameras, snapping pictures. I joined Mimi at the piñata, an orange paper pumpkin.

A tall teenage ghost tried to hit it but the mother in charge took away the stick. "Let the little kids go first, Buddy."

A mother dragged a pink-pajamaed daughter over but she lay on the floor kicking and refused to do it.

"I will! I will!" The small frog ran up and was blindfolded; he swung energetically several times but missed.

Then the pink ballerina who'd been the first to be eliminated in musical chairs was pushed forward, all golden curls and shrinking femininity, but she, too, was afraid to use the stick.

"Hit it, hit it, hit it real hard!" The frog yelled enthusiastically, but she just stood there, cowering and starting to sniffle. Raising girls who could be strong and hit out when they needed to—these didn't seem to be high on the list, or maybe even on the list, in Scott Bar. Perhaps their parents believed their girls' lives would be better later that way, easier. But they wouldn't; they'd be harder. I asked Mimi if she didn't want to try, and she nodded her head excitedly. I pushed her forward.

She stood very still while the mother put on the blindfold, holding the stick like a baseball bat.

Then the lights went out.

There was dead silence for a moment, then a few screams. They were silly screams—people thinking the blackout was part of the entertainment. Was it? I moved uneasily toward the place I'd last seen Mimi, but kept bumping into people, finally gave up. A small light across the room showed a fat, perspiring face, moved across another unknown face, lit up Joey Brown, who blinked, then the light went out. It didn't go back on. There was laughter now, mixed with the screams, and a low buzzing murmur as half the people in the room talked to the other half about the lights going out. I cautiously started moving again—toward Mimi, I hoped—but too many people were in the way still. After a while, the lights came on.

FIFTEEN

"OH MY *GOD*—TURN HIM OVER, CAREFUL . . ."

Several people were standing by the stove, one bending down over someone lying on the floor. Then others moved in front of me and I couldn't see. There was loud, excited talking all over the room and I couldn't hear anything else distinguishable, either.

I blinked and looked around for Mimi. She was standing against the wall, blindfold off but still holding the piñata stick. She looked all right. I caught her eye and she smiled nervously. I went over, told her to stay there while I tried to find out what was going on. She said she would, didn't seem to mind.

I inched my way toward the stove. The person on the floor had been turned over and I saw that it was Joey Brown. There was a horrible dent in his face surrounded by terrible burns. The binoculars still hung sadly from his neck.

The man leaning over him looked up and called out, "Is there a doctor here? Is there a nurse?"

A young woman with long brown hair in a cowgirl costume came up, knelt down. She took Joey's pulse, put her ear to his chest. Then she took the red cotton scarf from around her neck and placed it gently over the ruined face, which no longer had a mouth. She shook her head, got up. I looked back to be sure Mimi was still all right, moved closer.

"Gone, I'm afraid," I heard her tell the big man who'd been leaning over the body. I saw now he'd stood up that he was in a skeleton costume. "He must've stumbled in the dark," she said, "fell on the stove. Maybe someone should call the sheriff. We better not move him till they get here."

The big skeleton called out in a loud voice to the rest of the room, "Just a terrible accident, maybe better get the kids home now. Anybody who knows anything about this, though, stay and talk to the sheriff."

I looked around for the blond man Joey had been talking to before the lights went out. I didn't see him anywhere so I went back to Mimi, who was still holding the stick, and pried it from her hand. "A horrible accident, I guess, honey. I want to talk to the sheriff for a minute when they come, then we'll go home."

She nodded but clung to my hand. "What happened?" she asked.

"A man fell on the stove in the dark. He's dead, I'm afraid. You rather come with me?"

She nodded a yes, her eyes wide and interested. I kept hold of her hand and returned the stick to the mother who'd organized the piñata. "No, kids," she was saying, "no, we can't break it for the candy. There's a man hurt real bad over there."

I looked carefully around the room again, but there was no sign of the blond man. The group by Joey's body had grown larger and now included Darlene and Betsy and their father, Bill Dawson, Robby Rowe, and others I didn't know. Bill was talking to Darlene while looking avidly down at her breasts. Who could blame him? The dress was cut so low, it practically gave out engraved invitations. Why had Darlene's father let her out like that? Maybe he was into incest; was that what Bill had been hinting at? There was the faint sound of a siren. It grew louder, then abruptly cut off. Two deputies came through the door and walked over to the crowd around the stove.

Darlene was watching eagerly. Betsy was looking on with great interest also. Still holding hands, Mimi and I went over to the second deputy. He stood quietly listening to the other one who was apparently in charge.

"Excuse me—I saw something I wanted to tell you about?"

He was tall and skinny, a prominent Adam's apple, ginger hair. Small green eyes with pale lashes. He said politely, taking out his notebook, "Yes, ma'am?"

"My name is Maggie Elliott and I live in the Thornton cabin on the other side of Scott Bar." He wrote down the name. "I'm a California licensed private investigator, number 364998." He looked at me sharply, then wrote that down.

"And your name is—?"

"Deputy Sam Hill, ma'am."

"Well, a minute or so after the lights went out, a flashlight came on near the woodstove. It passed over a couple of faces, nobody I knew, then lit up Joey Brown's face—that's the mu—the man who was killed. It passed to his face and went out. I thought it was funny because the light didn't go back on again." I paused, thinking back.

"You expected to see the flashlight go on again," he prompted.

"Right. People were screaming, laughing, I guess most of them thought the lights going out was on purpose, part of the party. But you'd think anyone with a flashlight would keep it on at that point, wouldn't you? Maybe they saw something . . . unusual, or saw Joey fall. Or if you don't find the person who had the light, if nobody admits to it, well, why not? Also, Joey was talking to a blond man not long before the lights went off. A little under six feet, early forties, narrow face, short pale blond hair, dark brown turtleneck sweater. His ears kind of stuck out." The deputy started nodding his head. "I looked around when the lights came back on but didn't see him. If you could locate him, maybe he could tell you something more."

"That sounds like Robert Gerald, Miss. He's the head ranger for the Klamath National Forest." The way he said it, he was also telling me I'd picked on a pillar of the community. He might be asked for information, but politely.

The deputy wrote rapidly for a couple of minutes, then looked up with a noncommittal expression. "Thank you, ma'am. Phone number?"

I gave it to him and he said if there were any further questions, they'd be in touch. Robert Gerald, I said it over to myself, head ranger for the Klamath.

Mimi and I slipped out into the cool night air. Car engines were revving up, a half moon was sailing through a dark immensity of clouds and scattered stars, a good Halloween wind was shrieking in the trees.

I was tired, so was Mimi—she was almost sleeping by the time we got home. I quickly got her to bed, then crawled gratefully into my own. Thoughts churned tiredly in my skull: Poor old curious Joey . . . Where had the blond man disappeared to, Robert Gerald? The horrible gash that had been Joey's face . . . What had he been going to tell me about someone else suspicious? Who?

But I was already sliding down fast into blackness, and after a while came out into a beautiful sunny valley surrounded by mountains that were green all the way to the top and had a sort of postcard look. I knew I was up at high altitude, yet the air was soft and warm, filled with brightly colored fluttering birds and huge blue butterflies.

I looked down at my arm and saw that it was covered with soft brown fur. There was a loud noise that I thought at first was a helicopter but then realized was a gunshot, and I scurried back into the cave on furry paws that ended in delicately pointed pink claws. I scratched tentatively at the soft dirt floor of the cave, then was brought abruptly back to the cabin in Scott Bar by the dogs, a pandemonium of barking.

Confused, I sat up, shoved my feet into slippers, stumbled into the living room. Had that shot in my dream been a real shot? All three dogs were underneath the big side window barking furiously, hysterically. The window was quite black, but then a soft streak of moonlight escaped the clouds and something moved out there, moved away from the lower right corner of the window, something pale. A *face?*

The dogs rushed toward the kitchen, still barking like mad.

I was suddenly certain I'd forgotten to lock the back door. I moved somehow and got there panting, but it *was* locked. I didn't want to turn on any lights and make myself a target, so I crept as fast as I could through the darkness, bumping into things, to check the front door. It was locked, too.

Mimi. He was after Mimi. I stumbled over and yanked open her door, half-expecting to find her gone, or dead. But she was sleeping quietly. I hurried to my bedroom and got the shotgun. When I came out, the dogs had stopped barking and were settling down again, walking in slow circles in the moonlight, scratching at the floor, getting ready to lie down.

Should I call someone? Who? Hank didn't have a phone. Maybe Bill Dawson. And if he came crunching up the driveway, whoever or whatever it was would be long gone. Probably gone by now anyway, or the dogs wouldn't be going back to sleep. But if they weren't gone?

I've never been one to crouch huddled in a corner, waiting for the ax to fall. I felt my way to the bedroom, got my flashlight with the tiny beam from the bedside table, and located black sweatpants and a sweater. I put them on quickly, along with my black Reeboks, moved silently to the closet for a dark jacket, and took my revolver from the shelf. Then I moved quietly to Mimi's room, closed the curtains. She was sound asleep. I closed her door behind me.

I tiptoed back through the living room, turned the lock and inched the door open. It was well oiled and made no sound. A porch board creaked as I stepped on it and I stood still a minute or so but heard nothing respond, so I quietly locked the door and continued down the steps. I turned right and went slowly and silently around the corner, then paused, leaning against the side of the house. The moon had gone behind a cloud so black that no light escaped, and I couldn't see anything at all, could only feel my way along the edge of the house. I waited. And heard nothing but the wind rustling the dry leaves of the apple trees just beyond. If only I could see just a little—without being seen myself.

I crept along under the big window toward a bush on the far side, feeling along the wall of the house with my elbow.

I held the pistol close to my body and pointed straight out in front in case there was anyone hiding there. When I got to the bush, I cautiously stuck my left hand around and was just thinking with relief that the space was empty when someone grabbed me from behind.

I let out a shriek, which was cut off by a rough hand over my mouth and a whisper in my ear to shut up or he'd cut my head off. I shut up, gasping but trying to do it quietly. Why hadn't I stayed inside? I'd seen one curious man die tonight; you'd think that would have given me a hint.

The voice at my ear whispered, "Oh ... it's you. Stay here. Don't move." He let go and moved off fast, switching on a powerful light that caught the apple trees. I realized I'd heard the voice before; it was Mimi's stepfather or whatever—Hank. Relief swept through me like a flash flood. His steps pounded loudly on the frozen ground, heading toward the woods. His light picked out more trees but I couldn't see anyone. I thought I heard another set of pounding footsteps, ahead of him. The light disappeared into the woods.

I picked my revolver up from the ground where I'd wimpily dropped it and stood still, waiting for a long time. After a while the black clouds passed on and the moon, high and small, created an eerie landscape of soft white patches with deep black trenches like open graves. Then Hank said, not more than a couple of feet away, "Maggie?"

"Hank. Did you see who it was?"

"No. He got away. I almost had him. *Shit.*"

"My coming alerted him, I guess. I'm sorry. But I had no idea you were out here. Let's go inside."

I turned and he followed. I unlocked the door and we went into the living room. I drew the heavy curtains and turned on a small lamp. I looked in on Mimi; she was still asleep. I closed her door again.

"What happened? You didn't go home then. You stayed to guard Mimi. I mean, Hermina."

"After you got back, I was over near that shed. I could see most of the house that way, especially the back. I didn't figure he'd come up the drive."

He paused, took a pack of Marlboros out of his jacket pocket, shook one out, and lit it. Then he offered me one but I shook my head. Just one is all it would take. Just one and I'd be back to three packs a day before you could say cowboy hunk. Quite a few of them dead now of lung cancer. But I'd loved Marlboros, in the bad old days.

Hank blew three perfect smoke rings toward the ceiling. "I didn't hear him at all, then all of a sudden I saw him under the big window, looking in. Happened from one second to the next—he wasn't there, then he was. I started over. He didn't hear me—wind in the trees probably covered me. Got over by the side of the house. I was going to go for him. Then the dogs started barking and he ran around toward the back. I think maybe he tried the door but couldn't get in. Anyway he backed off, went over to those apple trees and that's when I heard you coming along. The moon was gone then—I couldn't get any kind of look at him except just his general shape. Big guy, or anyway heavyset."

"How big?"

He shrugged. "Hard to say, in moonlight like that."

"Well, Hank." I took a deep breath, let it out slowly. "I sure am glad you were out there. I was really scared."

"Why'd you come out then? And," he smiled narrowly, but this time it reached his eyes, "what's a nice girl like you doing with a pistol like that?"

"I do private investigation work. I got sick, came up here to rest and get over it. Was there any particular reason you expected danger? Tonight, I mean?"

"I expect it every night. I've run someone off from the cabin twice now at night like this. Didn't get any look at all before tonight. But they're after Hermina, all right. Not going to get her while I'm around."

"You know why someone is after her?"

"Same old same old—like he went after those hikers. And the poor fools fishing up there."

"Yes, but Hermina—I was asking her tonight if she'd seen anyone when she was up there looking for gold. You knew about that, her looking for gold the Indian children supposedly left on the trail before the whites came?"

He nodded. "I don't let her go up there now."

"She said she saw a man up there, I think it would be the day the hikers were killed. She said he had a gun and she ran and he chased her. But his face was in shadow; she didn't get a good look. But if it was the killer—he doesn't *know* she didn't get a good look at him."

"I'm thinking maybe we should all go back to town for a while."

"Redding, you mean?"

He nodded.

"Where would you stay? Would it be easy to find you there?"

"Friend of mine has a place we can use. Everything's in his name."

"Good." I stretched, leaned back again. I was so tired. "Hank, that first time I came up to the cabin—when I was leaving, Hermina's mother fell on the floor and didn't get up."

"Yeah, she drinks. Sometimes, not all the time. Off, then on. Can't handle it."

"I thought she looked like she was on something more than alcohol. Along with the alcohol, I mean."

"Yeah, she does 'ludes sometimes. I try and keep them from her, throw 'em away if I find any. But she's got a million hiding places."

"What about you? You drink, too?"

"Sure, a little. Only one trouble with my friend in Redding." His voice was very quiet now, and hostile. "The one with the house where I stay? He just goes on and on about AA. I just can't stand that. It's okay if he wants to go pray, but me, I'm a person who doesn't need that kind of crutch. I'm looking after Clara, I'm working on her problem with her, and," he added with almost a snarl, "I'm looking after her kid. My own sister was murdered when I was ten years old. That's not going to happen to Hermina."

A shock of corn fully ripe.

TOMBSTONE, SCOTT BAR CEMETERY

SIXTEEN

LATE THE NEXT DAY I HEADED DOWNRIVER ABOUT FIFTEEN miles to the Rainbow Grocery. Late, because poor Joey had said the Chinese man was gone all day, busy with his search.

The cluster of small cabins to the left of the store looked shabby in the fading light. A coat of white paint would have helped a little but not much. They sagged—the proportions were wrong. There were a couple of beat-up old cars parked outside, but neither was the Chinese man's, so I went into the store. It was small but crammed with stuff—fishing equipment and at the back a lot of nails and tools, along with the groceries. A faded sign, worn at the edges, said in homemade lettering that rafts and inner tubes could be rented by the hour or the day.

A medium-sized, balding man was behind the counter, adding up some figures on a small piece of paper. He looked about thirty, with abundant light brown hair on the long side, hazel eyes, a little bit of belly beginning to crawl over the top of his wide brown belt. He looked up inquiringly. He had a direct, intelligent look and I dropped the story I'd manufactured and told the truth—to a point.

"Yeah, well I want to see this killer caught as much as anyone, more than some—I lost a lot of business since it happened and they won't come around this spring, either, if

154

the bastard isn't caught. If it's true what you say that Brad-shaw has an alibi—how can I help?"

I asked him many of the things I'd asked Robby Rowe, writing down the names of everyone he'd seen from August until now in the mountains near where the four men were attacked. The approximate times he'd seen them. There weren't many—Robby Rowe, Ullrich, Bill Dawson, looking, he noted wryly, for Bigfoot, two men he didn't know. Neither had bushy eyebrows, but his description of one of them matched pretty well with the blond man I'd seen talking to Joey.

I asked him what he knew about the four fishermen. The one he'd known was an Oakland cop who came most years to fish. "He was a damn tough guy, alert. I tell you, that killer must be something else." Arnie hadn't known any of the others and had no new information. Then I asked about the Chinese man.

"Came in August, around the middle of August, usually I don't have a cabin available then but somebody'd canceled. He leaves every morning before daylight, gets back around dark. And that's about all I know. Real close-mouthed fella, never said what he's doing here. I asked roundabout you know and then more blunt. But he doesn't answer. Just acts like I hadn't asked. Buys his few groceries here, regular basis. No phone calls, no visitors. You think *he*'s the killer?"

"I don't have any reason to think so. But I want to talk to him."

"Well I hope you have better luck than I did. I—"

"Aaaaarnie?" A loud female voice came from outside, then the door burst open and what seemed to be a dozen children tumbled in, followed by a blowsy, pretty woman with long blond hair who was carrying a baby. The children were all over the place, from toddler age to about ten, but when I counted, I found there were only five, plus the baby.

"Like you to meet my wife," Arnie said. "Melody, this is Maggie, from Scott Bar. She's looking into the murders."

"Glad to hear somebody is besides that dingbat sheriff," she said cheerfully.

"Aw, he's not so bad—he and her old man are enemies," Arnie explained. "You want to come back to the house with us? I got to close up now."

"I think I'll just wait here, catch the Chinese man, thanks. But call me if you think of anything else, okay? And if I do I'll call you, or come by again."

I scribbled out my number, took his, then went back to my car and waited. Soon they came out and all got into an old VW van and drove off.

Arnie had no alibi for the time the fishermen were murdered. No one would—it covered too long a time. He remembered being in the store all day with his wife when the hikers were attacked. They'd been doing inventory and heard about it on the radio. But a wife isn't exactly a reliable alibi; I'd have to get background on him, too. As Joey had said, it might be a group of killers. A car pulled up, late-model, gray. The Chinese man got out and started for his door.

I stepped from my car and got there just as he did. "Excuse me," I said, "I need to talk to you."

He took the key back from the lock and turned to me, expressionless. As we stood on the concrete apron in front of the cabin, barely able to see each other because it was getting so dark, I explained that I was looking into the murders but didn't say why or for whom. "Perhaps we could go inside?"

Still quite expressionless and silent, he put the key back in, opened the door, went in. I followed, feeling kind of mean, as if I were hounding some poor immigrant. The tiny room was very neat, the bed made, no clothes around. I held my open billfold with the private-eye license right up to his face. People don't usually read it carefully if you push it at them like that, and the card makes you look like some kind of state official. Maybe this was the wrong way to go about it, but nice, warm, friendly Arnie hadn't gotten anywhere so I'd try a tougher approach. I explained he wasn't a suspect but that we had to check everything. I didn't say who "we" were.

I sat on the one chair, a rickety wooden thing, and he sat down on the bed, very straight-backed. Looking at me, saying nothing.

"Where are you from?" I asked.

"Hong Kong."

"What are you doing here?"

"Tourist."

The accent was clipped, clear—British.

"People say you go walking around in the mountains a lot. Looking for something, they say."

"No. Tourist."

"I need a description from you—any men you've seen up there, where you go."

"I have seen no one. I go no particular place."

"Never? Never seen anyone, even once?"

"Never."

He was lying. He must at least have seen Joey, but how to get him to admit it? "You know of a town called Locke?" I felt frustrated, wanted to find a connection if I could. "It's down near Sacramento, it's mostly Chinese people. They came over here from China when things were real bad over there, stayed. You know Locke?"

"No."

"As a tourist, maybe you'd like to visit it. I've spent some time there, it's peaceful, beautiful." The faces of the old people were kindly and sweet, communicating the friendliness they couldn't speak in English. But this man's face was hard and suspicious. Wisely, perhaps. Trying for a more conversational tone, I asked, "What's so interesting to a tourist from Hong Kong, up here in the middle of nowhere? You have ancestors who came here in the old days?"

"No."

"So why are you here?"

"I am driving around America. Tourist. I stopped here

one night. I liked it. I decided I would stay here for a period of time."

"For months? How much longer?"

"Perhaps one month more. I like it here. I shall decide
later."

I could feel it in the air—his story was bullshit and he
wasn't going to tell me one single thing. Why should he?

"Name and address? Phone?" I took out my notebook, a
pen.

"Leong. Six seven eight three King Street, Hong Kong.
No phone."

"First name?"

"Chan."

I could get up early one morning and follow him as Joey
had. Joey, who was dead. I hadn't seen the Chinese man at
the party, but that didn't mean anything, with so many people in costumes, masks. Still, it didn't feel good, the way I
was talking to him—trying to sound like a cop, someone he
had to answer to after I'd pushed my way into his sad little
room. Probably that had been a mistake. If it had, it was
too late now. He stood up, walked to the door, opened it.

"I have answered your questions. I know nothing of
these affairs you inquire into. Please be so good as to leave
now."

I walked uphill on the dirt road behind the post office,
past Bill Dawson's trailer, and after a few minutes came to
a dark stone wall on the left. A concrete plaque said WPA
1936, and a painted sign read SCOTT BAR CEMETERY ORIGI-
NATED 1857.

The wide wire gate was open and I walked quietly over
dry pine needles to the far side, where a small group of
people were standing clustered together for Joey Brown's
funeral. A minister, his cheeks scarred with old acne, was
speaking, and a closed gray metal casket lay above an open
grave on four-by-fours.

"You look at me," the minister was saying, "and you
think you see a good man. Because I am a minister of God,

you think you see a good man. But I, too, have sinned; I, too, have suffered; I, too, have done wrong; I, too, have required forgiveness; I, too, have been in darkness and struggled to find the light; I, too . . ."

This went on and on and did not include any mention of Joey Brown. I soon grew tired of the self-important face droning on about itself, and switched my attention to the people around the grave. Most of them were old—white-haired or bald, slump-backed, wrinkled, and sad-looking. No one was crying or showing open grief; the impression was rather of a group of old people seeing yet another reminder of their own mortality, which would probably be coming right along. They didn't look like people who had enjoyed or were enjoying life very much—but they didn't look ready to let go of it, either. Frank Ullrich was there, apparently listening carefully, Bill Dawson beside him. No Darlene. I caught Bill's eye and smiled slightly.

I saw Robby Rowe standing on the far side. He also seemed to be giving his full attention to the preacher. There was a sudden silence, into which the man said, "The Lord giveth and the Lord taketh away," and he turned and started talking to the woman next to him. People began murmuring among themselves and moving away from the grave. I'd gotten there late. Robby came over and I asked if he'd been a particular friend of Joey Brown.

"Friend? I guess, in a way. Sometimes he'd stop by my place and talk . . . well, you'd have to call it gossip. It gave him some sort of kick, knowing things about people. Especially things other people *didn't* know, if you see what I mean."

I nodded thoughtfully. "He seemed like a competent sort of person, not like someone who'd fall onto a wood stove with a hot fire going."

"Well, I don't know. . . . He was alert for his age, but you know he was really kind of frail. He was old—seventy, anyway. It was dark and people were moving around. If somebody bumped into him he could have been knocked over pretty easily, I think."

"Who bumped into him?" I asked.

"Well, I don't know, but then maybe the person wouldn't want to say—or might not even realize, you know?"

"Every time I saw him, he had binoculars, powerful ones. The police have no question it *was* an accident, do they?"

"Oh, I don't think so—he wasn't malicious. Like I said he enjoyed knowing things about people, but he wasn't the blackmailing type if that's what you mean."

"There was a man Joey was talking to—tall, blond. One of the deputies said it was probably Robert Gerald. You said you know him, right?"

He grinned. "I sure do; he's my boss. Chief ranger for the Klamath."

I waited and he continued. "I kind of wondered what he was doing there, matter of fact. He's divorced. The ex-wife has the kids in Mount Shasta. It was more a party for people with kids. Course, I was there without kids, and you, too—Saturday night, looking for something to do. . . ."

"This ex-wife, did she keep his name?"

"Mmmm . . . I'm not sure. She hates him, what I hear, and I think maybe she took her own name back. I can find out if you want—but why do you want to know? You doing your private-eye bit? You suspect my poor boss of something?"

"I'm just curious," I said vaguely. "But if you'd find out, I'd appreciate it."

After Robby left I found myself alone in the graveyard but for two old, weak-looking men who were shoveling dirt into Joey's grave. The afternoon was warm, with the sharp, good smell of pine needles in the air, the *zit-zit-zit-zit* of insects, the varied songs of birds from thick brush that covered the hills at the back of the graveyard. Loudest were the jays, an incessant *squawk squawk squawk* that was, somehow, not unpleasant. The scattered trees were pine, cedar, oak, a few fruit trees, and manzanita, but they were all rather thin-leaved, so the sun got down through and the cemetery was sunny, quiet, and charming. I could think of many worse places to end up, and there was still quite a bit of room left.

I began to wander. The very oldest headstones were of dark, thin wood in oval shapes a couple of feet high; one said simply, "Negro Jimmie." I walked on, looking for anyone named Jane, or Jed, or Alma. The place reminded me of the cemetery in the small east Texas town where several generations of my mother's family lie, awaiting Judgment Day of a Presbyterian sort. That plastic awning at my mother's funeral or maybe it was canvas. The metal folding chairs in neat rows, all so machinelike somehow. My anguished father; yet he'd remarried before five months had passed. . . . Which one would he be buried next to? That white haired ex–University of Texas bluebonnet beauty, somehow always just a little too gracious, or my mother? My mother, who betrayed me . . .

A small grave dated 1882 read, "Walter rest gently in Heaven." Next to this, there was a tall rectangular marble with a curly-haired, sweet-faced sheep kneeling before a cross:

> Four children dear lie buried here,
> Their death caused tears to flow,
> But He on high who rules the sky
> Hath willed it to be so.
> John aged 9,
> Henry and William (twins) aged 3 years;
> d Nov 20 1865, also infant daughter.

They'd all died the same day. What had happened?

From Joey Brown's grave, the steady sound of shoveling and of dirt being loosened into the grave suddenly stopped. The two old men had put their shovels down, were taking a break. I walked over.

"Quite a job," I said.

"Yep," agreed the shorter of the two, who had tired brown eyes and an unruly shock of white hair, "pretty good funeral. What do you think of our cemetery here?"

"It's beautiful. Peaceful. And awfully well kept."

"Yep. Lot of work, though, keepin' the woods back, grass cut. Sometimes the graves fall in."

"Were you friends of Joey Brown?"

"Forty years, give or take," the taller, bald-headed man said loudly, like a somewhat deaf person. He had a strained look, too, of someone always straining after something, but I had no idea what. "Joey and me, we both came here after the war. He bein' from back East someplace. Real bad luck."

"Did either of you know a Spencer family here? Or a Jane Thornton or a Jed? I don't know the last name."

The bald man shrugged his shoulders, but the short, thin one said, "Sure, there was a lot of Spencers here one time. All moved away now, though. There's a George Spencer, I believe, over in that section back of you."

"Did you know him?"

"I can kinda remember him, I think—he was some older'n me."

"Did he have a daughter named Alma? Or a sister?"

"Well, there was a girl named Alma, come to think of it. His daughter, she was."

I felt pleased, excited. I didn't know exactly why I wanted to know more about those people, but I did. I smiled. "What was she like?"

"Real pretty, yeah I do remember her now you mention it."

"Can you remember what she looked like? What was so pretty about her?"

"Well . . . now that's kinda hard to say. Had a lot of real curly black hair . . . and she had a way about her. She was just a kid but there was something—she had a way about her. I don't know how to put it better than that."

Sex appeal would probably be one way. Even prepuberty. She must've been quite something. "She still around this area, by any chance?"

"Naw, she got married young, moved away."

"Where to?"

"Now that, I don't know."

"What about Jane Thornton or Jed?"

"Seems like there was a Jed maybe." He shook his head. "But I'm not sure. It's a long time ago. I grew up here, but I left to go work on the coast in 1934, then there was the war. I was here to visit off and on, but I just come back to live a few years ago."

He picked up a shovel, wanting to get back to work. I went over to the section he'd indicated and found George Spencer among the many who'd chosen their standing in the military as the one extra piece of information to be known by to eternity: "Co H, 8 Cal Inf, Spanish American War"; "Cook, US Army, WWI." WW2, Korea, Vietnam . . . George was a private, 132nd Infantry, WWI. Father to Alma of the good figure and clingy dress, probably had his hands full keeping track of her. Like poor tired Frank, with Darlene. Or poor Darlene, depending on what was really going on. There were several other Spencers nearby, but none of them was Alma.

The shoveling stopped again, and I looked around and saw the men leaning the four-by-fours against the far wall, beside another gate. I went back over. "What's over there on the other side? Looks like—is it for more graves?"

The tall man answered in his loud voice, almost a bark against the silence of the sleeping dead. "Aw, that's the old Chinese graveyard—just holes now."

Then I remembered—Jane had talked about it in the diary.

"See, the Chinese," the short man said eagerly, "when they come here to this country to work, they had a contract with a company paid their way, had to pay 'em back. Then if they died here, well, they was buried right away a course. Can't put a thing like that off, can you? But then the company had to dig 'em back up later and ship the body to China. None left there now except for one of 'em died later. Men come along in a big black car, right about 1923 it was. I was a kid here then. Had 'em dug up and shipped back. Well, we got to be goin'."

They picked up the shovels and gave a backhanded wave as they went off, and then I was alone.

I walked over to the rusty gate, read the small tin marker next to it: "King Cole." The gate opened with a loud screech. The other side was much darker, the ground thick with pine needles and overgrown with brush. There was a thin creek running through and a small breeze was gently moving the leaves; then it picked up and blew harder.

I sat down on one of the mounds and looked around. I could almost see an ancestor of the Chinese man at the Rainbow. He was smaller than Chan Leong and had a long pigtail, wore a pajamalike garment. A big rock fell on him and then a lot of Chinese men gathered here for the burial. But today there were only forty or so empty holes about six feet in diameter, with plants and small trees growing in them and mounds of earth by their sides—the company men in the black cars hadn't bothered to put the dirt back. Had they been in a hurry, time is money, time is money? It looked to me as if all the remains and all the ghosts were gone. I saw no sign of the one grave. Then almost before my brain had computed the sounds of something big moving through brush, a man came out on my left carrying a rifle that was pointed at me.

I jumped about a foot and looked for something to leap behind or burrow into, my heart thudding and my head screeching senselessly, The murderer! The murderer! Then I saw that it was Frank Ullrich. His beak-nosed face still looked tired but also quite pleased. He gave a chuckle and lowered the gun, a .30-.30 with a telescopic sight. A vampire when last seen, today he wore raggedy outdoor clothes and looked a little like the Scarecrow of Oz—but not so sweet.

"Scared you, did I? Bet you thought I was that killer!" He chuckled happily as if sure I'd share the good joke. But just because he was making a joke about it didn't mean he *wasn't* the killer.

"Hello, Mr. Ullrich." I smiled weakly, hoping to seem as if I thought his odd behavior was perfectly ordinary, as if

I saw the joke and joined in. "Frank, I mean. You did startle me just at first. Have you been out hunting?"

"Not specially—always carry my gun in the woods these days. Fact is, I've kind of got in the habit of it now. I was going to say hello after the funeral, but you looked occupied. You sure seem to know a lot of people around here already. By the way, who was that little Indian girl you had with you at the Halloween party? You called her Mimi, I believe."

"That's right."

"She live around here?"

"Well—sometimes she stays with her grandmother. But most of the time she's with her mother, over in Modoc County or somewhere." I didn't trust him at all. But how exhausting it was, seeing everyone as a suspect, thinking over everything before I answered, lying.

"Didn't think I'd seen her around. Who's the grandmother, then?"

"Her name is—I'm not sure, come to think of it. But she's away a lot, too." I shivered. "I guess I'd better be going. My car's down at the post office. Are you headed that way?"

"No, little lady, I'm on my way home. I take a shortcut up above the cemetery."

"So long, then."

I got up and walked quickly away, my knees feeling watery, wondering if I'd be shot in the back and then scalped. A hen-pecked husband's repressed years of buried rage exploding in bizarre murders, was that the answer? But nothing happened.

*. . . dreamers and creatures both are caught in
time's current, which indifferently carries the
most primitive and advanced of organisms,
and which sometimes abandons apparent
paragons of development, such as the
dinosaurs, for reasons that remain obscure.*
—DAVID RAINS WALLACE,
THE KLAMATH KNOT

SEVENTEEN

IN THE LATE AFTERNOON I WROTE SOME LONG-OVERDUE LET-
ters. While rummaging in the desk for envelopes I came
across the diaries and felt the old curiosity click in at the
sight of the faded covers. I made a cup of hyssop tea, settled on the couch and opened the second volume: 1939. It
didn't begin until March 10.

> Dearest Diary, Nothing ever happens—good or bad.
> Look after Mama. Clean the house. Go to Church. I
> heard Jed and Alma had a baby, a little girl. That was
> depressing. . . .

The rest of 1939 had only a few entries with more of the
same non-happenings, and I skimmed through quickly.
Then I picked up the final volume—1940—hoping to find
Jane's life somehow moved out of its rut.

> February 27: Dear Diary, Something has happened
> which I never thought it would—Mama has agreed to
> go to live with Bessie in Yreka and I am to go to the
> college in Ashland! I feel kind of like those Biblical
> people must have felt when the sea parted and there
> was suddenly a way through. I'd rather have had Jed,
> but this is at least something. Miss Louise told me
> their parents never hear from them. Jane

The next entry wasn't until June 15:

> I have seen him. Just right there walking up the road
> when I went to the post office. I felt like my heart was
> turning over inside my chest, and I couldn't get my
> breath. . . . He came over and we talked. I hardly
> heard what he said, it was like my ears were stopped
> up or something. Those same blue eyes, looking down
> at me the way he did on July Fourth when he kissed
> me. I could hardly talk, just managed something about
> glad he was back and I had to run off. Then of course
> when I got home I was dying to see him again, and
> wished I hadn't left in such a hurry. No mention of
> Alma, oh could it be they've separated? Jane

I hurriedly turned the page. June 16:

> Dear Diary, They have, they have—Miss Louise told
> me! She didn't know why, only that Jed has come
> back here with the little girl, and Alma is still up in
> Washington and isn't coming back. I wonder where I
> could go that I might possibly run in to him? He's
> staying up on Mill Creek with his family. Do I dare
> casually walk out that way? Jane

Nothing more for a couple of weeks, then another July 4:

> Dear Diary, We were together the whole time at the
> picnic today, and he danced mostly with me at the
> dance. People were noticing, of course. I just hope no-
> body says anything to Mama. She would forbid me to
> see him I know—a married man. But I will see him.
> We went off for a walk by ourselves—he said he and
> Alma are finished and he will get a divorce, but it will
> take some time. He said—he said just about every-
> thing I wanted to hear. He realized only at that other
> picnic that he cared for me, and then Alma told him
> she was pregnant. He said their marriage was a night-

mare. She got a job as a singer in a bar where she was waitressing, and then was never home and left their daughter alone. He said she wasn't faithful and she's pregnant again, but not by him. So finally he left, and his folks are looking after his little girl, and he's certain he can make a living mining. We are going for a hike next weekend to some special place he wants to show me. I'll tell Mama I'm spending the day at Susanna's. Jane

July 13: Dear Diary, Yesterday I went with Jed far up into the mountains. I am going to start hiding this notebook. He says he's found nuggets in the old mine we went to. It's a deserted Chinese mine, a place they all left in a big hurry for some reason. He says he was always thinking about me, up in Washington, about what a mistake he made.

But I want to write about the whole day, yesterday. I left the house early in the direction of Susanna's and then cut off on the trail to the cemetery and met Jed there. No one was around. We went on a long, steep trail far up that mountain, and down, and then up another mountain. Then there was a big rock on the side of the trail shaped like a turkey—a turkey when it has its feathers all ruffled up in back. We cut up behind it, leaving the trail, but it was pine trees there and not much brush and fairly easy going. After a while we came to a tree blackened by lightning, and we turned straight up hill there. It got more rocky, big boulders and lots of trees. It was kind of a ravine, actually. I was getting hungry and suggested we stop and eat the lunch we'd brought, but Jed said it wasn't much farther and he'd rather we ate at "the lost cabin," so I followed him into the ravine, which was thick with brush but once we got well in, there was a very faint trail. It seemed like we were just heading into the side of the mountain but after a bit we squeezed around a cliff and there was a tiny little pocket valley down there, and an old falling-apart cabin, and a pretty good-size stream running through. Inside the cabin there wasn't anything except some broken glass and some old opium tins, and rubbish. It was all falling apart, but behind that there was a circle of trees with pine needles on the ground. Jed made a small fire, and after that he put his arm around me and he leaned over and kissed me. And kissed me again. We were lying down on the ground and I hardly knew where I was. Then his hands were on my breasts but somehow I made him stop. It was so hard I didn't want to. . . . I could see right through his blue eyes down into his soul. . . . He pulled away, said he was sorry. His voice was shaking. I was shaking all over, too. He said he's going to get the money, and not to worry, we will get married. Then he got a surprised look on his face and said, "But hell! I never asked you!" He sat up, and leaned down over me, and took my face in both his hands, and looked deep into my eyes, and said, very formally, "Jane Ellen, will you marry me? I love you so much. Will you marry me, Janey?" Of course I said I would. . . . Oh, God. I want to be with him right now. It's early evening and Mama and I just had dinner—I'm going to meet him after she goes to sleep, at the school . . . and next weekend we'll go up to the "lost cabin" again. Good night, dear diary. Jane.

They got a lot more out of a few kisses in those days. I put the diary down, feeling happy that things were turning out so well, after all, for that Janey of over half a century ago. Why had Jed called the place the "lost cabin"? Might it still be there?

In gold country all the way into Alaska there are hundreds of stories of a "lost cabin," all much the same: A couple of miners, down on their luck and hungry because the game as well as the gold have given out, see a deer, or maybe a bear, and chase after it into some gully or ravine much like the one Jane described. And at the end of it, they find incredibly rich deposits of gold—as nuggets in a stream, or as a rich vein in a wall of quartz, or whatever. They build a cabin and mine the gold and bury it, and finally leave the cabin, with most of the gold hidden, to go down to civilization for supplies. They take just a little of the gold, just what they need to get the supplies, not wanting anyone to know they've made a rich strike until they've gotten it all out. But when they come back they can't find that trail that the bear or the deer first led them on; they can't find the cave or the creek; they can't find the place where they built their little cabin. Or the gold. They look everywhere, but they never find it again. They tell the story in bars for the rest of their lives.

I got up and stretched, then let Diana out and stood on the porch, breathing in the spicy autumn air. I realized I hadn't talked to Hallie for a while, so I went inside and called her. It was pretty late and she was at home. I told her about Joey getting killed, my belief that it hadn't been an accident. "That would mean," I said, "that the killer is someone who was at the party. Joey was an extremely curious man. I think he found out something the killer didn't want him to spread around. So if I concentrate first on men who were at the party who *also* have been seen up in the mountains where the attacks were—"

"You'll find out who it is! Oh Maggie, that's wonderful news! But I knew you could do it, I just knew it!"

"I haven't done it yet," I cautioned. "How's Sally?"

"I have the impression," Hallie said slowly, "that she's a little better, but I don't know why I think that. There's nothing overt; the doctors haven't said anything. It's just an impression."

After we hung up, I let Diana in, then settled back with the diaries. What had happened next for Janey and Jed?

August 20: Jed and I have managed to get up to the cabin two more times. Being with him is all I ever think about. And I'm supposed to leave in three weeks. It's all arranged for Mama to move to Bessie's.

Jed says he's going to see a lawyer in Yreka next week about getting a divorce. This is far sooner than I could ever have hoped. So maybe one semester, or at the most two, and then we can be together Forever. His little girl is so darling—named Florence—luckily she looks just like him, not at all like Alma except for the hair. Jane.

August 27: Jed's seen the lawyer, who said he has a clear case of desertion and it's pretty sure to come through by summer. We've been up to the lost cabin whenever we can manage, which isn't often. He always makes very, very sure no one is following us. He wants to make certain the place stays lost to everyone but us. Since he doesn't have a legal claim, the gold he's finding isn't legally his. He has claims other places but he doesn't want to stake a claim here because he's afraid that might just draw attention to the old mine. We were talking about all that last time we were up there, and I asked him when he had found the place. He said it was in May two years ago—and looked very uncomfortable. I felt like I'd suddenly been stabbed with a huge terrible Sword right in my Heart—I realized he must've taken Alma there. Perhaps they made Love in the special place that is Ours. But I didn't say anything, what good would it do? I am going to marry him, and I am going to forget Alma ever existed. Later I noticed some marks on one of the trees and looked closer. It was AS–JB and I felt stabbed again. He's so cautious about no one finding out where the place is but I guess he doesn't worry about Alma since she's so far away. And doesn't know about the gold he's found. It's an odd stream there— comes out the side of the mountain in the woods back behind the clearing, goes right past the old cabin and pretty soon goes underground again, before the ravine. So no one else would know there was a creek back

there by following it. It comes out again later, but far
below.

That one wasn't signed. The final entry was a hasty scrawl
on July 3, 1941:

> Dear Diary, We'll be married tomorrow, it is so per-
> fect: three years from that July Fourth when he first
> realized he loved me, first really saw me. When I was
> wearing a borrowed dress. The Scott Bar house is
> opened up for the wedding and Uncle Seth will give
> me away. It's a small wedding, because of Jed being
> divorced and anyway a big one would cost too much.
> But I have a beautiful white dress that belonged to
> Aunt Millie. We had to let out all the seams. And Jed
> and I will live here in this house when we get back
> from San Francisco, which will be in about three
> weeks. Mama will stay with Bessie for now. Florrie
> will be with Jed's parents while we are gone but then
> live here with us. I am so happy, it hurts! Your Jane.
> P.S. Tomorrow I will have a New Name!

The rest of the pages were blank. I closed the book. A nice
happy ending, as endings go. But what had happened after
that? What had Janey meant in the diary about Alma not
knowing about the gold Jed found at the old mine? Maybe
that was a key somehow. Maybe this was the place the
killer was protecting.

Could I find that mine myself? I'd go look for it one day
soon. Maybe Jim would go with me on the weekend.
Maybe there was an old-timer still around who'd know of
them. The woman at the post office, she might know. . . .

The woman who shared the post office job with Bill was
somewhere in her sixties, tall and spare, with rather purply
dark brown hair that surely came out of a bottle. Shiny
round brown eyes, inquisitive like a squirrel's. Chatty and

friendly, like Joey. Elvira, she said to call her. Elvira Messenger.

"With that name, people remark on my working here—and it's true this is just the perfect job for me!" Delighted every single time she thought of the fortuitous coincidence. I smiled, too.

"Elvira, I'm glad it's you here. I'm trying to find out about some people who lived in Scott Bar about fifty years ago—Jane Thornton and Jed something that begins with *B*, and an Alma Spencer. Do you know any of them?"

She shook her head. "Sorry, I don't. I grew up downriver in Orleans, I didn't come to Scott Bar until about twenty years ago."

"Can you think of anyone who might remember them?"

"I bet Elizabeth Petersen would. She's real old and an invalid now but she still has her brain. She was the postmistress here almost forever before me and Bill. She lives in Yreka now but she'd know if anyone would."

"Would you mind calling her, asking if I could stop by? I'd love to meet her."

"Sure, when do you want to go?"

I looked at my watch. "I think I'd like to go this afternoon."

Elvira looked up the number and dialed it, waited, looking expectant. "Elizabeth? This is Elvira ... fine thanks. But there's a friend of mine here would like to talk to you, wants to ask you about some Scott Bar old-timers. Okay if she stops by?"

She listened for a minute, then said, "That's wonderful—she thought she'd probably come this afternoon. Maggie Elliott is her name." She listened a bit more. "Keep well, then. I'll stop by next time I'm in town." She hung up and said, "She's an invalid, always home. She said you can stop by anytime. This afternoon's fine."

I went left on Miner Street, where turn-of-the-century buildings on either side give the area a certain charm. After a few blocks the businesses thinned and I turned right on a tree-lined street where one and two-story Victorians, all of them white or cream, were sunning quietly through the years of their old age.

Mrs. Elizabeth Petersen's house was in mid-block, narrow, with a deep front porch and lots of gimcrack, a big bay window to one side. It hadn't been painted for a while. I walked up the shallow steps and rang the bell. I could hear it echoing inside, and after a few minutes a hefty middle-aged woman in a white uniform appeared and let me in.

"Oh yes, she's expecting you."

The hall was rather crowded with hat stands and small tables and old photographs. Odd how we live on, after we're gone, in those flat pieces of black and white or colored paper. Reduced to one expression forever, to one certain dress or suit or bathing suit that soon begins to look quaint, or bizarre. The hall was dimly lit and smelled of old house, used-up lives.

I followed the woman into a big room on the right where a very elderly woman sat in a wheelchair in a big bay of four windows that looked out onto the shady street. She had a shawl over her legs, though it was a warm day. She was large-boned and thin, with a badly humped back and sharp black eyes that looked incongruously alive in her shriveled face. Her hair was gray but still had a few dark streaks. With a hand well ringed with small diamonds in old settings, she waved me to a comfortable easy chair opposite. I wished I'd asked Elvira more about her. Why was she living in Yreka now instead of Scott Bar? I smiled.

"Elvira called about me this morning? I'm Maggie Elliott."

"I'm eighty-nine years old," she said, "ninety next month. Elvira said you wanted to ask me . . ." Her voice faded in confusion. Oh, dear. But she rallied, got it back. "People who lived in Scott Bar in the old days."

"That's right. I'm trying to locate a couple named Jane and Jed who lived in Scott Bar about fifty years ago. I don't know his last name, but she was—"

"Janey Thornton, you must mean," she interrupted in a high, quavery voice, "and Jed Bow."

"Oh good"—I smiled—"you do know them. Are they living anywhere in the area, by any chance?"

Slowly, she shook her head, running her hand along the edge of the hair net in back. "You won't be able to talk to *them*—they're in the cemetery, here in Yreka." Her hand was on the arm of the wheelchair now, stroking it, back and forth slowly, back and forth. Her eyes were looking at something far, far away. "They died on the way back from their honeymoon. . . ."

I felt shocked, cheated. As if a dear childhood cousin I hadn't seen in years but was just about to find again had been run over crossing the street to meet me. I tried to take it in. "What happened? They were young. How did they die?"

Her eyes became focused and sharp again. "It was a car accident—that Klamath road was even worse in those days than it is now. Do you know the part where it climbs up real steep and then there's a very sharp bend to the right?"

"Tree of Heaven it's called—that place? There's a Forest Service campground down below?"

She nodded, stroking the arm of her chair. The small hand was freckled with liver spots, plump, weak-looking. The diamonds were a little dull but they were strong, would endure. "There wasn't back then. But that's the place. One of those big logging trucks it was, came straight at them and forced them right over the edge, it said in the newspaper. Both dead, of course, probably before they hit the ground." She put her hand back to the hair net, looking out the window, her voice dreamy. "I went to their wedding. I can still see them, the way they looked, you know, before they went down to San Francisco. Oh, they were very much in love—you could see it."

I felt as sad at the news as if Janey and Jed had been good friends, as if I'd known them. Well, I had known them, even if they'd never known me.

Elizabeth Petersen sat silently, looking out, nodding her

head, far away again. I looked around the room: large, with a deep plum-colored carpet, spotless. There were several brocade upholstered chairs, all with doilies—white lacy squares carefully placed at the back so no hair oil would mar the material. Doilies were also placed on the arms so no one's dirty hands would streak the expensive cloth. But who would have dared have dirty hands here? There was a lot of stuff about, tables, knickknacks, pictures in silver frames, but all in their place, all dusted. It was perhaps the cleanest room I'd ever been in.

She went on, "And things had just started going so well for them; there finally seemed to be plenty of money. . . ."

When she didn't continue, I said, "I thought they didn't have any money . . . or not much. Did one of them suddenly come into an inheritance or something?"

The small black eyes glittered, looked amused. "Not an inheritance, no. Neither of their families had anything to leave them. It was right after the Depression, you know. Jed just suddenly seemed to have money. Where before— you're right—he'd barely had two quarters to rub together. It was gold, but nobody knew really where it came from. He must have made a big strike, but afterward . . ." Her face saddened again.

"Afterward . . ." I prompted.

"Well, a couple of local boys bought up his claims but they didn't find anything. I always thought myself, maybe he found old Indian Mary's gold."

"Oh," I said, wanting to keep her talking, though I'd heard the story, "that sounds interesting. And mysterious. What was that?"

She smiled, looking pleased, and repeated the story Joey had told me. Joey. So many dead people. I was sick of it, sick.

She added, "Probably be worth an awful lot these days."

Then she said no more but just sat, gently nodding and looking out the window. I looked too, but nothing at all seemed to be going on out there—not even a cat or a bird. No one walking their dog. It must be very lonely, being old and housebound. She was suddenly looking tired, and I hurried on with my questions.

"What about Alma Spencer? Did you know her, too? Did she ever come back?"

"Alma? She never came back to *live* in Scott Bar, no. She was up in Washington state somewhere, as I recall. She was back a few times, but never to stay. Left off her boys with her parents sometimes."

"Do you remember what their names were, her boys? How many were there?"

She thought but finally shook her head. "No, now that, I don't remember. Larry, perhaps Johnny, Frankie, Bobby—they were just ordinary boys' names, dear, but I'm afraid I don't remember just what they were. I never knew those boys well. I never cared much for Alma."

"What was it you didn't like about her? I guess Janey didn't like her much, either."

"Cheap. She was just cheap. I never understood why—her family was perfectly nice. But Alma was . . ." Her voice trailed off. Perhaps she didn't have the words she needed in her ladies' vocabulary. *Slut*—

She interrupted my thoughts. "A floozy!" she cried triumphantly, leaning forward and then sinking back again, tired by the unusual effort.

I smiled. "That gives me the picture, all right. How many boys of Alma's were there?"

"Three or four, I believe. Perhaps even five. I think there was one boy older than the others . . . perhaps a stepson. She and Jed had a daughter, but the little girl wasn't in Scott Bar for very long after her father was killed. She was brought up by his parents, Jed's parents, but they moved away soon after the accident."

"Florence, her name was—the little girl."

"That's right, Florence. Silly name, I always thought. She was a darling child, though. Those lovely black curls all over her head, just like Alma had . . . although overall, she looked more like Jed."

The nurse had been hovering and took the opportunity to

interrupt: "It's time for your afternoon nap now, Mrs. Petersen. Will you be finishing up your visit soon? And we'll want to take our tonic, as well."

"And Alma," I asked quickly, "did she remarry? Do you know what her boys' *last* name was?"

"No, no I never knew. . . ."

The nurse strode forward.

"Well . . . thank you very much. If I think of any more questions, may I call you or stop by again?"

"Yes, dear," she said tiredly, "that will be fine. Now where did I put—oh, yes." She took a small leather case from the table beside her, opened it, took out a metal nail file. "Fingernails grow so fast, don't they?"

Hallie sounded revitalized, reborn, bubbling over.

"Not only have the vital signs picked up, Maggie— they're almost certain now she'll regain consciousness! They expect it to happen sometime in the next few days. Oh, Maggie, I'm so excited and so *nervous*."

"God, I wish I could be there with you—maybe I can come up soon. Do they think she'll be able to tell them anything about who attacked her?"

She gave a kind of moan. "That's a lot farther down the road, I think. Of course they don't really know, but they expect at least a certain period of amnesia apparently—which might go away or might not."

Things were even more urgent now—if somehow the killer heard the news. . . . I was tired, and after we hung up, I lay down on the bed and thought about all the things I wanted to do next. But I fell asleep, and then Jim came by. I was still half-asleep when I let him in. "You get your business done in Hoopa?"

"Yeah, more or less. What was the funeral like?"

As I made him coffee I told him about it, yawning and still collecting my thoughts. "I was thinking—maybe it would pay to find out who among the men around here haven't been here long."

"Because?"

"Because the murders were so bizarre—maybe they weren't the first. Maybe if we found out about the men who came here before August, during the past year or so, and where they came from, we could discover whether there were any weird killings where they lived before."

He nodded. "We could get a list easy enough from the post offices. I'll take Happy Camp. You want to do Scott Bar? And we should get Horse Creek and Seiad, too. The killer may not be from right around here but then again, he might. How're you feeling?"

"Not bad. It was a tiring day, but I feel pretty good. Oh! I haven't told you—I talked to Hallie. Sally's expected to regain consciousness very soon! In the next few days, she said."

"Really? That's wonderful. You want to go up? I could take some time off, drive you. Next weekend maybe."

"I'd love that. But to get back to what we were talking about before for a minute. Do you know anything about Robert Gerald? Specifically, how long he's worked around here?"

"Huh? The Klamath National Forest's head ranger?"

"He was talking to Joey just before Joey was killed. At the Halloween party. After the lights came on I looked for him. I wanted to ask him what they were talking about. But he wasn't there."

Jim smiled. "Now that would be an interesting solution. He's an arrogant bastard, doing real well in the Forest Service—he's responsible for cutting more board feet of timber than anyone ever has before. How long has he been here? About a year. But hey—there's a hearing tomorrow, appeal on the Forest Service plans to develop Bear Creek. He'll be there; Robby Rowe, too. You could look him over, maybe ask him some questions. Want to come? But we'd have to take two cars, I'm going to Redding afterwards."

*There's always the possibility they've
simply outgrown our neotenic vanities,
that they would no more dream of
lording it over their own ecosystem than
we would dream of eating our parents.*

DAVID RAINS WALLACE,
THE KLAMATH KNOT

EIGHTEEN

Bob Gerald looked up as we came into the room and
said to me, though the hearing was theoretically public,
"Who are *you*?"

Robby Rowe murmured something and made introduc-
tions. A man in a beige suit was Bill Keber of the regional
office in San Francisco, appeals coordinator. A corpulent,
putty-faced man in a gray-brown suit, cream shirt, and gray
and brown striped tie was from Coast Timber Corporation;
his name was Dixon. Gerald was the local Forest Service
representative—the defendant, in a sense. A tall, thin man
in shirtsleeves from the Audubon Society was a coplaintiff
with the Karuk tribe.

Keber looked down at the papers in front of him and
read rather rapidly: "Number two: 'We support multiple-use
management at a level consistent with protection of the
whole area.' Any questions on number two?" He hurried on
before anyone had a chance to speak. "Number three
claims the Forest Service plan does not adequately assess
water quality and wildlife, merely restates the decision notice and doesn't address any of these issues. Points out the
GO Road decision says the plan *must* consider cumulative
effects. . . ."

I looked around the small room: no windows, beige
walls, beige carpet, several black-framed color photos of
trees, all rather bland, labeled this or that National Forest.

Three large dish-shaped lights in the ceiling provided a cold, even illumination. Bob Gerald, brightly lit, seemed not to be listening, as if he had better things to think about. Those ears that stuck out had probably caused him a lot of pain growing up, but now he gave off an aura of being better than everyone else. He had thinning blond hair, rather large blue eyes.

Jim interrupted Keber: "Water quality also includes fisheries, and adherence to DMPs does *not* assure compliance." I felt my blood heating up—go after them, Jim! "Fish and Game concurred with the analysis—it's an important and significant stream for both steelhead and salmon. We need better cooperation with DFG's spotted-owl management—"

Gerald looked bored; Robby Rowe looked sleepy. The bastards. I imagined first one and then the other as the killer.

Jim went on. "The original study figured one thousand acres to sustain a pair of spotted owls and now they're saying spotted owls need two thousand acres to survive. If you go in and one thousand isn't enough, if you go in with intensive management, build logging roads, and destroy it, then it's gone. We say it's not a *necessity* to enter Bear Creek now. We need to document the spotted owl needs which are not documented in the EA. And the Forest Service *had* the information before they came out with the decision plan."

Gerald scowled, cleared his throat. The habitat of the spotted owl was an important issue because they're an endangered species, a flag species, which, if it can be saved, will guarantee the survival of several other species who share the same habitat. Their extermination would automatically mean the extinction of the others as well.

Keber continued. "Number four: 'We'—that's Audubon Society and Karuk Tribe—'are not receiving the current six-month listing of EAs and don't believe the Forest Service has met its procedural requirements.'"

Robby Rowe, behind his politely attentive but rather glazed dark blue eyes, was a million miles away. Where?

Dixon, the timber rep, said, "I hate to agree with them but we had exactly the same problem—we only discovered by accident an appeal had been filed. We should be kept informed as well."

Gerald tightened his lips, shifted position. He was no longer looking bored; he was looking pissed. As if he were some kind of royalty, forced to attend a meeting of shoemakers and then they had the audacity to say things he didn't like. Of course, I was terribly prejudiced. Maybe that wasn't what he was feeling at all. Maybe he was feeling remorse for his dirty tricks, for not working fairly with the environmentalists. Maybe he was having second thoughts about the little owls, thinking they should be saved, after all.

Dixon went on, "Unemployment is now about twenty to twenty-five percent. Our wealth is in our resources and we think economic health needs to be based on wise management of these resources. The survival of the timber industry in this country, saving the jobs and livelihood of countless families, depends on wise harvesting of old growth."

The Audubon man said quietly, "The timber industry has logged ninety-nine percent of their privately owned old growth and ninety percent of the public's old growth, and now they want to get the last ten percent of this region's old-growth heritage, which is public. Obviously their old growth–based industry is already dead."

Jim said, "We want some balanced management from the Klamath office. We know it's new, and difficult, for the Forest Service and the lumber companies to have to deal with the conservation community. We tend to get to adversary positions right away and I believe we need to move beyond that. We get a lot of PR, but when we get down to substantive issues we don't feel we are getting very far."

I felt a surge of pride. He could stand up and fight for what he believed but be reasonable, too, work toward cooperation. I'm hopeless at that sort of thing once I get emotionally involved. I just want to have the other side taken out and shot—the sooner, the better.

Keber nodded and said, "Okay, that's it then. If we could have a written summary on the appeal within ten days. A decision will take a while, a few weeks."

Gerald said in a rather disdainful way, "We can't overlook how our direction is given through congressional funding. It's impossible to come up with a decision that satisfies all segments of the public—zealots who are devoted to old growth. . . ."

Zealots! If there was a zealot here, it was Gerald! Well, and me, of course.

Dixon of Coast Timber added, smiling, "I have spent the last twenty years of my life working with timber and I've yet to see or hear a spotted owl and I don't believe they exist."

The Audubon man rolled his eyes.

Keber picked up his neatly stacked papers, nodded in a general way to everyone, and left the room. Gerald and Robby Rowe followed, in company with Dixon.

I hurried after them. The hall was already empty but when I turned the corner, the four men were standing just inside one of the offices, a big room with five or six metal desks and people working quietly at a couple of them. The others had their backs to me but Keber saw me, looked inquiring.

"Excuse me," I said, going around so I could face the others, "Mr. Gerald—could you tell me where you lived before you came to the Klamath? I understand you've only been here about a year."

He looked at Robby and Keber as if they might know the answer. Then he frowned and said coldly, "That's really none of your business. I don't see what business it is of yours. No, I *couldn't* tell you."

Back at home in the afternoon, I was daydreaming about going up to Ashland with Jim. I wished there were three minutes until the weekend, not three days. Still, I could get a lot done by then, maybe get much closer to the killer. I called Robby Rowe at work to see whether he'd found out the current name of Bob Gerald's ex-wife.

"Louise Redmond," he said. "Four ten East Mountainview. She works at home—some kind of writing, my friend said. When do you want to see her?"

"Tomorrow morning. You think your friend could call her, tell her I'm coming, smooth the way?"

"Sure. Say, did you hear the news about the girl hiker? The girl in the coma?"

"Uh—what? What news?"

"She's expected to regain consciousness any day now. Isn't that great?"

"Where'd you hear that, Robby?"

"It was on TV, on the late news last night."

If he'd heard that, so would the killer. Or maybe he was the killer. I pulled my scattered thoughts together. "Did they say where she is?"

"No, that's still a secret."

"I'm glad of that, anyway," I said grumpily. "Well— thanks very much for the name and address." I put the phone down, feeling furious, frightened for Sally. I dialed her room at the hospital. Hallie answered, her voice vibrant, excited, the old Hallie.

"Oh, Maggie—she's come out of the coma! This morning! And best of all—she seems to be all right. She can talk; she can see! God I'm so happy I could—I could—I don't know what, but isn't it *wonderful*?"

I sat down. "Oh, Hallie. Should I come up?"

"I'd love it, but not yet. They've said absolutely no visitors for the first week or so. And that'd be sort of frustrating, wouldn't it? To be here and not be able to see her? Maybe by next week."

"Okay, but Hallie—it was on the news, that she was expected to regain consciousness. How did that happen? I think you should double all the precautions, *now*. Can you do that?"

"I'll try. I don't know how the news got out—here's the doctor. I'll call you back when I know more."

After we hung up I headed for the post office.

"Seems like months since we've talked, Maggie." Bill Dawson beamed. "Saw you at the Halloween party, but then"—his face clouded over—"poor Joey . . . what a terrible thing. . . ." He arranged a stack of envelopes to make the edges straight, looked up again. "Caught a glimpse of you at the funeral, but you were busy talking to Robby Rowe and I had to get back to work. How are you?"

"Fine, thanks. What's been going on with you?"

"Same old things. Working, studying. Try and get out whenever I can. I don't know if I mentioned it to you, but I've been on the lookout for Bigfoot. There've been lots of sightings of Bigfoot prints in these mountains, stories go a long way back. People have seen 'em at night in their headlights several times."

"Who have you seen when you've been out looking for Bigfoot?"

"Why . . . just locals. I mean like Frank Ullrich, Robby Rowe . . . Arnie. And that Chinese man. I've seen him up in the mountains—wonder what he wants."

"Don't you ever worry about going up there, Bill? With that killer still loose?"

"Oh, I keep my eyes open, don't worry about that. I know people think I'm kind of a nut on the subject of Bigfoot, but you know, there's a real good chance they're really there. That would be quite a big thing, scientifically speaking, if a person could actually discover 'em, talk to 'em."

"You think they speak English?"

"Well, that's the trouble of course, language. But it could just be that in some ways they've developed way beyond us humans and could understand us—to stay hidden the way they have, that would take a lot of skill. They don't seem to be neotenic the way we are."

"Neotenic?"

"That's a biology term, Maggie. Means when a species stays in a juvenile state—like us humans. Ha ha! Have their offspring early, curious, not very serious—vain, self-centered, things like that."

"Oh."

"They're descended from a different branch of apes than us, did you know that? For instance, their eyes shine in the dark—shine red, people who've seen 'em say. We gave that up—the ability to see in the dark—you know, so we could have binocular vision. We needed that when we came down out of the trees."

I could just see our ancestors, standing in a long line at God's door. Handing Him or Her back little packages of that part of the eye that lets you see in the dark, getting back little boxes of binocular vision in return.

"I have a book here on Bigfoot if you'd like to borrow it." He felt around under the counter and pulled out a slim yellow hardcover.

"Thanks, I would."

Then I explained my idea about checking on men who'd moved to the area in the last year or two, which was really what I'd come for.

"That's a good idea," Bill said slowly. "Sure, I'll be glad to do that. Might not anything come of it, but no harm in finding out, is there? I can make you up the Scott Bar list easy enough. Give me a day or two and I'll have it. I imagine Seiad and Horse Creek could get theirs ready pretty quick, too. I'll call 'em for you. Meanwhile, here's your mail." He smiled and handed over a thin letter from O'Reagan.

That night I went to bed thinking about the many things I wanted to do next, worrying about someone at the hospital—it must have been—letting the news out about Sally. Stupid, stupid, dangerous . . . After a while, I started thinking about Jim, then fell asleep. Stars swirled in black layers of some fluffy magical stuff that reached forever, and there was something about birds, a lot of brightly colored birds. One was a quetzal, huge, brilliant emerald green, snow white, blood red. Flying through the cloud forest so high, so gracefully.

The next morning, the dream stayed with me, like a talisman of happy times to come, until the phone rang.

"Is this Maggie Elliott?"

"Yes?"

"Well, my name is Junior Cornell. I'm a neighbor of yours in Horse Crick. I'm a bachelor fella. I thought it would be nice if we could meet. How about if I stop by and see you sometime? I could come by now."

My overwhelming feeling was, No! And so I hurriedly said, "I'm just leaving."

"How about this evening, then?"

My curiosity, which often gets me into trouble, began to get the better of me. Besides, I was in no position to reject any bachelor fella that fate was throwing my way, without at least having a look. Maybe I'd like him; maybe I could console myself with him if the thing with Jim continued as friendship, nothing more. And he was a male who lived in the area, so he might be the killer. Maybe he'd been at the Halloween party, wanted to find out something about Mimi, knowing now that I knew her.

"Not in the evening—you can stop by this afternoon if you'd like. Late afternoon, after four."

"Good. I'll bring us a couple six-packs. Do you drink?"

"No."

"No?" There was a very long silence, and finally he said, "Do you cook?"

Oh, God. I should have paid attention to that immediate feeling, potential murderer or not. I sighed and said, "As little as possible."

Another silence, but not as long as the first. "Well, I'll see you this afternoon, then."

As I put down the phone with a feeling of dread about what I'd let myself in for, depressed at the contrast between my dream and the unromantic phone call, it rang again. I picked up the receiver, still thinking of the weird conversation with—what had he said his name was? Junior? It was Nancy Odum.

"Maggie? There's been *another murder*—I just heard about it from my cousin works dispatch. It's that ranger— the one found the hikers, took the girl to the hospital? He wasn't scalped but he'd been *tortured.* Isn't that terrible?"

Tortured, I thought. *Sally.* Robby Rowe had said his partner, the ranger, talked to Hallie sometimes. He therefore must have known where she was. Hallie and I hadn't talked about him—I'd forgotten to ask. The killer would be on his way to the hospital now with the location extracted from the poor ranger—if he wasn't there already. A wave of panic swept over me, nearly took charge.

"When did this happen?"

"Real recent, my cousin said—early this morning, they think. Cigarette burns all over 'im and his privates was all cut up, too. Body was in a old abandoned mine up back a Seiad. Nobody never goes in there, but it just so happened some kids was playing, exploring. They found 'im about an hour ago. Coulda been there weeks nobody noticed, hadn't a been for those kids."

"Thanks for letting me know, Nancy—I have to make a call right away. But I'll get back to you, okay?"

I dialed Hallie's number, my heart in my throat. It rang six times before it was picked up. But it wasn't Hallie who answered. I asked for her, said it was an emergency.

"She's just down the hall. You want to wait while I get her?"

It seemed to take forever but was probably only two or three minutes.

"Have you heard from the sheriff's department down there this morning?"

"No! Why? What's happened?"

"The ranger who found Sally—he's been murdered, but he was tortured first. So the killer may know where you are. You had better get Sally moved right away. Or put a lot tighter security on than whatever you've got now until you *can* move her. Call me as soon as you can with whatever your new number is."

"Yes . . . yes. Oh, God—" She hung up.

I wanted to get in my car and go. But even if I rushed right up there this minute, they'd be gone by the time I got there. At least I certainly hoped they would.

I called Nancy back. When she answered, I asked without preamble, "Do you think your cousin could get me a copy of the sheriff's report on this murder? And also what they have on the murder of the four men? I'm working on the case for the girl's mother, the girl in the coma. I could ask the sheriff myself, but usually they really hate private detectives. If I ask and he says no, then I might never get it."

"Why—why—you're working for the poor girl's *mother*? I bet I could, sure. We were talking about you being a private detective and all, my cousin and me, just the other day. She's real interested, I'm sure she'll help. And she thinks the sheriff is way too bossy with her; she's no big fan of his. I'll go over this afternoon. If she can get it for you I'll mail it today, you oughta get it tomorra."

> *"Animals don't behave like men," he said. "If
> they have to fight, they fight; and if they have
> to kill, they kill. But they don't sit down and
> set their wits to work to devise ways of
> spoiling other creatures' lives and hurting
> them. They have dignity and animality."*
>
> —RICHARD ADAMS,
> WATERSHIP DOWN

NINETEEN

WHEN I'D PASSED THROUGH MT. SHASTA YEARS BEFORE ON
the way to the mountain with David, the place had seemed
just a dinky little town of not much interest. Today, after
the months downriver, it seemed almost a big city, a place
of diversity and complexity. So many stores, so much to
choose from.

At four thousand feet it was cooler here than Scott Bar's
fifteen hundred, but still unseasonably warm for early November. But in spite of the warm day I felt an underlying
chill. What was happening up at the hospital in Ashland?
Were they somewhere else by now, somewhere safe? I
stopped for lunch at a restaurant called The Bagel, sat at a
small table and worked my way through a large quiche. I
felt I needed fortifying for the interview. Robby had said
Louise Redmond hated her husband, but that didn't neces-
sarily mean she'd have any use for me. Relationships . . .

Through the window I could see the gigantic, glistening
white mountain. Twelve thousand feet high, it hung over
the town like a mirage. Panther Meadow was tucked away
in there somewhere, covered with snow now, but it had
been so lovely that summer. A narrow high-mountain creek
running through, it looked almost like the Alps. I smiled,
remembering David's exasperation, my own frenzy, the
sight of his bare legs sticking out from a hastily grabbed
tarp as the rain poured down and we tried to gather up all

190

the things we'd left strewn about, in a special hurry the night before to make love for some reason. We'd gone to sleep beneath such a starry, starry sky, the foam arranged so our heads stuck well out from the tent. Never thinking it would rain like that. The sound of the door opening right by my table brought me back to a Mt. Shasta that was five years older. An old man came in with a young woman clearly not his daughter. They were holding hands, leaning close together, as if their skins wanted to be touching all the time. Relationships. They made me think of Frank Ullrich and his gorgeous daughter. Darlene. What exactly was going on there?

On the way out I paused to look at the bulletin board. Handwritten scraps of paper pleaded for low-cost rentals. Printed fliers in several colors offered yoga, body work, t'ai chi, tap dancing. A petition was tacked up asking for signatures: SAVE PANTHER MEADOW FROM THE FOREST SERVICE. I read the details; apparently they'd given a concession to some ski resort and had the meadow marked for a parking lot. I signed the petition. Was I healthy enough now to go for throwing myself in front of bulldozers? Probably not and anyway my first responsibility was to Sally. Beside the petition, a hand-scribbled note asked for others who had seen flying saucers, especially if they had spoken with the saucers' occupants, to get in touch with Richard at 647-0378. I'd always heard Mt. Shasta was just a little bit weird.

Robby's directions were good and I easily found the one-story white stucco house, sitting far back in a narrow lot, where Louise Redmond lived. The yard had lots of trees, with many bright piles of yellow leaves on the ground. In summer, the house would probably be completely hidden by green. I rang the brass bell, inserted in the belly of a porpoise or perhaps it was a whale. The mountain glistened high and pure above the treetops to the left. Relationships . . . what would she be like?

The door opened almost immediately. "You're Maggie? Come on in," the woman said, sounding more friendly than not. She was tall, skinny, had frizzy dark brown hair pulled back in a ponytail, wide hazel eyes in a lightly tanned face that had a clean, scrubbed look. A little girl's face almost, in spite of her almost six-foot frame and maybe forty years of age. She had on loose jeans, a red sweatshirt that said GREENPEACE, and Birkenstock sandals. But her eyes weren't a child's eyes; they burned with some inner passion. She started talking right away, her back to me as I followed her down a narrow hall.

"I can't say I was completely surprised to hear someone was investigating Gerald as the scalper murderer," she said with what sounded like satisfaction. "I was always a little afraid of him even when we first met, when I was unfortunately in love with him. . . ." Her voice trailed off. Perhaps she was remembering with surprise and annoyance that she once *had* been in love with her ex-husband.

We entered a long room at the back whose far wall was glass and looked out on a big vegetable garden, rich brown dirt mostly picked over and empty now. There was also a small patio with an attractive blue ceramic fountain where birds fluttered and played. At one end of the room a door laid down on filing cabinets, the low kind with only two drawers, made a big desk. It was piled high with stacks of papers. There was a floor-to-ceiling bookshelf, two comfortable tweedy chairs, and a coffee table. A teapot and two cups stood waiting. I could smell the mint. And I could sense already that she was so pissed, I'd probably hardly have to ask a single question—just listen to the steady anger-fueled stream that all her friends were no doubt sick to death of by now. I'd done it myself. Excellent—the timing couldn't be better.

"I appreciate your taking time for me," I said. "I know you work at home and you're busy."

"That's all right." She shrugged. "I'm always behind anyway, a little more won't matter. Betsy said you're investigating the scalper murders. What's the connection with Robert?"

"None at all probably, but I'm making a routine check on several people. I got interested in your husband because of a man named Joey Brown—he was killed at the Halloween party in Scott Bar, maybe an accident and maybe not. Your husband was talking to him right before it happened, but when I tried to ask him a couple of questions later, he wouldn't tell me anything."

A bitter smile pulled at her lips. "Sounds like Robert. Even if he had nothing to hide—anal to the end. I guess I read something about the accident in the paper—the guy who fell on a woodstove?"

"That's right. Do you know if he and Joey Brown were friends or had some other connection?"

She shook her head. "I never heard of the man till I saw the piece in the papers, or maybe it was on the news. I remember because it was such a—such an unlikely way to die. If Robert knew him, it was probably after we split up, which was about a year ago. About eleven months, eight days, four hours. He's not exactly my favorite person. What do you want to know? If I can help you, I will. The bastard. I'll be glad to answer your questions as long as you don't tell him you've talked to me. He has ways—he can cause me a lot of trouble."

She got up, paced nervously to the end of the room and back, sat down again, her gray eyes burning bright. "He insists on using his visiting privileges with my children. They aren't *his*, but in that first fine glow of our romance I was a fool and let him legally adopt them. And don't think it's because he came to care for them; he doesn't. He knows it irritates me, infuriates me, that's why he does it. They hate it, too. They never did like him. They were a lot smarter than I was when it came to a husband. Shit. Four battle-weary years freezing to death in Bellingham, Washington. The job down here was a promotion for him."

She looked around, wanting something. Then she got up and flicked out a cigarette from a pack on the desk, lit it, and took a deep drag. She went on, standing, looking out at the yard. "When we got married, I thought the Forest Service was about, you know, Smokey the Bear and all that, taking care of our priceless wildlands et cetera et cetera. I thought I was marrying someone who did that. At first I—I guess I didn't *let* myself see what it's really all about. Board feet of timber—first, last, and forever. Anyway, I innocently started working on a local environmental effort for wild rivers, up in Washington. At first I just didn't understand why Robert was so angry."

She paused, looked down and noticed the tea. "I made us tea and forgot—you want some?"

"Sure, thanks." She sat down again, poured a cup from a brown glazed pot that looked as if it had been made by someone just starting out, perhaps one of her children. She handed me the matching cup. As she poured one for herself I watched the birds outside—about half blue jays, half sparrows, who seemed to exist on eternally parallel lines, never touching. "So was that the main issue, that's when the battles started?"

"Well, let's just say it was the main issue our irreconcilable differences got expressed around. Anyway, after three more miserable years, right after he got transferred down here, I finally left him. The divorce became final about a month ago. Like I said, he's legally my kids' father and he provides some child support, but I'm doing okay now with this technical writing. I'd rather not have the support since he gets the visits, too. But that's what the judge ordered, dammit."

"I can see it must be infuriating. Your lawyer can't appeal it?"

"Maybe. We're talking about it. But unfortunately, Robert's never done anything you could point a finger at. I mean he jabs at the kids but it's all psychological stuff. The kind of thing, if it was repeated in court, it would probably sound okay. That's his style, Mr. Clean on the outside but rotten underneath. I tell you, Maggie—he could *easily* be this murderer."

"Do you happen to remember . . . were there any unsolved murders while you were in Washington?"

She looked at me sharply. "Why—yes there was. Some people were killed with a shotgun, out in the woods—about six months before we left. Three people, two men and a woman. They weren't scalped or anything like that, though. It was thought to be drug-connected, but they never found out who did it. Or not while I was still there, anyway. There was a big to-do about it because the woman was a state senator's daughter." She nodded her head, thinking. "It was a while before they found the bodies—so nobody could have an alibi because they never knew exactly when it happened. It was in the National Forest, like here. Robert's National Forest."

"Does he do drugs? Did he ever deal or anything like that?"

She shook her head. "Frankly, I'd like to tell you he did every despicable damn thing, but I'll stick to the truth. No drugs for Robert. In fact, I smoked dope occasionally, but when we got together I gave it up, because he was rabid on the subject."

"Before he was in the Forest Service, was he in the military?"

She stared back at me, seeming not to comprehend, as if her thoughts had flown many miles away. Then she blinked her eyes, said, "Sorry. I'm afraid I wasn't listening. What did you ask?"

I repeated the question.

"Marines," she said. "He was very gung ho at one time, I gather—that was long before I knew him, but his father told me proudly all about it. Two tours in Vietnam, special training and all that."

"Special training?"

"Well, for jungle war, you know, counterguerrilla stuff I guess you'd call it. His enthusiasm was considerably dampened when he got rather badly wounded. But he got over it."

Special training and all that . . . "What's his date of birth?"

"Valentine's Day, oddly enough, but would it be—wait a minute. I have it here somewhere." She got up and went over to the desk, opened the drawer in one of the filing cabinets, and pulled out a manila folder. She flipped through loose papers, found what she was looking for, and copied the date down, gave it to me. "Valentine's Day," she repeated wryly. "Robert, the man without a heart."

I asked my final question, for whatever it was worth, looking into her glittering eyes. "Do you really think he would be capable of doing something like the scalper murders?"

She looked back at me, a woman who hadn't lived with Gerald for a year now but was still almost consumed with rage. Of course, maybe she'd always been that way, long before she met Robert Gerald.

"After my friend called to ask about your coming here," she said, "I tried to think about it objectively—did I think he could have done those murders, scalp people. I remember how cold he is, cold as glass. The result? Yes, I really think he could have."

We sat there looking at each other. Finally she said, "I need to take the kids somewhere, get away. He could kill us all. What do you think, really? Or let me put it this way, what would you do if you were me?"

I said slowly, consideringly, "If I were you, Louise . . . there's no reason to think he's the killer any more than several other men I'm investigating. Maybe none of them is the one. But to be on the safe side, if it were me, I think I'd take my kids and go on a vacation. And not tell anyone where I'd gone."

The bachelor fella from Horse Crick was waiting in his car when I got home. He got out and followed me up to the porch. He was overweight, fifty or maybe only forty going on seventy, with four or five dark bags under each eye, one under the other like stairs, and he was wearing bedroom slippers. The very picture of a far-gone alcoholic. He carried a six-pack in each hand and I reluctantly invited him inside.

He sat on the couch and popped open one of the beers, pouring about half of it down his throat in a hurry. I sat on the edge of a chair not very near the couch, most of my attention on the telephone, willing it to ring and be Hallie, who would say everything was fine.

"Sure you won't join me?"

"No, thanks."

"What do you do with yourself all alone here? Ain't you lonely?"

"Oh, I like to be alone."

"Well, I don't. I was married, but I come home one night—I'm a logger; that's hard work, let me tell you. I come home one night and my wife and kid was gone; she just took off. I never did know why."

"That's too bad."

"It's awful. I don't know how to cook. You should see the garbage I eat. Come home tired from a hard day's work and have to face that stove, that awful food. House is a mess, too."

"That's too bad." My replies were a little monotonous, but he didn't seem to mind. Why didn't Hallie call?

"It sure is. You ought to see the place. Oh, it's a real terrible mess since my wife left." He opened another beer and drank deeply.

"How long ago did she leave?"

"Been about six years now. I had a young girl livin' there with me for a while after the wife left, but she didn't stay, neither. I didn't ask much of her, neither. I mean, not much sex, not often . . . just to keep the house clean, reasonably clean you know, and cook somethin' decent for dinner to come home to. She left, too. I don't know why."

He didn't know why? He continued. "Why don't you come over there with me now and have a look at my place?" He had a rather high voice, kind of squeaky. He could use some new parts himself, if he could find God's door, get in the line. "It's a real nice house, nothin' wrong with the *house*, just needs a real good cleanin'. Oh, you should see the couch. It was a nice couch once, but now it's piled so high with junk, and there's all those cats. . . . My mother used to clean it for me, but she got all crippled up, then she died. How about it? Let's go on over there."

"I don't think so, thanks."

"Sure, we could go over there right now. You could stay over. I'd pay you if you'd straighten up that house for me. Or you could live there. Let's go on over now and just take a look."

"No." The poor fellow was desperate, but how could he imagine I would have any desire to take care of him?

"Well why *not*? Why don't you just come have a look, anyway?"

"Because I don't want to go to your house, I don't want to have a look at it, and I don't want to help you clean it up."

"Oh," he said morosely, opening another beer. "But I need some help. I *need* to have someone there. Lately it's gettin' so hard to get up in the mornin's, go to work. I just about can't do it no more. Get to work late. If I wasn't workin' for my brother, I don't think I could keep a job. I'm so tired."

I could sympathize with that, all right—and with his very real misery. "There's no solution in just getting someone else to come dig you out, Junior. I mean that would be fine, except it doesn't work. How much do you drink every day?"

"Oh I do drink too much—I'll be the first to admit it. I could drink less, see, if somebody'd come help me out. Way things are, I just can't face it. You ought to see that garbage I eat every night. I can't cook. I bet *you're* a real good cook. Why don't we go over to my place right now—"

"No way, Junior," I said firmly. "Tell you what. I'm an alcoholic myself and I don't drink *because* I'm an alcoholic. The only way out, believe me, is to stop drinking. Go get help. Go to AA. That's what helped me."

He opened another beer and drank quickly.

"Well, I probably could quit if I had a nice pretty girl like you to help me. Let's go over to my place and—"

"You think you can't quit drinking till your life gets better, but the way it works is the other way around. You have to quit drinking first, *then* your life gets better. Anyway, I already told you I don't want to go over to your place. Nobody's going to want to go over to your place, Junior, the way you describe it! But if you ever decide you want to go to an AA meeting, call me. We can go together. Okay?"

"Sure, but I still think we should—"

"What do you think about all these terrible murders?"

"Aw, it's just some crazy Indian. I'm back up in there all the time. My brother works for a big time lumber company, see. Headquarters in Canada someplace. Surprised we didn't come across some of those bodies ourselves. Man, that would've been somethin'!"

"It sure would. Were you ever in the military, Junior?"

"The military?" He looked at me blankly, as if he'd never heard the word, didn't know what it meant. Perhaps the brain cells holding that information had been poisoned off.

"You know, like the army, the Green Berets, that sort of thing. Were you ever in Vietnam?"

He looked away, didn't answer, swigged down the rest of his beer. He put the can on the floor, popped open another. "I wouldn't bother you much," he said hurriedly, ignoring my question, "I wouldn't ask much for sex, you know, just— wouldn't it be nice to have some companionship, now be honest. We could go over there right now and you could just stay. Save you considerable rent, I imagine. How about it?"

"Were you ever in the army, Junior? Ever in Vietnam or someplace like that?"

He picked up the unopened six-pack, got up. A pathetic wreck in his old slippers, the big belly over the belt, the shoulders hunched probably since early childhood, saying. Oh, don't hit me . . . But you can't get another person sober; they have to do it themselves. Or anyway, put themselves in the place where it can happen. He went over to the door.

"I got to go now, but I'll come see you again soon, okay?"

"Don't come unless you want to go to an AA meeting. In which case call first."

"Aw . . . don't be like that."

"I mean it, Junior. What's your date of birth?"

"Huh?"

"When's your birthday?"

"Why . . ." His face cleared for a moment, thinking perhaps I wanted to know so I could give him a present. He was that far away from reality. "It's in about a week or two."

"What year, Junior? What *year* were you born? You have a driver's license? Let me see it." I held out my hand.

Looking puzzled, he pulled a wallet from his back pocket and flipped through a couple of plastic envelopes, handed it over. He'd probably been quite docile with his mother, too. I noted the date of birth and gave it back.

"Thanks. Were you ever in the army, Junior? Special Forces maybe?"

He turned and went out the door, then shuffled hopelessly back to his car, which was an old wreck like himself. He turned it around and drove away, back to his messy house. I could just imagine it after six years of not being cleaned and the *couch* and the *cats*!

I called the office and asked Harold to check out James William Cornell, Jr. I gave the date of birth and asked him to check especially for military service. Although he was in such bad shape, I didn't see how he could possibly have killed all those people—unless he wasn't always like this or was acting. But the greatest actor in the universe couldn't create that row of bags under his eyes. Probably he was just what he seemed, a sad, damaged man in no shape to kill anyone. Except for the slow job he was doing on himself.

Also, I told Harold, they should run a check on Robert Gerald. I gave him that date of birth and the information about the marines. And I told him he should find out everything he could about unsolved murders in the Bellingham, Washington, area over the past five years.

I waited by the phone all evening, but it didn't ring at all. I tried the number at Hallie's house several times, but there was still no answer. I finally went to bed but didn't sleep well; most of me was alert for the phone that never rang.

The next morning when I called the hospital for Sally's room, they said the phone was disconnected. They couldn't or wouldn't give any further information. They must have moved her, then. For the life of me I couldn't remember the name of Sally's doctor. I called Hallie's house, still no answer. I called the number Jim had left, where he'd be in Hoopa, but that didn't answer either. I waited by the phone for another hour, then I couldn't stand it any longer.

I took my drops, then got out my day pack and put in some trail mix and a canteen and my revolver, drove to the cemetery. I had to do something. I might as well see whether I could find at least the beginning of that trail to Jed's old Chinese mine.

I walked along the back of the graveyard and saw only thick brush. But at the far edge of the Chinese ex–burial ground there was a small gate I hadn't noticed before. I opened it and went through.

It was not a well-traveled path and the going was slow; often it took a little searching and thinking, sometimes with false starts, to keep to the trail. I followed it over the top of the first mountain and started down the other side. There were occasional crackling noises in the brush but nobody shot at me; though each time, I felt a streak of fear rush through my body, hunched my shoulder as if about to be hit, looked around apprehensively.

Then I heard the light but definite sound of footsteps around the bend on the trail ahead, coming toward me.

Without even thinking, I dived into a bunch of manzanita bushes at the side of the trail, holding the gun pointed at the footsteps. By the time the man came in sight I was—I hoped—well hidden.

The steps came closer and then I saw Frank Ullrich. He was carrying that big gun again and whistling. I held my breath, was utterly silent.

As he came nearer, he slowed, looking around uneasily. Then he took the gun down off his shoulder and pointed it back the way he'd come—but not at me. He stopped, seeming to listen, then backed quietly off the trail, disappearing behind a patch of brush opposite me.

Other footsteps approached. When the tall figure appeared around the bend, I saw it was Robby Rowe. He, too, carried a big rifle, but it was slung across his back with a leather strap. He also wore a holster on his belt with a pistol in it. Ullrich stepped out from the brush.

"Afternoon, Robby. Heard you comin' and it gave me quite a turn for a minute till I saw it was you. Thought it might be that crazy Indian killer, ha ha!" Ullrich lowered his gun, pointed it down toward the ground.

Robby, who'd sort of flinched as Ullrich emerged from the bushes, smiled weakly and said, "Nothing to the scare you gave me, Frank. What're *you* doing up here?"

"Not much that's good. My spring's up this way and the water's comin' in dirty. I came up to fix it, but it's caved in. Be a bigger job than I expected, I'll have to get some help."

"Too bad. If it's not one thing it's another, I guess."

"Yep. You out lookin' for dope growers?"

"That's about it, Frank."

"Say, wasn't that a terrible thing about that bombin' up in Oregon?"

I felt like I'd been slugged. Bombing up in Oregon?

Robby nodded, his face going long and sad. "Just terrible. When will they find this maniac, put him away? Well—I'll head on back to town too, I guess."

Surely, I told myself, surely it was something else. Don't get upset, I told myself, until you find out. But he'd also said, "When will they find this maniac? . . ."

Ullrich went on down the trail, Robby Rowe following. After they'd been gone a few minutes, I came out, hurried after them. It seemed to take forever to get back, images of Sally and Hallie filling my head the whole way, along with the fear. There was no sign of Ullrich or Rowe.

I ran across the Chinese cemetery, wound my way through the old Scott Bar graves, my lungs hurting, a pain in my side. I turned the car around and drove downhill fast to the post office. There were no other cars, but Bill might know something, or the woman, if it was her shift. What was her name? I turned off the ignition with a shaking hand, went inside. Elvira.

I stood there looking at her. My mouth was dry; it was hard to form the words.

"The guy's late today," she said, "so there's no mail yet . . . why Maggie—what's wrong?"

Finally, I heard myself, as if from a distance, someone else speaking.

"I heard there was a . . . a bombing in Oregon. Where was it—what was it all about?"

Her usually cheerful face turned fierce. "That poor little girl in the coma—the news said it was that killer; he got her after all. Oh, it's too bad. And the girl's poor mother, they showed her on TV all hysterical. . . ."

The room went dark around me; after what seemed a long time, the light gradually seeped back, wavering. "Uh . . . when did it happen?"

"Yesterday late afternoon it was—at that hospital in Ashland where it turns out they were hiding the poor little thing. In case she regained consciousness, you know, and could identify the killer. Remember that ranger was murdered and *tortured*. They think he musta told the killer where the girl was. The ranger'd been in touch with the mother all along, they said."

On the way home, I kept remembering a time at the beach over by Lands End. Hallie fake-chasing Sally along the edge of the water, Sally squealing and screaming in pure delight. . . . She'd been about seven. Oh God. Couldn't I somehow choose that day, from that lost pack, and throw away this one? Throw away yesterday; that was the one that needed to be gotten rid of.

I dialed Hallie's number but there was still no answer, though I let it ring twenty or thirty times.

Over the river, the shining moon;
in the pine trees, sighing wind;
All night long so tranquil—
why? And for whom?

—HSUANCHUEH,
CHENG-TAO KE

TWENTY

I WANDERED AROUND BUT COULDN'T SETTLE ON ANYTHING; waited for the phone to ring and tell me it was all a bad dream, did a little housework. Finally I decided to go back to the post office. Bill should be there by now; maybe I could get his list and start to work on it. Locking the barn door, the horse gone. But there was still Mimi.

As I pulled up on the small gravel drive in front, I saw bulldozers at work down by the bridge. I hadn't talked to those guys yet. I needed to do that. But not now, I felt too scattered.

A girl was on the porch, leaning back against the railing and looking up flirtatiously at a man I'd not seen before. It was the blond bombshell from the Halloween party, Frank Ullrich's daughter. The man was a lot older than she was, the kind of older that's in excellent, tough condition and tends to be very appealing to women. He wasn't my type, though; there was something about him that I didn't like—a kind of coarseness, a thuggish quality. Another candidate for murderer maybe. Who was he?

I went inside, where Bill was reading, as usual. He looked up and asked, "You see any scorpions around your place?"

"Scorpions? Not so far."

"Remember how I told you the worms were the first ones to crawl out onto the land? Well, scorpions were next,

204

but the interesting thing is, back when they first came out of the water, some of 'em used to be nine feet long. Isn't that something?" He grinned happily.

"It sure is. Imagine running into one."

"No, thanks." He turned and reached into my box. "Here's your mail. You got three letters today."

"Thanks. Did you make that list for me?"

He lightly hit the side of his head. "Glad you asked; sure I did. The places they came from before here, I put that down, too."

I looked at the paper he handed me and saw about ten names. The only ones I recognized were Frank Ullrich, previously Eureka, and Bill Dawson himself, previously Los Angeles.

"Very thorough," I said, "I didn't know you'd lived in L.A. What were you doing there?"

"Worked for the post office, like here. Didn't have any time to read, though, down there. Say, did you hear about that bombing? That girl in the coma—they'd hid her up in Ashland, but the killer figured out where she was somehow and got to 'er." He shook his head sorrowfully. "They let that Indian go, you know—'spose he did it, after all? Was runnin' around free to do this?"

"He had an alibi for when she was shot, Bill—from two different people, and one wasn't a friend of his, more like an enemy. So he's clear."

He shook his head again, unconvinced. "Well, I don't know."

"I see they've started work on the bridge again. Did you put those people on the list?"

"Sure I did. They're the ones, previous place Anaheim." I looked down. That took care of three more names. Bill went on, "Prob'ly hard for you to believe it but before last August, Maggie, this was just the most peaceful, tranquil little place you could imagine. What's gone wrong with the world, anyhow?"

I thought of the elderly medicine man that Ruther had seen, thin, bony hands scrabbling at a rock, trying to stay upright, slipping and falling. The world made wrong for Indians and everybody, the whole year. But now about the worst that could happen had already happened. Sally. I felt like a total failure at everything. If I hadn't gotten sick, maybe I could have found the killer in time. Sometimes I wished the whole world would just blow up and take all us neotenic humans with it. Leaving the other animals intact somehow, the trees and rivers. I asked Bill, "Who's that guy outside with Frank Ullrich's daughter?"

"Darlene? Why—I don't know. Let me look." He peered through one of the mailboxes that was open on the other side, turned back. "You know Robby Rowe, don't you? That's his brother Randall. Works down in Central America but comes up to visit, usually around steelhead time."

"Oh . . . Robby mentioned him. Said he works selling pharmaceuticals down there. What company does he work for, do you know?"

"I did . . . let me think. Carlton, I believe it was. Yes, Carlton, I'm pretty sure. Has quite a time of it down there, from what he says. Adventures. There's all those Communists down there in Central America you know, revolutions."

Outside, Darlene was still listening intently to the handsome Randall Rowe. As I walked past she hastily said hi but made no move to introduce us. Naturally not. Up closer, the man was even better-looking, with the kind of deeply sun-browned skin that's taken years in a hot place to acquire, with piercing blue eyes that looked as though he could see all the way through you. He had a biggish nose that had once been broken, so it was rather flat; wide cheekbones; neatly trimmed dark hair going gray in an interesting way; and a lithe, muscular body that looked as if it had very quick reactions when needed. There was an air about him, too, that gave one the idea he lived the kind of life where they often *were* needed. He looked like too much for a kid like Darlene to handle, but maybe I was underestimating her. He was much older, anyway, somewhere in his forties, I thought.

I got into my car and opened a letter from O'Reagan. "The world's eighth wonder has occurred," he wrote. "That skinflint Patterson sent us a check—only fourteen months late. I deposited your share in your account here— $17,563.27—which is after taking out your part of office expenses for that period. I'll have your information in a day or two. More later. I'll call you—POR."

I sat back, astonished. It had been so long, I hadn't expected ever to see that fee. Now I wouldn't have to be continually worrying about money for a while, for quite a while. I let out a deep breath I hadn't realized I'd been holding in and opened the long letter from my friend Julie. It was mostly about the work-brigade plans for the coming summer in Nicaragua—would I be able to come? Maybe I just might. With Sally dead, the pressure was gone to find the killer. Maybe I could get Hallie to go with me. Mimi seemed safe enough in Redding, I hadn't accomplished anything on the murders, I'd been feeling good physically. And I was now relatively rich.

Then I became sharply aware of the desire I still felt— stronger than ever now—to find the rotten bastard, string him up by the balls, strangle him with my bare hands. I felt a rush of hatred so strong, it made me dizzy. I couldn't go anywhere yet. When my head had cleared again, I drove off.

Back at the cabin, I tried Hallie again but got no answer. I cross-referenced Bill's list with what I had for men who'd been at the Halloween party, which gave me Bill himself, Frank Ullrich, and possibly the three construction guys from Anaheim. I added Randall Rowe to the list, then Robby Rowe, and finally Jonathan Farrell, who'd never been seen since the shootout.

O'Reagan wasn't in and Harold was out to lunch, so I left a message that they should concentrate on those eight, along with Junior Cornell and Bob Gerald. My ten prime suspects. Would they please find out absolutely everything they could about them?

Then I remembered I had another letter. I went and got

it out of my purse, looked at the return address: Nancy Odum. It seemed so long ago that I'd asked her to try and get the reports for me. I took out several pages, copies of the scene-of-crime description on the four murdered men, as recorded by the deputies. I read through quickly, trying to picture the scene just before the murders and then as they happened.

It looked as if the four Vs had been in the process of cooking dinner after a day of successful fishing. A large Coleman stove knocked over, a big frying pan containing three fish beneath it. V 1, later identified as George Stuckey, a mason from Oakland, shot through the chest with the same high-powered rifle that had hit the hikers. Bullets matched. Stuckey was sprawled on his back next to the Coleman, shot from in front. V 2, also shot from the front, was lying by the campfire. He was Joe Ellison, bricklayer, Oakland. V 3 was shot in the face and flung backward over the fire, badly burned. He'd been Mickey Jones, car salesman, San Leandro. V 4, holding his rifle, was shot in the right shoulder and then again, half his head blown off. All were scalped, even the one with the partly blown-off head. He was the Oakland cop, Sidney Vinson. All four were Caucasian males in good health but for the holes blown through them and the scalping. The Vs were thought to have been shot more or less in the order named; in any case, V 4 was thought to have been last, giving him time to grab his gun but not time to fire it. So some of them had time to see it coming, knew what hit them. A strong sense of their panic and confusion hit me, hard. For a moment I could feel the disbelief, the terror.

The phone finally rang, the caller's words at first so rushed and breathless, I could hardly understand.

"Sally's okay she wasn't in the room I knew you'd be worried they wouldn't let me call you they said they had to check you out first—Oh, God, Maggie, I'm sorry—"

"Slow down," I interrupted. "She's *okay*? Everyone's been saying—it was on the news—what *happened*?"

"It was thanks to your call—they got her moved right away to another room and then soon after that to another hospital. We're in Redding. I just couldn't call before now; I'm so sorry. I know how awful it must have been for you. They never thought of a hand grenade—explosive device they called it. The bedroom windows had heavy bars, but it was apparently thrown in *through* them; it broke the window. They think it was thrown from the room above, it just went right through the glass. . . . But Sally is *fine*." She paused to get her breath.

"Oh thank God . . ."

"They wouldn't let me tell anyone she's still alive but finally they agreed I could tell you, after I said I'd hired you and they checked you're really a licensed private detective. And since it was you who called in the warning—anyway, they cooked up the idea to say Sally was killed in the explosion, which will buy us some time. They had me go on TV all distraught. It was easy to act hysterical 'cause I *was*—oh, Maggie, if they don't find this guy soon—she can't live the rest of her life in a hospital and anyway the police won't keep guards on her forever. They'd already loosened up a lot when this happened. Maggie, are you making any progress at all?"

"Some," I said, which was what she needed to hear though not very truthful. "But it's very difficult to find a killer like this. It may be a long time. Do they think she might remember soon about what happened, could describe him?"

"They say probably eventually but it may not be *soon*. They said it could be a year or two, or five, and then it might start coming back. What do you mean, a killer like this? Why's he harder to find than any other murderer? I'd think with these really flamboyant things he does—doesn't that help?"

"I just meant—the people he's killed weren't because of *who* they were; it was something else. I have a few ideas on that and I'm doing everything I can think of. How is Sally?"

"She's doing pretty well—we didn't tell her about the bombing of course. But she's so thin, weak. She's been in bed so long all her muscles—she's getting a lot of physical therapy."

"Give her my love, tell her I want to come see her, soon as I can. Can you give me your new number?"

If I'd been restless before, I was really hyped up now. Tired but wired. I wasn't hungry but ate a banana anyway, then called Diana back from dreams and was just about to take her out when the phone rang. It was the drunk, Junior Cornell.

"Hi ya, Maggie honey, say, where ya been? I been tryin' to get a holt a ya, thought I'd drop over, chew the fat, we could have a few beers and then maybe come over to my place—"

"I'm just going out now," I interrupted. "But remember, if you want to try to stop drinking and go to an AA meeting, I'll take you. Otherwise, don't come by. And don't call, either, Junior."

The only requirement for membership is a desire to stop drinking, AA tradition number three. Junior clearly didn't have the desire, but at least the AA pitch should keep him from bothering *me*. I went out with Diana and walked for a long time, from afternoon into evening, feeling euphoric about Sally, trying to work out how best to use my second chance. When I got home the phone was ringing and I hurried inside, thinking it might be Hallie again or Jim, but there was only a dial tone. I put the receiver down and then it rang again immediately.

"Hi there, darlin', it's me, Junior! Ain't you never home, you got a boyfriend you're havin' sex with now or what, why ain't you never home no more? Or is it you're in bed all the time with your boyfriend?"

I listened for a minute to the drunken, abusive voice, waiting for a pause to insert my AA message, but there wasn't one soon enough and I hung up. He called right back and again a few minutes later just as I was about to get into the bathtub. I let it ring, then unplugged the phone and got into the wonderful hot water.

I stayed there a long time, still trying to work out some plan of action, then soft-boiled a couple of eggs for dinner. I opened Bill's Bigfoot book but couldn't keep my attention on it. As I was standing by the bookshelf looking for something else, there was a loud banging on the front door and before I could get to it I heard the very drunk voice of Junior Cornell.

"Maaaagie, Maaaagie, come on out, Maaaagie . . ." *Bang bang bang!*

I retreated into the kitchen and after about ten minutes he went away.

A nearly full moon was riding high in the sky out my window. Cougars were screaming in the woods on the mountain behind the house, sounding as restless as I felt.

The night was noisy with insects, with frogs from the small creek behind the house. The cougars wailed along in the background like some weird harmony. I got tired of tossing and turning and thinking circular, speeded-up thoughts about Sally, the murderer, how I might find him. I went out to the rocking chair on the porch and studied the moon for a while; I felt like howling at it myself. Diana came out with me and, catching my restless mood, ran around the yard sniffing the trails of small night animals. *Alone alone alone,* the crickets chirped; *arghhaiii arghhaiii,* the cougars screamed; *I want I want I want I want,* my mind churned out.

It grew chilly out. I went back to bed and tried again to sleep. The clock said 3:00 A.M. I lay there turning endlessly, thinking how infuriating it was that I couldn't sleep, how I'd have to sleep through the whole morning if I wanted to be rested enough. The next thing I knew the sun was streaming in through the window, accompanied by loud noises. Finally I woke up enough to realize the noises weren't attached to the sunshine; it was someone banging on the door.

I struggled out of bed, furious, knowing it was the drunk, fumbled my way into my flowered Japanese robe as I stalked to the living room ready to kill. But when I looked through the glass, I saw that it was Jim. I undid the safety chain and as I opened the door, he moved in and grabbed me.

"I called and called and you didn't answer—I was so worried," he said into my hair, then took my chin in his hand and moved his head down and kissed me, a long, fierce kiss that seemed to go on and on. Finally, I pulled back and gasped.

"Come on inside . . . the rest of the way." Watery-kneed, I led him to the couch, where we sat down facing each other, both his hands holding both of mine.

"This awful pathetic drunken alcoholic came to see me and I got him to leave, but then he kept calling—finally I unplugged the phone. . . . I thought you weren't getting back till tomorrow?"

"I got back early, wanted to see you. Thought I should call first—then when you didn't answer—there was that bombing—I kept worrying something had happened to you. Maybe Farrell had found you somehow—I was afraid you were lying out there dead—scalped—you name it, I thought of it. I told myself there were a thousand places you could be, and be fine. But then when I woke up early this morning and you still didn't answer—I didn't think you had a boyfriend up here—"

"No . . . I don't have a boyfriend here. But listen—" I wasn't supposed to tell anyone about Sally, but I had to tell Jim. I'd never be able to pull it off, pretending for any length of time I was heartbroken she was dead. "Sally's *alive*; Hallie called. She's all right—they'd moved her in time."

"So all that on the news . . ."

"Was fake. To buy some time."

"Good idea. I'm very glad."

"You want some coffee? Breakfast?"

"Sure, we could have coffee out on the porch or go for

an early morning walk or talk about literature if you want to. But," he added quietly, "I'd rather make love to you."

I drew in my breath. Now that what I'd wanted for so long was finally here, I felt shy, nervous. Finally I said, "I've thought you didn't want that kind of . . . involvement with me, for some reason."

He raised one of his hands, still holding mine, and brushed it lightly down my cheek, across my lips. "I was trying to avoid getting involved, that's true enough. I thought it wasn't a good idea so soon after my marriage breaking up. I wasn't at all sure I wanted anything to do with another white woman, you want to know the truth. . . ."

"Just another rotten racist, huh?" But I said it gently.

He shrugged. "Maybe so. But then you were so sick. I convinced myself what I felt was maybe just a passing thing, a reaction, I should wait and see. And what if you just stayed sick. I was scared, in other words."

I leaned into his hands. "I wasn't scared. I've wanted you to be with me like this since the Deerskin Dance, or maybe since you first came here."

Looking into his flat black eyes, so close, my heart pounding, I added, "Maybe I should have been scared. I am now."

Survival, as Jim Prideaux liked to recall, is an infinite capacity for suspicion.

—JOHN LE CARRÉ,
TINKER, TAILOR, SOLDIER, SPY

TWENTY-ONE

WE TOOK MY CAR, SMALLER AND LESS CONSPICUOUS THAN the truck, and parked beyond thick brush at the cemetery. Jim followed me to the small gate at the other side, our feet passing silently over the pine needles.

After about an hour of steady hiking—a little beyond the place I'd hidden when I heard Frank Ullrich coming two days before—we came out on a small clearing by a creek. A big bird convention was going on there, a noisy potpourri of jays and sparrows and small yellow-bellied birds I'd not seen before. I could hardly believe it was November, it was still so warm.

We stopped and sat down, sipped peppermint tea from a thermos. We'd had a long honeymoon night and morning, luxuriating in bed with occasional forays to the kitchen. A tingling warmth flared through me as I remembered those hours, the unexpected slow easiness of it, the intensity. . . . I reached over and took Jim's hand. He smiled with his eyes, then leaned over and began nibbling on my neck.

I ran my fingers down his broad muscular chest, thinly covered in a blue cotton work shirt, then yanked them back. The honeymoon was over; it was back-to-work time now.

"We'll never get to that mine." I sighed. "We'd better go."

A little farther along, the trail straightened to cross a small ledge, where we stopped for a minute to look down at the tiny silver river winding through its twisty canyon. Far above us jagged white tips pointed into the blue, blue sky. Densely black buzzards circled and floated on thermals rising from mountain ridges below, and I felt incredibly content, euphoric.

Soon we saw the big boulder that did, in fact, look like a turkey with its tail feathers spread. We turned uphill as Janey and Jed had, and not long afterward came to the lightning-struck tree. We almost missed it because it was no longer standing but lay pointing downhill, the remains of its enormous roots sticking far up in the air.

We began making our way through thick brush. Birds chittered, a slight breeze ruffled the leaves, a creek rushed by somewhere below. The terrain grew rocky. Large boulders were strewn carelessly, perhaps from the rough-and-tumble day the mountains were formed. Ahead the rocks were even bigger, and beyond them I could see a high white cliff face. The air smelled of pine needles, of a beautiful earth empty of humans.

We scrambled around the bigger boulders, scratching ourselves as we pushed through thick manzanita brush. I fell behind when my pack snagged on a malevolent branch, but just as I was getting it free Jim came back for me.

"I've found the path, I think," he whispered. "Here, let me—no, you have it, good. I looked around and didn't see you—scared me for a minute. Come look."

Sure enough, there was a faint trail through the underbrush. It seemed to head straight for the high rock wall that stretched above and to the right and left, but when we followed the path, so faint we couldn't really be sure it was one, it led us behind a big boulder to an opening in the cliff face and passed behind, seemingly straight into the rock.

Jim went first through the opening, which, because of the way it was angled, was quite a bit wider than it had looked—big enough for a horse, in fact.

Janey had come this way, and Jed. Also Alma. I could almost see them, a blue-eyed man with a pretty woman whose wild black hair was blowing free, a woman who "had something special." And later, Janey with that same blue-eyed man. Her hair I imagined to be blond, silky and fine, not so abundant. It brushed her shoulders; Jed reached over and gave her a hand. . . .

Jim took my hand and we slipped through quietly. Occasionally, one of us would dislodge a rock and as it went clattering down the hill with a horrible noise, we'd freeze. Would the ghosts of that old love triangle be waiting for us on the other side? Or the killer . . . "Eee-your-eeeka," I said softly. "We've found it."

A small high-mountain meadow lay below, sleeping away in the warm twilight. Birds sang, and there was a little stream, not too deep and about two feet across. It meandered around through grass that was still emerald green, providing the pleasant sound of water moving through shallow banks over rocks. Drifts of wildflowers—pink, yellow, blue, and white—nestled like bright jewels in the softly waving grasses, delicately scenting the air. Cow parsnips, I recognized, and corn lilies. I could almost see them: Janey in a summer dress, picking the flowers while Jed watched, smiling.

"It fits the directions and there's the stream," Jim whispered, "but where's the cabin?"

"And the mine," I murmured. "Anyway it feels quite empty, don't you think?"

We cautiously descended and found, on the far side of the meadow, the cabin's collapsed remains. A big gray lizard darted around on the ragged boards, caught a bug with the sudden flick of his long tongue, then paused to swallow it. The birds were quiet now, waiting to see what we would do and whether we were going to be dangerous.

"Well, you've found your lost cabin," Jim said quietly, lightly kicking a piece of rotted wood. "Let's see if there're still any signs of the mine."

We put our packs down behind some bushes and walked back toward the big rock outcropping. After pushing through the underbrush that grew along its side, we found an open area between the brush and the side of the mountain. It soon curved around to the left. Jim, ahead of me, stumbled and almost fell but caught himself. I looked down and saw some old rotting four-by-fours lying on the ground.

"Here it is," he said softly. "Don't think we'd want to go in tonight, though."

In the side of the mountain was a large hole, shored up with moth-eaten timbers. The inside gaped dark and dank.

Jim said, "Now we know it's here—we can come back tomorrow, okay?"

I nodded. "Let's go find a good place to make camp."

We walked quickly back to the meadow and looked around.

"There's supposed to be a place with a ring of trees around it," I said. "Over there, I think. Let's look."

But when we found the spot, which was surely the one where Jed had proposed, Jim thought it was too close to the clearing. A part of that long-ago time was still here; I could feel it. Ghosts hovered just at the edge of the trees, watching. "Let's try further into the woods," Jim said.

"Wait a minute, look—there're carvings on this tree, they look old . . ."

With difficulty we made out something that looked like Bobby, and a Billy; there was part of a date, 194. . . . But Jane and Jed had had no children. Alma's, then? Alma's boys?

I looked at several other trees before I found the A S and J B that Janey had seen all those years ago; it was mostly overgrown, almost indecipherable.

We picked our way through more brush and trees on the far side of the clearing. Soon we came to a small open space beneath tall trees, the ground covered in pine needles and protected on the meadow side with thick bushes.

Half an hour later we were comfortably settled, with food spread out on a tablecloth that had been Aunt Bessie's: Faded red cherries popped abundantly from equally faded round green trees, with a boy and a brown dog beneath each identical tree—the same boy and the same dog. I'd taken my revolver out, put it on the ground beside us within easy reach. I cut the broiled chicken and passed the breasts on a thin plate to Jim, then helped myself to the drumsticks, thinking how fortuitous that we liked different parts. With bottled artichoke hearts for the vegetable and sweetrolls for dessert, it was a pretty good meal and there weren't any leftovers.

We sat companionably side by side, backs propped against a big tree, watching the sky darken through the branches above us. Stars began coming out in bunches while birds still sang. Robins, I realized. Singing their hearts out.

"I don't know when I've felt such peace," Jim said, gazing at the tall, tall trees surrounded by bird song and stars and the sound of rambling water. "Not for a long time. This is as good a house as I've known."

He pulled me closer and stopped looking at the stars, looked at me.

The mine was dug into the side of the mountain, the walls of rock and a dark red earth shored up by timbers. It went downward, curving after about thirty feet. It didn't look quite so creepy in daytime but you wouldn't have called it inviting, either.

"Gentlemen before blondes," I said.

He grinned. "Maybe you're really not up to this. You sure you don't want to wait out here while I check it out?"

I reached over and socked him on the arm. "I hope you're being funny and not a you-know-what," I said. "I wouldn't dream of staying behind. There's going to be something in there. I want to see it, drugs or gold, whatever."

He looked amused. "Sometimes you slip back into twelve-year-old-dom, do you know that? It's very endearing. Okay, let's go look for your treasure."

"You laugh now," I muttered. "Just wait."

Jim stooped under the low portal and I followed. The ground was packed down hard beneath our feet. He walked cautiously and flicked on his flashlight before he went around the corner into the greater darkness, and I put mine on, too. The passage narrowed, but we were still able to stand upright. Occasionally our lights would pick out a rotting timber or a pile of rubble to one side but mostly the place was bare and empty. It was cool and there seemed to be a slight breeze coming toward us as we walked farther down under the mountain. Those busy Chinese hands, all those years ago, shoveling and chiseling out so big a space . . . I had a sudden unpleasant thought.

"I don't think these are very fresh batteries," I whispered, "in either flashlight. In fact they were both in the house when I came and I never put in new ones."

"Let's just use mine, then. Hang on to my belt and turn yours off. Ah—what's this?" He played the light over some mounds of rubble and earth. "Look, here's something. . . ." He reached down and held up part of an old bottle, dark blue, read the raised letters around the bottom: " '—agne Française.' Guess they must've done all right, if they drank imported champagne. And here's something else. . . ." He bent over and picked up a small round silver tin with raised Chinese characters on one side. "Opium tins."

There was a small pile of them, mixed with broken glass—more of the dark blue—and a few grayish ceramic pieces with a rice pattern. I ran my light slowly over the walls but saw nothing special, no wall of glittering gold, just the dark earth mixed with rock and held up every few feet by thick timbers. Jim returned the broken bottle to the pile and we went on, the tunnel soon ending but another going off to the right.

I flicked on my flashlight again and peered at the walls and ceiling, but they looked all right, no sign of any cave-ins. I turned it off and held on to Jim's belt as we squeezed past the timbers of the opening. The tunnel curved almost immediately, went a short distance, curved again. I counted the curves, five . . . six. . . . The passage grew narrower.

Jim's light seemed to be dimming but maybe I was just imagining it.

"Let's just—" He broke off abruptly and stopped; the light went out. Then above us, I heard the unmistakable sound of footsteps.

They were coming down toward us.

Making no effort, it seemed, to be quiet.

A thought came through in my fear-frozen brain: If they weren't trying to be quiet, they must not know we were here.

Well, my brain corrected, it *probably* meant they didn't know we were here. They? No, probably not, it sounded like just one person.... Jim pulled me farther into the tunnel.

Silently, we drifted deeper into the mine. I felt for the large side pocket of my pants but even before my hand got there, I knew perfectly well I'd find it empty. I could remember quite clearly putting the gun in the top of my pack, before we cleared away all traces of our presence in the clearing. Thinking I'd get the gun out when we headed for the mine—and then we'd made love again, unexpectedly, on the bare pine needles, a little scratchy but I'd soon forgotten that. And I had never given the gun another thought.

There was a very faint light behind us now. Jim pulled and I followed, stiff with fear. Remembering what I'd heard about the murders—bodies blown apart, the scalpings. The rape. The torture and sexual mutilation. Remembering movies about old earthen tunnels caving in. Remembering how rotten those timbers were outside the entrance. Dangerous to move when the man behind wasn't moving, but probably even more dangerous to stay where we could see the edges of his light.

Swoosh, swish, swoosh—our bodies hissed as they brushed the walls. I didn't know for certain it was the murderer, I reminded myself. Could be a separate problem. But if it was, then *who* was it? I wanted desperately to be able to see—but I had too little courage, or too much sense, to take the chance of trying to sneak up on him and have a look.

Jim whispered, "You have the gun?"

"In the pack. Sorry."

We kept going in tiny increments, like snails, or worms, slowly and blindly. I remembered Bill Dawson saying we're descended from worms—maybe ancient instincts still remaining in the lower, most primitive parts of our brains would kick in now, and help us. Why oh why had I put the gun in the pack?

The tunnel seemed to open out into a kind of room. Had we been traveling down into the darkness for minutes? Hours? Decades? All sense of time had gone with the loss of a visible, measurable world. I felt cautiously around the walls, thinking of things like tarantulas, scorpions, and snakes. We hastily patted the walls, trying to be quiet, looking for a continuation of the tunnel. If the man behind found us trapped here, if he had a gun, if he was the killer ...

Finally Jim guided me into another opening. The relief! The footsteps behind got suddenly louder, echoed. He must be in that open space now, not far behind at all.

I felt a pile of rubble by my leg, gradually lowered myself onto it. I was tired, my legs were shaking. Jim sat, too. It was cold so far underground and we huddled together with our arms around each other.

In the room behind, there were scraping noises now, something being dragged across the dirt. Then more footsteps, a voice, a muffled scream!

I clutched Jim's arm as two voices murmured now—one briefly, the other at length. Answering questions maybe? More scraping sounds; it went on for what seemed like a long time but probably wasn't. I settled back against Jim and tried to relax. I'd been holding myself so rigidly I'd soon be completely exhausted. Finally the scraping sounds stopped. The voice that had done the least talking murmured again. There was the sound of something being dragged, of rocks tumbling. Then two sets of footsteps walked slowly away and soon there was only silence. After what seemed another very long wait, Jim's lips were at my ear.

"Haven't heard anything, think I'll go look."

"Okay," I whispered. "We'll both go."

Soon I could sense the open space around us. "Let's see if we can find out what they were doing," Jim whispered.

His light moved about the room: close-packed dark earth, small rocks, a vast and empty space. On the far side, there was a pile of rubble and old wood. We went over quietly and began pulling away the wood. A large hole gaped beneath, filled about three-quarters to the top. I flicked on my light; it joined Jim's, traveling across the dull golden surface of what must be a king's ransom in nuggets.

"Jesus," Jim said softly. He picked one up. It was big. I

don't know much about gold or nuggets, but it looked very pure. "So this is what it's all about. . . ."

I didn't say anything. I couldn't. The sight was astonishing, overwhelming. The money that gold represented—very few people in the world had ever seen that much at one time. Kings in the old days maybe. Major drug dealers. So much money . . . Mimi, I thought. Now she can get a house. "Let's take some of it with us," I whispered. "I want to give some to that little girl. That little Shasta girl."

"We'll have to think about that. There's probably some legalities here, little Miss Twelve-Year-Old." His hand brushing my arm made the words affectionate, not condescending. "But first we need to get out of here without being seen. No gold's worth dying for, is it?"

"Let's just put some in your pack real fast, then." There was room in Jim's pack now, from where the food had been. Soon it was about a quarter filled, and too heavy to add more.

After what seemed like years of creeping, muscles stiff and tense with fear, we rounded the last corner and began to see faint daylight ahead.

"I'll go first," Jim whispered. "You stay here until I make sure he's gone."

"No." I tightened my hold on his belt and we continued on together. When we reached the entrance and peered out, I saw nothing but two gray lizards chasing each other on the fallen timbers in the blessed sunshine.

We pushed our way through the brush, getting plenty of scratches. When we got to my pack, Jim took the gun out and checked the safety, then held it out.

"You can keep it if you want," I said.

Okay." He stuck it in his belt and shrugged off his pack. After we divided the nuggets, we hoisted the heavy packs onto our backs, Jim took the gun out, and we cautiously set off.

We saw no one, heard nothing for a long time: no voices, no footsteps. I was beginning to relax just a little bit as we started down the last mountain and was about to suggest we stop and rest a minute when the silence was broken by a loud *boom!* in the distance ahead, followed immediately by another *boom!*

I'd dived under a bush in two seconds flat, Jim right behind me. When I could hear again over my thudding heart, which seemed to have moved up into my head, there was silence again. A breeze in the trees, no birds.

"Came from over near the cemetery, I'd guess," Jim murmured softly. "I want to have a look. Stay here."

"No," I said, more firmly than I felt. "You're not going without me, but Jim—if it's the killer—"

"We'll be careful."

So we made our way slowly, staying mostly behind the cover of trees and brush at the edge of the trail. Maybe it was just a hunter, I thought. It's deer season, isn't it? Maybe we won't find anything, maybe it's just a big waste, feeling so scared. We reached the place I'd seen Frank Ullrich and Robby. Jim, ahead of me, held his hand back, signaling to stop. I waited. Finally, he moved ahead again, very, very slowly, not making a sound. I followed.

He stopped where the trail bent to the left just before the cemetery, and when I caught up to him and peered out through the bushes, I saw a dark bundle of rags that hadn't been there before, lying across the trail. We hurried over. Dark jeans and . . . oh, God. I hastily looked away but the afterimage burned in my brain, a face beneath a mass of sticky looking red. *Scalped,* my brain shrieked, *scalped!* I could feel the hair on my own head rise up. I looked again and realized it was the Chinese man. At first I thought he was still alive, looking at us with that terrified look of a wounded animal that knows he's had it. Jim had knelt down, was trying to do something about the bloody hole in the man's chest, but suddenly I knew it was useless. The eyes were blank, the eyes of a dead man.

Tears came, ran down my face. I felt in that moment the sadness of all those thousands of Chinese, persecuted, murdered. They'd worked so hard—what had the books said?—they worked at jobs no white man would touch, built the railroads ... and it wasn't all that different, in spirit, the way I'd been to him at the Rainbow. Snarl, snarl, answer my questions. But I hadn't *meant* it; it was strategy. Did that make it better? In a good cause, et cetera? Probably just what the robber barons said, over cigars. ...

Jim leaned over and closed the man's eyes, then stood. "Nothing we can do for him. Poor bastard."

We made our way through the cemetery, still cautious but seeing no one. We got into the car; Jim drove home. I felt so tired I almost hated being jumped on by my happy Diana, but I made an effort not to be so grumpy.

I sank down into one of the rocking chairs. In a couple of minutes Jim came out with two tall glasses of water and some sweetrolls. I drank thirstily, wolfed them down. Jim said, "I'll call the sheriff."

"Yes," I said. But neither of us moved. A small, blue bird flew down, hopped along the porch railing. Diana watched, unmoving but at full attention.

Was Jim by any chance thinking what I was thinking? "Uh, Jim," I said. "Don't you think it seems a kind of a pity ..."

"For the sheriff to get all that gold? Or the Forest Service, more likely."

"Especially since the poor Chinese man is dead, anyway. We don't have to mention the mine, do we?"

"Of course, the main thing is to catch that killer."

"Maybe we could go back, stake the place out. Well-armed, this time."

"I don't like the idea of you going back there. And that gold won't be worth a damn cent to us if we're dead."

"But think how much it'd be worth to, say, the Sierra Club, Greenpeace, Earth First, Save the Bay, the Karuk tribe. And a house for Mimi. It's not that I'm greedy for *me*. What would you do with it?"

His eyes lit up just thinking about it. "Well, the tribe. If we had a nice fat legal fund, we could do a lot more about the Forest Service around here, for one thing. And we could maybe buy some of our land back. But I don't want you going up there again."

"Both of us or nothing," I said in a hard and determined voice.

He grimaced; he could see I meant it. "We also need to consider . . . if the government nailed us on it. Might mean prison, you think of that?"

"Didn't you tell me the treaties the whites made with the Indians, the congressmen saw to it the treaties weren't ratified, so the Indians were cheated out of that land too? Probably the mine's on land that really belongs to the Indians, anyway. Plus, if those government scumbags cared anything about *America*, instead of grabbing everything they can, lining their own pockets, shit, this wouldn't be necessary. All these places would already be protected, for the future 'Americans' they're always mouthing off about so hypocritically. If they minded the idea at all of a world without trees or a beach to go to for everybody's children, if they cared at all . . ." I paused to catch my breath.

"Now, now," Jim said, "now, now. Okay. I agree, in principle. If we can figure out a way the gold goes to the tribe, the environmental groups, back to the land—without putting our own asses in a sling—I'll go for it."

"I guess I do get a little wound up sometimes," I said. "We should try to find that Chinese man's family and see they get some of it, too."

He laughed, reached over and took my hand. "That's two of the things I like about you most," he said, "your passionate nature and your sense of fairness. But why don't you go and take a nice hot bath while I think about this whole thing?"

We wouldn't be criminals, I thought as I lay in the marvelous hot water; we wouldn't be criminals if we kept the gold but gave most of it away. No more than Robin Hood was. He'd always been my favorite historical character. Though there are people, I know, stuffy people, who say he never existed at all.

TWENTY-TWO

"**S**heriff's out of town, so I'm in charge on this. Deputy Sam Hill. We found the body all right, just where you said. How did you happen to come across the deceased?"

It was the same man I'd talked to after the Halloween party—had that only been a week or so ago? It seemed like years. He'd arrived about an hour after Jim called, and we were all sitting out on the porch with cups of coffee and tea. Jim answered with our prepared story, that we'd been out walking, just looking around, found the body on our way back. I could almost see the sequence of thoughts behind the deputy's small blue eyes, the freckled forehead: Went out walking where they know there's been all these killings? Not likely ... maybe *they* killed him. ...

I hastened to add, "I've known the mother of the girl hiker who was attacked for a long time. I did some private inquiry work before coming up here, and she asked me to look around, see if I could find any, ah, clues."

226

"You know the girl's mother?" he repeated, as if he didn't believe me.

"That's right, from San Francisco, years ago. Hallie Stephens. I got in touch when I realized it was her daughter, Sally, in the coma."

He nodded slowly, still looking dubious.

"So that's how I happened to go and see this Chinese man," I continued.

"The deceased? You talked to the deceased?"

"That's right. I talked to him in his cabin at the Rainbow. Asked what he was doing around here so long, what was he doing walking around all the time in the mountains— several different people had reported seeing him—and that's about it, I'm afraid. He said his name was Chan Leong and he gave me an address in Hong Kong." I handed what I'd written down to the deputy, the address and the date I'd seen the man. "He claimed to be just a tourist."

We made camp behind a screen of brush that gave a clear view of the path coming down from the cliff face. We'd come a back way Jim knew, to avoid the sheriff's people, who would still be searching the trail near where the body had been. Jim had an AK-47 he'd gotten from somewhere in a hurry; I had Bessie's shotgun and my revolver. We also had trail mix, cheese, nuts, oranges, pills to kill the *Giardia lamblia* in the water—enough for three days. We'd been there most of the day now, but no one had come.

The night before we'd talked a lot of logistics. We didn't have a definite plan yet, but Jim thought it might be possible to route the gold through the Karuk tribal council somehow. The tribe already had a relationship with most of the environmental groups because they'd gone to court with them as coplaintiffs in a lot of cases against the Forest Service.

With only another hour of daylight left I'd stayed at camp, covering the trail down from the cliff while Jim went off to the mine. We didn't think the killer would be coming this late. It was almost dark when Jim got back and sat down beside me, breathing heavily.

"No sign of anyone. That big nugget I left with the little one balanced on top—they're still in the same place. I don't think he's been back."

"Good." I sighed with relief, although a large part of the purpose of our being here was in hopes he *would* come back and we could capture him. "Move over a little, will you? I want to lean back on your shoulder. Right . . . there."

It was about seven, a softness darkening all the edges of the strangely warm autumn evening. Birds were singing, the stars beginning to come out. We ate some cheese and crackers, sitting companionably side by side. Jim took my hand, absentmindedly poking with his free hand at some lichen on a low rock. "Funny thing, this stuff. The mountains up there that look so permanent, they're pretty young really, took shape only two or three million years ago. But these rocks now, these rocks that make up the mountains, they were here a couple hundred million years ago, around the time of the dinosaurs. And this lichen"—he brushed our locked hands across a patch of rusty yellow—"it's descended from ancestors even older than the two-hundred-million-year-old rocks it grows on—which makes it at least a hundred times older than those big permanent mountains out there. It's the way things like that bend my mind around that I like about biology, natural history."

We sat chatting about interesting things armed to the teeth, pretending life was still ordinary. Jim yawned, let go of my hand, and slid his arm behind me.

As we lay in the hot midday shade of the concealing bushes, one of us always keeping an eye on the trail, I asked, "Once you get the degree, you'd work in this area?"

"Don't know. . . . Most of the jobs around here are with the Forest Service; I wouldn't work for them. Anyway, I've a yen to go down to the Tropics. I have this strange longing to see the quetzal, maybe work in the cloud forest. . . ."

"You *do*?" My eyes left the trail, swept his face, which was contemplative, smiling. This man kept surprising me. "I'm hoping to go to Nicaragua again this summer, and Guatemala—the quetzal's their national bird. If we get this killer locked up or—or killed, if it has to be that way—why don't you come, too?"

"I don't think there're many quetzals left now in Guatemala. I wouldn't mind going to Costa Rica, though. Maybe I will. Now that I'm not married anymore, or soon won't be, anything seems possible.

"You're going ahead with the divorce, then?"

"You think I'd be here with you if I weren't?"

"I didn't know. I hoped not, but . . ."

"Anything's possible?"

"Something like that."

He pulled me closer.

The third night, and no one had come. Jim had to be in Eureka the next day, couldn't put it off. We'd eaten our meager dinner, gone off to pee, were settling down for the night. It seemed so unlikely the killer would come at night, we'd almost decided to leave, then changed our minds.

"I know a real good love charm," Jim murmured, leaning over and kissing my eyes, my neck. "Absolutely foolproof. You interested in that?"

"Mmmm—tempting. But . . . I guess not. Seems a little unfair to the poor man involved. And then, I'd always know that it was the charm and not me he really cared for. Anyway, I have everything I need, at the moment. . . . Birds and stars," I said softly, unbuttoning his shirt, "all at once, together. And—and you, as well."

The stars were white in an indigo sky over Jim's shoulder and I'd never seen so many in any sky anywhere, ever before. The air smelled of fir trees and mountains, of stars and of Jim. We'd spread the sleeping bag on the thick pine needles, and small objects kept poking into my back and arms and legs no matter how I rearranged myself. But I didn't really care or even notice them very much.

Later the moon rose over the tops of the black trees, a moon just off full, and bleached out the stars. I could almost see Jane and Jed again, hovering at the edge of the trail to the mine, smiling, sharing my happiness. I fell asleep, and the day hurried off to join all those others, stacked up in that dusty corner somewhere.

Nothing else happened; we saw no one. When we got home early the next morning, Jim left right away for the coast. I made a huge breakfast, feeling starved. I got out Aunt Bessie's Chinese pamphlet, reading as I ate. It said the first Chinese arrived from Hong Kong in 1848, two men and one woman. The numbers increased dramatically every month, most coming on the credit-ticket system. In San Francisco they were issued clean clothes and money to buy boots, supplies, and shovels, then sent to a mining site. The sponsoring company kept back their salaries until they'd paid back the forty-dollar passage and cost of supplies. Twenty or thirty Chinese inhabited cabins "so small that a couple of Americans wouldn't be able to breathe in it."

They stuck together with other Chinese, ate food often brought from China, and the Americans who were already here felt mystified, irritated, and threatened. By 1865, there was widespread agitation: "These Chinese must go!" Samuel Bowles noted in his account of traveling between the Mississippi River and the Pacific Ocean in 1869:

> Terrible are some of the cases of robbery and wanton maiming and murder reported from the mining districts. They had been wantonly assaulted and shot down or stabbed by bad men, as sportsmen would surprise and shoot their game in the woods.

Even so, by 1870 they were the largest single ethnic group working the California gold fields, and one-fifth of all the labor in California. There used to be Chinese fishing villages from Baja California to Oregon. The violence intensified, culminating in the "Driving Out," when white mobs burned and plundered Chinese communities. There were major massacres in California, Wyoming, and Oregon in the 1880s and many of the Chinese still remaining fled back to China. The Chinese Exclusion Act of 1882 stopped the flow of Chinese entering the country.

I thought the dead man must be a descendant of one of those driven-out miners. Who'd been in such a hurry he'd not been able to get back to the mine and dig up his hidden nuggets. But it was an enormous stash. Had perhaps all the Chinese in the area gathered together, put their gold there, then fled for their lives?

And one of them had passed down the secret to his family in China, until it came to the one who'd come after the gold. Leong, he'd said. But he hadn't known exactly where it was. Say he'd finally found the place, sometime before the day Jim and I were there. But the killer must have found it a long time ago, considered it his. Say he'd seen the Chinese man go in but not us, followed and talked to him down there. Maybe he'd convinced the Chinese man they could share the gold, and the victim had walked back out, to the place he'd been shot.

I called my office. O'Reagan was out, but Harold said he thought they had something on my inquiry. He went away and came back to say there was no Chan Leong or anyone else at the Hong Kong address—there was no such address. Shit. I really wanted some of that gold to go to his family.

I called Hallie. I didn't tell her any of the details but said Jim and I had had some luck and could well be on to something, maybe closing in.

"Oh, Maggie—that's the best news I've had except for Sally coming out of the coma! I'd almost gotten myself resigned to our living in hiding for the rest of our lives. . . . She doesn't remember anything about the killer, though. You have some idea who it is, then?"

"Not exactly—we've found a place up in the mountains where he goes. We had to come back down but we'll go up again tomorrow. Don't worry, we're well armed. I'll let you know as soon as I know anything. I hope it'll all be over soon, then I can come. I want to see Sally so much. How is she?"

"Better and better, every day in every way. She really is. She's gained ten pounds and she seems to be accepting it about Bobby, wants to get on with her life. She's worried about all the school she's missed but they've done a lot of tests now. There's no brain damage, thank God. She wants to see you too. Come down as soon as you can, okay?"

I took a long nap and then went to the post office. O'Reagan's promised letter with information on at least some of the names must surely be there by now. Frank Ullrich was on the porch, opening mail. I looked at him carefully, but if he'd been the other man at the mine five days before, there was nothing to show it now.

"Hello there, young lady," he greeted me, "how's the world treating you?"

"Fine, thanks, Frank. How're you?"

"Got more time than money. Got more time than money, I'm afraid." He began going through the pile of papers he'd taken from his box, which looked like mostly bills and junk mail, and I went inside.

Elvira said excitedly, "Do you know about Bill? He got bit by a rattler, nearly died? He's in the hospital in Yreka!"

"Oh, no," I said. "Is he going to be all right?"

She nodded, her round brown eyes excited. "But it was real close there for a while. He was out looking for that Bigfoot; rattler got him in the leg."

"The poor guy—how long will he be in the hospital?"

"Just a day or two, I think. Oh, he was pretty bad though."

"I'll try to go see him. Can you think of anything he'd like, that I could take? Are any of his books here?"

She rummaged around under the counter and handed over a large volume about dinosaurs. "You have some mail, too."

At last. She gave me two letters and one was from O'Reagan, but it was thin. I opened it and skimmed through hurriedly but to my disappointment, it was all negative. In Eureka, where Frank Ullrich had lived, eight long-dead migrant workers had been found in shallow graves in a wooded area north of town the month before, all garroted and none scalped. They were thought to have been killed over a period of time extending back three or four years to about a year ago. The Bellingham shootings that Louise Redmond had told me about were the only crimes of that sort in the area where the Geralds had lived. O'Reagan had no details yet but would get them. Nothing similar to the murders had occurred in Tulelake or in the Sacramento area, so nothing implicated Jonathan Farrell. Apart from the most recent crimes, nothing was reported in this area "except your ordinary bar and domestic stabbings and shootings." Robby Rowe didn't seem to fit in, therefore. There'd been many bizarre murders in the L.A./Anaheim/San Diego areas—where Bill and the three construction guys came from—but none involved scalping or anything similar.

"Didn't seem to me," O'Reagan wrote, "that any of them had the feel of the killings up there. I checked back five years, I thought that should be plenty. On Randall Rowe—I talked to Carlton. They claim he's an ordinary salesman headquartered in Guatemala City, but they were unwilling to provide an address or say anything about where he worked before. I have someone working on that. Nothing on the military backgrounds yet, but I'll get it to you as soon as I have anything. Meanwhile, good luck, and be careful."

A scrawled "Love POR" was at the bottom. And that was it. Damn. I'd been hoping for a lot from my "place previously lived" idea—similar crimes, maybe even scalpings. I felt terribly disappointed. But life keeps urging me to grow up. Anyway, now we had a good chance to catch the man red-handed, so to speak, coming to the mine. Language is so strange, our use and perception of it. Only now, for the first time I suddenly understood that term. Red-handed. Blood covered, in other words.

A small, cheap envelope with no return address had writing I didn't recognize. I opened it and looked at the signature—Hank. Oh, good. Some news of Mimi at last.

"Dear Maggie," I read. "Plans have changed—Clara got real bad and went to a rehab place. Maybe you'll be surprised after what I said about not liking my friend to talk about AA. I visited her a few times and went to some of the meetings there they have for family. Well, I decided to check in myself! The place is called the Redwoods Program. Don't have the address offhand but it's in the book. Lillian and Hermina went to stay with a family friend, Joe Hornaday. Phone's 683-9261. Maybe you could check on them. Thing is, Lillian wanted to go back up to the cabin. I tried to make her realize about Hermina being in danger, but not sure I succeeded. Maybe you could call them at Joe's, and if they did leave, maybe you could go over and see if they're there, convince her not to stay. Just till I get out, that's in a couple weeks, then we can all go back to the cabin if Lillian wants to, tell her. Well that's all I guess. Hope you're doing okay. This place is not too bad. Not like I thought it'd be. Well I'll tell you all about it when I see you. Sincerely, Hank."

The writing was small and shaky. He hadn't said how long they'd been there. How long had Lillian been itching to get back to the cabin?

TWENTY-THREE

THERE WAS AN ACRID, UNPLEASANT SMELL IN THE AIR AS I turned up the last steep switchback to Mimi's. Diana raced ahead, barking excitedly, sensing trouble as the smell grew stronger. I began to run.

When I reached the clearing I saw the cabin burning, a lot of Forest Service men in their green uniforms, and several of their trucks and a car or two. Then I saw Lillian Goss. She was on the far side, standing very still, watching her house burn. Mimi was holding her hand, watching also, with a completely expressionless face. Prince and Little Dog were sort of cowering behind them.

The cabin was about half-gone and various belongings—I recognized the wood box Mimi kept her clothes in, the big living room chairs, and there were pots and pans and dishes and piles of bedding—were stacked haphazardly at the edge of the clearing. I rushed over.

"Can't anyone do anything?"

Lillian turned and looked at me dully; she looked terrible. Her face was a kind of putty color and she was breathing in short, jerky gasps.

"They made the fire," Mimi screamed, glaring at the tall Forest Service man standing nearest, who I suddenly realized was Robert Gerald.

I turned to him furiously. "You really came up here and

made them move all their things outside and—and *set fire* to their *house*?"

"*We* moved their things out, and—you're the woman who came to the hearing. What are you doing here, anyway?"

"I'm a friend of theirs. Who are you to be doing this?"

"Robert Gerald," he said formally, as if we'd not met at the hearing, "chief ranger at the United States Forest Service station in Oak Knoll. In charge of this removal."

"*Removal!*"

"The old woman had plenty of warning," he said angrily. "She was informed of the decision to terminate the cabin— it's on National Forest land; she doesn't own it—she was informed over a year ago. And she has refused to leave. So, of course, we had no alternative but to come up here and get them out. I don't know why they didn't leave like they were supposed to, like they were told to. They knew this would happen."

"Maybe they didn't understand how the government could come destroy their home when they've lived on this land so many years before there even *were* any National Forests or 'government' or—or people who … *work* for them." This last I said with scathing contempt; I couldn't control it.

"We're just doing our job," he said stiffly, "as mandated by the United States Congress. We can't have people freeloading on the National Forests. Okay! Get back to work over there!"

Lillian gave a gasp and then a soft moan and fell forward, clutching her chest. Mimi knelt down and took one of her hands, crying, "Granny, Granny, oh, what is it, Granny?"

I squatted down and turned Lillian over, put my head to her chest, cursing that I'd never gotten around to learning CPR. I couldn't hear any heartbeat but the fire was making a lot of noise. I called out loudly, panicked, "Anybody know CPR? There's a heart attack over here. Anyone know CPR?"

A huge ranger with long black hair in a ponytail rushed over and flipped Lillian onto her stomach. He gave a hard jolt to her back with his fist, then flipped her over again and, with one hand over the other, pressed down on her chest several times in a regular rhythm. Mimi was standing with her hand to her mouth, looking horrified.

"They're not hurting her, honey," I said quietly. "That's to help her start breathing good again."

Several of the rangers were standing around now, heads straining forward, anxious expressions, willing help to the one doing CPR. He leaned down and breathed into Lillian's mouth while holding her nostrils pinched closed and then began pressing on her chest again. He did this several times, then looked up and told one of the others to take her pulse as he continued. A young blond guy knelt down and held Lillian's wrist, and everyone was very quiet. But she was breathing now—we could all hear it—raspy and uneven but the sounds of life. After working on her a few more minutes, the big man picked her up and carried her to the back seat of a Forest Service station wagon. I climbed in too and held Lillian's head on my lap. Mimi pushed all three dogs into the back and scrambled in after them.

"Okay, Jack," Gerald called to the man as he turned the car around, "get her to Yreka as fast as you can. I'm sorry this happened, but they should've been out of here and it *wouldn't* have happened!"

Mimi was looking down at her great-grandmother over the back of the seat and crying soundlessly. Lillian was still breathing, if raggedly, and still unconscious. I held on tight as the car streaked around the endless curves, trying to keep her as still as possible. Jack made the one-hour drive in forty minutes.

He pulled up at the emergency entrance with a loud squeal of the brakes, jumped out and picked up Lillian and carried her inside. White-suited attendants put her on a gurney and took her away while Mimi and I were ushered into a small office to give the necessary information for the paperwork.

I doubted Lillian would have private insurance but thought she must be eligible for Medicare. Mimi sat silently while we talked, looking petrified. When we finished, the woman directed us to another part of the hospital, upstairs, where she said we could wait for news. She also said a social worker would be coming to talk with us, since Mimi was a minor and I was not her legal guardian.

Mimi pulled on my hand, wanting to go faster, to get to wherever they had Lillian.

"We won't be able to see her, honey. We'll have to wait for the doctor."

When we got there, I told the nurse at the desk who we were. She said a doctor would be out as soon as possible to let us know what was happening. We sat down. We waited.

"Mimi—that heart attack looked pretty serious, so I imagine your granny will have to stay in the hospital for a while."

"She dying," Mimi said, looking down, "she dying now. I *hate* the piss-firs!"

I hesitated. What to say? "We don't know that yet, honey. She may be fine after the doctors help her. Let's wait and see. But I want you to come stay with me, okay? Hank wrote me he and your mother went into a rehab place in Redding. I'll call them. And you stay with me until they get finished there." I suddenly realized I wasn't expecting Lillian to come out of this.

A young woman in a pink dress and a doctor in white came in, wearing carefully noncommittal faces. He was middle-aged, a bit overweight, with short black hair going gray. He had metal-rimmed glasses. Behind them his gray eyes looked remote. But the woman, young, large breasts pushing out of some silky jersey-type material, a tall but plain blonde with a big smile, was warmth itself.

"Are you the granddaughter?" she asked Mimi gently. "And you're a friend of the family?" she said to me.

We both nodded and the doctor said, his voice low and a little hard to hear, "I'm Dr. Conrad. This is Miss Appleby.

We won't really know anything about Mrs. Goss for an hour or two, maybe longer. Do you want to wait?"

"Of course," I said.

He looked at his watch. "Well ... then ..." he mumbled, "I'll let you know as soon as I know anything." Doctors are in the life-saving business and many of them don't handle it very well when it's not working out. Judging by this man's manner, it didn't look good for Lillian. Oh, God. Wouldn't it ever stop?

The young woman sat down on a chair opposite.

"I'm the family social worker here," she said, "Mary Appleby. This little girl lives with her grandmother?"

"Yes—Mrs. Goss is her great-grandmother. Usually Hermina's mother lives there, too, and her mother's boyfriend. Clara Goss and Hank Preston. They should be notified. I just got a letter from him today saying they've both gone into an alcohol rehab place in Redding—the Redwoods Program? Can you have someone there talk to them, break the news and maybe get them up here? Mimi can stay with me meanwhile. Or if they're not ready to leave the program yet, I'll keep Mimi until they're finished. Or until Mrs. Goss is able to take over again."

The social worker nodded. "Give me your phone number so I can let you know what I find out in case I don't reach them before you leave here."

"I thought I'd call them myself now."

She shook her head. "They have pretty tight schedules at that place. You wouldn't be able to get through to them at this time of day. But as an official of the hospital, more or less, I'll be able to talk to them. I'll go try now. And don't worry, honey. The doctors are doing everything they can."

Mimi's face was squeezed tight and she was trying hard not to cry. She didn't acknowledge the social worker's encouragement, probably would have burst into tears if she'd tried to talk. I put my arm around her, pulled her close.

"Cry if you want to, Mimi. This is terrible. Anybody would want to cry."

But she shook her head and kept back the tears. Maybe

if we did something. It was horrible just sitting here choking back tears and waiting for what I was afraid was going to be very bad news. Maybe we should go out and get a hamburger or something. I didn't feel like eating, which didn't matter, but probably Mimi didn't, either. Then I remembered Bill Dawson. He was here. We'd go see him. That would give Mimi maybe a slight distraction. And I wanted to see poor Bill.

He lay with his eyes closed on a bed in a medium-sized room with several other patients. Two of the beds had elderly men asleep in them. One man was bald and one had wispy white hair. Both had their mouths open, snoring gently. One of them didn't have any teeth. This was an old hospital and it looked it, in this section. Dingy somehow, everything a little worn and shabby. It smelled of old age and sickness. We walked over to the bed and Bill opened his eyes and looked at me, then at Mimi. He looked almost frightened.

"Maggie!" he cried. "What—"

"Sorry, I didn't mean to startle you," I said softly.

He gave a shaky grin. "Aw, I'm all upset from that damn rattler."

"Elvira told me you were here. How are you feeling, or is that a dumb question?"

"Well, I tell you," he said, smiling, looking more his old self, sitting partway up, "I feel better than I did. Thought I'd die for sure, oh Lord. Maggie, you just can't imagine how it feels, all that poison running around loose inside you. Who's this little girl?"

"Sorry," I said. "This is Mimi—this is Bill."

She was looking at him, round-eyed and impressed to see the survivor of a rattlesnake bite. "My granny say . . ." she began, then swallowed and closed her eyes. She opened them and looked at him again, "Lotta people get bit by a rattler, they die pretty quick."

Bill nodded solemnly. "That's right, but I'm too tough to kill, I guess. I was over there by Tomkins Creek. A Bigfoot print was spotted there not so long ago, and I wanted to check it out." He shrugged. "Usually I'm pretty careful about rattlers, but I saw what looked like a giant footprint right by the creek, just the other side of an old rotted-out log. I jumped over and that's when the bastard—excuse me, little girl—that's when he got me."

"And was it a footprint?"

"Don't know for sure. Looked like one, but I knew right away I was in big trouble, so far back to town. I didn't think about that print anymore. I took it real, real slow so the poison wouldn't spread so much, but I guess it spread pretty good, anyway. Now they're still trying to clean me out somehow."

"I meant to bring one of your books, that big one on dinosaurs, but then everything got too—rushed. I'm sorry. If I can get back up, I'll bring it."

"Now that would be a real kindness, Maggie. A real kindness. But don't worry about it—I'm getting out tomorrow or the next day."

"I'm sorry." The doctor shook his dark head, looked down at his feet. Then he looked up again, at me; he wouldn't look at Mimi. He seemed tired almost to death himself, defeated. "Her heart was in bad shape. We just couldn't save her. I'm sorry." He dropped his gaze and turned away. The social worker sat down on the chair opposite.

I looked at Mimi. She'd understood, all right. Her face was frozen, immobile, holding back a hundred thousand tears, a scream. I took her hand. "I'm so sorry, Mimi. I know how much you loved Lillian. And she loved you so much. I love you too, and I'll help all I can."

Mimi looked back at me, unblinking, silent.

The social worker said, "They tried, honey. I'm so sorry she didn't make it. Do you go to church?"

Mimi looked at her but didn't respond.

"I just ask because sometimes it's helpful at a time like this if you have a church you go to."

Mimi still didn't say anything.

"She lives pretty far out in the country," I said. "I doubt they went to church."

"Well . . ." She raised her eyebrows in a way that made her face look sad but resigned. "I have a call in to her mother and Mr. Preston, but they've all gone on a field trip somewhere, I'm afraid. I won't be able to talk to them until late this afternoon, maybe early evening. I'll still be on. I'll call you after I talk to them. Maybe you'd step over to the desk with me for a minute, Mrs. Elliott?"

When we got there she asked whether I wanted the addresses of a few funeral homes. "Since the little girl's mother can't be reached right away, maybe won't be in any shape to . . . or who would be making the arrangements?"

"I'll start on it, I guess. Thanks."

*There are always dances going on in
heaven, and plenty of hunting and
fishing, with no game laws or canneries
down river to interfere with you. It
seems well to know as little of the bad
trail as possible, but at one place you
have to pass through a burning forest,
and Luther says the hot stones burn
your feet terrible.*
—MARY ELLICOTT ARNOLD AND MABEL REED,
IN THE LAND OF THE GRASSHOPPER SONG

TWENTY-FOUR

IT WAS COMPLETELY DARK WHEN WE CAME OUT OF THE HOSPITAL. A lot of stars, no moon yet. Mimi sat rigid and silent all the way home. When Jack let us off back in Scott Bar, he said, his voice strained and awkward, "I sure feel bad this happened. I sure am sorry."

"Thanks for all your help," I said. "You did your best."

We went inside. I got out sheets and asked Mimi to help me make up the bed in the spare room. Then the phone rang; it was the social worker.

"I'm afraid the mother won't be able to take over the child's care immediately—it's a twenty-eight-day program and they have a couple of weeks left. Since her grandmother's already died so she can't see her, they really don't want her to leave yet, except to go to the funeral. The county could arrange for a foster home in the interim—"

"I definitely want to keep Mimi until her mother and the boyfriend—he's very good with Mimi; I know him—can take her," I interrupted.

"Oh, I was hoping you might say that. Her mother said it would be fine with her, if you really don't mind. I gave her your number and she should be calling you any time now."

I went back to the bedroom and told Mimi what the so-cial worker had said. She didn't respond, really, just contin-ued to look miserable. Then I explained about beating pil-lows. That it wasn't good to hold in a lot of unhappy feelings but that sometimes it wasn't so easy to let them out, either. I wanted her to start hitting the pillow as hard as she could. She should try to yell, too. She shook her head and pulled back. She didn't want to. But I insisted and she hit down at the big feather pillow halfheartedly, then a little harder, and finally worked up to a good strong rage, screaming with the heavy blows.

"I hate the piss-firs!" she yelled, over and over.

After she'd worn herself out, I held her as she cried and cried and cried.

"I *hate* the piss-firs," she said, sobbing.

"I know. But honey, everybody dies. It was partly their fault—but not totally. She did have a bad heart, you know that." I wanted Mimi to get her feelings out, feel however she felt. But I didn't want her poisoned with hatred for the rest of her life.

She didn't acknowledge what I'd said, but finally she'd cried as many tears as she had in her, for the present. I gently laid her back on the bed and soon she was asleep.

It was Hank who called. We talked a little about what had happened and then he asked, "How's the kid taking it?"

"Pretty hard—just what you'd expect, they were so close. But she's as fine here as she'd be anywhere, till you two get through down there. Hey, I'm so glad you've done this, you and Clara. I went through it myself. It wasn't easy, but now I wouldn't trade anything for it. How you doing?"

"The first week was bad, but I'm more or less okay now, I guess. And Clara—oh, you should see the change in Clara. She's had a real hard time, harder than me, but she's getting a hold on things now. She wants to talk to you—here."

The voice I'd never heard in the cabin was round and clear, like a beautiful old handmade bell. "Maggie. You sure you don't mind keeping Hermina?"

"I'm *glad* to have her. For as long as you need, I mean it. And I'm so sorry about your grandmother." I told her about the arrangements I'd made for the funeral so far. "She said, one time I came to the cabin—she said when she died, she wanted to be buried the Indian way. Is there somebody I could call who'd know what to do?"

"That's right. She was real traditional; she would want that. If you could call Bella Merton—she's in Etna. She'll know. It'll be listed under Marvin Merton."

Mimi and I were sitting out on the porch the next morning when the sky blue pickup came up the drive.

"That's Jim," I told her, "a very good friend of mine you haven't met yet. How about you go inside and wash your hands? After I talk to him a minute, we can do something about lunch."

She went inside obediently but looked back curiously. I ran toward him, along with all three dogs, who seemed as happy to see him as I was. He put his arms around me and kissed me thoroughly. Finally, I pulled away and said breathlessly, "That was Mimi—she's going to stay with me a couple of weeks the Forest Service burned down their cabin her great-grandmother had a heart attack—"

"Whoa," he said, looking concerned, "slow down. The Forest Service burned down their cabin and her great-grandmother had a heart attack? Where is she?"

"We took her to the hospital in Yreka but she—oh Jim, she—she *died.*"

"Oh *shit.*" He pulled me closer, put his hand on the back of my head and held it tightly against his shoulder. "I'm sorry."

"I'm all clean, Maggie," Mimi interrupted, calling from the front door. "You comin'?"

I took Jim's hand and we climbed the steps to the porch, where I introduced them.

"Those are fine-looking dogs," he said to her. "They yours?"

"Yes," Mimi said, "well, Diana's not mine but the other two are."

"What do you call them?"

"Uh . . . this one's Prince, and that's Little Dog."

"Pretty good names," he said, nodding thoughtfully. "How about helping me bring some things inside while Maggie makes us some lemonade?"

"Sure," she said shyly, glad to be of use. They walked back to the truck while I went to the kitchen and heated water to dissolve the sugar. A couple of minutes later they came in with several large grocery bags. Jim handed me a package of lemons, then got Mimi to help him set the table on the porch and carried a third chair out while I made a salad.

Finally we had everything on the table and began helping ourselves. Jim ate a lot, Mimi only a little, and I was medium. We all drank a lot of lemonade, though, it was a hot day. When we'd finished, I yawned and said, "I want a nap. You too, Mimi—later we can go for a walk with the dogs."

After I had Mimi stashed away with her door closed I went to my room, where Jim was lying on his back, his shirt off, his hands clasped behind his head. I closed the door and unbuttoned my blouse, slipped it off and stepped out of my shorts, walked over to the bed. Jim reached up and I knelt down beside him and rested my chin on his chest as his arms came around me.

"Look," he said, "now that you have Mimi here, you won't be able to go back up to the mine with me. I've been thinking about that. I'll draft Ruther to help. With all that's happened, I haven't told you—he and Lucy are leaving, going up to Spokane. Ruther has an army buddy there and the sheriff's helping them get new names and new identities to use till they find Farrell. Fixing that up will all take a little time, though, so he'll be here a while yet. I talked to George Demmings—he's the head of the tribal council. We still have to work out some of the details, but we've agreed in principle—Ruther'll stake a claim up there for the tribe. It's a nonprofit entity, see. Probably we'll do a bunch more claims, too, just to confuse the issue. Ruther's done some mining, so he knows how. Then the tribe'll say they found the gold on their claim, or several of them. Meanwhile, Ruther and I will keep the place staked out to grab the killer when he shows up. How does that sound?"

"It sounds like a terrific plan except," I said anxiously, "like you said, the gold's not worth dying for. But that *is* the only likely way to catch him. . . . Sally can't stay hidden forever . . . I wish I could be up there with you, though. Also—I really want to see at least half that money go to Greenpeace and a few others. Were you thinking the tribe would take all of it?"

"No, no, what we thought was maybe two-thirds would go to the groups, directly back to the land, you might say. The tribe will donate it to them. We still have to work out the details, as I said."

"Wonderful. My only other question is, can the tribe also buy Mimi a house somehow?"

"We'll work it out. Did you find out anything about the Chinese man?"

I shook my head, swiveling my chin on Jim's lovely warm chest. "It was a fake name, fake address, so I don't see how we can trace him. If they ever *do* find out who he was, though—some of the money could be put aside for his family."

"Sure," he said, running his fingers up my arm, across my lips, "but let's forget about all that now. Let's make love very quietly so we don't freak out the kid."

Jim woke me up to say O'Reagan was on the phone.

"Finally got something more than tidbits," he said. "The military stuff."

I was still half-asleep but the news gave me a pleasant jolt, woke me up. Things were starting to fall into place at last. And if I could track the killer down from a paper trail, then Jim and Ruther wouldn't have to keep putting themselves in so much danger at the mine. O'Reagan was saying, ". . . goes, you ready?"

"Wait," I said, grabbing a pencil, finding a piece of paper that wasn't written on. "Okay. Shoot."

"First, on Gerald: Bellingham reported three people killed in the woods with a shotgun like you said, a year and a half ago. But not scalped or mutilated in any other way and not a .30-.30. Never solved, thought to be drug-connected. His military service record is still to come. I've tried to light a fire under those people, but they have thick behinds."

"Gerald sounds like a good possibility, don't you think?"

"Don't know. . . . We can tell better when we get the military sheet. Frank Ullrich spent an undistinguished two years in the army at a desk job in San Antonio, Texas, twenty-two years ago. No opportunities to learn about bombs or even electrical wiring; there was no commando or guerrilla tie-in. No record of any deaths involving scalping in the area during the time he was there, no other murders with any kind of feel like the ones up there."

I wrote fast, making the weird abbreviations I'd developed years before for art history notes in a darkened lecture room. "No sim mrds SA," I completed. "Go on; I'm ready."

"Bill Dawson was six years in the marines, worked as a cook. No commando training. Stationed San Diego, Guam. No murders with scalpings or anything similar either place. The post office rated him a very good worker in one of their L.A. branches prior to his transfer to Scott Bar about a year ago."

"Poor guy was bitten by a rattlesnake," I said. "He's been in the hospital but he's recovering."

"I'm not surprised—they're all over the place up there. Think I've seen one every time I've been up."

"I've never seen even one."

"Anyway, Jonathan Farrell was two years in the navy, in minor trouble the whole time—for fighting, bar-fight-type stuff. Eventually he picked on a captain and barely missed a dishonorable discharge. He was stationed in the Philippines. Record doesn't show, what I have so far, but that location might have included training and maybe experience in guerrilla warfare, including explosives."

"That sounds promising. Although he's never seemed the type to me ... for these particular murders."

"Why not?"

"Well ... he seems to get into personal confrontations—even the way he used to pick on migrants came from strong feelings. And it seems pretty clear now this all has to do with money." I told him about the old mine and the nuggets, about finding the Chinese man and staking the place out.

He whistled. "Sounds like you're really getting somewhere. Please try to remember what I said about being careful and not doing anything alone, okay? I have a little more. Robert Lucas Rowe was also navy, stationed in the Philippines but quite a few years before Farrell. Possible guerrilla training but not yet confirmed. No military record yet on Randall Rowe. I told you I got confirmation from Carlton that he's a salesman based in Guatemala but nothing more. They're damn stingy with information. I'm working on that. And that's it."

After we hung up I started thinking about how I could approach Gerald—was there any chance Robby Rowe might get me copies of time sheets, if there were such things, from his office? See if Gerald had been away at significant times, like when the hospital was bombed. . . .

After dinner, in a twilight noisy with the many birds flying about, Jim told Mimi some of the old Karuk stories, which, he said generously, were from the Shastas, too.

"Here's one about the river: A weird thing came up here from the south, because they didn't have any water down there, and no salmon, either. This weird being started on his journey so he'd get here during fishing season. When he got up here, he found out there was a big pond hidden real carefully in this big sweat house, filled with fish."

"What's a sweat house?"

"You don't—" Jim looked at her quizzically, one Indian

to another. "A sweat house is a little building Indians make out of logs with deerskin or something like that stretched across, for walls and the top. They make a fire in there and sit around it and it gets real, real hot, so they sweat. It's how Indians keep from getting sick. The sweat takes the sickness out of their body. If you want to, we'll go to one sometime."

"Oh." Big-eyed, she nodded thoughtfully. "What happen next, in the story?"

"Well, let's see. . . . Weird Being watched the men at that big pond they had hidden, and saw them take out a whole lot of fish. Later on, when the men were all asleep, he thought he'd like to get some fish for himself, so he pulled at the gate that shut the water in, and the water burst out so strong, it broke the dam, and that was the beginning of the Klamath River."

Soon after breakfast we set off south on River Road. After a few miles, Jim turned sharply right up a steep dirt road for about a hundred yards, to a large old log cabin where the first part of the funeral would be. The house was on a pleasant knoll that looked down over the tops of trees to a partial view of the winding silver river.

Mimi and I followed Jim up a shallow flight of worn wooden steps. Inside, an open black casket, not very big, was set up on a table against a window. About fifteen people were seated facing it in metal chairs. The room was rather small but generously decorated with pictures: mountain scenes and pinup girls from old lumber company calendars, as well as three puppies and a kitten playing, and some darling baby bears, both torn from magazines. There was a wood plaque on the wall next to the window, titled INDIAN PRAYER:

> Lord, I pray that I may not
> criticize my neighbor, until
> I have walked a mile in his
> moccasins.

Then I saw Clara and Hank, sitting in the front row with an empty seat between them. I hadn't recognized them at first; they looked almost like different people. Clara was in a dark blue dress, plain but quite lovely on her, stockings, and shiny black high heels. She looked alive now, no longer like a shop dummy—and in pain, purple circles under her eyes. Hank had on a jacket and tie, dark pants. Both jacket and pants were a little tight, quite possibly borrowed. He too looked a lot better, rested, not red-eyed and exhausted.

I pushed Mimi forward. Clara smiled when she saw her, held out her hand, nodded at me. Jim and I sat down in the back row and a woman minister in a dark dress began to speak, mentioning Jesus Christ and resurrection and other Christian things. Mimi didn't cry but sat stolidly at attention.

The minister, a large woman with shining black hair in a bun at the back of her head, spoke about Lillian. As she talked, I thought about what a strong person Lillian had been, what a hard life she'd had. How she'd been doing no one any harm at all, living in the cabin her father had built for her when she married. I felt a surge of hatred for Bob Gerald, for the Forest Service. I remembered from something I'd read somewhere: The evil that you see has always been here; don't get torn up in hatred. . . . How could I help Mimi to be free to have her real feelings but not get torn up in hatred . . . and myself, too. She had to understand somehow that the Forest Service hadn't set out to kill her great-grandmother. Lillian had had a bad heart and might have died soon, anyway. It wasn't purposeful; it was indifference. But was that really much better? Maybe it was worse.

The people in the room were elderly, as they had been at Joey Brown's funeral, but they looked somehow healthier, or sturdier. They all seemed to be sitting very straight, unlike most of the people at that other funeral, who'd stood slumped over, flabby, as if they'd given up at some internal post where it really matters. A thin woman with a deeply wrinkled face and long gray hair twisted into a knot at the back of her head, particularly straight-backed, was weeping softly.

The minister was saying Lillian Goss had been a good, hardworking woman, generous with her friends and neighbors, a woman who could surely expect resurrection and the good life in the hereafter. Then she stepped away.

The weeping gray-haired woman nodded to Clara and Mimi, and they all stood up and went to the casket. A man pushed up the large window in the wall behind it, and then several men lifted the casket and, with some difficulty, passed it outside to other men waiting, who carried it to the back of an ordinary funeral-parlor hearse.

"If a body is carried through a doorway," Jim said softly, "then its spirit will come back and take the other people in the house. We all go to the graveyard now, for the ceremonies Indian way."

Scott Bar cemetery again, the second time in less than three months. To say good-bye to a person I'd liked a lot. The burial was in a corner of the old graveyard surrounded by tall trees, with sun filtering through, enclosing a feeling of remoteness in time, of peace.

At the grave the open casket rested on four-by-fours over the yawning hole. Mimi stood near the casket between Clara and Hank, each holding one of her hands. The gray-haired woman, the one who'd been crying earlier at the house, stood with them. I thought it must be Bella Merton, who'd told me she'd been a lifelong friend of Lillian's. An elderly man with a round face held what looked like a long piece of straw; he struck a match and lit it, then passed it rapidly over the body.

"That frees the spirit," Jim whispered. "It goes away in the smoke."

"What's that—" I whispered, too, "is it food burning? Next to the grave?"

"That's so the spirit—well see, when a person dies the spirit flies around for several days, maybe visiting all the places it's ever been, or maybe going into the body of a moth, or, well, eventually it goes down with the body into the earth, to the spirit world. But, so, until the burial, the food is burned so the spirit can get sustenance; a spirit can't eat solid food, but it can inhale the smoke and get it that way."

The round-faced man began sprinkling something into the open coffin.

"What's he doing now?" I asked quietly.

"Those are ashes. He sprinkles those in, and sand, then they put in some money, too, so the spirits she meets will know she's wealthy."

The man stepped back and the coffin was closed. Several other men came up to help lower it into the ground. More sand was scattered on top, and then the gray-haired woman who had been Lillian's friend leaned over and spoke softly down into the grave. Clara joined her, speaking quietly too. Mimi looked on with a worried expression, working hard not to cry. Clara murmured something to her and then Mimi said something into the grave.

"They're talking for the last time with the spirit," Jim said. "It's come forth because of that straw they burned, with the smoke. Afterwards, the spirit goes down the Red Dirt Road, and it's not supposed to look back, so it's important to have this last talk now, before it leaves."

"Where does it go, the Red Dirt Road?"

"Well, at the end of it there's a river, a big river. There's a boat there, with a spirit in it, who takes her across. When she gets to the other side, she goes right into the Deerskin Dance."

I liked that, to think of Lillian free and lithe, young again maybe, dancing. . . . The two women and Mimi stepped back; the men began filling the grave. Clara and Hank came over with Mimi.

Clara said, "I don't know what would have become of the child if you hadn't been there."

"Oh, Clara," I said, taking her hand, "I love Mimi. I'm just so happy to have her. And I'm really glad to see you looking so good. How do you feel?"

"Well, not too bad, tired. Kinda nervous."

I nodded. "I went through what you're going through now. It gets better. It really does. You'll hardly be able to believe it a year from now, how much your life has changed. But ... I'm awfully sorry about Lillian."

She wiped away a tear, nodded. "We go to these meetings," she said. "They talk a lot about acceptance, I'm trying to learn."

Hank touched my arm. "You'll be real careful, won't you, until I can get back up here? You got anything but that revolver?"

"A shotgun," I said. "Don't worry."

Then a man in a suit who'd been kind of hanging back said something to Hank and Clara. They nodded and said good-bye: Clara told Mimi to be good and do what I told her. They went off with the man to a small van with THE REDWOODS stenciled on the side.

As they drove off I wondered how long Lillian's spirit would spend on the Red Dirt Road. Was it a long distance she had to travel before she crossed that river and entered the eternal dance?

Apruan! Essie yelled. *It was a devil all*
right. I could see it plain.
——MARY ELLICOTT ARNOLD AND MABEL REED,
IN THE LAND OF THE GRASSHOPPER SONG

TWENTY-FIVE

WHEN I WOKE UP, FEELING QUITE LICENTIOUS, I REACHED
for Jim but found only an empty place. Damn. He'd gone
back to the mine the day before, right after the funeral. That
space had been empty all night. I sighed, and started thinking about what I needed to do that day. So much had been
happening, I realized I'd never gotten the lists from Seiad
and Horse Creek. I'd pick those up, then try and talk to
some of the men on my master list, my ten most likely.

I heard kitchen sounds, got up, and found Mimi making
coffee. She didn't look too bad. At least her face wasn't all
swollen from crying the way it had been the night before.
I wished she wouldn't drink coffee, but this was hardly the
time to push for diet reform. . . . I'd have to think of someplace safe to put her while I talked to suspects.

It was almost hot out; how could it be November? September and October are the warmest months in San
Francisco, but not so far north, it should be getting cold by
now. Maybe it was the greenhouse effect, all those spray
cans and refrigerators making the ozone hole bigger and the
consequences come sooner than they'd thought. We're such
ostriches, we humans. No wonder, though, descended from
worms. It must come quite naturally, burrowing our heads,
covering our eyes and ears with dark, comforting earth and
ignorance.

Mimi helped fix breakfast and we ate, as usual, on the

255

porch. I kept refilling my glass from a big pitcher of iced mint tea. What to do with Mimi? Who could be trusted? I thought of Lillian's friend Bella Merton, but Etna was too far. I thought of Elvira, but she'd be working, with Bill off.

"Mimi, I have a bunch of things I need to do today. Do you think you could stay here by yourself for a few hours? Stay inside, with the doors locked?"

"Sure, I stay by myself lots of times. Where you goin'?"

"I have to see some people, talk to them. But Mimi—if anyone comes, don't answer the door, just pretend there's no one home. I'll be gone a couple of hours probably."

She looked at me, questioning.

"It's because you saw that man on the trail, that time after the hikers were attacked. Hank and I think he might be the killer—and he might be after you because you saw him. But whoever he is, he doesn't know you're here—so just don't open the door if anyone comes, okay?"

"Okay. Don't worry, I'm not scared."

"But you won't open the door, right?"

Across from the post office, the bulldozers were hard at work on the hideous new bridge to Mill Creek, putting the concrete foundations into the river. How do they get them to stay up, not be washed away before they get them all in place?

Inside, Elvira was busy sorting mail that had just come in, taking out handfuls from two large, heavy U.S. Mail bags on the floor of the little cubbyhole.

"You're looked a little peaked," she said, examining my face more closely. "You all right?"

"I'm fine, thanks. What's the word on Bill? I saw him the other day in the hospital; he didn't look so good."

"Oh, he's back home. He's doin' pretty good, except his trailer's right back of here, you know, and all those machines they got going for that new bridge, how will he get any rest?"

"Well, he must be glad to be home anyway. I'll go see him later, see if he needs anything."

"Did you hear the big news?"

"News?"

"You know Darlene Ullrich, don't you?" I nodded. 'She's run off with a forty-nine-year-old man! Now isn't that terrible? Man old enough to be her grandfather, if you think about it—she's just fifteen. Her Dad's fit to be tied. Nobody knows where they are—they just found this note she left."

"That's awful," I said. "Who was it—anybody I know?"

"I don't know if you know 'im or not, but it's that brother of Robby Rowe's, that one came up here from Central America."

"Uh-oh," I said.

She nodded agreement. "Good-looking fella and she's been wanting to get away from home real bad. I guess she thought this would be an improvement. Frying pan into the fire's what I say. I just hope he'll marry her, that's all."

"But Elvira—if he's wrong for her . . ."

"Yes, times may have changed, but a girl still needs her reputation, I don't care what anybody says."

"Poor Darlene," I said.

I asked the Horse Creek postmaster what he knew about the four names on his list, where they'd lived before, and wrote down what he said. Another Los Angeles, a Yreka, a Redding, and a Provo, Utah. I didn't know any of the names. I thanked him for his trouble and drove downriver the twenty minutes to Seiad Valley. A note tacked to the post office door said "Back Soon" and was signed Myra. I went into the grocery store and asked the young girl behind the counter whether she had any idea when *soon* would be. She looked at her watch, wide and plastic and brilliantly colored.

"Myra had to go over to the school, but she should be back in about a half hour."

"Thanks—I'll come back. Could you give me directions for Robby Rowe's house?"

"Sure. Go up Seiad Creek Road about maybe five, six

miles. You'll go around a big curve to the right, then down below the road you'll see a silver-colored trailer. Take your first right after that. It's a dirt road and it'll wind around some, but eventually you'll come to an open field and a big two-story house with woods behind. That's him; there aren't any more houses down that road."

After about fifteen minutes and ten miles, not five or six, I came to the silver trailer and, just beyond, the dirt road to the right. It wound down and crossed a narrow creek, then flattened out in a small valley with a big house at the end— two-story, natural wood, attractive. Was Robby Rowe married, with a family? I'd thought of him as single but realized he'd never actually said he was. The yard was neat but uninteresting—close-cropped grass, no flowers, and none of the old junk lying around that decorated most people's yards on the rivers. A graceful stand of oak trees stood by a stream over on the left.

Robby came through the door as I pulled up. I got out and his face lit with such a nice smile, I wished I was making a social call, after all.

"Welcome to my humble abode, Maggie. What brings you my way?"

"Just passing by." I grinned. "No, really, I wanted to ask you about some things."

"Sure, come on in."

I followed him into a big long room with a lot of windows that looked out on the creek and the oak trees. The walls were beautiful wide boards of natural wood the color of cinnamon. A lot of old photographs in various sizes hung on them in patterns that looked awkward. One wall had large old iron implements of some kind, for farming or perhaps mining. The furniture was like the yard, newish and neat but in dull colors and shapes.

"This is a beautiful house. Did you build it?"

"No, it was built by some young kids, came up from the city but then found they didn't like living in the country, after all. They were in a hurry to sell, so I got a good price on it."

"How long have you lived here?"

"About six months. You see Bob Gerald's wife?"

I nodded. "I did. Thanks again for the address and everything."

"She any help?"

"Sort of. That's what I'm doing now, in fact. This isn't just a social call, I'm afraid. I'm trying to eliminate whoever I can from my list of possibles."

The happy expression left his face. "Me, you mean. Well, sit down, take the load off your feet. You want some coffee or something?"

"Not right now. Maybe later, thanks. I'm sorry if it's offensive to you, my asking. But you know, I've always believed Joey Brown was murdered, so you're on my list because you were at the Halloween party. I'd like to cross you off, though."

He was sitting on the couch at the other end from me, quite a long couch. He'd been sitting upright, stiffly, on the edge of the cushion, but leaned back now, nodding his head. I continued.

"I thought if you could tell me where you were August twenty-first, when the hikers were attacked. And then if I can verify it, I can forget about you as a suspect, which I'd like very much to do. Or, ditto for November eighth."

He turned sideways to face me, a frown on his face. "What's your interest in all this, Maggie? I've never been able to figure that out. I didn't think private detectives usually worked for nothing."

"I'm sorry. I can't say who it is, but someone has hired me to find the killer. So how about it, and please don't hate me for asking, okay?"

"Shit," he said. "Well. Let's see. When the hikers were killed, I wasn't in the chopper, obviously. I was just out walking around, looking for anything suspicious, any signs of marijuana, over by Bear Creek. I remember because of hearing about the murder when I got back to the office."

"You were by yourself?"

He nodded.

"What about November eighth? In the afternoon, early evening?"

"November eighth? Why are you asking about November eighth?"

"That's when the girl in the coma was ... killed by the bomb. That's a definite time, not like when the four men were killed, or the ranger."

Robby sighed and got up, went over to a brown painted desk in the corner, a schoolboy's desk. He opened the long center drawer and took out a black date book, flipped back a few pages. "Nothing here," he said, sounding irritated. "It was a weekday. I wasn't on the chopper or I'd have put it in here, so I must've been out by myself again looking for dope, but I don't remember specifically."

"Do you have time sheets or sign-out sheets or anything like that at your office?"

"No, there's a record kept of sick leave but not where people are if they're just out working routine. If they're somewhere special and people need to know where to find them, then we tell the secretary."

"Damn. I was hoping there would be something like that. Not just for you—I thought it might be a way to get a line on Robert Gerald. I like him a lot better than you as a suspect." Which was neither a lie nor soft soap. I could still smell Mimi's cabin burning. "Let me ask you something else, then. What about your brother?"

He got up again, went over to a table against the wall, and turned his back to me. Something in the atmosphere changed perceptibly. "My brother?"

"Did you know Darlene Ullrich has run off with him, maybe all the way to Central America?"

He turned, holding a cigarette in one hand and a lighter in the other. "Randall always did have a way with the ladies."

"Does your brother's interest in a particular lady tend to be long-term or short-term?"

He flicked open the Zippo and the flame jumped up, caught the end of the cigarette. He smiled slightly. "Short-term, I'd say. But I don't really know. He just comes up once or twice a year, if he can, for the fishing."

"Do you know where he is now?"

"No, sorry. He just shows up when he shows up. Once or twice a year, usually in the fall, like I said."

"When was he here, exactly, this year?"

He didn't answer for a minute, then said reluctantly, "He was here two, three times—in the spring, then again in August or September for a week or two when the steelhead started to run. Then he went away to take care of some business and came back in . . . I guess it was the middle of October. But so was most of the population of Siskiyou County here, those times. Why pick on *us*?" He was watching me intently.

"Just a place to start." I tried to sound soothing, non-threatening. "Please don't take it personally. Randall stays with you when he's here?"

"No. If he doesn't have a lady friend he's seeing, or if she's married or something, he likes to stay at the Rainbow cabins. Right where he wants to be for fishing. But he's been gone a couple days now, maybe back to Central America, for all I know."

"You have an address for him down there? Is it always Guatemala, where he is?"

"Why do you think he lives in Guatemala?"

"Why—you told me."

"Did I? Well, as far as I know he doesn't live any one particular place; he goes all over down there. He's traveling most of the time for his company. As I said, I don't know any details. But that kid's a real looker—she'll do all right for herself even if Randall's interest is . . . short-term, I think you called it."

"She's a little young, though, to be on her own, doing all right for herself in a foreign country, don't you think? She's only fifteen. If your brother was convicted of sexual conduct with a minor, he'd go to prison."

"Not Randall," he said. "Anyway, that girl's older than her years, as they say. Maybe they haven't left the country;

maybe she just went off for a fling for a few days. She'll probably turn up again at home."

This was getting me nowhere. All that iced tea I'd had for breakfast made me think of the bathroom—which would give me a chance to look around a little, too. "Could I use your bathroom?"

"Sure. This way."

He pointed me through another big room, a sort of game room with a pool table and not much else. "Just off that hall at the other end."

On the far wall was a gun rack with five or six guns, and one of them had a telescopic sight and looked just right for the murder weapon. Surely he wouldn't keep it out like that if it was. On the side wall as I passed were ten or fifteen large black and white photos, old ones, framed. They all seemed to be of the same person, a woman with a mass of curly dark hair and heavily painted pouting lips. The style was 1940s, early 1950s. I looked more closely at one where she was wearing an ostrich feather halfway down her large breasts. At the bottom right the inscription was bold and clear: "With love from Alma Lancelot." Along the bottom in small fancy letters, the name of a club was printed in white: THE HIDEAWAY, SPOKANE, WASHINGTON.

A jolt went through me like a charge of electricity. Alma ... who'd gone off to Washington with Jed, who'd worked as a singer in a club, who'd kept on living in Washington when Jed came back. Robby had said he'd lived in this area all his life—hadn't he said that at the Halloween party? But "Bobby" was carved on the tree at the mine, a more usual nickname for Robert than Robby. . . . Maybe as a child, he'd been called Bobby. Or maybe it'd been Robby on the tree, not Bobby.

I looked back and saw him still standing in the door to the living room, watching me. "Who is this beautiful woman?" I asked.

"My mother, she was in show business."

"Oh really, where was that?"

"Different places. We moved around a lot, but we lived up in Washington State mostly, I guess. Spokane."

"She was really lovely—is she still alive?"

"No, she died quite a few years ago."

"You didn't grow up here, then? I thought you said—I remember at the Halloween party you said your mother's family was from around here and you were a native and I thought you said you'd always lived here—that you'd stayed home, that your brother was the wanderer in the family."

"No," he said, "I grew up mostly in Washington, but we came here summers sometimes. So I've known the area since I was a kid. When I had a chance to come back, transfer here, I was real glad."

"Oh," I said, and went into the bathroom and closed the door, my mind buzzing. Robby, Alma's son. Robby and Randall, Alma's boys—two of them, anyway. They'd visited summers and would know about the old mine; she'd surely told her sons about it. Make a nice adventure for a pack of wild little boys, get them out of the way for a while.

Did *not* always live here, after all. What sorts of weird crimes had there been, the place Robby had lived before here, or the place before that? I hadn't given O'Reagan a previous town to check on him because I hadn't known there was one. His information on murders where Robby had been stationed in the navy had showed nothing. I'd believed my best bet for tracking the killer was to match him up with similar or at least equally bizarre murders where he'd been in the past, so I hadn't given Robby much real consideration as the killer. I'd come here thinking mostly about Randall, not Robby.

Directly in front of me was an old oak chest with four drawers. I opened the top drawer, quietly; it had just towels, new-looking, dark green. I felt around underneath but that was all it was, a drawerful of towels. I opened the next: more towels. The third down had toilet paper, four bars of Dial soap still in their green paper wrappers, hydrogen peroxide, Q-Tips, and shaving cream. Well, what had I expected? A signed confession? In the spare bathroom?

The bottom drawer had just a green baseball cap, not new, sitting on a pile of newspapers. Just a green baseball cap. Just a . . . so it had been Robby whom Mimi had seen, run from. I thought back, remembered she hadn't been with me when I was talking to him at the Halloween party. But even if she'd seen him there, she'd said she hadn't seen him clearly, hadn't really seen his face. . . .

I'd been too focused on Robert Gerald, Frank Ullrich, even Jonathan Farrell and the brother, Randall. Too focused on them to consider very seriously the Robby Rowe who was waiting for me to come out of his bathroom. Well, I couldn't cower in here forever. But I wished I had my gun. I opened the third drawer again and took out the bottle of peroxide, put it in one of the big pockets of my skirt. It was a glass bottle, not plastic. Maybe I could bash him with it if things turned bad—which wasn't likely, I told myself, not likely at all. He didn't know I knew anything about Alma, about the mine; there was no reason at all he shouldn't continue to be quite pleasant. I flushed the toilet and went out.

I paused to look at the pictures of Alma again. Yes, she'd had something all right, floozy or not. She was like some of those thirties movie stars, not pretty so much as compelling: Joan Crawford, Bette Davis. Dark, dark eyes, bottomless, that promised something. What, wasn't so clear, but men had sold their souls for it long before Alma came along. I pulled my eyes away and noticed a picture in a smaller frame, a boy's face from a newspaper and the article that went with it. I could just make out the small print in the dim room.

The dateline was Spokane thirty-five years before. It was a front-page account of a household electrical accident that had killed seven-year-old Lawrence "Larry" Lancelot. The child's mother, Mrs. Alma Lancelot, said he'd gone to his room and when he plugged in his electric train set, there was an explosion. The child was dead on arrival at Spokane Memorial Hospital.

Child's electric toy. Explosion. Child dead. Click, click, click.

Any lingering doubts died a fast death. What more did I need? That signed confession I hadn't found in the bathroom? Electrical accident . . . I read quickly through the rest of the article. Authorities believed that old, inadequate wiring in the fifty-year-old house had caused the death.

"Are you all right?" The voice was so close, I jumped. Robby was standing in the doorway again.

"Sorry," I said, "I was just looking at your mother's pictures again. They're so . . . kind of compelling. Did she die up in Washington?"

"Yes," said Robby. He turned and I followed him back to the living room.

"How *interesting* it is, all this stuff you have on your walls—better than a museum because it's real, it's your family." I walked over to an old picture of six or seven miners, an expression, I hoped, of naïve bright interest on my face. On the long table beneath, where Robby had stood earlier lighting a cigarette, were several *Time* magazines and a pile of *National Geographic*s. There was also a large copper dish with small change, a lot of pennies, paper clips, a marble, something shiny. . . . My back was to him. I reached over and poked through the stuff in the dish. "Marvelous picture, these old miners," I said. Among the jumble was a small gold locket. It said ELIZABETH across the front in old-fashioned lettering. "Were they . . . your ancestors?" The locket was old, some of the gold wearing off—just as Hallie had described it all those weeks ago in Ashland. The locket that Sally lost somewhere, on the hiking trip. I was careful not to touch it with my shaking hand.

"The one on the far left," Robby said, close behind me now. I hurriedly pushed some of the pennies over the small locket, turned, and smiled. Jesus. What an arrogant bastard, to keep it here like this.

"He looks a little like you—handsome!" I said, trying to sound sexy, fascinated with him. "Maybe I could come back sometime; we could have that social visit we didn't have today. I have to be somewhere now, but I'd love to know more about your ancestors." I even fluttered my eyelashes a bit, looked at him through them with my big green eyes.

He seemed to fluff out, smiled happily, and held my eyes with his.

"Please do. I'd like that."

We went outside, said good-bye. He stood watching as I turned the car and drove away. Thinking what?

I drove as fast as I dared down the twisty road to the post office, where Myra was back and I asked her for the list. She had to go back into her records for Robby Rowe's previous address—Laramie, Wyoming. I said I'd call her later if I wanted the others, and then I sent the Karmann Ghia at max speed—only about seventy, unfortunately—down the highway to Happy Camp.

The deputy I'd seen before, at the Halloween party, was on duty in the sheriff's small office. Sam Hill. I could hear a woman's voice on dispatch in the next room.

"Sam, is the sheriff here?"

"Stepped out for a minute, but he'll be back soon. Can I help you?"

"I need to talk to him, I think."

"Sit down then; he'll be right back."

O'Reagan had said he knew the guy, had worked with him in San Jose, an ex-cop. I hoped that being O'Reagan's partner would give me enough credibility.

As I was working out what to say a medium-tall man with a big potbelly, wearing khaki trousers and a short-sleeve blue polyester shirt, walked through the door. He had heavy eyebrows, a sharp nose a little small for the rest of his face, small pale eyes.

"Here he is now," Sam said. "Sheriff Mack Olson."

I told him who I was, emphasizing my close connection with O'Reagan. A smile broke out on the puffy red face; he must be a drinker, I thought. "Any friend of Pat's is already a friend of mine," he said. "This a social call or can I do something for you?"

I took a deep breath, collected my thoughts again, laid it out for him as briefly and clearly as I could. I left out the part about Alma and Jed and the mine, of course.

"You say you know that locket yourself? You'd seen it when you knew the girl before?"

"That's right. I'm sure it was the same one. I didn't touch it."

Then I told him what Mimi had said about the man on the trail, the green baseball cap, that there was one like that in Robby's bathroom.

"It was the baseball cap that got me really looking around, you see. It was because of the baseball cap that I dragged out the time there and looked at everything I could in the living room."

"Robby Rowe," he said, shaking his head. "I sure never would've thought it. Never knew him well, of course—but I never would have guessed." Then he brightened. "Be good to get this thing cleared up, though. Such horrible crimes and everybody's been on my back, I mean everybody. We'll go over there now. You say he's home? He wasn't suspicious, you said. Book him, then have a real good look around his place. Get that locket, check the gun. . . ." He was thinking out loud.

"Denise!" he bellowed into the other room, "get the judge on the phone. I need a warrant!" He hurried out, telling Sam to take my statement and be quick about it.

I stopped at the Rainbow Grocery on the way home, chose fruit, the makings for a salad, and some candy bars that I hoped Bill would like. In Scott Bar I pulled up behind the post office, in front of his trailer. I'd been gone just on two hours and found myself thinking, a few more minutes wouldn't hurt. Then I realized with a surge of relief that I didn't have to worry about Mimi anymore—or Sally. The sheriff should be at the killer's house right now, taking him into custody. A momentary sadness clouded the relief—that it was Robby, not Gerald or even Frank Ullrich. I'd liked Robby in spite of his profession, his racist jokes.

But when I thought of Sally, of Mimi, free to live their lives now in safety, the sadness instantly disappeared.

Bill opened the door himself, looked at me inquiringly, then his face cleared and he broke into a big smile as I handed over the bag of "get well soon" stuff. "Maggie." He beamed. "How kind." He seemed his old self except for a slight limp I noticed as I followed him inside.

"I can only stay a few minutes, Bill. How are you feeling?"

"Not bad, not bad at all. But you look like the cat who swallowed the canary—what you been up to?"

Was there any reason not to tell him? No, I decided, there wasn't. So I filled him in on the visit to Robby's, what I'd discovered. "He should be arrested by now," I concluded. "The locket itself should be enough, but they'll probably find more evidence when they search his house. Oh, it's such a relief!"

"Well, good for you, Maggie." He smiled, shaking his head. "You just put that pretty head of yours to work and law enforcement wasn't even in the race! Good for you!"

"I think they were a little handicapped by their belief it was an Indian," I said modestly. I was secretly delighted, however, and thinking, Good for me, good for me! We talked a few minutes more, but for once Bill wasn't full of some interesting piece of ancient natural history and we seemed to run out of things to talk about. I felt restless, wanted to get home, so I said how glad I was he was better and that I'd stop in again in a day or so.

Back at home, Mimi had covered about half the pages of typing paper I'd left with bright, dramatic Crayola pictures. Maybe she was an artist, I thought, looking them over. Dogs, houses, trees—no people.

"They're *beautiful*!" I told her sincerely, and gave her a big hug. Then I called Hallie.

"Oh, thank God," she said. I could hear the tension leave her voice just in those three short words. "I knew you'd do it; I knew it! Oh, when can you come down? Oh, we don't have to hide anymore! Oh, Maggie . . ."

"Better wait," I cautioned. "Stay hidden a little longer till we see what else they find, and charge him. I don't see how there's any doubt with that locket, and there was also the baseball cap, but—just to be on the safe side. Then I'll come down. Right now, I need to go up to the mine, tell Jim and Ruther they can come down."

"The mine?"

"Oh . . . that's another story; I'll tell you when I see you. I'll let you know."

I looked at more of Mimi's pictures and asked her about them until I thought enough time had passed, then called the sheriff. Sam answered, said they had Robby in custody. He'd been booked and they were getting ready to charge him on what Sam was still calling the Indian murders. They didn't know whether the gun checked out yet, but in a superficial search they'd found two small packages of cocaine in the house and about a pound of marijuana, which Sam said would be plenty to get going on. A more thorough search was being made now.

"Guilty as hell," Sam said, "you can see it in his eyes. Soon as he saw we had the locket—first he said he never saw it before, had no idea how it got there, had no idea it belonged to the girl, then he started talking lawyer, clammed right up. But don't worry. Thing like this, he's not going to get bail or, anyway, nothing low enough he can pay it. I'll keep you posted."

I felt pounds lighter, not having to worry about Mimi's safety all the time, or Sally's. I told Mimi what had happened, that she didn't need to be worried about the man she'd seen on the trail anymore. "You want to come with me up in the mountains?" I asked her. "Jim's there. He was looking for the killer. I want to tell him he can come back home."

She cocked her head, looking interested. "Maybe we can find some gold," she said.

*Whatever you see, that is in front, behind, in
all the ten directions. No thought, no
reflection, no analysis, no cultivation, no
intention; let it settle itself.*

—ALAN WATTS,
THE WAY OF ZEN

TWENTY-SIX

THERE WAS NO SIGN ON THE OTHER SIDE OF THE CEMETERY
that a man had died there recently, and all the investigators
were gone. We got to the path going down from the cliff in
good time, since we didn't have to worry about being seen,
or being followed, or being shot. I made Mimi wait while
I descended halfway, waving and calling to Jim. He
emerged from the bushes and I signaled to Mimi to follow,
ran to him.

"It's over," I said. "It was Robby Rowe—"

"It's *over*? Rowe? How—"

"I went to his house to ask him some questions. I found
a green baseball cap, like Mimi saw on the man on the
trail. And more important—I found Sally's *locket*, the one
Hallie told me she lost on the hike! It's *over*; you and
Ruther don't have to stay. . . ." He grinned and gave me a
long kiss, as if I was something he'd been starving for.
Then he swung Mimi up in the air and she screamed with
delight. He put her down and as we walked back through
the bushes to the camp, I realized there was no sign of
Ruther. "But where is he?" I asked.

"He had to go take care of some business." Jim smiled,
holding Mimi's hand now, his other arm still around me.
"He'll be back pretty soon but hell, let's go. I'll leave him
a note."

He couldn't find any paper but finally retrieved his jacket

270

from under the sleeping bag, found an old envelope, a ball-point in one of the pockets, scribbled a few words. "Now, where to put it so he'll see it right away?" He looked around the small campsite.

"Put it on his sleeping bag," I suggested. "Wait a minute." I undid the safety pin I always keep on my day pack's strap, handing it over. Jim attached the note and began packing up the rest of the things. I filled my pack; Jim filled his; even Mimi had a small bag we put things in, leaving not too much for Ruther to bring down.

"Oh, I feel so happy," I said, practically singing the words. "It's over, it's over, it's *over*!" I did a little amateur dance on the pine needles.

What will it take till I learn—to paraphrase Bob Dylan—never to say things like that? There was a funny soft plopping sound, or maybe the sound of a hundred thousand butterflies, flying by fast and close together. Ruther's sleeping bag jumped off the ground but it was in pieces now, fragments. There was a loud *boom* as the bits of sleeping bag and pieces of a canvas pack that had been lying on top drifted slowly back to earth. What I was seeing had no meaning, no reality, but Jim had jumped in front of Mimi and me, pushing us to the ground. I fell, hit my cheek on a rock.

"Don't move," said a calm voice.

I knew that voice. It was one of the three or four I knew best on the rivers. I did as it said and lay very, very still, not moving at all.

"All right," said the voice. "You, Indian, sit up real slow. If I have to blow a hole through you it'll go through them too, you know." The voice was conversational, imparting information—as usual.

"Now you, Maggie, sit up slow. That's right. Little girl, you just keep laying down for now."

Mimi was huddled into herself, a tiny, terrified shape. Jim and I, larger terrified shapes. Although Jim's face, looking at Bill Dawson, had no expression at all.

"Hi, Bill," I said feebly, still with that feeling of unreality. Everything seemed to have a slight haze on it, to be slightly out of focus. "Uh, what are you doing here?"

"I really thought you were different, Maggie," he said in a pained voice. "When you first moved here, before you started going around with the Indians, I really thought you weren't going to be like the others. Like Alma . . . I thought you might finally be the one I could *trust.* I had so much to offer you, Maggie. I've applied to Harvard and we could have shared the gold. I'm going to be a famous scientist, world-famous. You could've been my beautiful wife, receiving all the accolades with me. Why'd you have to bring this Indian in on it, throw me over for him?"

"Throw you over? But Bill, I didn't know—"

"What gold?' Jim interrupted. "What are you talking about?"

Bill smiled slightly and shook his head. "No, that's not going to work. You may as well stop that right now, Indian. I saw you and her go in the mine. But then the Chinaman showed up; had to do something about him first. Would have come back and done something about you afterwards too wasn't for that rattler got me."

He rubbed his chin, which was bristly, needed a shave. "Harvard doesn't know me as Bill Dawson. I have a whole new life waiting over there, a whole new life. That's why I can afford to let you folks go, if you behave."

Oh, sure. My head was beginning to clear just a little. Some things were in focus now, sharp focus, while others stayed fuzzy. The long, smooth gray metal barrel of the powerful gun pointing at Jim, that was sharp, and Jim's face, the back of Mimi's head. Bill's lips were in focus, too, moving, talking, but his eyes were fuzzy. I shook my head, tried to think. Jim had said Ruther would be back. Keep him talking. Back soon. How soon, soon enough? "Bill, what did you mean when you said . . . about Alma? Were *you* one of her sons, too? Was she your *mother?*"

"My dad left me with her when he went off to work on the railroad, got himself killed. After that, why I just kind of stepped into his shoes. I was fifteen, strong for my age.

Alma was happy with me. I made her happy, for a while."
A sad look crossed his face, as sad as death. Elizabeth
Petersen had told me there was maybe a stepson, I remembered. "Alma got restless, though, dumped me just like she
did every man she ever went with except my dad—he didn't
live long enough." He gave a wild little laugh. The gun had
dropped slightly while he talked, but he raised it again, dead
on Jim's gut.

"You're mistaken about one thing, though," Jim said in
a slow, even voice. "Maggie and I were never *lovers*; she
wouldn't have me. God knows, I tried"—he shook his
head—"but she just wouldn't have me. I got the idea
maybe she was interested in *you*."

A wistful look crossed Bill's face briefly, swiftly replaced by anger. His face turned red and seemed to glow.
A streak of sunshine came through a hole in the canopy of
pine trees and his face turned gold, seemed to waver in the
bright light. "Liar," he said loudly, then shouted, "*liar!* Get
up real slow, Indian, or I'll shoot you just where you sit.
That's right. Now, Maggie . . . okay. Little girl, you *get up
now*."

Mimi rose and I moved my hand slightly to take hers,
squeezed it. She was looking at the ground, not at Bill, not
at me. Jim was still expressionless, but I felt certain he was
calculating the distance, figuring whether he could jump
Bill, get the gun. *No, Jim,* I prayed silently, willing him to
hear somehow, *no, you're not close enough. . . .*

Jim spoke brusquely. "Why'd you kill all those people,
Dawson?" Jim the bad cop, me the nice cop, setting it up?

"Had to keep people away from my gold, didn't I?" Bill
asked in a soft, reasonable voice. "Indian, you go first, then
the kid and you together, Maggie. Keep ahold of her hand.
Nice and slow. I'll be right behind you. Head over to the
left, to those big Doug firs."

Keep him talking. As we started for the trees, I asked,
"Did Alma take you to the mine, Bill? Is that how you
knew about it? When you came here summers?"

"Not the mine, just the old cabin. She really liked it up

here, for some reason. It was Randall found the mine but it was me who found the gold. Years later, when I came back. I was always a lot smarter than the others, see, always yards ahead of those boys. No, don't stop. Keep going. *Move*."

There was a quality to his voice that made a person want to do what he said. We moved—away from the trail over the cliff into deep woods, where there was a faint path. Oh, Ruther, I thought, *please* be out here somewhere, watching us, waiting for your chance. . . . Jim was just ahead, walking slow. His arm reached back toward me. I tucked my elbow to my waist, moved my hand in front of my body where Bill couldn't see, took Jim's hand a moment, let go. Keep him talking. Alma. Alma had really gotten to him.

"You told me you didn't know any Alma when I asked you, Bill. Why didn't you want me to know about Alma?"

"Why—you ought to be able to figure that out yourself, Maggie. Because Alma connected up with the mine."

"But you said she didn't know about the mine. Randall and Robby—they didn't know about the gold, you said, so I don't—"

"*Nobody* knew about the gold. You know how much those nuggets are worth? At least six million dollars! They don't make 'em like that anymore! Chinaman told me the Chinese back then, his honorable ancestors, see, they saw the trouble coming, had to get out fast and couldn't take the gold with 'em. So they all joined together, put everything they had down there in the mine, covered it over. Probably *more* than six million, that's just a rough estimate." He gave a high, crazy laugh.

"How many people have you killed now, Dawson?" Jim asked, the mean cop again. "Just out of curiosity. How many?"

"They were nothing but *worms*," Bill said in a fast, furious voice. "People are just *worms*—I bet you didn't know that, Indian! Worms! *Worms!* And they act like it, too. Look how these so-called wise men *act*! *Homo sapiens?* Ruining the planet, aren't they? A few more or less don't matter, except ... What I say—the fewer, the better." He took a breath and his voice slowed, grew calm again. "I'm doing the planet a favor, way I see it."

Worms. "But Bill," I said, "*you're* a human, too. You wouldn't like anyone to kill you. Why don't we talk this over." I could see us in a small circle, sitting on the pine needles, streaks of sun highlighting first Jim and Mimi, then the man I'd thought was my friend who was now poking a gun in my back. Sitting down and calmly talking it over. You don't really want to kill us, Bill. I'm your friend. Maybe you're right, Maggie, he would say, smiling, the old Bill. Bill, with his first-class brain, long ago crossed over into the dark world of madness. Very long ago ... there was the kid electrocuted by the train set, his stepbrother. . . .

"Say," Bill went on, as conversational as though we were in the post office again, he behind the counter, me listening happily, "did you know a giant forest just like this here once covered all of North America? This where we are now is rare, very rare. . . ."

The green leaves on either side of the path, the dark trunks, remnants of that other forest, wavered and glittered where the sun hit, going into focus, out again as we passed by. The forest primeval, without mercy. Like Bill. I wondered whether I might have a concussion. My ears were buzzing, but I hadn't hit my head when I fell, only my cheek. It hurt.

Bill continued talking in the chatty, agreeable voice. "The world got a lot cooler at a certain point, see, so the beech and magnolias, most of the hardwoods migrated thousands of miles away. They picked up and went to the Atlantic coast." I could just see them with their little suitcases. Perhaps they went on outings to the beach after they got there, tentatively sticking their delicate roots into the nice warm surf. . . . I shook my head, tried to clear it. I must be going crazy myself. None of this seemed real, even Jim's back in the blue work shirt, ahead of me, something in a dream.

Bill continued, in full lecturing mode now. "But the fir

and pine and redwoods, they stayed here. I bet you didn't know that, did you? These trees you see all around you, all growin' in the same place together, pine and magnolia, softwood and hardwood—why, everywhere else, they haven't been seen together for about forty million years. Now isn't that something?' His voice hardened. *"Stop dragging your feet, little girl."*

Mimi walked a little faster; I did, too. The gun poked me harder in the back. "A nice steady pace is what I want. That's better. Hurry up a little, Indian, but not *too* much. That's right."

"Oh!" I cried spontaneously, "Oh, *look*!"

"Cut the—uh-oh—cubs, huh? Two of 'em, now where's the mother?"

I turned my head and saw that Bill was looking around, searching the bushes with his eyes. Jim was looking back, too, now, every muscle tense, ready to spring. But the gun was still firmly in my back.

The mother bear, huge, walked out onto the trail.

Mimi said in a desperate, strangled voice, "We better get outta here, mister—"

Bill didn't think to shoot me in the back before he swiveled the gun to get the bear, only a couple of feet away now—furious and attacking because of her cubs. I shoved against Bill and he swung the gun back toward me but the bear was coming up so fast, he changed his mind in midswing and moved the gun back around to shoot the bear—*my* bear. She had that same torn ear. Jim knocked into me and pushed Bill heavily to one side. I fell backward as the shot went wild but caught myself on a bush as Jim shoved again, so the next shot went wide too. Then all Bill's attention was on the bear, who was reaching for him and there was no more time to get the gun lined up, no time to try again.

Jim grabbed Mimi's hand and we raced down the trail. We were just rounding the big rock when we heard the sounds I still hear sometimes when I wake in the middle of the night and they're ringing in my ears. As we ran the sounds stopped and then there was silence, except for the beating of our feet on the path, the beating of my heart, which was pounding loudly right between my ears.

Three beams of light moved across the dull, lumpy gold. We'd already made two trips with the mules and only now were finally nearing the bottom of the pile of nuggets.

"God, I'm sick of the sight of this stuff," Jim complained.

"Me, too," Ruther agreed.

"Me, too." I sighed.

I'd been half-afraid we'd turn into the kind of gold-crazed freaks I remembered from *The Treasure of the Sierra Madre*, Humphrey Bogart and the others suddenly changed from friends to enemies, each wanting all the gold for himself. That gold was dust and blew away in the wind. This gold was solid and incredibly heavy. All the details had been worked out, with half the money going to the Karuk tribal council, the other divided among Greenpeace, Save the Bay, Earth First, the Sierra Club. And a house for Mimi. The Chinese man, no other identity found, had been buried as Chan Leong in the Chinese graveyard next to old Chicken Hans.

I often think of the bear, wish there was something I could do for her and her babies. But all she really needs from humans is to be left alone, with enough wild space to make her home. I hoped the gold would trickle down to her in that way, or at least to her kind.

Meanwhile, we'd worked through most of the night and all any of us wanted at the moment was to see the last of the damn nuggets. None of us was really a money person. Not that any of us disliked it, but it wasn't what came first, or even second or third, for any of us. I was so tired, I'd even lost touch with the pleasure of giving it back to the earth that produced it.

"Say, Maggie," Ruther said. "I've been thinking. If it was Bill Dawson who shot the hikers—how come was that girl's locket at Robby Rowe's place?"

"Probably Bill Dawson put it there. Robby told the sheriff that Bill stopped by to visit him a couple of times this fall—he never had before. Bill maybe had the idea of setting Robby up as the killer all along but I guess we'll never know for sure."

"Yeah, makes sense . . . say—that's the end of it!"

"Then let's get out of here. Ho!" Jim slapped the first mule on the bit of rump not covered by heavy saddlebags, and the tired animal slowly began to move up the passage. The other three mules followed, not really wanting to be down here any more than we did.

I like to travel light and at the same time not part with anything I care about, or am likely to change my mind and decide *later* that I care about. It's a leftover from being really poor, I think, those years I was drinking. I closed the lid of my suitcase for what I promised myself was the last time. But it was still so hard to close. Maybe I didn't *really* need those black sweatpants, they were pretty ratty. . . . I opened it up again.

People started arriving; I wasn't expecting them. Ruther and Lucy, Hank and Clara and Mimi, Elvira, even Nancy Odum. Hallie and Sally weren't there, but Sally was fine now, and I see them in San Francisco. Certain people were missing—Lillian, Joey Brown, also Janey and Jed, even Alma in a way. All just cards now, in that deck in the dusty corner somewhere. Jonathan Farrell had never been found. Robby Rowe was in jail for drugs. And Bill Dawson. Did murderers go down the Red Dirt Road? What awaited him on the other side? Not the Deerskin Dance, I thought.

Jim turned up with a big stack of pizzas. There was plenty of beer for those who drank and plenty of lemonade for those who didn't. They'd all brought food so there was more than we could finish, even though we tried.

It was a crisp autumn evening, still not really cold. Late flowers and falling leaves mixed with pine and Douglas fir, making the air scented and spicy. A moon that was still low enough to be big and orange rose over the canyon. The Nitty Gritty Dirt Band sang from the cassette recorder:

warm as mountain su-un shine
on the edge of the sno-ow line
in a meadow of
colum-biii-ine . . .

Mimi was laughing, a vibrant little girl again, showing Hank something. I went over, saw it was one of the pictures she'd done when I went to see Robby: a bright red bear, blue trees. She looked up and saw me, smiled that transcendent smile of hers. Clara and Hank and Mimi would be staying at the cabin, while they looked for a house, and the dogs.

They said this party tonight wasn't to celebrate my going but just to say good-bye temporarily. They said I was part of their lives now. They said I'd better come back. My eyes misted over as I looked at them, these friends who'd made me, a stranger, welcome in the Klamath country, where I had a home now the way it could never be in a city. . . . Had it really been only four months, less than four months? Would I ever be back? From time to time to visit at least, to see Jim. But life has a funny way of taking you on, forward, of not letting you go back, like a big, powerful river that only flows one way. There was Mimi, I reminded myself. There was no way I wouldn't be back to see her, to help her any way I could; I wouldn't let her drift out of my life. And Jim, so much of his life was here, in spite of what he said about wanting to work elsewhere. We'd have a commuter relationship; we'd see what would happen. . . .

But my bags were packed, my health apparently recovered, or anyway much improved, my purpose here fulfilled. The big river doesn't stop moving, and it was moving me on.

I couldn't get to sleep and then it was morning, sun and bird song streaming in through the window together like one single sweet piece of beauty, impossible to separate out into this part, that one.

Jim fixed breakfast while I wandered around the cabin

feeling spacy and strange. Wandered around the good, solid
hundred-year-old house that had welcomed me, given me
sanctuary. That had brought Mimi into my life, and Jim.

My bags stood waiting by the door. The dogs were out
in the yard, optimistically hoping to catch some birds. Mimi
was in the kitchen, helping with breakfast. The sun coming
through the old wavy glass windowpanes dappled the room,
burnished it, made me feel, as it had for so many mornings
and perhaps for the final time now, like a figure in a paint-
ing by Vermeer.

The Klamath Knot was lying open on the table. I walked
over, to see what its parting message would be. Before I
left the Klamath country, and went down below . . .

Conquering civilization could cut the Klamath knot,
and that of every other wilderness; dam every river,
log every forest, plow every meadow, until the last
gasp of splendor subsides from the earth. "What
now?" the serpent might whisper, as it perhaps whispered to Alexander on the banks of the Ganges.